AN UNWELCOME GUEST

The rogue blink of the alarm and the dead phone line were hardly needed to tell me that I was in immediate danger. I reached into the drawer and groped for a doorbell-like button that would send an emergency radio signal directly to Hertfordshire Constabulary. I only hoped the damned thing worked.

Where was it? I rummaged amongst suburban detritus—a remote control, snippets of paper, pens and pencils, a deck of cards—and heard a floorboard creak in the hallway.

Instantly, the house was plunged into darkness. Every sound stood out in relief to the utter quiet. The house was so familiar to me that I knew its every sound, knew precisely where my intruder was. He lurked just inside the doorway. I could tell from the timbre of the creak that he was ̶n̶o̶t̶ ̶h̶e̶a̶v̶y̶. I imagined a small, catlike ̶f̶i̶g̶u̶r̶e̶ ̶

As he inc̶_____could to the sofa, and ̶_____wling on hands and kn̶_____ heard silenced bullets ̶_____occupied only moments ̶b̶e̶f̶o̶r̶e̶. . . .

The Booklover's Mysteries
by Julie Kaewert

UNPRINTABLE*
UNBOUND*
UNTITLED*
UNSOLICITED*

and coming soon

UNCATALOGUED

Available from Bantam Books

UNSIGNED

A BOOKLOVER'S MYSTERY

Julie Kaewert

BANTAM BOOKS

NEW YORK   TORONTO   LONDON   SYDNEY   AUCKLAND

UNSIGNED

A Bantam Crime Line Book / January 2001

Crime Line and the portrayal of a boxed "cl" are trademarks of
Bantam Books, a division of Random House, Inc.

Quotations from *Beowulf the Warrior* copyright © 1954
by Ian Serraillier, used with permission of
Bethlehem Books, Bathgate, ND. All rights reserved.

ISBN 0-553-58219-4

Published simultaneously in the United States and Canada

Bantam Books are published by Bantam Books, a division of Random
House, Inc. Its trademark, consisting of the words "Bantam Books"
and the portrayal of a rooster, is Registered in U.S. Patent and
Trademark Office and in other countries. Marca Registrada.
Bantam Books, 1540 Broadway, New York, New York 10036.

PRINTED IN THE UNITED STATES OF AMERICA

OPM   10   9   8   7   6   5   4   3   2   1

For Brian and Lauren

Acknowledgments

Alex Plumtree wouldn't enjoy his many extraordinary exploits without the generous help of talented and downright indulgent experts. As usual, their advice has been perfect. Any mistakes are entirely my own.

Sincere thanks to the following: Timothy and Kathryn Beecroft, long-suffering friends and UK editors; the many exceptional reference librarians of the Boulder Public Library; Nicholas Brealey of Nicholas Brealey Publishing in London; Brad Churchill of the University of Colorado Latin Department; Nick Clee of the *Bookseller* (who does not resemble the *Bookseller* journalist in the novel in a single respect); Suzanne Collier and the Society of Young Publishers; Phil Cronenwett, Rauner Special Collections Library archivist at Dartmouth College; Diane Mott Davidson; Adam Douglas of Simon Finch Rare Books, London; Daniel and Nancy Fleming; Janet Fogg; Alan, Libbie, and Rebecca Groves; Jim and Adrienne Hester; Andrew Hunter of Quaritch, London; Christopher Hurst, Christopher Hurst Publisher Ltd, London; Doyle Kersey; Karen Lin; Ed Maggs of Maggs Bros, London; Kate Miciak; Christine and Bill Mottram; Connie Munro; Laura Blake Peterson; Kathy Saideman; Tom and Enid Schantz of the Rue Morgue Press; Leslie Socash of the University of

Colorado Germanic Languages Department; John Stevenson and Charlotte Sussman of the University of Colorado Department of English; John Windle of John Windle Antiquarian Books, San Francisco; and University of Colorado's Norlin Library's very helpful Special Collections librarians Chris McCusker, Chris Vincent, and Deborah Hollis.

Prologue

Hrothgar, King of the Danes, glorious in battle,
Built him a huge hall—its gleaming roof
Towering high to heaven—strong to withstand
The buffet of war. He called it Heorot
And lived there with his Queen. At time of feasting
He gave to his followers rings and ornaments
And bracelets of bright gold, cunningly wrought,
Graved with runes and deeds of dead heroes.
Here they enjoyed feasts and high fellowship,
Story and song and the pride of armed peace.
But away in the treacherous fens, beyond the moor,
A hideous monster lurked, fiend from hell . . .
He, one night, when the warriors of Hrothgar lay
Slumbering after banquet, came to Heorot,
Broke down the door, seized in his fell grip
A score and more of the sleeping sons of men
And carried them home for meat. At break of day
The hall of Heorot rang loud and long
With woe of warriors and grief of the great King.
Thereafter, from dark lake and dripping caves
Night after night over the misty moor
Came Grendel, gross and grim, famished for flesh.
Empty the beds, no man dared sleep at Heorot,
But Grendel smelt them out of their hiding place,
And many a meal he made of warriors.
For twelve years he waged war with Hrothgar,
Piling grief upon grief. For twelve years
He haunted great Heorot.

—BEOWULF, *seventh- (or tenth-) century Anglo-Saxon epic*

CHAPTER 1

Now there lived overseas
In the land of the Geats a youth of valiance abounding,
Mightiest yet mildest of men, his name Beowulf,
Who, hearing of Grendel [was] minded to destroy him . . .

— BEOWULF

The moment before the bullet struck, I was glaring at a journalist I didn't like over a cup of coffee I didn't want. At eleven o'clock on this Saturday night, I was meant to be sipping champagne next door at the literary event of the year; instead, I had just burnt my tongue. The lights of the Meridien Hotel opposite twinkled gaily, illuminating this stretch of Piccadilly as its flags flapped to and fro in the October gale. It was the opening night of National Book Week, and it wasn't supposed to happen this way.

"Let me get this straight, Nathan," I said, replacing my cup on its saucer with studied composure. "You expect me to believe that Trevor Gravesend—owner of Britain's most eminent publishing company and president of the Publishers Association—had his star author *murdered* to increase sales?"

Before answering, Nathan Griffith sucked hard on a cigarette, his fingers shaking, and cast suspicious glances at the few others populating the coffee bar. Nate, a staff writer for Britain's publishing and bookselling organ, the *Bookseller*, looked more gaunt than usual. The twenty-something journalist was cursed with an old man's body: his prematurely wrinkled face, ashen from frightening excesses of nicotine and alcohol, was sadly consistent with his balding pate and cadaverous frame. With the hand holding the cigarette he raked a few tenacious hairs across the top of his head and blew smoke to one side.

"I don't like it any more than you do, Plumtree. But that anonymous caller was very serious indeed. It *could* have happened as he said. Think about it: Gravesend was quite concerned about Montague's book, between the obscene advance he had to pay, and its wandering nature. You saw the reviews. And the title! I mean, really—*Beowulf's Blood*? What could Gravesend have been thinking of?" Out of habit, Nate fingered the terrifically tattered and grimy notebook he dragged with him everywhere for recording industry secrets.

I stifled my irritation, vowing to give Nate a badly needed lesson in literature—and no more than three minutes of my time. It was beyond me why Nate had chosen *me* as his father confessor. "Actually, *Beowulf* strikes me as a rather nice association for a novel about a monstrous serial killer—noble Beowulf versus the hideous Grendel, the timeless battle of good versus evil. You're an avid Trekkie—don't you discuss this very sort of thing at your *Star Trek* sci-fi conferences? Use your common sense, Nate. McKinley Montague's signing takes place in less than an hour. Why haven't we heard anything about the author's tragic death? Besides, to make such an accusation about Trevor Gravesend—of all people—on the basis of an anonymous caller . . . really, Nathan, you should be more careful. Perhaps your libel law needs swotting up."

"Plumtree, *listen* to me." Nathan looked ready to

jump out of his skin in his desperation to convince me. "Please! Try for once to expect the worst in someone. Someone who stands to lose a hell of a lot if he doesn't have a best-seller in his pocket on his way to the Frankfurt Book Fair and Merger Mania. Someone who cares about money *more* than—"

Crack! Instinctively, I raised my arm to shield my face from the cascade of glass that rained down next to me. The deafening collapse of the window seemed to carry on and on, as if all the glass in Piccadilly had just shattered at my elbow. Sheets and shards exploded into a million pieces, flying in all directions and tinkling endlessly onto the marble floor of the small establishment.

In the next moment, all was eerily quiet. I looked across at Nathan, who appeared stunned but unhurt.

A bullet. Through the window. I knew the sound all too well.

Reaching across the table, I shoved Nathan down by his shoulder. We scrambled down on our hands and knees, unsuccessfully avoiding the sharp shards of glass as we sought protection beneath the absurdly small table. Nate reached up and groped for his precious notebook; he found it and clutched it to his chest.

I caught Nate's eye. If the bullet had been intended to silence him, then perhaps it was true: England's most respected publishing house had literally *killed* to sell books. Good Lord.

But how had they got on to Nate? Someone must have followed us. . . . Quickly, I thought back over the rather extraordinary few minutes that had preceded Nate's appearance that evening.

The excitement had begun as Nicola Beauchamp,

my trade editor, and I were making our way through the windy night to a bookshop grand opening and signing party. Bang in the middle of Piccadilly Circus, a vicious October gale whipped Nicola's skirt up round her waist and held it there. She'd whooped in surprise and fought to clamp it down again, but not before I'd caught a glimpse of her rather stunning legs (and equally note-worthy knickers). Though I failed to stifle a smile, I did avert my eyes—only to see an approaching cluster of yobbos gesturing lewdly at poor Nicola and calling out surprisingly creative compliments. I'd reached down to put an arm round my diminutive employee's shoulders, drawing her close as the louts passed.

When the danger was gone, I dropped my arm again and tried to alleviate her embarrassment. "I'm curious to see what Wellbrook's Books has made of the old Simpson's building. Bit of a challenge to imagine New Fiction in men's haberdashery."

"I'll say. But all that white marble and glass should set off the books nicely. What I find hard to imagine is the idea of a midnight signing. What sort of a turnout can they possibly expect?" My dignified, petite, very lit-erary editor and I were on our way to a coveted cham-pagne reception celebrating the official opening of the grandest new bookshop in Britain—a superstore on the American model, complete with gourmet coffee bar. Everyone was desperately curious to see the transfor-mation of the elegant institution formerly known as Simpson's, where Britain's upper classes had purchased their clothes for generations, into the Wellbrook chain's flagship store.

But the real highlight of the evening was to be a signing by McKinley Montague, the most sensational novelist in Britain and author of a new serial-killer chiller. Wellbrook's had thoughtfully timed both its opening and Montague's signing to coincide with the launch of National Book Week, now moved to autumn from spring. Personally, I thought it should be moved right back again, because it was too close to the Frankfurt Book Fair, beginning at the very end of this same week. Bit of a cock-up in the NBW planning department.

At the same moment I'd heard Nate's high-pitched voice calling from behind us—*Plumtree! Wait!*—Nicola and I found ourselves caught in the vortex of a small tornado of dried leaves and dust. We stopped in our tracks, Nicola clamping her arms round her thighs prudently as I shut my eyes against a hail of grit. In retrospect, as a publisher of books, I see that dirty little whirlwind as a bit of foreshadowing by the Omniscient Narrator in the Sky—the rather obvious sort used by the gooseflesh-generating McKinley Montague. A dirty little whirlwind was about to sweep away British publishing as we knew it . . . but who'd have suspected that such malignant and unsuspected forces would be at work in our gentle world of books?

Quite right—*I* should have suspected.

When the whirlwind subsided I blinked half of London out of my contact lenses and glimpsed Nathan Griffith jogging toward us, famous notebook in hand . . . Nathan, who never jogged anywhere, and who had written a rather flattering profile of Plumtree Press for the most recent issue of the *Bookseller*. He caught us up with a disturbing gasp for breath.

"Nathan! You know Nicola Beauchamp, don't you?" They nodded at one another in greeting and we continued to battle our way down Piccadilly. Between the short, intense young journalist panting on my right and tiny Nicola, I felt a veritable giant. At six foot four, I tower over most people and often worry that it is intimidating.

"Big night for bookselling news," I shouted cheerfully to Nathan. Ahead of us, the rabble queued for entry to the daringly innovative midnight signing while the bigwigs of the book world walked past them through the door, presenting their invitations to the reception.

"You don't know the half of it," Nate wheezed. "Alex, I need to talk to you. *Alone*," he added pointedly, with an obvious glance at Nicola. And so, though I wasn't eager to hear Nathan's latest conspiracy theory regarding the acquisition of publishing companies, I'd agreed to a quick chat. Given his recent complimentary profile of the Press, I felt it would be rude not to do as he asked.

I left Nicola at the Simpson's—I mean *Wellbrook's*—glowing glass front, which shone like the sun onto Piccadilly and revealed acres of white marble floor within. It was disconcerting, as I'd suspected, to look through the doors and see a table of books labelled "New Fiction" where there had always, as long as I could remember, been a mannequin sporting a mackintosh and a brolly. A bit wistfully, I followed Nate as he oozed down the street, gliding away from the party with a liquid motion that always made me feel he was trying to slip away from someone.

Drawing up next to him, I teased, "Okay, Nate— what is it now?" Privately, I was amused by his perpetual assumption that something sinister lurked behind every publishing deal, and every bookcase in the corner shop. But he glanced back as if convinced we were being watched, and without answering did a swift double-take before thrusting me through the door of the coffee bar.

Was that it, I thought now, under the table with Nate? Had someone followed us from Wellbrook's?

No fusillade of bullets had followed the single shot over our table; no gun-toting assassins lurked in the street outside. The rotund, mustachioed coffee shop proprietor seemed stunned, gaping out from behind his massive stainless steel Italian coffee machine. His young washer-up, however, sporting rings through every conceivable (and inconceivable, no doubt) bit of flesh, seemed to instantly assess the situation and take charge.

Voices began to surge around us, and the ultrahip dishwasher shouted at the half-dozen dazed patrons to stay down as he rushed from behind the worktop to the phone. I saw that the bullet had lodged in a framed photograph of Piccadilly at the turn of the century, a site uncannily close to where the coffee bar now stood. With a creeping certainty I felt the attack had not been a random act of violence. That bullet had been intended for Nathan . . . or perhaps for me. Heaven knew I'd been involved in enough political and publishing intrigue to last a lifetime. Either way, we had to get out of there fast. Someone knew where we were, and we were very exposed indeed.

"Come on," I hissed to Nathan. We slipped and slid on the glass, which skated along under us as we struggled to our feet. Everyone seemed too distracted to pay much attention as I pulled him to the rear of the shop. I opened the exit door and glanced both ways down the narrow, pungent alley. "Let's get you out of here," I breathed, and tugged him past polythene bags full of rubbish down to the corner and into Jermyn Street, utterly deserted at this hour. I kept moving past the dark shops of antiquated tailors into St James's Square, past the London Library, and down towards Pall Mall. At last I ducked into the shadows of a recessed doorway, the offices of a well-known software company, and Nathan stumbled up to me. His face was grey.

"So," he said, wheezing horribly. "They're after me"—*gasp*—"at last." His feeble attempt at humour was tragic; his chuckle ended in a frightening coughing fit. "Always thought this might happen—" *Wheeze.* "Bound to." *Gasp.* "My career—" *Wheeze.* "Built on other people's dirt." He glanced up at me and winced. "You've blood—on your face—Plumtree. Bits—of window glass."

"You, too, I'm afraid." As we stood huddled in the doorway collecting ourselves, Nathan reached inside his pocket and drew out a folded tissue. He began to wipe at his face with one hand, while reaching for his packet of cigarettes with the other. Odd, I reflected, how we resort to routine activities—clean the face, light the cigarette—to escape the terror of more disconcerting thoughts. I suddenly felt simultaneously sweaty and cold. *Concentrate, Alex. . . .*

I latched on to the possibility that the shot was *not* deliberately targetted at Nathan. It would be much less disturbing—and perhaps more reasonable—to believe that it had been a random act of violence. Sadly, those were not as uncommon as they used to be. But try as I might, I couldn't persuade myself the shot hadn't been intentional. As I folded Nathan's tissue over to a clean surface and began to wipe the blood off my face, I felt sharp stabs of pain where tiny bits of glass had lodged in my skin. I brushed them off and counted myself lucky indeed.

Though he still hadn't caught his breath, I watched in amazement as Nathan groped for a lighter. "Alex," he said around the fag, stuffing the rest of the packet away again.

"Mmm?"

The cigarette trembled so violently in his hand that I felt a wave of pity for him. "Watch yourself," he said. "They know I was talking to you."

They. "Nate, who are 'they'? And come to think of it, why *did* you tell me?"

He took a greedy drag of his cigarette, then lifted it out of his mouth. A wry, shaky smile began at one corner. "Because you're a bloody superman, Plumtree, aren't you? I mean, look at you, for heaven's sake. You're known for getting to the bottom of this sort of thing."

"Hardly. But I do think we should ring the police. After that call you received—"

"You wouldn't do that to me, would you? 'Nate Griffith is helping the police with their enquiries, as the only person with information pertaining to the murder of McKinley Montague?' Come on, Alex."

"Nathan, you received a tip about a *murder.* And someone might have just tried to kill you!"

"I know it. But I have my reasons, and I'm not ringing the police."

I sighed. Strictly speaking, after gunfire one is obliged to call the police . . . but I supposed the omni-pierced dishwasher had done that. Meanwhile, time was creeping on . . . not only was Nicola waiting for me at the party, but I wanted to find out what would happen at Wellbrook's. Would McKinley Montague appear or not?

First I'd have to find a safe place to leave Nathan—if I could persuade him to stay away.

"You *will* agree that it's too dangerous for you to appear at Wellbrook's?"

He exhaled a cloud of smoke and nodded. "I'd dearly love to go and investigate. But . . . you're right. That bullet was close enough."

"Come with me, then. I've an idea." I hailed a taxi on the Mall, enduring the driver's curious glances at our imperfectly cleaned faces, and climbed out at a rather special place just off Berkeley Square in Curzon Street.

"*Botkin's?!*" Nate exclaimed, turning to me with an incredulous frown. "What on earth are we doing at Botkin's?"

I unlocked the door to the narrow little building, one of London's finest jewels of a bookshop—an institution, in fact—and let him in. I switched on the lights, and we took in the lovely wooden round table in the hallway, piled with contemporary fiction. Beyond that was a seating area in front of the large and elegantly fronted fireplace, where Botkin's customers used to come for tea—or something stronger—and a chat. This had ensured that the smell of the place was a mixture of old ashes, aromatic tea, and the inevitable mustiness of hundreds and hundreds of very old books. The walls were lined with them, from front to back, and two charming little alcoves were recessed halfway back. One of the alcoves held my favourite bit of the entire shop: an entire wall of a bookcase, perhaps five feet wide by six feet high, pertaining solely to the writing, printing, binding, publishing, and selling of books.

"Welcome to my new shop. Sleep here, if you like—Botkin used to live upstairs, you know. It's been thoroughly cleared out up there, but I've left the furniture. There are clean linens and flannels and things, and you can always ring out to have food delivered. You should be safe enough here for a bit."

"What?" He was staring at me incredulously, as if I were joking. "*You?* Own Botkin's?"

"I said the same thing to my accountant. Bookshops aren't exactly known for making money, as you know all too well. But weeks before Nottingham Botkin died in a nasty fall down his cellar stairs, when word got round that he was selling, my accountant insisted it was the thing to do. And you know about Botkin's collection. That alone would have made the purchase worthwhile."

"Of course." Nathan, deep in thought, sank into one of Botkin's famous overstuffed chairs. "I wrote a feature on him two years ago. He was the only antiquarian bookseller to also sell contemporary blockbusters—and to greet every customer by name. But *you*—"

I knew it was unusual for Plumtree Press to have purchased a bookshop, but I didn't understand why Nathan should be quite so shocked by the fact. I had, after all, told him when he'd interviewed me about the shop my grandfather had owned in Paternoster Row, near St Paul's, in the 1920's. From everything I'd heard about my father's father, he was more a bookseller at heart than a publisher.

"You know, Nathan, I still think it might be wise to ring the police and tell them about all of this—the phone call and the gunshot. In fact, the more I think about it, the more I think we're obliged to tell them."

He fixed me with a cynical eye. "I told you, I *can't* go to the police. I'd be their first suspect where Montague's concerned. Besides, what shall I say? That an anonymous caller told me McKinley Montague had been murdered to increase sales of his book? And that a bullet nearly missed me in a coffee bar tonight?"

I saw his point; the police were unlikely to come to any vital conclusion from those bits of information. It wasn't as if he had actual evidence, such as a tape recording of the call or a glimpse of his assailant. "Well, then, you might at least try to get away for a bit for your own sake. Whoever shot at you seemed quite serious."

Nathan didn't seem to be listening; as best I could tell, he was still pondering the impenetrable mystery of my owning Botkin's. He thumbed distractedly through a copy of Ian McEwan's *Enduring Love* on a round Victorian table piled high with contemporary fiction. I went upstairs and washed my face; with satisfaction I noticed in Botkin's old splotched mirror that my white shirt and tie had escaped unscathed. When I returned to the shop downstairs, I don't think poor beleaguered Nate had even realised I'd gone.

"Nathan?"

"Hmm?" He looked up from the book. "Oh, right. Yes. Thanks, Alex."

"Feel free to look around . . . plenty to keep you entertained, I should think." Only London's finest collection of *comfortable,* thumbable antiquarian books, I thought, as I watched him sink into a chair near the empty fireplace. Botkin had collected and stocked books that people liked to actually *read,* and not merely collect to sit on their shelves. I turned on a lamp near Nate, feeling rather protective of him. "The shop's not open these days, so soon after Botkin's untimely death, so no one should be coming in tomorrow. If you do go out, use the back door; it doesn't have to be locked from the outside. The spare key's under the tea caddy."

He didn't answer. I promised I'd be back to check on him, and left a very thoughtful *Bookseller* reporter behind, crumpled in one of Botkin's armchairs with the light of one ancient lamp shining over his shoulder.

I locked the front door behind me and was lucky to catch a taxi back to Wellbrook's, more curious than ever about McKinley Montague's signing. The shining white marble, brilliantly illuminated bookshop was full to overflowing; the queue from outside had been allowed to enter. Still, hundreds of bibliophiles desperate for a glimpse of the desperately handsome Montague gently competed for admittance, clustered round the doorway. Seeing that it would take much too long to work my way inside from the front, I moved round to the back door, showed my engraved invitation to the guard, and simply stepped inside.

Fascinating, what makes an author the object of such adoration: In Montague's case, his chiselled good looks, complete with aquiline nose and thick shock of black hair, didn't hurt. But the reclusiveness that kept him from appearing on chat shows and even in the pages of the *Bookseller* made him all the more appealing. Women couldn't get enough of him because they never *did* get him on the radio or telly, and that alluring photo on his dust jackets teased them mercilessly.

What they didn't know, I thought, was that he was reclusive because there really wasn't much to McKinley Montague, behind those prominent cheekbones and that plentiful hair. Just as he wrote his series to a strict formula, one grisly suspense thriller following another with remarkable regularity for twelve years, Montague was a predictable commodity—and a rather prosaic disappointment. Still, it worked for the great British public and, increasingly, for the world.

I found myself in a quiet, plush backwater of an alcove and saw at eye level a shelf labelled "*People——M.*" Biographies . . . I caught sight of the biography of John Murray, the present-day incarnation of one of London's early publishers and booksellers, and vowed to read it one day soon. Murray's empire was the only independent publishing firm in London to have endured for more generations than the Plumtrees', and the current John Murray had just finished his term as chairman of the Publishers Association board several years before.

Sinking practically to my ankles in plush carpeting, the scent of which still permeated the air, I was very much impressed by the mammoth, elegantly appointed new shop. A sweeping circular staircase ascended from the middle of the ground floor, as I well knew from my childhood visits to Simpson's. Wellbrook's had added a gallery with overstuffed chairs on the far side of the first floor level; this was encased by glass to waist level, overlooking the ground floor. Perhaps fifty people from the champagne party had found their way onto it, looking hugely pleased with themselves for having achieved their vantage point.

A huge golden "W" had been painted on the glass on the far side from Piccadilly—all rather unusual, and quite breathtaking, for a bookshop. The lighting was tastefully recessed, focussed and subdued, and the shop carried out the Wellbrook's theme of black and gold. Against all the white marble and plush white carpeting,

the effect was brilliant . . . and I couldn't help but wonder at the massive debt Wellbrooks' must have incurred.

Flowing with the teeming masses towards the staircase, I noted with approval a table of independent publishers' fiction in pride of place. Thoughtful touch,
that; a number of our Plumtree Press books would be
featured there if I could be bothered to fight through
the crowd for a look. I climbed to the first floor,
where I knew from the noise level the party must be.
Chairs and tables had been cleared from a coffee bar
half the size of a football pitch to make room for the
party-goers; the remainder of the large area had been
allocated to portable chairs, hundreds of them, for
Montague's fans.

As I reached the buzzing crowd of fellow publishers, journalists, and booksellers, I saw Nicola with her
champagne flute. I raised my hand and she waved; she
was chatting to Sabera Khan, my old friend who'd been
named manager of the new store. I was relieved to see
him; I wanted to tell him the extraordinary news I'd
heard in the last hour.

Sabera smiled, and gestured that I should join
them. He was short, like Nicola, but as broad, strong,
and dark as she was narrow, swanlike, and fair. Sabera
had heavy, inky hair that fell flat against his head,
which always seemed to be inclined to one side or the
other as he decided which book to recommend or how
to answer a question. He was always intense, though
he'd learned how to put people at ease with a smile.
Above all, he was scrupulously honest, which I appreciated more than all his literary knowledge.

As I made my way over, I reflected on how far Sabera
had come, and how quickly. We'd met at Cambridge,

where he'd worked at a small bookshop near my college, Magdalene. His was the only shop I patronised during my time as a postgraduate, because I found that the quiet, Iranian-born Sabera knew far more than anyone I'd ever met about new books, and never failed to recommend winners for pleasure reading as well.

After I'd been sucked into the publishing business, an old friend at Hatchards—the prestigious grandfather of all London bookshops—had asked if I knew of anyone legendary to take the post of assistant manager at his venerable store (he'd had a string of disappointments from his up-and-coming employees). I'd recommended Sabera, and he'd always been grateful; there was no more prestigious pedigree than Hatchards, even now that it was owned by Wellbrook's.

I reached Sabera and Nicola just as Ferdinand Worth, an aesthete known for his Fu Manchu beard as much as for being Trevor Gravesend's head of publicity at Hanford Banner Publishers Ltd, gestured wildly for Sabera to join him.

"Sabera, I must tell you—"

"I'm so sorry, Alex. It's time," Sabera said in his soft accent. His brilliant white teeth flashed against his dark face. "They need me. I must go."

"But you don't understand," I said, catching his arm. "It's McKinley Montague, Sabera. He might be—"

"Late, I know. He's been held up in traffic, and couldn't make the reception. Fairly typical, actually. But he is on his way. I'll see you afterwards, Alex? Nicola?" With a swift glance he saw that the rabble was being let upstairs for the signing. "I'd grab a seat now, before it's too late." With a friendly wave he was gone.

"What's happened to you?" Nicola was frowning at my face. "Is that tomato sauce? Or blood? Alex, are you all *right*?"

I took her to a seat near the front of the empty rows of portable chairs. In hushed tones, I told her about Nathan's and my far-from-quiet coffee. She listened in amazement as she did her best to cleanse a spot of "tomato sauce" I'd missed with a tissue and some lotion from her handbag. "Nothing's been said about McKinley Montague *not* being here, except for the traffic delay that kept him from the party. Just look at the crowds." Indeed, it appeared that fans were pouring in to see the best-selling author in remarkable numbers.

"I know. I'm not sure what to make of it all, but that bullet was real."

The noise level around us soared to new heights as the crowd from outside reached the top of the staircase and swooped in to claim seats. Nicola and I fell silent and watched the spectacle around us. Although admittedly this was an unusual signing, because of the hour and the grand opening, I found myself touched and encouraged by the atmosphere of excitement that Montague and his books had created. *This* was why we published books; this was the thrill of it, putting great (well, enjoyable, at least) novels in people's hands for their benefit and pleasure. The hushed anticipation in the room was palpable: National Book Week was the only week of the year that Montague showed his handsome face in public.

If the feted author, I speculated with a stab of dread, were still alive to show his face. . . . I searched the cherry-wood panelled area at the rear of the coffee bar/party/signing floor for a glimpse of Montague, but couldn't spot him. Seeing these crowds, it was very difficult to believe that Montague could be dead, much less murdered. If he were—and surely he hadn't been, so I could afford to be cynical about it—I couldn't wait to see how the publicity ploy was handled.

The startlingly loud *clonk* of a finger tapping on a live microphone intruded on my speculations. The crowd, silenced, strained for a glimpse of McKinley Montague, but it was not he who stood before us. Instead, the calmly competent Sabera appeared under the oh-so-subtle lights of Wellbrook's. "May I have your attention, please. I'm afraid I have some bad news."

Suddenly I was all ears. "I regret to inform you that there's been an accident—a tragic accident." Sabera met my eyes as if he might have remembered that I'd tried to tell him something; I saw them flick to Nicola next to me. Another pause as he licked his lips. "McKinley Montague is dead."

McKinley Montague is dead echoed in the unnatural silence that fell over the room so deafeningly filled with chatter mere moments ago. Sabera gazed grimly at his audience, discharging this difficult job with dignity and poise. "He was lost from his yacht forty-eight hours ago in a squall off Portsmouth. After a lengthy search, he is presumed dead. Evidently the conditions have been quite harsh at sea, and the authorities claim he cannot have survived."

In the next moment a hum rose from the crowd that sent gooseflesh rippling up my back. The collective response of Montague's fans was nearly as powerful as the news itself—an undulating torrent of sound that rose and fell, punctuated by horrified exclamations of disbelief.

Sabera raised his hands; the crowd went quiet.

"Wellbrook's will remain open for one hour. I am very sorry that McKinley's books must go unsigned tonight . . . and always," he finished softly. You could have heard a bookmark drop, so complete was the silence. Sabera left the podium, and I could almost feel the realisation dawning on the crowd that they would somehow have to rouse themselves to go home.

Nicola turned to me with that intent look so characteristic of her. My own response astonished me.

"I must find Trevor," I said, "and get to Sabera. Come with me?"

We were some of the first to get to our feet. As we walked past the stunned crowd, I noticed that people were clutching *Beowulf's Blood* as if it were sacred literature, holding the A-format hardcover close to their chests. The novel had acquired the status of a holy relic since its author was now, like Beowulf himself, a lost hero.

I watched as several customers reached for more books from an Everest-sized display, and realised I was witnessing the start of a buying frenzy. A conservative, British buying frenzy, mind you, but an uncharacteristically acquisitive spate nonetheless—especially considering that these were hardcovers at £24.99 apiece. Montague's untimely death had indeed done a world of good for his sales.

As Nicola and I approached Sabera, he was exchanging grave words with Trevor and Nando Worth. ". . . could be record sales," I heard Trevor conclude with a shake of his head.

"Alex. Terrible, isn't it?" I wasn't certain, but again I saw something in Sabera's eye that told me he recalled my attempt to tell him something before Nando had called him away.

"Simply dreadful. I'm so sorry. Trevor, Nando, you know Nicola Beauchamp, our trade editor at the Press."

Nando put out a hand to Nicola, while Trevor blinked an acknowledgment. Putting a friendly hand on my back for an instant, Trevor said, "Alex, this is Sabera Khan, manager of—"

"Sabera and I are old friends," I informed Trevor, who appeared taken aback by this bit of information. I never bragged about who or what I knew, and as a result people often underestimated me. It was actually quite useful. "What a shock about Montague. There's been nothing in the news. . . ."

"I know it," Trevor said. He glanced at Nando, who gnawed at his thumbnail with abandon. "I think everyone fully expected he'd be found. McKinley was an experienced seaman. Really, it hardly seems possible. But it could be the same weather system we're experiencing with this wind tonight. By the time the storm had passed and someone got to the yacht, he was gone. His family rang me just an hour ago with the news—and of course who could blame them for not thinking of us sooner? I raced over straightaway and gave the news to Nando and Sabera myself." Trevor gave a sad little shrug as if to say, *and that's that.* But a tic in his left eye betrayed him. In his own way, he was as distraught as Nando . . . or was he guilty? Again, I surprised myself: this time by doubting Trevor at all, now that I was in his presence. I had intended to take him aside and tell him of the phone call Nathan had received. Now that I had the opportunity, something made me hesitate.

The tic diminished as Trevor added, "By the way, Plumtree, I always meant to tell you. Montague was very grateful for the compliments from your *Beowulf* author—you know, that scholarly chap who brought out the new facts about the history of the poem."

"Hammonds, you mean."

"Yes, that's the fellow. It meant a lot to Montague that your fellow thought he'd got the lit crit bit right."

I smiled sadly; Nicola looked at the floor. A moment of excruciating silence followed as we considered how to get past the embarrassment of it. Hammonds, my *Beowulf* scholar, had been pilloried in the *Times* for fabricating the evidence that led to his new and radical theory. Though it hardly mattered now, Hammonds had proposed that *Beowulf* had been written several centuries later than previously thought, an announcement that sparked vitriolic debate in Anglo-Saxon-scholar circles. Hammonds himself had written a grovelling apology for what he admitted had been a deception. Since then—several weeks ago now—he seemed to have disappeared from the face of the earth.

"If I ever speak to him again"—this drew a smile from them all—"I'll tell Hammonds you said so. Truth to tell, I think he was shocked that anyone trusted to-day's readers of popular fiction to grasp the significance of *Beowulf*. Quite encouraging, when you think of it."

"The world's simplest story of good versus evil—monsters against honourable men. The seventh-century version of *Star Wars*. Or should I say tenth-century?" Sabera's eyes twinkled, albeit sadly, as he repeated what I'd said to Nate earlier—nearly word for word.

"The debate rages on," I acknowledged.

Nando Worth had been shifting from one foot to the other, eyeing the crowd. "If you'll excuse me," he said, "I must do my duty and—er—*mingle* with the fourth estate. I'll need you in a moment, Trevor—if you would." He straightened his tie, cleared his throat nervously, and moved off towards a barrage of flashes on the other side of the room. No doubt the press were having a large time interviewing distraught fans.

I came to my senses; there was no need for us to hang about. It was after midnight, we had yet to drive home, and I still had to go to Botkin's to look in on Nathan. "Right. We'd best be off. I am sorry about Montague, Trevor. I don't suppose you'll be coming to the PA meeting tomorrow?" The Publishers Association board was meeting over lunch the next day.

"Good God! I might've forgotten—thanks, Plumtree. Life does carry on, doesn't it?"

We said subdued good-byes. As Nicola and I moved off towards the staircase, I heard someone ask Trevor in a low voice that wasn't quite low enough, "Any word on his fiancée?"

Nicola stiffened. I'd long ago grown used to whispered words behind my back, but it didn't stop me spinning headlong down a chasm of loneliness at the unexpected mention of Sarah Townsend.

"No," I heard Trevor say. "Everyone but Plumtree, poor chap, believes her dead—there was an article in the *Times* not two weeks ago about an American raid on the Iraqi terrorist group holding her. Everyone was believed killed. Tragic loss. Lovely woman, too—and brilliant. Glad to see he's out with this Beauchamp girl now."

When there was bad news, I'd learned, people didn't know what to say, so they said nothing at all—*until* one was out of earshot. Unfortunately, in my day-to-day running of the eighth generation of my family publishing firm, Plumtree Press, I'd got into enough scrapes that the trade knew all too well who I was. Since my American fiancée's disappearance, and then the report of her presumed death in late September, I'd ignored sideways looks and whispered comments in abundance. They must have thought I was deaf *and* blind.

Nicola looked at me aghast. "Oh, Alex, I'm sorry. How awful for you."

"It's all right. Happens more than you'd think. Sorry you've been swept into the gossip mill as well." We'd both heard people talking about the fact that we spent time together these days, but the fact was that there were many social events in the book publishing world—most of them in the evening. There was no romantic attachment whatever between us; I was still wedded to Sarah in my mind, and Nicola was grieving over the loss of her fiancé to another woman. He'd moved out just the month before.

Still, it only made sense to travel from the Press to certain occasions together. On this particular evening, we'd worked through the afternoon and had a late dinner together to while away the time until the Wellbrook's reception at eleven. Over dinner, Nicola had casually suggested I join her on a sailing holiday she'd planned for some time, and it seemed quite natural that we might go as friends.

Stepping out onto the Piccadilly pavement, I couldn't help but notice a couple laughing as they strolled past arm in arm. I felt the usual stab of dismay that it wasn't Sarah on my arm, but immediately on its heels came—what was it? *Guilt.* Then in the next instant I understood; the epiphany came to me with such clarity that I slowed in wonder. The wind had subsided into bracing gusts, and fellow bibliophiles surrounded us toting elegant black carrier bags, subtly emblazoned in gold with the name *Wellbrook's*. I heard Nicola say, "All right, Alex?"

"Mmm. Fine. It's a lovely night, except for poor Montague." *I am alive.* Perhaps it was the narrow scrape with the bullet or the author's death that had made me see it. True, Sarah might be gone, my future irreparably shattered. But the world and all its delights—including glorious, infinite London, twinkling Piccadilly at night, and scores of glossy-covered books—were still here. Could it be that I was regaining an appreciation for life? Was I accepting that it was possible to go on living without Sarah?

I got Nicola a taxi, but she lingered a moment before getting in. "So what do you think, Alex? Do you really think Montague might have been—er—deliberately . . . ?" She slid her eyes to the back of the taxi driver's head to explain her reticence.

"I only wish I knew, Nicola. But I do intend to find out." And to find out, too, who'd shot at us in the coffee bar.

"Of all the things I've seen in publishing, this—if it's true . . ." She shook her head and got into the taxi, looking a bit wilted.

"Good night, Nicola. I hope you can get some sleep."

As I set out for nearby Curzon Street and Botkin's, I was dogged by the unthinkable: that Hanford Banner, and therefore Trevor Gravesend, might actually have had something to do with McKinley Montague's untimely death. But it didn't quite ring true. Why would an already successful publisher risk everything to dispatch the author who might earn many more millions of pounds for him in the future? And who would call Nathan with the tip? And for what reason?

So wrapped up was I in these musings that I nearly missed the—er—vision that appeared before me, brief and fleeting as a dream. As I stepped into Berkeley Square, I caught a glimpse of a woman just hailing a taxi—but not just any woman. My breath caught in my throat; I stopped short. It couldn't be . . . but it was.

Sarah!?

All I caught was a flash of a sheet of flowing dark hair, with that perfect slight curve at the bottom, as it swung round to hide her face when she climbed into the taxi. The woman wore a coat just like the one Sarah had always worn in blustery weather like this—khaki, hooded and belted. And I knew Sarah so very intimately that I was certain I saw *her* way of moving, *her* way of turning and getting into the taxi. . . .

My heart leapt. *"Sarah!"* I ran into the road after the cab, frantically searching at the same time for another in which to follow her, to catch her up. But true to the ancient law of taxi lore, now that I needed one desperately there were none at hand—hardly surprising at just past midnight. Defeated, I strained desperately to spy the taxi's number plate. At least I might be able to track down the driver later, find out where she'd gone . . . but my abysmal night vision obscured the vital numbers and letters from me, and the car rumbled away noisily into the dark. I ran towards the taxi, bellowing like a madman, but it was already too far from me—all the way at the opposite side of the square. The driver accelerated and they were gone.

I had lost her . . . again.

When I got my wits about me I was standing in the middle of the road. I somehow got myself back onto the pavement and stood gazing after the taxi, now out of sight. It only took a moment for reality to return; there were thousands—no, millions of women with long dark hair in mackintoshes who climbed into taxis after midnight in Mayfair. My mind was playing a cruel trick. Besides, if Sarah were alive, and in *London*, for heaven's sake, she'd have come straight to me.

Wouldn't she?

In ten minutes I stood at the heavy front door that old Nottingham Botkin had always left open in welcome when the weather allowed. But as I stood on the shop's step fumbling for the key, I was surprised to find the door on the latch. Frustrated, since I'd specifically asked Nathan to leave by the back door, I gave it a shove with my shoulder and stepped in. The armchair by the fire was empty, and the silence, taken with the open door, seemed ominous. My anger turned to foreboding.

"Nathan? Are you there?"

Beyond the pleasant alcove where Botkin had entertained many a customer by his fire with tea—and often something a bit stronger—a chair clattered over inside the office.

My initial unease turned to alarm. "Who's there?"

Silence. I crept forward, adrenalin flowing as I picked up the stepladder, bracing for a confrontation. Perhaps someone had taken Nathan into the office, was doing something awful to him . . .

"Plumtree? Is that you?"

To my immense surprise, Duncan Whitticombe, Publisher of the Year and proprietor of Perseverance Press, closed his eyes dramatically, clapping a hand to his chest. "Lord! You startled me." Breathing heavily, he gave me a rueful smile. Sweat glistened on his skin.

"*I* startled—" An incredulous laugh escaped before I could stifle it. "Duncan, I *am* sorry, but . . ." I went to the door of the office and looked in at the litter of papers on Botkin's desk. "It's past midnight, for heaven's sake. What on earth are you doing here?"

The portly sixty-five-year-old nodded, as if he knew his presence in my shop looked odd. "Sorry, Plumtree. Hope you don't mind. I—Well. Botkin didn't tell you, then." I sensed Whitticombe sizing me up anew, buying time with his rhetorical question while he took a decision.

Whitticombe's most unfortunate—and misleading— physical feature was a set of lids that drooped over half-closed eyes, suggesting they couldn't be bothered to remain fully open. But everyone knew that Whitticombe was as clever as they came.

"*What* didn't Botkin tell me?" Inwardly, I groaned.

"Well, the old fellow was going to sell the shop to *me,* you see, until you and your accountant got involved."

I opened my mouth.

"No, it's all right. No hard feelings, Plumtree. I only wanted to retrieve the cheque I'd sent him as earnest money. Rang your office earlier, and Khasnouri lent me a key. I was on my way back home from that Wellbrook's opening over in Piccadilly—left before all that signing madness, of course—and since it was so close . . ."

He didn't know about Montague, then.

"Can't seem to find the blasted cheque anywhere, though. . . . Old Botkin wouldn't have done anything with it. Nor would you." He cast a quizzical glance at the immense fire hazard of untended papers that rose from the surface of the desk, then turned back to me with a bitter laugh. "Hardly surprising it's lost, in all this mess. Who'd have thought, Plumtree, that a couple of publishers like us would ever want to buy an old, run-down bookshop like Botkin's?" He shook his head, and I thought I detected in his tone the same wistful regret I felt about Botkin's deadly tumble down his own shop's stairs.

"Too true." He was right; publishers rarely crossed over to the "other" side of the books business. What Duncan and I knew only too well was that along with a fairly affable camaraderie, there was an unbreachable chasm between book publishers and booksellers. This historic, traditional distance had only been broadened and deepened by deep discounting by publishers, booksellers, and distributors alike. The recent demise of the Net Book Agreement, which had guaranteed that all books would be sold at the same price across the UK, had brought the dispute closer to all-out war.

As small, independent publishers, Duncan and I knew that our little world was changing faster than we could keep up with it. Publishing in Britain had never been more alive, more exciting—or more risky. Firms were acquiring one another faster than you could say "erosion of territorial rights," the very issue that had started the merger-spree in the first place.

Or so I thought then. As I offered Duncan a coffee, asked him whether Nathan Griffith had been in the shop when he'd arrived (his answer was a puzzled no), and related the tragedy of McKinley Montague's death, I hadn't a clue how much *more* was about to change in the publishing world. If old Botkin had come back from the dead and told me that I'd unwittingly become part of a vast Machiavellian scheme, I'd have laughed in his ghostly face.

CHAPTER 2

*For we have heard of thy wisdom and thy policies,
and it is reported in all the earth, that thou only are
excellent in all the kingdom . . .*

—JUDITH 11:8

After Whitticombe had taken his leave, with a
promise from me to return his cheque to him
if I should find it, I sat for a moment in the quiet of
the cosy shop. Aside from a lingering worry about
Nathan's whereabouts and well-being, questions on the
Whitticombe-and-Botkin front plagued me. First, what
was the *real* reason for Whitticombe's presence in the
shop tonight? I found it hard to believe that he was rummaging for cheques past midnight on a Saturday. And
why hadn't Botkin mentioned that he was already selling the shop to Whitticombe? What had made him
change his mind?

The last words Botkin had spoken to me there
seemed to echo in the musty air. *"Now, Plumtree, if you
should run into trouble, you might need a—er, a little
something I've saved for you."*

"Botkin, no," I'd said, troubled that the elderly gent
might have set aside any portion of his meager earn-
ings for me. He'd held up a hand in protest; out of respect I'd fallen silent.

*"I won't tell you where it is now—least said best.
But if you do have trouble, God forbid"*—it might have

been my imagination, but I do believe the old man shuddered—"*ask Ed Maggs. Do you understand? Go to Ed Maggs for help, Plumtree, and don't tell another living soul.*"

As I recalled that exchange, remembering how drawn and defeated the old bookseller had looked in the days before his death, I wondered if he'd known he was not long for this world. He seemed to think that I might get in to some sort of trouble . . . what sort, I couldn't imagine, though finding trouble of any sort had hardly been a challenge in the past.

Odd that he'd suggested I go to Maggs, of all people . . . though Ed Maggs, one of London's most prestigious sellers of rare books, was a good friend of mine. He, too, was the eighth-generation proprietor of his family firm, and we frequently compared notes on the trials and joys of a family business. In the two weeks since Botkin's death I hadn't spoken to Ed, and couldn't imagine how he might help me with my yet-to-be-discovered problems.

I turned off the fire, put out the lights, and closed the door on the lovely old place, deeply curious about what Botkin had known . . . and what I had yet to discover.

With relief I drove to the Plumtree family home, the Orchard, which for centuries had stood on the border of Buckinghamshire and Hertfordshire on an unpaved road called Old Shire Lane. The parcel of tenant-farmed land, house, and garden was a positive sanctuary from most of the cares of the world. I'd grown up in a haven of peace and love here. I longed for nothing more than to give my own children what I'd been given, the same safe, sane existence with ponies and a printing barn beyond . . . but all of this depended upon a rather extraordinary person, who was no longer here.

The next morning, Sunday, I slept late for once. Knowing that I'd be knackered after the midnight signing, I'd signed up a fellow parishioner at Christ Church Chenies to read the *early* early service lessons in my stead. As I rose at ten and tried unsuccessfully to reach Nate before trundling wet-haired off to the late service, I found that sleep had at least sorted out the tangle of highly disturbing questions that had troubled me the night before.

First, there was the Nate-related set. Where had Nate gone, and why hadn't he let me know? Who had called him about Montague's death, and why? Why, for heaven's sake, had he told *me*? And why had we been shot at—because we knew about Montague's murder?

Which brought me to the Montague-related set of questions. I was grateful for the Publishers Association Board meeting the next day, because I could ask Trevor about these—though it might be tricky. *"Good morning, Trevor . . . did you have McKinley Montague murdered to increase sales?"* I could hardly wait. At least I could ask if the police had found any sign of force, or if other parties had seemed to be involved in Montague's death.

On to the Botkin set of questions: Why had he been ready to sell to Whitticombe, but then let the sale fall through in lieu of selling to me? What had Whitticombe *really* been doing in Botkin's? Was I meant to get in touch with Ed Maggs now, and why?

As for the appearance of Sarah in London, or someone who looked very much like her, I found myself torn: if I'd mistaken someone else for Sarah, I didn't have to deal with the issue of why she hadn't come to me, or at least told me she was alive. But if I allowed myself to believe I'd seen Sarah, at least I knew she was alive . . . and perhaps then I wouldn't even *mind* that she hadn't come to me. My mind ran over all of this endlessly.

After lunching and sharing these troubles with my childhood friend Martyn Blakely, who now also happened to be my vicar, I feverishly continued to ring Nate at every number I had for him, but received only recorded responses. I toyed with ringing the police, but decided this was overreacting; Nate might merely have got out of London for a bit, as I'd advised him. All the same, I wished he would ring me.

When I got home at about three, I retired to the library with the papers. When I opened the Sunday *Times,* I gaped at page one, unable to get beyond the thought that this news had been waiting for hours, had existed for probably an entire day when all the writing and printing was said and done. Trevor Gravesend's firm, Hanford Banner, had been purchased by Megacom. This media giant was synonymous with movies, recordings of all sorts, and newspapers round the world. Why had Trevor not said a *word* about all of this? He had suddenly gone from being the owner and director of Hanford Banner, half of a relatively small merged publishing company, to being a multimillionaire. How could he not have given it away?

The shock necessitated a cup of strong tea— something with backbone. Smoky lapsang souchong it was. I went back to the papers again with my hot tea, noting with fascination the sparely written article on Montague's demise. The dust jacket photo peered out from the paper in all its morose glory, along with photos of the distraught crowd at the *Beowulf's Blood* signing. What a price to pay for publicity.

The next morning I led the staff meeting at the Press, now moved to Monday mornings, and looked with longing at my copy of the *Bookseller*. Though there wasn't time, I flipped to the news page and scanned the headlines, then indulged myself in a brief look at Bookworm—the page where the mighty were brought low by an anonymous columnist.

The acerbic wit and juicy titbits shared by the excellent writer of this page were a delight in the often mundane world of commercial journalism. I chuckled to read about the pompous managing director of a publishing firm who had made some outrageously arrogant remarks after drinking too much at an industry event. Bookworm had pilloried him to the point that I doubted the gentleman would show his face in public for several weeks. Towards the bottom of the page was an interesting little squib urging us to watch for more mergers in the near future; I marvelled that Bookworm had somehow known about Hanford Banner/Megacom beforehand. Whoever he or she was, Bookworm was extremely well connected.

A corner boxed feature of the Bookworm page called "Manglo-Saxon" was always good for a laugh; it was here that hilarious misuses of the English language were spelled out in all their shameful glory. Usually this was a snippet from a letter to a bookseller or publisher that transformed, through bad grammar or misuse, a perfectly normal request into a flagrant sexual or other innuendo. Today it was a mocking reference to McKinley Montague's *Beowulf's Blood*, remarking that the Anglo-Saxon author of *Beowulf* in the seventh century would have been stunned to learn how ignoble his hero had become in the twenty-first century. The comment took on a sour note, now that Montague was gone.

Then, suddenly, it was half past ten, time to leave for the Publishers Association meeting if I was going to walk. I stepped out of the building and took stock of the day; the wind over the weekend seemed to have cleared away the clouds. It was gloriously clear and almost balmy.

I set out for Number One Kingsway feeling fairly cheerful, darker thoughts held at bay by the urgency of the remarkably busy day ahead. First, the PA board of directors meeting until two o'clock, then a meeting with our new Godwin Fellow—the equivalent of an international publishing ambassador-cum-intern—from America. I hardly knew what to expect of her, whether she would be a help or a hindrance during her one-year stint with Plumtree Press.

Our Fellow, Samantha Stone, happened to be heiress to America's greatest publishing empire, Stone & Stone—now of course owned by the largest movie, television, and music conglomerate in the world, but still with significant stock holdings by the Stone family. For some unimaginable reason, Samantha Stone had specifically requested to be placed with Plumtree Press, which could only be described as a small but diverse independent publisher with some very brisk-selling—even best-selling—titles. It was difficult not to be honoured by her request, but I'd learned that pride went before a fall.

I ran into Trevor Gravesend one street away from the PA offices, in High Holborn. Aside from the bags beneath his eyes, he looked his usual dapper self—trim, fashionably cut hair swept back off his forehead, well-cut suit and expensive shirt. Even at school Trevor had always looked as if the uniform had been custom-tailored for him.

He greeted me with a smile. "You must regret that the PA offices moved from Bedford Square, Plumtree. If we'd stayed, you might have rolled right out of your front door to our meetings." It had escaped no one's attention that what used to amount to a gentlemen's club was now a less than elegant set of cubicled offices. There was an unsettling aura of rather grimy defeat about the Publishers Association offices now, in fact. None of us even discussed this sea change; that, when I thought of it, was even more disturbing.

"Ah, well—at least my father and grandfather had that pleasure. Just as well they couldn't see the future."

Trevor *humphed* in agreement.

"I understand congratulations are in order. Well done."

"Oh, Megacom? Yes, that should keep us solvent for a while."

Silence. I marched into the breach.

"Trevor, I need to discuss something with you . . . I'm afraid it's not entirely pleasant. Last night, just before the announcement about Montague at Wellbrook's, Nate Griffith told me about a disturbing call he'd received."

"Oh?"

"An anonymous caller told him that Montague had been murdered—by Hanford Banner. For publicity."

"Good Lord!" Trevor stopped cold, mid-pavement, and stared at me. "What utter rubbish! Who would make a vile accusation like that? And why would Griffith pass on such nonsense?"

As if Trevor's angry stare and heated words weren't

stimulation enough for my senses, the throb of a taxi idling at the kerb just behind us was superimposed on it all. "Alex! Alex Plumtree!" Trevor and I turned in unison to look in the direction of the mid-Atlantic accent of the assertively pleasant female voice. This could mean only one thing: Samantha Stone, my Godwin Fellow from New York City. Early, evidently. I muttered as much to Trevor as I went to meet her.

As first one sculpted, high-heeled leg and then another emerged and planted itself on the pavement. I took in a woman in her late twenties, perhaps, with extraordinary golden hazel eyes. She had a strong, jutting jaw that made her look rather defiant, and finely chiselled features. Her golden-blond hair, light complexion, and mustard-coloured suit made her a rather startling vision of gold—as if I were gazing over a field of late-September grain.

"Samantha!" I said, reaching to hold the door of the taxi open for her. "I'm very pleased to meet you at last."

"Please call me Sam," she replied with a blazing smile. "And I'm delighted to meet you. In fact, I couldn't resist coming early—I arrived yesterday. No doubt it's shockingly rude of me, Alex. But now that I'm here, may I join you for the board meeting?"

Ah. So behind the smile she was tough as nails. This was uncharted territory. I sensed Trevor looking at me askance. As I closed the door of the taxi, I said, "I'm sure it's no problem," and introduced them. "Sam Stone, meet Trevor Gravesend. Chairman of the board of the Publishers Association."

A quiet recognition seemed to pass between them as he bowed his head slightly and said, "Delighted. I hope you will have a pleasant year here in London,

Miss Stone. You've done well to get yourself in with Plumtree, here. One of the best."

"So I've heard," she responded, eyeing me.

Neither Trevor nor I wanted to broach the subject, but PA directors' meetings were strictly private. How did one communicate to the heiress of the single most powerful and prestigious publishing firm on earth that she was not welcome?

Fascinated, I watched her turn and pay the cabbie the precise amount I'd have given him, then take our arms as if *we* were the newcomers. "Is this it?" she asked, glancing up at the unprepossessing locus of publishing power in the United Kingdom. To her credit, she kept her voice neutral. "Now seriously, you don't have to worry about me. I'll keep my mouth shut. Remember, I'm just here to see how you do things. And I can't afford to embarrass Alex, can I?"

She smiled at me then, with her super-sharp eyes and perfect teeth, and I felt the beginnings of a sort of dread.

Inside the rather dreary, cubicle-walled boardroom, things got off to a brisk and embarrassing start.

"Bringing tarts in to our board meetings now, Plumtree? Who's this?" Portly Harold Hoskins, coatless and wearing red braces that framed his outlandish paunch, rumbled with dissatisfaction when he saw us enter with Sam. We were all used to Hoskins's brusqueness these days; he was in the midst of a rancorous divorce and had little tolerance for anything. His behaviour would have been intolerable if we hadn't known him for years as a kind person with a keen sense of humour that had saved many a meeting.

I cleared my throat gently, hoping that Samantha didn't know what the word *tart* meant in England, but doubting we could be so lucky. "Hardly, Harold—this is our new Godwin Fellow for the year, Samantha Stone. Just arrived from New York."

The name, I knew, bore down on the assembled group of seven men and one woman like a lorry-load of honey. Everyone, but everyone, knew about the most powerful publishing house in the world, Stone & Stone. All mumbled a welcome; no one, I noticed, asked her to leave.

I motioned her to a seat next to mine as I began. "Sam, let me introduce you to the best of British publishing. You've already met Trevor, of Hanford Banner. This is Harold Hoskins, head of Peterson International; Esha Muchmore, of Orangutan; Duncan Whitticombe, of Perseverance Press; and Matthew Ireland, of Eponymous."

I watched Sam Stone's mental gears click through what all this meant, translating my brief introduction into who was owned by whom. I felt certain she was savvy enough to know that Hanford Banner was the merged result of two longtime independent British firms, now part of the Megacom empire. Gravesend *had* been on the board to represent the middle ground: fairly large firms that were not yet multinational or linked to film, television, and recording studios. Now, of course, all of that had changed.

Peterson International, represented by Hoskins, was a giant educational publisher that had swallowed up a large number of other, smaller fish in the educational market. It was difficult to imagine it getting any larger, but presumably they would find a way. Hoskins primarily represented the educational end of things, though as a smaller independent I had my say there, too.

Esha Muchmore, of Orangutan, was not as vested

in ownership as Gravesend and Hoskins. She was, however, acknowledged by all to be a "formidable" force in the industry, cowed by no one and fiercely outspoken. She was a tall, dark-skinned, muscular woman who on that day, as on most, wore a flowing purple caftan. The dramatic fall of frizzy dark-brown hair cascading halfway down her back would have made quite an overwhelming impression on its own. Orangutan was the feminist imprint of Petrel Press, an eminent English firm now owned by one of the big three movie/recording/print media conglomerates. Esha herself had been instrumental in founding the Orange Prize, the most coveted award for women's fiction worldwide. Enormously respected, Esha did a very conscientious job of representing not only the feminist side of the industry, but her larger parent company as well. Until recently Petrel had been the only one to own a thriving bookshop carrying books from all publishers; the chains had finally done them in.

Duncan Whitticombe of Perseverance and Matthew Ireland of Eponymous were independents, like me. Two years ago the board had realised that the Publishers Association was losing many of its independents to the Independent Publishers Association, and had taken a decision to stem the flow—and better represent the industry—by being more inclusive. While I knew and respected down-at-the-heel Duncan with his hooded eyes and trademark fallen lock of hair, elderly Matt Ireland was a dear old friend of my father's. Together they had founded the Independent Publishers Association many years ago.

I could still remember "Mr Ireland" coming for dinner at the Orchard, regaling us with stories of the book trade. When he was hardly more than a boy, Matt had gone from publisher to publisher with a large burlap bag slung over his shoulder, fulfilling orders for bookshops. He'd told us that most publishers would pretend to have more books in print than they really did, so that quite often his burlap bag was nearly empty after a long morning of trying to get books that were actually no longer in print for his customers. Evidently he was one of the very last of that dying breed of "bagmen"; he was also one of the last of the "uneducated" publishers. I use the word *uneducated*, but refer only to his lack of formal education. He was one of the very best educated among us, in terms of knowledge of books—after all, he'd been in both the bookselling and publishing businesses, which at times were very different indeed. In the old days, many publishers had not even finished school, let alone university. For Matt, knowledge of and possession of books gave him a feeling of value and worth, the same thing that a prestigious university degree did for other men.

Matt and I now belonged to the same club, and dined together several times each year. Matt was showing signs of aging, particularly today, I thought. Like my father, he'd been a tall man, but seemed to have shrunk. He was, however, bright of eye, spry and enthusiastic as always, neatly dressed in an ancient grey suit and old school tie. His white hair shone like a beacon.

"Welcome, Sam." Esha conferred all the dignity of royalty on my Godwin Fellow and her arrival. "And, Trevor, I'm very sorry for what's happened to McKinley Montague. A wretched end to a brilliant career . . . and a tremendous loss for you."

Trevor bowed his head in acknowledgment; I saw the tic in his eye start up again. "Thank you, Esha. I must admit it's come as quite a shock."

"Like everything else in this business," boomed Hoskins. "Now, if we might get on," he said, glancing at his watch. "I've a busy day stacking up. If you don't mind."

"Not at all," Trevor said mildly as he picked up his agenda from the conference table. "As we discussed last time, this meeting will be dedicated to discussing the PA's role in the increasingly international world of publishing. Miss Stone, we're partly referring to the gradual erosion of territorial rights, and partly to the swallowing up of British firms by larger, er, *non-British* fish."

Trevor cast a glance at Sam to see if she understood. Her confident look and brisk nod said she knew all about the subject; in fact, she managed to give the impression that she could tell us a thing or two about it. I didn't suppose territorial rights stood for as much in America, but we cared very much indeed in Britain. Normally an author sold publishers rights for a book by areas, receiving separate money and royalties for each deal: North American rights for the US and Canada; UK rights for England, Ireland, and the rest of the UK; and then Australia, Japan, Holland, Germany, and other countries individually. Now that E-sales had come into play, however, books that were not yet sold in the UK but were available in America could be sold anywhere in the world, thereby shorting the UK publisher of profits (or even of breaking even). Recently I'd been in Paris and seen the works of an up-and-coming American thriller-writer in a chain store, when I knew good and well that her agent had not sold rights to France. It was pandemic; we publishers had to cope with it somehow.

"Well, ladies and gentlemen," Trevor continued, "where do these issues leave the Publishers Association? And what are our responsibilities in light of them?"

"There's no question," Matthew Ireland said decisively. "I've explained the importance of this before: We fight tooth and nail for the status quo, and get behind efforts to police piracy with all the moral and legal muscle we've got. Look at the mess we got into with the Net Book Agreement. If we'd stood firm, we'd never have got in such a state."

"Oh, right," Hoskins scoffed. "And go back to the horse and carriage while we're about it." He shook his head as Matt glowered at him. "When are you going to crawl out of your cave and see that we can't stop progress? Our only hope—the only hope of any industry, ever—has been to get on the *right side* of change, and make it work to our benefit."

"Well," Trevor said, lifting his spectacles off and wincing as he rubbed the bridge of his nose, "I suppose we already knew where the two of you stood. Anyone else?"

"It's a nonissue," Esha pronounced quietly. "With all the mergers going on, all publishers will have their own editorial branches in the major cities anyway. I see our role as an advisory one. For those British companies not yet acquired by international giants, the PA could perhaps facilitate shared offices for them in New York—and help them get on their feet over there, cope with differences in US law and so forth." She shrugged. "Perhaps Ms Stone could help us with this while she's here."

Sam nodded.

Matt Ireland stood, trembling, and placed his hands on the table. As he did so, he bumped into the caterer, who was just placing our lunches before us. One plate of lettuce, tomato, cold chicken, and salad cream ended up squashed against the pristine white of the caterer's uniform, while another smashed against the wall and fell messily to the floor. Matt whipped round, appalled at the commotion.

"I know what all this is about," he fumed, managing to look both injured and enraged. "Some of you are in on it, I know." He looked round the table at each of us, and I saw several of my fellow board members close their eyes in exasperation. When he looked at me, I thought his eyes held my gaze for an instant longer than the others. "Well, you won't get away with it, not if I can help it. Botkin was on to it, too. You'll have to kill me, like you did the others."

Kill him! *The others?* What on earth—Suddenly I thought of Montague. If Nate's mysterious informant had been telling the truth, someone—and someone associated with Hanford Banner—had murdered him. Was this what Matt was on about?

Then another thought struck me. Matt Ireland had been one of Botkin's closest friends, and had been very distraught at the old bookseller's funeral. Botkin, too, had died recently, as had another elderly bookseller. But those were booksellers: Ireland was a publisher. Was the old man tending a bit towards paranoia?

Ireland began to bumble his way round the back of the table toward the door, so upset that though he was slight, he knocked into nearly everyone and everything along the way.

"Now look, Matt," Trevor soothed. "Be reasonable! Just because—"

Wham. The door slammed shut behind the old man with a blast of enmity.

Sam's voice broke the stunned silence. "Are your

meetings always so dramatic? We could certainly take a leaf from your book there—ours could use a bit of livening up."

Perhaps it was the wry humour in her voice, or the suggestion in her tone that she was accustomed to defusing such fraught situations. Whatever it was, Samantha Stone caused even Harold Hoskins to chuckle. In doing so she promptly won herself a place in our affections and, unofficially, on the Publishers Association board of directors.

Nothing during the rest of the meeting caused half as much excitement. We came to a decision to act upon Esha Muchmore's proposal to facilitate international offices for our London publishers, and caught up on who was buying whom since we'd last convened.

Publishing had shaken out in England so that there were only seven major players. Everyone else was in the process of either going out of business, declaring fierce independence with resignation to voluntary penury, or being gobbled up by one of the big international players—of which there were also only about half a dozen remaining.

As I looked round the conference table, I realised that everyone left in the room, except me and Duncan Whitticombe, represented the Big Seven. Duncan Whitticombe . . . who, curiously, had also wanted to buy Botkin's Books.

The business of books was an incestuous one indeed.

Another odd dozen or so UK firms floated in never-never land, content to weather the storms of publishing alone, but one had to wonder how long they would survive. Among those were the fierce independents, represented by Matthew Ireland and yours truly. Fiercely independent though I was, at times selling Plumtree

Press had seemed an extremely attractive idea; most of my troubles had arisen from my profession. I'd not have lost Sarah had I been in another field—anything but the business of books.

Surprisingly dangerous things, books. But I suspected that, having come this far and paid so dearly, I'd resist the temptation of selling the press in its eighth generation of family ownership.

When the meeting broke up, Esha Muchmore went directly to Sam and struck up a conversation. I used the opportunity to take Trevor aside. "Trevor, I know you've got a lot on your mind. But what do you think Ireland was on about?"

Trevor blew air forcefully through his lips, shaking his head. But the tic was there. "I'm concerned for the old boy. I fear he's slipping."

"The odd thing is, I couldn't help but think of three people in the bookselling world who *have* died recently—Montague, of course, and Nottingham Botkin, and his elderly bookseller friend, whose name I can't recall. You don't suppose there *is* something dodgy going on. . . ."

Trevor drew back slightly and looked at me with what appeared to be honest surprise. "Plumtree, I know you've seen your share of dark doings in the publishing world, for heaven's sake. And Montague—well, who could have known he'd meet with such an unfortunate end? But you don't honestly mean to imply that there's some grand scheme afoot! What, to eliminate all the elderly booksellers in London?" He let out a short, good-natured laugh.

"It sounds ridiculous. But you must admit, there's an unprecedented amount of change in the air. In many respects."

He stared at me, musing, apparently debating whether I'd crossed the line to insanity.

"I don't suppose you've heard anything more about Montague—exactly how he died, what they've learned about his accident?"

He looked away and began replacing papers and folders into his briefcase. "Nothing. No."

I sensed that our conversation was over. "Ah, well. See you anon, Trevor."

Trevor nodded a brisk farewell and went to have a word with Hoskins.

As Sam and I walked out of the building after the meeting, my mobile tweeted in my pocket. "Alex Plumtree," I answered, throwing Sam an *excuse me* look.

No answer.

"Hello?"

Silence.

"No one there," I told Sam, shrugging, and turned it off. As I slid the phone back into my pocket it suddenly occurred to me that Nathan might have been ringing for help. Was he in trouble? Where had he gone?

Or perhaps . . . *No. Stop it,* I told myself. That couldn't possibly have been Sarah you saw last night.

Sam looked at me with an indecipherable glance as I held the door open for her at the street. "So," I began. "You've found a flat all right? Have you begun settling in?"

"Oh, yes." She sounded amused. "Didn't I tell you? We've had a place here for ages, in Cadogan Square. My family came from England, you know."

"No, I didn't know. How convenient." Good heavens. Cadogan Square wasn't your average address. What other surprises were up her sleeve? Contrary to my expectations of playing nursemaid to a homesick American, I began to suspect she'd be teaching me a thing or two during her time here. "You know London well, then."

"Well enough to know that we're walking in the direction of your office, and that you have time to take me in and introduce me to everyone. Since you no longer have to go to meet me."

I laughed. "Quite right. Everyone's been looking forward to meeting you; you'll get along fine. I must say, we have an extraordinary group of people at the Press. Most of us are friends as well as colleagues."

Sam raised her eyebrows. "I thought *you'd* be the cynical ones," she commented, just as my phone rang again. With some irritation I plucked it out. "Hello?"

I heard someone exhale, then Nathan's voice came down the line. "Alex. I need to talk to you."

"Nate! Are you all right? I went back to check on you Saturday, but you were gone."

"You went back—to Botkin's?" This seemed to catch him off guard.

"Mmm. Where are you now?"

I could tell he was smoking by the brief delay before he answered. "Never mind. But I must tell you something important—and I'm sorry, Alex. I'm really very sorry."

"It can't be *that* bad."

Sam clipped along gamely next to me in her heels, pretending she wasn't listening.

"It is. I lied to you, Alex. Well, sort of. Someone asked me to *tell* you that I received that phone call about Montague's death—I didn't, really. And they told me to mention Gravesend and Hanford Banner."

"But I went to the signing, Nathan. Nando Worth *did* announce Montague's death."

"I know."

Not only was I bitterly disappointed that he'd lied to me, I was shocked. "Who told you to lie to me? Do you have any idea what a total twit you've made me look?"

"Look. I can't tell you who. And I've *said* I'm sorry. I just thought I owed it to you—I mean, there's more to this than you know, Alex." He paused as this sank in. "That gunshot wasn't supposed to happen. And a while ago I went by my flat. It's been ransacked. I think something's going on, and you should know—because now you're involved."

"*I'm* involved? Why? How?"

Sam looked up at me with interest. I vowed to be more careful what I said.

"There's no more time—I've got to go. Don't try to find me; I won't be in London. It's starting, Alex. It wasn't to begin until the fair, but it's starting. Now." Click. He was gone.

It's starting? What wasn't to begin until the fair? And by "the fair," did he mean the Frankfurt Book Fair in Germany, starting this Thursday?

Far from starting anything, I was ready to have a few questions answered. I didn't like the tone of this at all, but could already tell it was too late. Grendel was knocking at my door.

CHAPTER 3

I tucked the phone away and tried to bring myself back to the present and Sam. We'd come as far as Bloomsbury Way, nearly to Museum Street.

"So it's true," she said abruptly.

"What?"

"I was told there would never be a dull moment at Plumtree Press."

Ruefully, I smiled. If that wasn't true, nothing ever had been.

I took her up past Museum Street and into Bedford Square. I felt the same old pride as I opened the big black door with its brass knocker and ushered her inside. Whatever had happened in the world of publishing in the last eighty-five years, this building had been an unchanging rock, as had the business that occupied it.

"Welcome to Plumtree Press," I said with a jocular sense of ceremony.

Sam tipped her head in arch acknowledgment and stepped inside. I watched her take in the way the rampart-like door shut out nearly all the traffic noise, the formality of the black-and-white marble chequered entrance hall, the graceful curves of the elaborate chandelier overhead.

Sometimes people were a bit bowled over by this glimpse into the elegant world of publishing past, but I had a feeling it suited Sam Stone perfectly.

"Come and meet Dee."

Dee, our heavily black-booted, black-nail-varnished, and utterly delightful receptionist, had told me the week before that she was quite overwhelmed at the thought of meeting Samantha Stone. This had nothing to do, however, with our Godwin Fellow's family publishing credentials. Sam's other, better-known claim to fame was her relationship with Geoffrey Noble, the aristocratic, heartthrob actor on the American television show—carried by the network that was part of the same conglomerate as Stone & Stone—*Emergency Doctors.* Noble had emerged as a sort of American royalty. Dee referred to him as "absolutely delicious," and wondered how Sam would ever endure a year away from him.

"Perhaps we could arrange an exchange," I'd teased her the week before. "You could go over and keep him company while she's here."

"You *are* naughty," Dee'd said, and hit me over the head affectionately with a catalogue. The staff seemed much happier now that my sense of humour was returning. I'd been quite dull for a while after Sarah's disappearance.

When Sam and I walked into reception, Dee ran anxious hands through her short blond hair. Then she jumped to her feet as if to receive the Queen, hands clasped in front of her chest. I'd never seen her so twitterpated. "Oh, hello! You've arrived early!"

"Sam, this is Dee; Dee, Sam. You should know that Dee actually runs the place—I'm here as decoration only. A mere figurehead."

Dee waved this off and pulled a face, relaxing a bit. "Don't listen to him. He's all cheek."

Sam smiled. "Thanks. I'll remember that."

Just then, something in the rather appreciative way she looked at me made me wonder if everything was all right in the Geoffrey Noble department. I hoped this year wasn't going to be an exercise in flirtation, because I wasn't going to play. Good heavens, that would be awkward.

Dee was picking something up from her desk. "This arrived for you not long ago, Alex. Lisette's out, or I'd have taken it straight up to her. Looks frightfully important, doesn't it? Or expensive, at any rate." She beamed at Sam.

I took it from her and turned it over. We all gazed down at the Duke of Bradford's insignia in gold on the back of the oversized envelope.

"A rise in the rent, I'll wager," I said. "Despite all his promises to the contrary before I renovated and increased the value. Or a spectacular party invitation. What do you think?"

"Party," Sam pronounced.

"I'll go along with that," Dee agreed.

"All right: Let's settle it right now." I picked up Dee's letter opener and slit the end of the envelope, then pulled out several sheets of what appeared to be business correspondence. "Hmm . . . no party, I'm afraid." I saw the duke's business agent's letterhead, took in the words *We regret to inform you of our need for the property at 58 Bedford Square,* and stuffed it all back into the envelope. Everything at once, as usual. I'd deal with it later.

"More like a rise in the rent," I said with a sigh, and

they groaned. "Well, let's show you your office, introduce you round. See you, then, Dee."

"Lovely to meet you, Sam."

"And you."

I led the way up the plum-carpeted staircase. "We do have a lift." I just caught myself before I told her that no one ever used it except for furniture or masses of books. "You're most welcome to it."

"I can't help but notice that you're very fit. All that can't come from walking up and down the stairs."

"I'm not certain how fit I am, but I row in a pair, and we never really stop training. Ah, here we are. Nicola? Do you have a minute?"

"Of course." She stood and came round her desk, ever poised and confident. I watched with fascination as the two women appraised each other in the moment it took me to introduce them.

"Sam, this is Nicola Beauchamp. She finds all those trend-setting books for our trade division."

"Delighted to meet you, Sam. It'll be lovely to have a partner for a year."

"Thanks. I'll try not to drive you out of your mind."

Nicola laughed. "If you're not doing anything tonight, I'll take you to dinner. Tell you all of Alex's secrets." Nicola and I had arranged this, since I was speaking to the Society of Young Publishers and wouldn't be able to take Sam out for a welcome dinner myself.

"Wonderful. I'd love it."

"I can see I'll have to watch out for you two," I said. "Come on out of her clutches, Sam, and meet the others." Proudly, I took her deep into the editorial bowels of the Press. Rachel Sigridsson, our phenomenal copy editor, and Timothy Haycroft, our academic acquisitions editor, were still at lunch. Ian Higginbotham, of course, had had lunch at his desk and was hard at work. I gave a little knock on the door frame and ushered Sam into his office. "Ian. This is Samantha Stone—Sam— our Godwin Fellow."

He stood, an awe-inspiring, utterly fit and tan man of seventy-something, and took off his glasses before coming out from behind his desk. Ian was much more than the head of our academic division and co-founder of the Press. He was Sarah's grandfather, and in a way had taken the place of my own father after his death. He came towards us smiling. "Sam. I'm so pleased." He took her hand and offered her a chair. I could see that Sam was as impressed by his mild, gentle force as the rest of us.

"I'll leave you to get acquainted with the academic side of things. I'll see you in a bit."

I was returning to my office when I ran into Lisette Stoneham, my managing director, in the hallway. She checked her watch and looked at me with the slightly crazed expression I'd seen her give her own two sons. "Alex! 'Ave you forgotten your meeting with Samantha Stone? It's after two o'clock!"

I smiled. "Ye of little faith, Lisette. No, she arrived early under her own power—just in time for the PA board meeting, in fact. Pulled up in a taxi just outside the PA offices."

She raised her eyebrows at this indication of intelligence and nerve that equalled her own. Lisette, my best rowing mate's French wife, had joined the Press when I had, four years ago. She'd begun as a secretary and had quickly proved herself indispensable—and tough as nails. Not only did Lisette swear like a sailor, she could handle any situation with aplomb and joke about it besides.

"She likes to be called *Sam*, by the way."

"Oh?" Lisette was frankly curious about this new member of our little family. Lowering her voice, she said, "Tell me more."

I led her into my office, where I fell into my office chair. Lisette leaned back on the sofa, crossing one high-heeled foot over the other. Lately I'd noticed that she'd entered a new phase of tailored clothing. Whereas she used to wear free-flowing dresses along the lines of Esha Muchmore's, now she had a library of suits in a remarkable variety of colours with high heels to match. Today's was an autumnal chestnut hue. They all made the most of the more voluptuous parts of her figure; Lisette was feminine with a bang.

I continued, "She's meeting with Ian just now. I must say, I think we're in for a whirlwind year. She's a live wire."

"I suppose we might 'ave known, the daughter of *the* Samuel Stone." Lisette widened her eyes briefly in mock awe.

I could see there might be a bit of competition for the role of alpha female. Somehow Lisette and Nicola had avoided this; they were so confident in their roles— Lisette as MD and Nicola as head of the trade division— and so very different in many other ways.

As if to illustrate this, Nicola came and stood in the doorway, single, petite, dark, and serious. Lisette, sprawled on the sofa, was motherly and relaxed, comfortingly plump, her lips curving up in a wry but good-humoured smile. Ian appeared in the doorway behind them, the picture of white-haired wisdom and kindness, looking particularly fatherly with young Sam in tow.

I wanted to ask them all to hold the pose for a moment. With the potential disaster of eviction from the historic home of Plumtree Press looming, I wanted to hang on to the picture of them—Lisette in her frank loveliness, Nicola in her earnest innocence, and Ian in his perpetual perfection—and all of them my close friends and colleagues. Except for Sam, of course.

"Ah. Since we're all here—do come in, Ian, and close the door while you're at it, if you would. I'm afraid I have some bad news."

The Plumtree Press veterans glanced at one another quickly; there had been bad news enough in recent months. I could see they were imagining something far worse than mere property problems, and that helped me put it all into perspective.

"The Duke of Bradford wants his building back."

I might have predicted their reactions . . . even Sam's.

"*What?*" Lisette blustered, jumping to her feet on her nut brown heels. " 'E *can't*! I thought your father bought the building. I don't care if 'e is the Duke of bloody Bradford, 'e can't just suddenly tell you to get out!" Her eyes flashed; I saw she'd found more fuel for the fire. "And what about the flat upstairs? It's preposterous."

Sam frowned. "I don't understand. I thought you owned this building."

I could see how she might be confused. "Properties like this in London are rarely freeholds; this entire square was granted to the duke by the Crown hundreds of years ago. It's his by a sort of divine right. The entire square is held by lease—but ours, by verbal agreement between the last duke and my grandfather, was to have been virtually perpetual."

"Ah. I see." Sam made a sad little face.

True to form, Nicola remained silent, with an air of intense concentration about her. It was as though she was certain she could solve this problem, given enough information and a bit of quiet thought.

Ian came and stood behind me, as I might have expected, taking the gold-crested paper into his hand. I watched his fingers take in the fine texture of the paper, and appreciated his sharing of responsibility. I had no idea where I'd be without him. He'd shared the running of Plumtree Press with my father for forty-some years; now he shared it with me.

He must have sensed how the duke's document had thrown me; he did something very rare and made a pronouncement.

"Actually, I'm sorry to say these *were* the terms of the agreement. The duke did reserve the right to revoke our occupation of the building; he just said he'd never do it." He sighed deeply. "I am surprised that he's being quite so abrupt with us. He's exercising his right to occupy fifty-eight Bedford Square in exactly one month from today. Including," he added, "Number fifty-eight-A."

I stared down at the plush new carpet I'd installed just a couple of years ago. The flat upstairs, 58A, was currently fulfilling a personal dream. When Claire, my freelance publicity agent, no longer needed the flat, I'd finally indulged the dream of many a year and given it to my literacy pupil, rent-free. Giving up the flat and informing my tenant disturbed me as much as losing the ideal business space in which I'd invested so much.

This was purely selfish: All my life, spent between

London and Boston, and eventually later in Hanover, New Hampshire, and Cambridge, England, I'd known that I was outrageously privileged. Planted deep within me by my aristocratic American mother and noblesse-oblige father was an awareness that I must find a way to share my privileges with others less fortunate.

So I'd become involved in my father's literacy tutoring organisation. My most recent tutee was a sixty-nine-year-old immigrant who had felt uncomfortable in the home of her son and his wife, and I'd had the perfect solution. My guilt for her freedom. It had created some interesting situations—such as her address so vastly superseding her son's in prestige that at first she'd thought she couldn't accept. And then the daughter-in-law, who'd made her so desperately unwelcome, resenting her for living in WC1.

"You can't be serious!" Lisette exclaimed, irate at the duke, whom she'd never met. She turned from me to Ian and back again, incredulous. Her English got worse when she was really angry. "What about the rights for squatters? What about the legal recourses?"

"I might be able to persuade him with more money. But if the duke really wants his building back, I'll not stand in his way." It wasn't seemly to fight the Duke of Bradford over his own ancestrally owned building if he asked for it back. I wasn't the king, nor even Henning Kruse, owner of the vast educational publishing empire Spitze-Verlag that dwarfed mine, who was expecting me in an hour and a half for a most unusual meeting.

Royalty though I may not be, Ian and Ian alone knew that I was, secretly and rather quaintly, Lord Sarratt. I'd only learned of my title several months before. Just my good fortune to learn that I was a hereditary peer in the midst of a campaign by New Labour to chuck such anachronisms out of the House of Lords.

Still, me aside, there was Mrs Bhatti to think about, and Plumtree Press. Meanwhile, Lisette, Ian, Nicola, and Sam were staring at me.

"Sorry." I smiled, though I knew it was a bit thin. "I've frankly no idea what I'll do if the duke won't settle for more money." They all looked so miserable, I could see something had to be done. "Anyone for tea?"

We processed into the little tea-and-coffee-making grotto that did double duty as the storeroom, and made desultory conversation over the tea strainer. Then we retreated to our respective caves, Sam going with Lisette to learn the ropes from the master. I suspected they got as little done as I did. My eyes kept creeping back to the odious missive from the duke's business agent. I couldn't help but lament the breach of trust it represented. After all these years, why should he need the property so urgently? If we couldn't bribe him with more money, the thought of moving to some empty building and losing our Bedford Square heritage was a bleak one indeed.

There was a knock, and I looked up to see Nicola there again, a piece of A4 paper in her hand. "Sorry—I forgot what I'd come about earlier."

She looked so deadly serious that I felt guilt for having caused her such worry. "It's not *quite* the end of the world, Nicola—and it's not absolutely certain yet."

"I wish it were just that, Alex." Her eyes fell to the paper in her hand. "It's *Her Flight*."

My stomach flip-flopped. We'd paid the rising literary star Julia Northrup £750,000 for her second novel, an advance that required plenty of sales to earn it back.

"I rang a couple of the critics—you know, the ones who worked for me at the literary review—to get some initial reactions from the advance copies. The name just isn't carrying her, Alex, and they're not ready for the new experimental style she's adopted in *Her Flight*. I didn't consider it a real risk, because Julia's become such a personality cult. But it seems I miscalculated badly."

"Not you, *we*," I corrected her, and had the sensation of sliding down a slippery slope. I'd noticed in the past that once things started this sort of a downhill turn, they gathered momentum from the massed disaster and just wouldn't stop. "Odd that the reviewers had such a uniform reaction."

"I thought so, too." She frowned.

"How many have you spoken to?"

"Two last week—I didn't want to trouble you until I knew for certain—one yesterday, and one just now. I'm so sorry, Alex."

Neither of us felt it necessary to state the full meaning of Julia Northrup's failure. The twenty-three-year-old author's first novel had taken the world by storm, and we'd pursued and won the chance to publish the second—at a price. One never knew if a literary author had more than one superb novel in her; it was always a gamble.

We'd lost.

"I'm well aware that this will be my first Frankfurt Book Fair representing Plumtree Press," Nicola continued, "and I'm afraid I haven't put us in a very strong position for negotiations with the top authors. Those reviews will be all over by then—the talk of the Fair, no doubt. 'Northrup flamed out, did you hear?' "

It was true. The book world loved to gossip about

the instant successes and failures of people like Julia Northrup, and Alex Plumtree.

"Believe me, Nicola—a good reputation doesn't disappear overnight. And it's very kind of you to take full responsibility for this, but I was behind you all the way. As I recall, I encouraged you to push on with her agent when you began to have doubts. There was no way to tell what she'd produce, or how it would strike the public. You're the authority on literature; you're not to blame if the public can't see it. I still think *Her Flight* will have a significant audience, even if the reviewers steer a few readers away. . . . After all, word of mouth is still what sells books. The shops have already ordered high, on the basis of her name alone. You're simply ahead of your time, Nicola."

She responded with a weak smile. "Have you decided whether you're coming to Frankfurt?"

"Mmmm . . . I think I'll leave it in your capable hands. And Ian's, of course. Claire and Lisette will handle the stand so you'll be free for your meetings with agents. You'll have Sam, too."

Nicola raised her eyebrows in confirmation. My trade editor knew exactly who Sam Stone was, and understood her pedigree.

"I know you've had all your meetings set up for ages, Nicola, but if you like we could sit down together this week and talk about ceilings for your negotiations."

"Thanks, Alex." She hesitated for a moment before leaving, which was most unlike her.

"Anything else? Seriously, try not to worry about those Northrup reviews, Nicola. These occasional setbacks are inevitable. Besides, we don't know for certain that there's a problem."

"No—yes. Okay." She turned and went to the door, then hesitated again. "Have you heard anything more from Nate—or Trevor—about McKinley Montague's death?"

I grimaced. "Meant to tell you about that. Can you believe that Nate was told to pass on the false rumour that Montague was killed by Hanford Banner? He was specifically asked to tell *me*. Why, I can't imagine. And he won't tell me who orchestrated it all." I shook my head in disgust.

"How bizarre," she replied. "So Montague's dead, but he probably wasn't dispatched by his publisher."

I shrugged. "Evidently."

Pensively, Nicola started through the door.

"Oh—Nicola." She turned round. "Could you possibly take charge of Sam for the rest of the afternoon? I've a meeting with Henning Kruse, and don't want her to feel neglected."

"Of course."

I couldn't avoid the feeling that Nicola was hiding something from me. From the day I'd interviewed her for the job, more than a year ago, now, we'd had a strange, almost telepathic understanding. Possibly it came from having been reared in the same sort of family, attending the same sort of schools, and travelling in similar circles. It certainly made communicating with her easy, as she was usually on the same page with me even before I spoke. But this was new and strange, this keeping something back. I wondered if she was having personal problems of some sort, beyond the loss of her fiancé to another woman.

I sipped my almost-cold tea, gazing at the framed photo of my great-grandfather standing in front of the Press just after he'd acquired the lease from the famous

Bloomsbury author, Marcus Stonecypher, in 1914. Before I could sink into a reverie about losing the building, Sam appeared at my door. "Is this a good time to talk?"

Mentally, I shrugged and resigned myself to getting no work at all done that day. One of the best things I'd ever done was to hand over day-to-day operations to people more capable than myself. I checked my watch: half an hour left before I needed to leave for Henning's club. "Yes, certainly. Come in and sit down."

In the time we had, I managed to brief her on most of our current projects, international copublishing deals included. When we got to the subject of Frankfurt, I felt trepidation. "Sam, as you know, it's something of a puzzle to me why you've chosen a small independent for your Godwin Fellowship year, given your experience— though I'm delighted you did." I smiled and received a thousand-watt smile in return. "Since you are now part of Plumtree Press, however, we need you to serve in the trenches at the Fair like any other employee. I'm afraid you will learn what it's like to be part of a small Press, warts and all."

"That's what I'd hoped. I wanted to see what a *real* publisher is like . . . someone who's more involved with books than deals with dot-coms and record companies. Believe me, it won't be a chore to man the booth for you at Frankfurt."

I was impressed with her equanimity. Perhaps this would be a very good year for everyone concerned.

"When will we leave for the Fair?"

"Ah, yes. You know, I'm not going, now that I have Nicola to wheel and deal for me. Let's see here . . ." I shuffled through the papers on my desk for the Frankfurt pile, and found the leaflet under a pile of reports from Nick in accounting. Squinting at it, I was disturbed to see that in the normal daylight of the room I couldn't make out the grey-tone print. Disconcerted over what might be another decline in the waning fortunes of my eyesight— and it didn't have much farther to go—I switched on my desk lamp and glanced at Sam to see if she'd noticed.

With typical American forthrightness, she asked, "Eye trouble?"

I sighed and looked down at the brochure, avoiding her gaze. There was no harm in her knowing; she'd find out soon enough, anyway. "My worst fear, actually, is that in a few more years I won't be able to read the books I publish. Usually it's no problem. Ah—here it is. We have people setting up the stand for us, so you, Nicola, Lisette, and Ian won't need to appear until about noon on Thursday. Lisette's had Shuna arrange all the flights; she'll get you your ticket and itinerary tomorrow or the next day."

With a start, I saw that it was time to leave for my meeting with Henning Kruse. I ushered Sam over the creaking floorboards to Lisette so they could get acquainted, gave Lisette a wink that said *behave,* and trotted down the stairs and out the door. My thoughts turned to the man I would meet, one of the most powerful men in the world, let alone the publishing world—the chairman of the board of Spitze-Verlag AG.

Kruse's empire—and a nice chunk of stock was his now—not only dominated the publishing industry, having accumulated six or seven leading publishers in as many years, but had taken over significant chunks of the Internet business. Though the general public didn't realise it, two major and four minor film studios fell under the Spitze umbrella, not to mention three recording companies, a network of television stations, and even an airline or two.

For several years now I'd kept a page in the back of my Filofax that recorded who had bought whom, a sort of flow chart of mergers and acquisitions affecting British publishing. It had grown outrageously complicated, and seemed to change by the week. Sadly, in all of the huge media conglomerates, book publishing was a relatively minor consideration, trailed along with the bigger moneymaking operations for prestige as much as profits. But I suspected Henning Kruse was a true bibliophile; I think he loved the business of publishing as I did.

Half an hour later, I arrived at the all-powerful Kruse's club in St James. The porter ushered me into a private room and Kruse, a tall, golden-haired man of perhaps fifty, stood from his place at a long mahogany conference table and came to shake my hand.

"Alex Plumtree. We meet at last. This is a very great pleasure for me." His English bore the barest trace of an accent.

"And for me." I was very surprised to find him waiting for me—a rare act of courtesy for someone of his lofty position.

"Please, do sit. Congratulations on your win at Henley, Alex. It was a most extraordinary contest." His eyes twinkled as he sat down across from me. George Stoneham, who happened to be Lisette's husband, and I, along with the other six of our eight from Threepwood, had battled it out to the bitter end with a boat from Leander. We had nearly killed ourselves winning, but we had done it.

"Thank you." I laughed. "I can safely say I'll never forget it. I saw your race, too. You won with ease, as I recall. Two lengths, wasn't it?" I'd also seen him race at Henley, the world's most famous and distinguished rowing regatta on the Thames in Oxfordshire.

He smiled and nodded, trying not to look too pleased. We had an immediate understanding from our shared experience on the water. Rowing with a crew was an extraordinary exercise in teamwork, and required putting mind over body to a degree few ever imagined possible. Eight disparate people came together to pool every last ounce of effort—more than they ever dreamed they could summon—to make the boat fly through the water. It was glorious.

"Well, I won't keep you in suspense, Alex." He began twiddling with his gold fountain pen. "You must be wondering why I've insisted upon meeting with you today. I've been quite impressed with Plumtree Press. Did you know that I knew your father? When I began with a small academic publisher in Berlin, he spoke at a conference there. Fifteen years ago. I've admired your business ever since, your publishing profile and expansion into trade publishing. I took a similar route myself, except that I have ended up with a giant, while you have a small jewel."

He sat back and eyed me, toying with the pen. "Alex, I want to buy Plumtree Press."

Was it the solution to all my problems . . . or the beginning of far worse?

CHAPTER 4

Over the misty moor
From the dark and dripping caves of his grim lair,
Grendel with fierce ravenous stride came stepping.
A shadow from under the pale moon he moved . . .
Angrily he prowled over the polished floor,
A terrible light in his eyes—a torch flaming!

—BEOWULF

If Henning wanted a dramatic reaction to his dramatic offer, he was disappointed. I suppose somewhere in the back of my mind I'd suspected this was what he wanted, though I hadn't admitted it even to myself. This was probably because I was a bit afraid of the possibility of selling the Press—afraid that a desire to sell might overwhelm my heartfelt, if self-inflicted, obligation to carry on. Ian, who was my partner in ownership as well as in the work of the Press, had always made it clear that it was my decision to sell or not to sell.

I nodded at Kruse. "I see."

"I already have tentative approval from my board, and they feel the shareholders would not have any objections. We would be willing to pay you twenty million pounds. Naturally, you would stay on as publisher—if you wish."

Now I *did* struggle not to react. This was much more than I'd ever dreamed of receiving for the Press.

It would almost be foolish to refuse such a sum. And since the possibility of fathering any young Plumtrees to carry on the family tradition had all but disappeared with Sarah, I was actually tempted for a moment.

I counted to ten to temper my response. "Thank you," I said, and smiled at him to let him know I appreciated the offer. "I will consider it carefully."

"Of course. This is a big decision for you. Perhaps some time over the next day or so you might let me know which way you're leaning; I leave for Frankfurt on Wednesday night."

I nodded acquiescence and stood; he followed suit.

"Let me assure you," he said, meeting my eyes, "that we would uphold your family's fine tradition. In every way."

Something about the way he said it made the assurance easy to believe. He walked me to the door of the room, tut-tutting about the unfortunate McKinley Montague. "Oh! And don't worry about Julia Northrup and *Her Flight*. I believe you took a wise decision— time will prove us right—and we are prepared to absorb these temporary losses." He winked at me. "If indeed there are any. We have our ear to the ground, as you see."

"Ah. Yes." We didn't even have until the Frankfurt Fair to posture about the Northrup debacle; the news was already on the street—or rather, at the rarified height of Henning Kruse's ear. I said thank you and good-bye and mused that Henning had gone to rather considerable lengths to ensure that I would sell. For Plumtree Press to absorb the loss of £750,000 was really quite damaging; again, we would have to eat into the resources of the academic division, our cash cow, to finance my fledgling trade list. Henning Kruse had made sure that I realised he was offering to purchase Plumtree Press at more than full price, *and* compensate for our expected Northrup loss. Why, I didn't know; but I did know that I trusted the man. I left his club deep in thought. Was this the time to sell?

Lost in the depths of that moral dilemma, with half an hour before I had to be at the Society of Young Publishers meeting, I fled to a refuge for a bit of quiet reflection in peaceful surroundings.

But the moment I'd turned the key and swung open Botkin's door, I nearly sank to my knees in despair. The room was destroyed; it was a tragedy. I could cope with the overturned table of contemporary fiction; trade paperbacks and hardcovers alike covered the hallway.

But as I stepped beyond these poor modern victims to the antiquarian volumes beyond, I was enraged. Someone had pulled out all of the books from several cases—oddly, only along one wall—with the result that hundreds of books lay on the floor, their brittle pages splayed like broken legs. Perhaps one tenth of the antiquarian content of the shop was fallen; still, every book was precious at Botkin's. I cringed at the very thought of their cracked bindings. To anyone who cared about books, this was far worse than an honest break-in. In fact, it was positively cruel of the intruders not to have broken windows, lamps, chairs—all of which were untouched—*anything* but the books. I cast a glance into the tiny, paper-strewn office; it didn't seem to have been disturbed.

The bindings, of course, could be repaired; a restorer could rebind a book authentically, with the sort of materials used originally. But a rebound book was never quite the same—that is to say, quite as valuable.

Like antique furniture, the truly sought-after pieces were those in their original state.

I knelt to see which category of volumes had been so mistreated; I saw only volumes about bookselling, book publishing, and the book arts . . . what could the significance of that be? I'd always been intrigued by Botkin's assortment of books, but particularly shared his fascination with volumes about publishers, printers, booksellers, and the book arts. In fact, he'd been my inspiration to begin a subscription series at the Press for bibliophiles. Had someone been looking for a particular volume that had to do with the history of the book trade?

I was turning this over in my mind with distaste when I heard a voice behind me.

"My God."

I wheeled to see Trevor Gravesend. Even through the shock of the break-in, I was aware of the strangeness of his appearance there. First Whitticombe, unannounced and uninvited, then the intruders, and now Trevor. Did everyone think it was open house at Botkin's? I felt indignation rise at Trevor's presence, but then saw that I'd left the door open in my haste to inspect the damage. I suppose I couldn't blame him if the door was open; perhaps he'd even thought he might help.

"Trevor. What are you doing here?"

"What on earth, Plumtree!" Gravesend, gazing at the carnage before him, delivered it as an indictment. I realised that he—and others—were of the opinion that trouble only followed people so far, and after that they made it themselves.

"Who could have done this to you? Vandals, perhaps?" He shook his head as I shrugged in response.

"Nothing's safe anymore, is it? I was just passing, and saw the door open. . . . What a frightful mess. Here, let me help you pick up some of these. Actually, I wanted a word with you anyway. . . ."

He knelt to pick up a tragically broken volume of *Bindings of the Sixteenth Century,* but I stopped him. "Wait, Trevor. I should leave it until after the police and insurers have been. I don't suppose they'll be terrifically pleased, either." My role would be a difficult one, because I'd have to decide whether the books would be better off in their original, now broken state, or rebound. Perhaps I would give my old friend and restorer, Diana Boillot, a call.

"Oh, right. Of course. What am I thinking." He nodded and stood again, glancing at his watch. "I'm sorry, Alex, I can see this isn't a particularly good time for you. But there's something quite important I need to discuss with you. Could we . . . ?"

Would this be about Montague at last, I wondered? The true story of what happened to the poor man?

Bare minutes now until I was due to speak at the Society of Young Publishers, and Trevor seemed to want to sit down in Botkin's alcove. The only possible response was to welcome him and offer him tea. It was unusual of him to want to stop to talk; at Merchant Taylors school governors' meetings he was always quick to leave and get on with his business. The same at the Publishers Association. This *must* be important, I thought.

"No, thank you—I'll make this quick and be on my way."

We'd no sooner settled in the chairs, Trevor's dapper presence instantly transforming the place's seediness into stylish understatement, than he said, "I won't mince words, Alex. We've known one another for a long time, and I think you know you can trust me. I know I can trust you. I want to buy Plumtree Press. We're prepared to offer in the neighbourhood of fifteen million." The tic started again as he looked me directly in the eye.

I barely managed to suppress an urge to laugh. I couldn't tell him about Kruse's offer, of course . . . but it was uncanny. The atmosphere of the bookshop, which was as timeless as if it had been there since the discovery of fire, and the two bizarre and unsuspected purchase offers, gave me the feeling I'd entered an alternative universe, one where only the unexpected happened.

"What is it?" He frowned; he knew me well enough to sense my reaction.

"Well, Trevor, not only do I find it ironic that yours is the second offer in as many hours, but I'm curious." I toyed with the tassels of a tapestry cushion. "We've seen each other at least once a month for four years or so now. You've never mentioned this before. I must say, this all seems a bit sudden." Privately, I wondered if it all had anything to do with Montague, and my mentioning to Trevor that his company had been implicated in his death.

I decided to be direct. "Why does Hanford Banner want to purchase Plumtree Press?"

"My dear boy, I should think you would be delighted at the offer, not suspicious. Why *shouldn't* we want to purchase Plumtree Press? For your size, you're remarkably profitable and prolific. You've high visibility, as well. We could do with a bit of that."

I thought about the recent pattern of mergers and acquisitions reflected in the scribblings in my Filofax. Hanford Banner had been the latest to succumb. Were there rumours circling in the publishing industry about Plumtree Press? Why would *two* publishing houses—well, one giant media conglomerate and one publishing house—suddenly be after us?

I had a feeling that a great tidal wave was sweeping across the British publishing industry in slow motion, and I was caught in the middle of it. "All right, Trevor; thank you. I promise to consider it."

"Good!" He rose with artificial conviviality, almost as if I'd agreed to sell. "Sorry, I must run, but you will let me know, won't you? The others will be waiting to hear."

"Of course. By the way, Trevor, about McKinley Montague—"

"Mmm?" He pushed his hair back and tried not to look so hurried. After all, he might reasonably expect a question or two after offering to buy my company.

"Nate Griffith rang me this morning. He claimed that someone—he wouldn't say who—*asked* him to tell me that Hanford Banner had had Montague killed. I thought it was wildly improbable all along, but Trevor—don't you think it's odd that he should die so suddenly, on the very eve of his book's release?"

"We're back to that again, are we?" Affronted, Trevor took a step back.

I found his apparent disregard for the poor author's death reprehensible. "Yes, we certainly are, Trevor. The man is dead!"

"I'm all too aware of that, Plumtree! Just what the devil are you getting at?"

"No one seems to care, that's all. I think Montague *might* have been killed . . . I'm not saying you knew anything about it, of course. But someone shot at Griffith and me the night of the signing, and I can only think it's because Griffith already knew Montague was dead. And he *pretended* to know that Hanford Banner had done it. All this made Nate and me sit up and take notice, if no one else." Only then did it occur to me that perhaps Nate had become afraid of what he'd got involved with, regretted telling me, and so rang me back with a lie. Perhaps the anonymous tip about Hanford Banner really had come just as he said, and he was backtracking now. And I'd just spilled the beans to Trevor.

My old friend's scowl softened into a look of concern. "*Shot* at you! I'd no idea."

"It certainly gave us pause."

"Don't you think it might have been a random shot? Look at the vandalism to this shop. Violence is rampant these days—at least compared to what it used to be. I don't mean to minimise it, Plumtree, but sometimes I marvel at your imagination. You should be writing these novels yourself, I think." He turned in the doorway. "You'll let me know what you're thinking, then? About selling the Press?"

"Right. Yes. Thanks, Trevor."

He lifted a hand in farewell and was off.

I, too, lifted a hand, and let it fall as the door closed behind him.

Now there was no doubt in my mind. *Something* quite bizarre was, as Nathan liked to say, afoot. As I made a mental inventory of the books unceremoniously dumped on the floor of Botkin's, I saw that the number of books seemed to correspond roughly with the number missing from the shelves. Odd; they hadn't taken much, if anything. Why, then, had they bothered? What had they been looking for?

I also reviewed my strange—and very unexpected—encounter with Trevor.

Not only had Trevor's response to my questions about Montague's death been odd, but so had been his reaction to the news that we'd been shot at. And two purchase offers in one day?

I sighed, rang the police, and asked Nick Khasnouri, our accountant, to meet them at Botkin's. Then I rang the insurance office, and made an appointment to meet them at the shop the next morning at ten. After a final regretful look round Botkin's, I locked up and stepped out into the brisk Mayfair dusk. The eager members of the Society of Young Publishers would not wait. After drawing a deep breath, I told myself to focus on what I'd decided was important. I hailed a taxi for Terra, the latest Terence Conran restaurant, near Covent Garden, where the future media moguls of the world were meeting.

My thoughts wandered as I relaxed on the ride eastward. I felt strongly about the SYP, though I'd come to it late. I'd never planned on a career in the family business, and had forsaken a lowly entry job in publishing as salesman or assistant dogsbody for a life of leading sailing holidays in the Aegean. (That is, until I could indulge in my real dream, which only Sarah and Ian knew about.) But whereas most publishers found ways to avoid this group of aspiring publishing professionals, I was inspired by their enthusiasm. They worked with painful eagerness for starvation wages to make photocopies and fetch tea, all for the most remote chance to advance to an editorial role in several years, or a more significant role—if they were lucky—in a decade. No question, their idealism was touching.

I was also trying to atone for my privilege in having been born, without any effort whatsoever, into the highest levels of British publishing. These young people were no fools; they knew it was unfair, and they knew *I* knew.

Fifteen minutes later, I pounded up the stairs at Terra, to find not only that I was well ahead of time, as intended, but that Sam Stone was in attendance—*not* as intended. "Sam—what about your dinner with Nicola?"

"I don't think she was offended—she had some sort of crisis at work, and I told her I wanted to learn more about publishing in England. She agreed that this was the place to be." Sam shrugged and unveiled her blinding smile. I didn't see how I could disagree, though I was a bit wary of her intentions, despite her TV doctor.

"Alex!" Brian Fortescue exclaimed, rising to shake my hand from his place at the bar next to Emma Lathrop. The organisers of the SYP affairs had obviously got to know Sam quite well already. All looked to be well along on a second drink. Tall and dark-haired, with elfin ears, Brian reminded me of his father—though he had a bit of gawkiness about him. "*Great* to see you again. Rotten time for publishing, though—for Hanford Banner—or should I say Megacom?—in particular," Brian said, giving me a meaningful look. He was the twenty-five-or-so-year-old heir to a well-known but struggling literary publishing firm. Unlike me, he was paying his dues ahead of time. "Isn't it remarkable?" he clucked. "All those royalties to the bereaved family, and all those profits to Hanford Banner."

"Brian, you frighten me. We'll have to have *you* speak on ethics one of these days."

He let loose a genuine, healthy guffaw. It was a bit

of a joke to have me speak on the topic of ethics. The year before I'd published a book with the sole aim of keeping a certain politician out of office—a questionable motive at best, though if you held a referendum today, the British population would thank me. Fortunately, all had ended well. But both my effort and the book I'd published had been badly misunderstood at the time . . . thus the focus on ethics.

"Mr. Plumtree! Alex, I mean. So glad you could come." Emma, who'd worked her way up the hard way through sales and was now head of promotion at Hanford Banner, showed every sign of making it to the top in publishing—if she wasn't lost in the merger shuffle. She was what I believed earlier generations had called "plain" in the physical sense, but happily, in the twenty-first century, this shouldn't matter. She unquestionably had the intelligence, intuition, and tenacity to make a go of it. I noticed that she'd taken to wearing her hair back, gathered into some sort of knot, which suited her nicely.

"Thanks for coming early," she said, and ordered me a drink. It was a time-honoured tradition to assemble in the bar before SYP dinners. "I know you're always terrifically well prepared for these things. You'd be surprised what we have to cope with from some of your peers. Sometimes I have to literally go in a taxi and drag them here. Now, then. What are you going to tell us?"

"In a nutshell, how dreadfully sorry I am that I ever published a book entitled *Cleansing,* no matter how meaningful its content. And that I would do it all again if I felt it was the *right* thing to do."

"Right. Okay. You'll do, then. Cheers."

The next forty-five minutes passed in a blur of eager young faces—some sycophantic, some purely perceptive and bright, some blatantly ambitious. I was touched by the fact that we all start out as such innocents, so eager to do the right thing. God willing, I would help them to stay that way by what I said that night. But I knew only too well that ethics were very personal indeed . . . and rather, well, *flexible* for most people.

It wasn't until the main course, after my informal lecture about ethics, that Emma asked her question. "What do you feel is the appropriate course of action if your employer asks you to do something you know is inappropriate?"

I raised my eyebrows. "Such as . . . ?"

She blushed. "To go along with something you know is wrong, for the sake of an author's success—and for . . . *profits*." She pronounced this last word as if it were obscene.

I met Emma's gaze and nodded to show I understood. "That is a difficult position indeed. On the one hand, you are obliged to your employer for your livelihood—and we all know how difficult it is to come by a job in publishing. On the other hand, you are also obliged to do the right thing. Last year, when I published *Cleansing* to keep what I felt was an odious politician from Number Ten, one of my employees was furious with me. She didn't quit, but she didn't speak to me for weeks, either. Eventually, we came to an understanding—but it wasn't pleasant, any of it.

"The clearest and most difficult thing about ethics," I said to the table of twenty-nine fresh young faces, "is that only *you* know for certain what the right thing is."

Next to me, I felt Sam relax a bit. Perhaps she agreed with me. I'd ignored her, by and large, as I'd related my experiences and chatted to Emma, and Sam had remained silent throughout the discussion. I felt she'd played along admirably, and with jet lag at that.

"Often we don't want to acknowledge it, but if you are honest with yourself, you know what's right. I encourage you to act upon it and stand by it with all your tenacity."

The table seemed to sense that this was the end of my comments, and applauded. It was then that the unfairness of it all struck me. I'd done the right thing in every instance I could remember, and where had it got me? My beloved fiancée had been kidnapped and probably killed. My father, too, had always done the right thing. Now he was gone, as well, under similarly strange and violent circumstances. I felt imminent hot tears. I had to leave, fast.

"Excuse me," I said. "Sorry, I really must go. Thank you for a most thought-provoking evening." I did what I could in the way of a smile and stood, motioning to a stunned Emma and Brian that all was well; they need not leave the group.

"Alex! I—"

"Thanks, Sam, I must be off. Good night." Aware that she knew her way about London very well indeed, I carried on at a speed she could not mistake for anything but a desire to escape.

Home was my only thought. Home to solitude which, in Sarah's absence, was the best comfort I could hope for. As I retrieved my car from outside the Press, I noticed that it was dark and quiet at Number 58; all seemed well, except for the fact that we were being thrown out like unwelcome guests. I lowered myself into my newly acquired Volkswagen Passat and made for Chorleywood.

My CD of Haydn's *Creation* got me as far as Rickmansworth. I drove on in silence, windows down. The ritual of negotiating the narrow drive off Old Shire Lane to the house was a comforting one; a mixture of boxwood and holly brushed against both sides of the car on the narrow drive. After parking in the garage I stepped outside again to hear the night sounds and enjoy the peace of the evening.

What a day. Thank God it was nearly over. I meandered inside, disarming and arming again my recently installed alarm. I'd installed it to protect Sarah mainly, and secondly the family's priceless collection of books. Every day I tried not to think about the duty it had failed to perform.

I gravitated towards the library, as always, enjoying the aroma of the many fine old books that lived there. After turning on the lights I poured myself a whisky and looked in on the answering machine before settling in to my favourite chair. Someone—or perhaps a series of callers—had reached the answering machine and hung up six times in a row. The most recent call had been just twenty minutes ago. These ominous blank messages had a very sinister feeling about them; I'd have given anything to confide in Sarah how I felt, how fearful I was of the deadly goings-on Nate had warned me I was now a part of. I would, I decided, ring Ian for a bit of friendly counsel and comfort after a bit.

I had only just sat down and taken a sip of my peaty drink, hefting a manuscript my *Beowulf* scholar Gabriel Hammonds had proposed a month ago entitled *A History of English Printing* into my lap, when the phone rang. I gazed at colour photocopies of portraits of eighteenth-century, powdered-haired men and their seventeenth-century predecessors just inside the title page as I picked up. "Alex Plumtree."

But as I spoke, the light on the house alarm panel caught my eye; the light had flashed to green and back to red again—all very quickly. I'd never seen that particular phenomenon before . . . perhaps a brief power outage, I told myself, though the skin on the back of my neck prickled. The small red monitor light, showing that the alarm was now on, glowed steadily as I watched it. "Hello? Is anyone there?"

"Alex—yes. Sorry, it's me. Gabriel Hammonds. Please—don't hang up."

It was our *Beowulf* scholar, the one who had discredited us so very publicly in the national press. My mind's eye called up the scholar's unruly, too-long hair and rumpled coat, the few whiskers he always missed when shaving, his squeaky rubber-soled shoes.

"Hammonds. Ian and I have been trying to reach you over the past few weeks. We'd nearly given up. Where've you been?"

"I—er—I had to go away for a bit. And I'm not exactly proud of what I've done, Alex, as you might imagine."

I'd thought long and hard about the *Beowulf* scholar's plight, the pressures that must have made him publicise a false but newsworthy theory. I'd liked him from the start; was stunned by his betrayal; would never have believed that he'd have been so unscrupulous. But I would never, ever invite him to give a speech on ethics.

"Hammonds, I suggest we let bygones be bygones. We will need your advance back, but—"

"Listen to me, Alex." I'd never heard the gentle

Beowulf scholar sound so forceful. "You have no idea what I've done. It's worse than you might imagine. I— They threatened me. I was frightened. They said if I didn't cooperate in pretending I'd fabricated the evidence, I'd . . . Well, it was horrible, what they said."

I was silent, aghast. It sounded uncannily like Nate, who'd called to recant what *he'd* said.

"I simply couldn't let the lie stand one moment longer. I leave it up to you what we do next. I'm prepared to face up to the truth—I've spent my academic life on *Beowulf*, and particularly on dating this epic. I'm so sorry, Alex."

"Hammonds, who did this? Who told you to—" Perhaps it was a horrible flaw in my personality, but I believed my ex-author.

But he was gone. There was a click, and dead silence. I pressed the redial button, but to my surprise, there was no dial tone. It was my line that was dead.

Hammonds's words, the rogue blink of the alarm, and the dead phone line were hardly needed to tell me that I was in immediate danger. I reached into the drawer and groped for a doorbell-like button that—the alarm company assured me—would send an emergency radio signal directly to Hertfordshire Constabulary. I only hoped the damned thing worked—I'd laughed when the fellow had suggested it and had never so much as tested the device.

Where was it? I rummaged amongst suburban detritus—a remote control, coasters, snippets of paper, pens and pencils, a deck of cards—and heard a floorboard creak in the hallway.

Instantly, the house was plunged into darkness. Every sound stood out in relief to the utter quiet. The house was so familiar to me that I knew its every sound, knew precisely where my intruder was. He lurked just inside the doorway. I could tell from the timbre of the creak that he was not heavy; I imagined a small, catlike man.

As he inched closer—I felt my attacker knew exactly where I was—I crept as silently as I could to the sofa, and took refuge behind it. I was crawling on hands and knees towards sanctuary when I heard silenced bullets snick into the leather chair I'd occupied only moments before.

Bullets; Nathan. Was the intruder here because of what Nathan had told me? Had it been true? As I struggled to preserve my life, I was aware of how very much I longed to survive . . . a month earlier, I couldn't have been bothered.

I made a dash for the hallway, cringing as I heard bullets plant themselves in the three-hundred-year-old mantel. But I smacked hard into a very solid form: *a second man,* larger, heavier than I. *Professionals,* the thought flew through my mind; *silent, deadly, leaving nothing to chance. . . .*

With both hands I gripped his thick, meaty right wrist, gloved in something smooth, and struggled with all my might to hold his arm straight, anything to keep his gun pointing *away.* But my attacker flung me with superhuman strength and agility against the wall; my head hit the wall hard, and my chest collided with a framed portrait of our family. It clattered to the floor as I clung doggedly to that deadly wrist, expecting his friend to spray bullets at me any second if the giant didn't.

But at that moment the blessed voice of Constable Mick Parsons came from just inside the front door.

"Drop it! Police!"

I threw myself around the corner into the kitchen and stumbled towards the outside door, cringing away from the awful smack of bullets all around me. *Dear God, please let me make it. . . .*

I grappled with the doorknob and deadbolt for several eternities before finally escaping from the kitchen and dashing for the hedge along the side of the back garden. In the shelter of the thick boxwood, trying to quiet my breathing, I listened. All was ominously quiet. With sick dread I thought what the silence might mean for Mick. He was a good man, broad, squat and strong like a mastiff, as well as self-conscious about his thinning blond hair. He was loyal to his colleagues and kind to the people he served, which all too often included me. Everyone liked him, enjoyed a jar at the pub with him when he was off duty. An expanding stomach testified to his happy, comfortable life now that he was thirty-five and well established with wife and kids. *Be careful, please be careful . . .*

I couldn't just stand there and let him die. Whatever was happening in there, I had to try to help him. I ran to the rear end of the hedge and emerged, planning to enter the house again through the french doors of the library. But as I crossed the rose garden and approached the doors, I perceived two dark forms fleeing through the french doors, not ten feet from me. If they'd looked my way, they'd have seen me; as it was, they seemed intent upon running round the east side of the house to the front, where presumably a car waited.

I stayed where I was, recovering from a second terrifying near-miss, and heard light, fast-as-lightning footfalls on the circle of gravel in front of the house.

Mick's heavier steps followed. A car door slammed. He revved up the police sedan, turned on his blue flashing light and siren, and gave chase to the car that had just started up outside the end of the drive.

I sat heavily on the doorstep, sweaty and quaking, straining for sounds of the chase. Dear God, how I wished assassins would stop coming to my paradise in the countryside and turning it into a living hell. When—how—would it all end? Hugging my rapidly chilling, damp shirtsleeves, I pondered the bizarre succession of events in the last few days. First McKinley Montague's death, Trevor's implication in it, and Emma Lathrop's question about her employer's ethics at the SYP meeting.

Nathan's revelation, so closely followed by the first bullet. Then his sudden disappearance and subsequent apologetic phone call of warning.

Sam Stone's arrival and attendance at the PA board of directors meeting.

The Duke of Bradford's prickly eviction notice. Not one, but *two* offers to purchase the Press.

The vandalism at Botkin's.

And finally, a *second* guilty confession— Hammonds's—and a private assault team in my home . . . one sophisticated enough to know how to get round a top-notch alarm system. A firecracker had certainly been tossed into the tinder box . . . but it was a long time until Guy Fawkes Night.

It was not, however, so very long—just three days— until the Frankfurt Book Fair . . . which, Nate had said, would play a part in whatever dangerous scheme had come to include me. The Fair motivated all sorts of wheeling and dealing, with plenty of posturing by publishers who felt the need to make a certain impression, including, I supposed, Hanford Banner and Spitze-Verlag. And I could see that if Montague *had* been murdered for Hanford Banner's bottom line, and they thought Nate had told me, they'd have to get rid of us. But what was Hanford Banner doing acquiring presses like mine for millions of pounds, if they were so desperate for sales that they had to murder Montague?

The tyres of a car sounded on the drive, approaching at normal speed. Mick pulled his car into the circle quietly, sans sound and light show. "Sorry, Alex. They're gone. Not your average gun-toting thugs, those—they knew what they were about. I've got the news out on the radio. Didn't see the number plates, but it was a black Mercedes." He paused to take a look at me. "Are you all right?"

"I'm fine . . . I was worried about you, though. Join me for a cup of tea? It's not much thanks for saving my life, but it's a start."

Half an hour later, fortified by Fortnum and Mason's Millennium Blend, he seemed quite taken aback by the rather questionable things I'd told him about McKinley Montague and Nate's call. I was without contest the most frequent recipient of police visits in our little corner of the countryside, and police in the area had come to accept it. They doled out sufficient measures of good-natured teasing to make sure I never forgot my special standing.

"So my little alarm gadget worked. I wasn't even sure I'd managed to hit the button."

"Oh, no, we didn't get an alarm signal from you." Mick set down his tea mug and stood, dusting biscuit crumbs off his uniform. "It was your neighbour down the road phoned us. Said she'd seen 'suspicious people creeping about' in the lane, and thought they might even have weapons. I was picking up a curry in the New Parade when the call came in, so they dispatched me, gun and all." He frowned. "Wait a minute . . . didn't your leaseholder move house?"

He and I looked at each other. I nodded. "Nearly a year ago, to be nearer her children."

"Then who . . . ?"

I shook my head as we walked to the door and out to his car. "God knows, Mick. Only God knows. If things get the slightest bit more insane round here, I'll sign myself into the loony bin—and it'll be a relief."

"I always said you Plumtrees read too many books for your own good."

I laughed. "Too right, Mick. Good night."

I might have known that things would indeed grow still more insane; in fact, events had only just begun to gather speed.

It didn't help matters that as I switched off the lights in the library before going to bed, I caught a whiff of Sarah's perfume—complicated, heady, it was without doubt the scent called Ysatis, by Givenchy. Was my mind playing tricks? My head whipped round, instinctively searching for her, certain that *she* must be there if her perfume was . . . but even in the dim light, I was utterly, unmistakably alone.

What was happening to me?

Over the course of a long, sleepless night, my mind, like my body, twisted and turned. At three o'clock, when both bed and brain were badly distressed jumbles, I gave it up and went downstairs.

What *had* old Matt Ireland meant at the PA meeting, anyway? He said they'd have to "kill him like the others." Had he meant Montague? But then why the plural? The only "others" I could think of—people who'd died recently whom Matt knew—were old Botkin and what's-his-name. But why would anyone kill the kindliest old bookseller in London? Nottingham Botkin was the most harmless person I knew, and one of the best loved by his customers and fellow booksellers.

His fellow booksellers . . . I poured full-cream milk into Sarah's Bateman's mug and thought of the changes Botkin had seen in his life—the giving way of small independent shops like his to international monoliths like Wellbrook's. Massive debt, deep discounts, the disregard of territorial rights—all had changed our business drastically. No one quite knew how it would all end.

As the kettle boiled and clicked off, I smiled at the memory of the eccentric old Botkin. Suddenly I wanted to do nothing so much as go to Botkin's and rummage about in his landslide of papers. Especially now that the shop had been broken into, I was more convinced than ever that Botkin was somehow connected to McKinley Montague's demise and Matt Ireland's odd accusation at the PA meeting. Matt had mentioned Botkin just after the comment about Trevor—or someone—having killed "the others," but I wasn't sure if he meant to include Nottingham Botkin in the ranks of the murdered. After all, Botkin's deadly tumble down the shop's cellar stairs had been represented as an accident. Much had been made at his high-church C of E funeral of the difficulty of reconciling such tragic accidents with God's will. I'd give Matt a call as soon as the hour was reasonable—I'd meant to do so the day before—and ask him. I needed to ring Ian, too.

I splashed some water on my face, cleaned my

teeth, threw on a pullover and trousers, and climbed into the Passat. As I backed out I caught sight of the alarm control box in the garage and hesitated. I didn't like leaving the library with a wonky alarm system, although it hadn't done much good anyway—*again*— in the end. I switched the ignition off, climbed out of the car, went to the control box, and opened the cover.

It had never occurred to me to have the garage included in the alarmed area, but obviously this was necessary—in my case, anyway. A clump of wires had been cut with meticulous neatness, but one lone wire still snaked up to the box. It was clear what the intruders had done: They'd cut the wires to the alarm system, but immediately supplied power again to make it look as if it were still working. Was this circumvention common thieves' and murderers' knowledge? I thought not, and felt a case of the heebie-jeebies coming on as I thought of them inspecting my system some time ago and working out how to get round it.

Worse, I knew this wasn't the end of it: They'd be back, as they'd failed to dispatch me. And the alarm, my only line of defence, wouldn't help at all. Grimly, I finished stripping the ends of the cut wires and twisting them back together again into their wire nuts, and closed the front of the metal control box. Who on earth was I up against here?

I stepped back into the house just long enough to rearm the system, for all the good it would do me, and went back out to the car. As I neared the corner, where I would turn right to reach the M25, I caught sight of a black Mercedes, half-hidden in the overgrown blackberry brambles. I accelerated past it, gooseflesh from the feeling of yet another encounter crawling up my arms, and rang Mick Parsons on my mobile.

"You be on your way, and leave this to us," he said with authority. "They're not following you, then?"

I assured him that they weren't . . . yet. Only too happy to comply with his instructions to get away, I gave him my mobile number and carried on to Botkin's in London.

Whoever the men in my house had been, they had been deadly serious. I didn't feel safe in my home, and they would no doubt track me down at the Press or wherever I might be.

When I pulled in to Curzon Street to park near Botkin's Books, it was almost four A.M. The streets were, for once, absolutely deserted. This was a great relief. The shop had already been broken into once—I didn't think they'd bother a second time—and no one but the inner circle at Plumtree Press, Duncan Whitticombe, Trevor Gravesend, and now Nathan knew that I owned the famous Botkin's. No commandos with silenced guns would seek me out there, I hoped, particularly in the middle of the night . . . unless Nathan had felt another bout of logorrhea coming on.

When I unlocked the rear door of the shop, I was reminded of the unfriendly visitors who'd tipped over Botkin's publishing, bookselling, and book arts shelves. Again I couldn't help but wonder: mere (mere!) vandalism, or a search? That they'd chosen only one category of antiquarian books made me suspect the latter, but there was no way to know for certain.

And were the book vandals the same people who'd hunted me down in my own home?

What in heaven's name was happening?

Deep in thought, I wandered into Botkin's office, where he'd had that final, intense word with me while handing over his keys. His old oak desk was still covered with the mess of papers. I'd meant to go through them for the several weeks I'd owned the shop, but just hadn't got to it. Now I was irresistibly driven to see what had been happening in old Botkin's life in the weeks preceding his death . . . and to see if there was, in fact, any cheque from Duncan Whitticombe.

I sifted through piles of receipts, for which the old man seemed to have had no system at all, bills, and correspondence. I began putting these into a semblance of order, in neat piles on the floor. Several inches down into the paper jungle I discovered a letter from a powerful London landowner who I now recalled was Botkin's landlord. The really fascinating thing about this particular gent being Botkin's landlord was that he happened to own many of the properties along Charing Cross Road and in Covent Garden. The booksellers' and publishers' landlord, so to speak. I happened to know, in fact, that this fellow was Matt Ireland's landlord in Covent Garden, and a friend of his from many years in the book trade.

But landlords tended to keep to the area of their speciality, and I found it hard to believe that Mr Charing Cross had suddenly purchased Botkin's tiny bit of Mayfair as well.

> *Dear Mr Botkin,*
>   *I am sorry to inform you that I will require the building in which your shop has been located for these many happy decades. I shall require Number Eighteen Curzon*

Street exactly one month from today, and
apologise for any inconvenience this may cause.

Still holding the letter, I backed up until I hit Botkin's solid desk chair and sank into it. Today was 14 October. The letter was dated 1 September. Not only was I taken aback by the similarity of the letter to the one I'd received from the Duke of Bradford, but I was quite surprised to learn that I'd purchased a shop that was being forced to move. This was no small issue, as Botkin's location was in large part responsible for its success.

It just so happened that Ed Maggs's family enterprise, Maggs Bros, one of London's most famous and highly respected antiquarian booksellers, was just round the corner in Berkeley Square. The stream of foreigners with oodles of money to spend on rare books, after Maggs, had a habit of popping round to see what they might find in the infinitely more humble—though in its way equally charming—Botkin's.

I rummaged through to see if I could find any further correspondence on the subject, but found only a letter from Folio B (an irregular acronym of "For the Life of Old Books"), the antiquarian bookselling ethics group, taking Botkin to task for misrepresenting a book he'd sold that summer at a Provincial Book Fair Association fair.

Botkin? Botkin would *never* have misrepresented a book under any circumstances. It was not something that would occur to him, nor that he would allow—even under coercion.

Intrigued, I rummaged further but found no more letters on the property eviction or anything else. Nor was there a cheque with Duncan Whitticombe's name on it.

Botkin seemed to have been the recipient of the same sort of all-fronts assault I'd received lately.

And then it struck me. When had Botkin decided to sell? Certainly within the last month, after the date of the letter from his landlord. And when had I been approached to sell the Press? Only after I'd been informed of my impending eviction, and been professionally worn down by the (apparently fraudulent) errors of Hammonds's book.

It was a reach, but I couldn't ignore the similarity of my situation and Botkin's. Fortunately, there was one difference: he was dead and I wasn't.

CHAPTER 5

Greedily he reached his hand for the next—
  little reckoning
For Beowulf.

— BEOWULF

Feeling that I stood at the edge of an abyss, I paced the length of the shop and thought. Why hadn't the Landlord of Charing Cross forcibly evicted Botkin's Books by now, if he was so bent on doing it? The tiny rare bookshops along Charing Cross Road certainly owed him for their demise. Had the shop's changing hands somehow changed things, or had Botkin's death simply confused the landlord—or more unlikely, perhaps struck a chord of mercy—and delayed the move? Perhaps Matt Ireland had intervened on his old friend Botkin's behalf.

I pulled out my mobile and rang Lisette's voice mail at the Press. "Lisette. Would you please ring Neville Greenslade this morning and have him approach the Duke of Bradford's business agent—in a very friendly way, of course—offering a lump sum payment of up to one hundred thousand pounds to let the Press stay? If that's refused—whether today or next week—have him try to find out why His Grace needs us to move. All right? Oh, and would you or Nick please meet the insurance investigator at Botkin's at ten this morning? Thanks, Lisette. I might make myself scarce today—something rather nasty's come up. Bye for now."

I glanced at my watch; another hour until I could reasonably call Ed Maggs and try to get to the bottom of this. Matt Ireland, too. There was no doubt now that I was in the sort of trouble Botkin had told me I'd recognise.

Very curious indeed.

It was, however, late enough to ring Ian, and to find coffee and a croissant nearby. I locked up the shop and wandered over to Shepherds Market, where there was a Starbucks, and entered Ian's number on my phone along the way. Ian was always up as early as five in the morning, so I knew I wouldn't disturb him. When he answered, out of breath, I knew he'd been for a run. "Good morning, Ian—it's me."

"Alex! Bit early for you, isn't it?"

"Yes . . . but things have gone a bit crazy again, I'm afraid. Hammonds rang me last night, claiming that he was threatened to recant his *Beowulf* dating theory—or else. I believe him, Ian. Perhaps we should try to meet with him in the next couple of days. . . . We didn't really get to finish the conversation. We were cut off, and then I was attacked."

"*Attacked*—didn't you have the alarm on?"

"Yes. They got round that without any trouble. I'm a bit confused at this point as to who might have been behind it . . . especially as someone shot at Nate Griffith and me the night of the Montague signing. I'm afraid we're in the midst of another kerfuffle, Ian."

I elaborated for him, spelling out every last bizarre occurrence of the last few days, including my glimpse of Sarah, Matt Ireland's outburst, the two purchase offers from Hanford Banner/Megacom and Spitze-Verlag, and the ruined books in Botkin's.

"Good heavens. Why on earth didn't you ring me sooner, Alex?"

I hesitated. Since Sarah's disappearance, I'd drifted away from the close relationship I'd always enjoyed with Ian. Not because I didn't care about him as if he were my father, but because, I suppose, I saw how the loss of his granddaughter had ripped him apart. And it had been my fault; I had left her alone at the Orchard, and she'd been taken because of another messy book incident arising from my very own library. Ian didn't blame me, but I blamed myself.

"Sorry . . . What about meeting with Hammonds?"

He sighed; we both knew I'd sidestepped his kind concern yet again. "I'm attending the *Beowulf* conference at Cambridge tomorrow. Perhaps he'll be there, if he plans to reclaim his position in the scholarly community. I'll give him a ring and let you know."

We rang off as I arrived at the Starbucks; I felt guilty about the way I'd shut Ian down, but didn't feel like dwelling on it. I bought a *Times* at the kiosk outside and stepped in. The woman behind the counter told me she'd bring my order to my table, so I sat and unfolded my newspaper. Yet another skirmish in Bosnia . . . Prince Charles and Camilla Parker-Bowles were starting a charity for starving artists together, and . . .

An article near the bottom of the page grabbed my attention just as my coffee and croissant arrived. "Good heavens!" I exclaimed.

"What is it, sir?"

"No, no, sorry," I assured her. "Thank you— everything's fine." But an awful certainty gripped me as I raced through the article.

WELLBROOK'S MEGASTORE ACQUIRES
HANFORD BANNER FROM MEGACOM

One of Britain's most respected publishing companies has been purchased by the new Australian book chain, Wellbrook's, now of Charing Cross Road and Piccadilly. The acquisition took industry watchers by surprise: Hanford Banner had only just been purchased by communications giant Megacom mere days before. The sale is also notable because until now, publishers have owned bookshops, but not vice versa. Wellbrook's, a private company, refuses to disclose the purchase price, as do Megacom and Hanford Banner. At a private meeting to announce the sale Tuesday, Chairman Trevor Gravesend said, "It was inevitable. Just as publishers used to print and sell their own books, we're all moving closer in the industry. Booksellers and publishers have always worked together very closely indeed—this should facilitate even closer cooperation."

I guffawed aloud, and the coffee shop's quiet population studied me guardedly. A nutcase in their midst? Quite likely.

"Sorry," I said aloud to the clientele. They went back to their espressos and lattes, some with smiles, some with looks of stern censure.

Trevor's words could not possibly be farther from the truth: Booksellers had very nearly put publishers out of business with deep discounting and rigid terms that hardly favoured publishers.

My eyes followed the inexorable print down the page.

When asked about the issues this raises for the publishing industry—for instance, publishers being required to show manuscripts to national Wellbrook's managers before accepting them for publication—Wellbrook's Piccadilly shop manager Sabera Khan said, "The book publishing industry is very healthy indeed. We just broke a worldwide sales record yesterday, in fact, with the sale of *Beowulf's Blood,* a Hanford Banner book by the late McKinley Montague. Tragic circumstances, but a positive sign for the industry. And who better to know which books will sell than the shops themselves?"

There was more, but my mind wandered to Sabera. I knew him well enough to be certain he wouldn't be happy about this change. He must have known about the sale when I saw him on Saturday night. His words in the *Times* had been carefully positive, though; Sabera was always professional and discreet.

Again: Why hadn't Trevor told me? If he expected me to sell my family press to him, he might have warned me to whom exactly I was selling. If nothing else, why hadn't he mentioned this to us at the PA, considering its groundbreaking effect on the UK books industry? Failing this, why not bring it up privately with me over a pint?

No wonder Trevor Gravesend had a nervous tic in his eye. I would, too, if I'd just received another cash injection hard on the heels of the acquisition by Megacom. How very odd that two such large deals involving Hanford Banner had taken place in the space of several days' time. And how bizarre indeed that Trevor should have made an offer for Plumtree Press in the midst of it all.

I made the mistake of glancing back at the page before folding the paper; in the lower right-hand corner of the page there was another shocker of a headline:

Keewer buys the *Bookseller* from Whitaker

If ever there had been a constant in the world of British books, it was the organ of the trade, Nathan Griffith's employer the *Bookseller,* long published by the Whitaker family. Suddenly it, too, was gone? I wondered what, if anything, this had to do with Nate's strange behaviour of the day before.

The coffee and croissant had lost their appeal. In the bookselling world, these events were akin to a quiet announcement that the earth would no longer be orbiting the sun.

I plonked several pound coins on the table and pushed out the door. My visit to Ed Maggs, friend, confidant, keeper of secrets for Nottingham Botkin, could wait no longer. But as I rounded the corner to Berkeley Square, home to the august establishment of Maggs Bros, my mobile rang. I checked the caller ID; it was an unknown number.

"Good morning." Sam Stone's broad vowels ripped assertively into my ear, though by American standards I knew they were tame indeed.

"You're up and at it early, aren't you? Not taking advantage of the jet lag excuse, then?"

She laughed. "There's too much to do and see—especially considering that it's Plumtree Press. Speaking of which, what's the plan for today?"

Good Lord, I'd hardly expected a barely arrived Godwin Fellow to be such a pit bull when it came to work. No wonder the Stones of New York were a world-wide sensation. "Ah, well. I thought you'd have your hands full. You were going to help Nicola and everyone prepare for Frankfurt, and draft that proposal for the PA on the international publishing liaison. No?"

I heard the disappointment in her hesitation. "Yes, but . . ."

"But what?"

"Well, I expected to get to work side by side with you, Alex. Frankly, I didn't come all this way to be shunted off onto secretarial projects. Next year I'll be running my own imprint at Stone and Stone, after all."

I sighed. I'd been afraid of this. "Sam, you're going to have to bear with me. Do you remember my telling you that from time to time things get rather intense here at the Press?"

"Yes, of course I do—like that time when you were built into the walls of your own building? Or the time you and your fiancée were held hostage at that chateau in France? Or the time you chased your anonymous, un-solicited author across the Atlantic? Everyone knows—but you don't mean—" Her voice dropped. "Alex, are you in danger right now?"

"Let's put it this way: People have been shooting at me, and I'm not going to get you involved. What would your father do to me if I sent you home with a bullet as a souvenir? London's supposed to be civilised . . . and I don't think I could tell him it was all in the line of duty at Plumtree Press."

"God, Alex, you're every woman's dream. Sorry, unprofessional . . . but do you have any idea how excit-ing your life is?"

Er, quite.

"Meet me for lunch," she said. "Pick some hole in

the wall—wherever you want. No! I know. Come to the house. I'll have the cook whip something up. One o'clock?"

"Yes, but Sam—"

"Twenty-one Cadogan Square. I'll be watching for you." *Click.*

I sighed again and trotted up the steps to the beautiful Georgian house occupied by Maggs just as the bells of Farm Street Chapel chimed eight o'clock. It was early by London standards, but Ed loved to come in early. I'd known him to bring homeless people in with him for a cup of coffee and a roll before his elite clientele started to arrive for the day.

The door swung open in response to my brisk knock, and I found myself looking into the large, brown eyes of my friend. His auburn mustache was thicker and longer than ever—his trademark feature—and his wiry reddish hair looked as if perhaps he'd been in a hurry that morning. He wore a pea green mohair cardigan and brown corduroy trousers.

The aroma of old books, furniture polish, and antique building drifted out to meet me.

"Alex! What're you doing here so early? Hoping I'll acquire Botkin's like Wellbrook's bought Hanford?" His laughter boomed out into the street as he stretched out an arm and welcomed me inside. "Incredible, isn't it? Come in, come in."

My friend was hardly what you'd expect of the scion of an aristocratic antiquarian bookseller to the Queen. In fact, Ed Maggs had a sort of earthy friendliness that put everyone at ease. Far from treating the Berkeley Square shop as some sort of rare book mecca, which it was to the hundreds of people who made pilgrimages from all over the world each year, Ed trotted amiably up and down the revered staircases of Maggs like an oversized schoolboy—just happy to be helping people with books, and happy to be around the things. He also possessed a larger-than-life quality, partly from his physical size, which was massive. Ed was my height of six foot four, and very solidly built. To see such an athletic, physically powerful man in a rare books shop was quite unusual.

Once I'd been in awe as he'd chuckled and pointed out three complete sets of *Cook's Travels,* of course the original edition. I'd burbled something to the effect that it must be remarkable to possess such treasures. I'd never forget Ed's response. He'd shrugged and boomed, "Ah, they're just books, aren't they?" and led me off to see another treasure. His one vanity, perhaps, was the Victorian-style handlebar mustache that gave him a sort of timeless quality.

But on this visit, Ed seemed to sense instantly that all was not well. "Alex—what is it?"

He saw me glance round reception and gestured for me to follow him. He loped up the two flights of stairs three at a time; his way of keeping in shape. Ed's sport was rugger, and he had the scars to prove it.

He closed the door to his office behind us and threw himself into the chair behind his desk, gesturing for me to sit. Almost as if it were a carefully planned backdrop, shelves of lovely old books pertaining to Ed's own interest, sport, covered the wall behind him. Light poured in through the large window at the side of the room; the yellow leaves of the trees in Berkeley Square were still. He lit a cigar and sat back. "All right, out with it."

I took a deep breath and coughed on his cigar smoke, an old joke between us. He broke into a grin when he saw me wave away the green cloud of smoke with exaggerated motions.

"I'll start with Botkin, Ed. Someone broke into the shop, and I'm trying to work out whether it has anything to do with some people who've been shooting at me lately."

"Oh. Well. Is that all?"

"No, there's quite a bit more, actually. I'd love to get your reading on it all. But first, Botkin. Please."

He exhaled another cloud of smoke, directly into my face by way of friendly teasing, and said, "All right. It didn't take you long, did it?"

"What do you mean?"

He shrugged again and stood, crossing to a painting of his great-grandfather at the opposite end of the room from the window. He slid the portrait aside to reveal a small metal box set into the wall and expertly twirled a knob on its front. "It might have been years before you came. We didn't know when, or if, you ever *would* come."

"What's the—why didn't someone just *tell* me?"

He pulled out a small box, quarto-sized, closed the safe, and replaced the painting. He sauntered over and lowered himself into the chair again without answering.

"Ed, why didn't Botkin tell me instead of you?"

"Ah. Well, now, that's a very old secret. And this is a very good time to tell you." He stopped for a puff and held it for a moment as he eyed me, looking very much like the Cheshire Cat.

"Oh, for heaven's sake, will you get *on* with it?!"

"All right, all right," he said, resting the cigar on a cut glass ashtray. "This goes no further than this room, of course." I nodded. "Nottingham Botkin was a rather special book collector, as you know. But he had to be quite careful who he trusted, because of the books he—er—kept." He pronounced this last word with an odd inflection, as if perhaps he'd misused it slightly. "When you decided to go off sailing instead of following in your father's footsteps in publishing, Botkin temporarily placed the collection in my care. But I think there must be something in the collection that pertains to you or your family, because the old man was determined that it should go to you." Momentarily distracted by the burbling sound of his automatic coffeemaker finishing its brew, he raised his eyebrows in invitation. I shook my head and he went to pour himself a cup.

"Did you ever wonder where we got some of those show-stoppers we'd come up with for the Paris Book Fair, or London?"

"The basement, of course—everyone knows about Maggs' miraculous basement. It's legendary."

He raised a finger. "Ah, yes. But Botkin had his own sort of basement collection, though it's not in his cellar. And he chose to deal through us on a few selected sales. He saw his brief as one of preservation, mainly, but now and again he'd let a lesser item go."

"Lesser item . . . you're calling those books *lesser items*?!"

My friend nodded gravely. "Indeed I am." He sipped his coffee and reached for the box he'd got from the safe. I'd always noticed how cavalierly he consumed caffeine, nicotine, alcohol, anything and everything in close proximity to the irreplaceable books surrounding him. I sometimes thought he did it on purpose, as a sort of thrill-inducing, risk-taking behaviour.

"Here. This is what Botkin told me to give you when you came round in dire straits. Which, by the way, you look as if you are." He smiled brightly.

"Well, thank you for that," I retorted sarcastically, and took the book box from him. When a sprinkler system goes off, accidentally or otherwise, and a £25,000 book is ruined, the insurance companies are not best pleased. So they require waterproof, smoke-proof book boxes like the one I was opening.

To my surprise and delight, it held a very famous book indeed—and one of which only one copy existed. It was a handwritten record of booksellers in London in the eighteenth century, when booksellers were also publishers and printers. The first John Murray had penned it for his son in 1780. It had been rumoured lost more than fifty years ago.

"This is unbelievable! The sly old fox," I said, gaping at the precious book. "But why would he give it to me?"

Ed gave me a blasé look over the rim of his coffee cup. "Much as he liked you, old son, I don't think it was solely for your pleasure."

"No?"

"No. Old Knotty Botty never told me as much, but I think there might be a message for us in that little book. See what you think."

I turned the pages carefully past a rather affecting inscription to Murray's son, penned painstakingly in perfect script, to a series of paragraphs describing the book scene in London. So-and-so printed x number of copies, so-and-so displayed them on the street in a cart instead of indoors, so-and-so used women as sales staff, and so on for twelve pages. Then I turned to a charming sketch of Little Britain, Paternoster Row, and St Paul's Churchyard, areas rich in bookselling history since the sixteenth and seventeenth centuries.

"Is this supposed to signify something profound? Am I being thick?"

"Just look at it. Let your mind roam. Free-associate, I believe the Americans say." He grinned, cigar in one hand, coffee in the other, watching me solve this puzzle. Obviously, he'd already worked it out, or Botkin had told him the answer.

> *Smithfield*
>
> > *Little Britain*
> >
> > > *St Paul's Churchyard*
>
> *Covent Garden*
>
> > *Strand*
> >
> > > *Temple*
> > >
> > > > *London Bridge*

Westminster

After studying it for its true meaning, I half-closed my eyes and thought of patterns. What pattern? Was there any pattern?

And then I saw it. "Botkin's bookcases! The way he's organised his book arts and publishing history section . . . he's put all the books where they'd physically have been sold in seventeenth-century London . . . miscellaneous old books in all languages in Little Britain and Paternoster Row, divinity and classics in St Paul's Churchyard, law, history, and plays at Temple Bar, French books in the Strand, law at Westminster, plays and novels in Covent Garden, and lesser stuff for people travelling out of town via Smithfield and London Bridge."

"Botkin would be well pleased with you," Ed said, nodding with satisfaction.

"What a love for books Botkin had," I said wistfully. "Would you believe someone broke in to Botkin's yesterday and tipped out those very books? As if they were looking for something."

"You're serious?"

"Never more."

"Bring the Murray book. Let's get over there now."

As he loped down the three flights of stairs, he told Violet, his receptionist, he'd be out for a bit.

Violet looked up from her papers. "Right. Hello, Alex!"

"Morning, Violet." I waved to her and then we were out the door, round the corner, across Berkeley Square, and—at Ed's breakneck pace and long-legged stride— at Botkin's front door in a matter of a few dozen steps.

"Good God." Ed stared at the disarray in the book arts alcove as I locked the door behind us. "It all depends on whether . . . ah, yes. Good. Whoever did this didn't understand. All right, we can work out which shelves these books came from without too much trouble."

"We can't replace them yet; the insurance company is coming round in an hour or so."

"Right." I thought he looked at me rather strangely, then, as I stood holding my priceless book. I imagined it was burning a hole through my right hand. Ed lowered his voice to a whisper. "This is it, Plumtree. Botkin's got the world's most priceless books hidden in the wall behind these shelves. At the time of his death, he was the sole surviving descendant of Sir Robert Bruce Cotton. No doubt that name means something to you."

I gaped at my friend. In the eighteenth century, Cotton's collection had formed the basis of the entire British Library. The Cotton Vitellius collection was unparalleled. In fact, the codex containing the earliest manuscript of *Beowulf*, about which Hammonds had written with such disastrous consequences, was part of the Cotton Vitellius collection.

Ed saw that I understood; *he* gave a little nod to acknowledge how extraordinary it all was. "Now. As you know all too well, there are a few unsavoury characters in the book world . . . the ones who came looking for the hidden collection, for instance. Botkin considered it his duty to ensure the safety of these books. Forever. And that's why he's sold to you now. They're yours— but only you—and I," he said with a wink, "know they're there." He smiled at me. "What d'you think?"

It was difficult for me to take in what he was saying. I heard the words, but they couldn't be real. They *couldn't.*

"This isn't one of your jokes . . . ?"

He laughed at the look on my face. "Most definitely *pas,* my friend."

"Why didn't he tell me? And how can the Cotton Collection be here, if it's in the British Library?"

Sadness clouded Ed's eyes. "I think he meant to tell you; probably to show you himself. But that fall down his stairs did him in before he had that final chat with you. And—sorry, I should have made this clearer—this is not the *entire* Cotton Collection, of course. It's only a small, forgotten portion that Botkin's eighteenth-century ancestor, who was related to Cotton, was able to rescue from the fire at Ashburnham House in 1731. I know—ironic name for a place that burned to the ground! For years this relative had been distressed about the way the books were being looked after in firetraps just like Ashburnham, so he took all he could for himself in the confusion of the fire. People were throwing books out of the library window as fast as they could that night, and this fellow—Botkin's ancestor—simply stood on the ground and caught them. They were all from the Vitellius case."

I'd read about the tragedy of the books lost in the fire . . . the world had written off the irreplaceable volumes. I'd also read about Cotton's obscure but workable system of cataloguing; the bibliophile had organised his books by the busts of various notable figures that sat on top of each of his library bookcases. A book labelled Cotton Vitellius B.IV, for instance, would have been in the case under the bust of the Roman emperor Vitellius, on the second shelf down—B—the fourth book from the left.

"Botkin organised it all so beautifully for you, according to the John Murray map . . . but he didn't set it up just so you'd enjoy his little reminder of the bookselling history of London. It's the key to his organisation of the Cotton Collection remnant. First, though, the mechanical details. To unlock the false front, lift on this shelf—yes, behind where St Paul's would be. It lifts ever so slightly, even with all the books on it, and releases a catch. I'll just have to move some of these out of the way. . . ." Delicately, he moved some of the fallen books a bit farther from the bookcase while I pressed up on the shelf, noting that it moved just a fraction—perhaps no more than a millimetre.

Ed then went to the side of the sadly empty case, its bolts into the wall showing like open wounds, and said, "You're going to have to help me move this—take the other side. It weighs a ton." I aligned myself with Ed on the opposite side of the case. With a mighty pull from Ed, the bookcase wall itself began to move, rolling on minute wheels that must have been no larger than ball bearings. As we pulled, I peered round the back of the moving wall.

Awestruck, I saw that roughly half the space revealed was taken up with a recessed shelf. The recessed shelf appeared to be filled with antique books, perhaps as many as a hundred of them. When the wall was about two feet away from the recessed case, we stopped and went in to have a look.

"I can't believe I'm seeing this," I muttered. My gaze fell first on what would be the "St Paul's" area, corresponding to ecclesiastical books, if I imagined John Murray's map. The wealth of the world's most precious books was almost beyond my ability to take it in, and I stood and struggled to get a grip on that section alone. There were:

. . . a Wycliff manuscript Bible in English, in oak boards, with a pigskin backstrip . . .

. . . a hitherto unrecorded copy of the Gutenberg Bible, the first printed book, in its original German calf binding . . .

. . . the Alacalá polyglot Bible, the first multilingual Bible, printed for Cardinal Ximenes, in contemporary red Spanish morocco with the cardinal's arms on the covers . . .

. . . a complete Coverdale Bible of 1535, the first Bible printed in English, in original calf with the extremely rare map in perfect condition (it was normally missing or torn, as it was a fold-out) . . .

. . . a Tyndale New Testament of 1525, of which

only two copies were known to exist, and a King James Bible of 1611 in its perfect original presentation binding for the King himself.

There were people who would kill for any one of these books.

Nearby, in the Little Britain/Paternoster Row area, I spotted an extremely ancient-looking *Beowulf* in alum-tawed vellum. I lifted out this last volume gingerly, scarcely able to credit the priceless books before me. The *Beowulf*'s vellum cover, smooth but singed on the corners, had been hand-printed in black ink in a rounded hand: *Beowulf. Beowulf* certainly seemed to be making a comeback these days—first Hammonds's *Beowulf* textbook, then Montague's *Beowulf's Blood*, and now perhaps an Anglo-Saxon copy of my very own.

"That's not the extremely valuable one, I'm sorry to tell you. The Cotton Vitellius A.fifteen *Beowulf* is on display at the British Library. But this one isn't much later, I understand. And it's *Beowulf* alone, not bound in with a load of other stories like Judith, as in the British Library's *Beowulf*. No one knows why Laurence Nowell, the first known private owner of the book in 1536, bound together two codices—the Nowell Codex and the Southwick Codex—into a book that came to be known as Cotton Vitellius A.fifteen. People of that era, as you know, were forever rearranging ancient fragments and binding disparate texts together."

"What's Judith?"

"Alex, Alex . . . and you have a Douay Bible in the Plumtree Collection! I've seen it. This is what comes of going to university in the Colonies."

I rolled my eyes. "All right, all right . . . out with it. So it's in the Catholic Bible, *and* . . . ?"

"Have you never heard of the Apocrypha? The books of the Bible of doubtful authenticity?"

"Yes, of course . . . so Judith is part of the Apocrypha? And the Anglo-Saxon story in Cotton Vitellius A.fifteen is based on it?"

"Exactly."

I backed into one of Botkin's easy chairs and studied the masterpiece in my hands. The scratched-in mark of the quill pen, the exquisite calligraphy of the monk, the hair side versus the smooth side of the calf skin, the absence of page numbers, showing the book was bound before the year 1200 . . . it was a bibliophile's dream.

"I'd have expected you to be a bit cheesed off with the whole *Beowulf* scenario," Ed said mildly.

"Interesting that you should bring that up. Hammonds rang me last night, Ed." I sighed. "He was threatened with grievous bodily harm unless he wrote that snarmy letter to the *Times*."

Ed looked as if I might push him over with a feather, which, in his case, was saying quite a lot. He licked his lips. "Er, when did all this come to light?"

"Rather late last night."

"I see."

Lost in thought, he seemed to stare at the book in my hands without seeing it.

"Ed, why didn't Botkin—or his ancestor—turn these over to the British Library if he really cared about preserving them?"

He shrugged. "All I can say is that he must have enjoyed owning this sort of book as much as you or I do. Think of your Malconbury Chronicles, the pride and joy of your library. It's a kick in the pants, isn't it?"

I had to laugh at his use of his American wife's expression—Sarah had used it on occasion herself. A kick in the pants it was. But I knew there was something else. Botkin had loved books too much to risk keeping them here without a reason.

Ed looked at his watch, and I was reminded of the passage of time. Friend that he was, he did have a thriving business to run. My own watch told me it was nearly half past nine.

"I'm sorry, Ed—you've Americans to see, books to sell."

He smiled and told me that I was, in fact, right; that morning he was to meet with a wealthy American woman who amused herself by collecting the writings of Jane Austen. He had a letter to show her.

"May I walk you back to the office and regale you with stories of deceit, terror, and doom?" I asked.

"Would you really?"

After sliding the wall back in to place, we set off at his lope. I told him about the shot at Nate and me on the night of Montague's signing—and the attack at home. I also filled him in on Matt Ireland's odd comment at the PA meeting, and dared to share one of my darkest suspicions with him. "Ed, what if Botkin was pushed down his cellar stairs? It's a horrible thought, but he'd never fallen before. And he was being pressured to sell the shop. Now, with the break-in and Matt Ireland's comment, I can't help but wonder. Maybe someone knew about the collection."

Ed nodded grudgingly. "It used to bother old Knotty terribly that a rumour had started somewhere. He did a good job of ignoring it and leading people off the subject." I could see that Ed, like me, didn't want to believe Botkin could have died this way. I told him about the Duke of Bradford's eviction notice, and its extraordinary similarity to the one I'd found in Botkin's office. Finally, I told him about the two efforts made to purchase Plumtree Press the day before.

"My friend," he said, after listening in silence, "you are most definitely under siege. Come with me."

We entered the front door of Maggs Bros. At the back of the building, he opened a locked door with a key from his pocket, and urged me through. It was a staircase, presumably the back way to the basement. He closed the door again behind us but didn't lock it.

"Now. You know this is where we keep all those marvels that no one ever gets to see, though I must say the book you're holding would perhaps be the best of the lot."

Following his eyes, I saw that I still clutched the John Murray book from Botkin. I suppose the tenacious clutching of books was one of the things I did best.

"But one thing even *you* do not know, Plummers, is that we have a sort of *luxe en prive* flat down here in the midst of bibliophile heaven. Sorry, am I going too fast for you?" He tossed the words over his shoulder.

Smiling, I trotted gamely down the stairs after him. I had seen him on the rugger field and knew his deceptive speed. "There's a reason for the saying 'Real athletes row; all others play games.' "

"Ha bloody ha, Plummers," he said. "All right. Here you are. Servants' quarters at one time, we reckon, but the location is great."

I gaped at my surroundings. To one side of the legendary basement of priceless books, any one of which would create a worldwide sensation were it to be sold at a major book fair, was a long, narrow room cheerily painted in a creamy yellow. Its rounded, arched ceiling made it look a bit like a narrow tube tunnel, or a passageway, shut off at one end. A canopied day bed sat to one side, and an Aga cooker graced the far wall.

"The Aga works. Stay as long as you like; you can squeeze your car into the spot round the back. But let me have a glimpse of that Murray text from time to time. Yeah?"

"Right," I said. "Thanks, Ed. Er—is there an unobtrusive way to get in and out?"

He winked again. "Never fear. Violet in reception need not witness your coming in and your going out." I could see that he hoped I'd bring a romantic interest there—like everyone else, Ed seemed convinced that Sarah had perished at the hands of the Iraqis. He had very high hopes for Nicola, and made no secret of it. I'd tried to explain to him before that I hadn't quite got to the point of considering Nicola as a romantic interest, and couldn't until I knew for certain about Sarah—but he tended to grow exasperated with me for not acknowledging the fact that Sarah was not coming back.

It wasn't that I hadn't thought of Nicola in this light. With the uncanny understanding Nicola and I had, we did have a close and very special relationship. It was the sort of understanding that could conceivably turn to love someday, when we were both done pining for our lost loves. But not just yet.

He took me to a door that opened onto the courtyard between the two Maggs buildings, front and rear, rather like Plumtree Press before the remodeling. "Just be sure to lock it, won't you?" he grunted, tossing me a key.

"Mmm," I said, thinking of the books inside for which there truly was no price.

"Ring if you need anything." Without a backward look he set off for regular business hours and the Jane Austen letter.

I went inside, locking the door behind me, and sat for a moment on the bed. "Sarah, Sarah," I said quietly. I longed to hold her, to bury my nose in her softly scented neck. "Darling, I miss you." In the silence I imagined a response—somehow I felt certain she'd heard me. In a mockery of my own exhaustion, I let myself fall back on the bed. As I did, I smelled Sarah's perfume.

My eyes snapped open and I sat up again with a start, chasing the scent with my nose like a blood-hound. I found it on the pillow and buried my face in it. *How could her perfume be on a pillow in the basement of Maggs?* But when I surfaced again sanity had returned: Thousands—perhaps tens or hundreds of thousands of women—wore her spicy, Oriental scent. Who knows what had last happened down here; who had brushed against this pillow wearing that particular perfume?

"Get a grip," I told myself, and sat bolt upright on the bed. I was losing it. I rubbed my face hard with both hands, stowed my newly acquired book under the sweet-smelling down pillow, and stood. It was time to do a little digging about Hanford Banner. "Move the car, then it's off to Companies House," I told myself firmly, and set off through my book-filled paradise towards the great out-of-doors.

Companies House, the public information office for which was ironically located just round the corner from Plumtree Press on Bloomsbury Street, was the records centre for all public companies operating in the United Kingdom. This was the first time I'd ever made use of it, but I had need of the place now. It had been troubling me ever since I'd read the article in that morning's paper: Why had Trevor been so secretive, first about the fact that Megacom had acquired Hanford Banner, and then about its acquisition by Wellbrook's? Though I wasn't seriously considering his offer to purchase the Press, I was more curious than ever about who owned whom . . . and about my two rather hurried offers.

The ground was shifting beneath the book business, but someone was at bedrock making it move. I *would* find out who it was. I did have the unfortunate feeling that I was the only one, besides those at bedrock, who suspected the shift. And the president of the Publishers Association, Trevor himself, was directly involved. I certainly couldn't go to him with my fears.

After moving the Passat from Botkin's, my head still spinning a bit at the thought of what I'd seen there, I made my way to the Bond Street tube station and so to Tottenham Court Road station. Along the way I rang both Matt Ireland and Nate at their offices. Neither answered, but I left them messages. I didn't feel close enough to Matt to ring him at home, but I did leave an additional message at Nate's home number. Carefully skirting Bedford Square, I arrived at Companies House via Bedford Avenue.

I walked through the modern glass doors of the Information Centre and along the corridor to the public records room. Rows of sparkling new computer terminals in comfortable carrels stretched the length and width of the room. Though there were people all around me tapping away at their keyboards, I saw that

I would need a bit of guidance. I approached one of the knowledgeable-looking women at the front desk.

"Good morning," I said. "Would it be possible for me to find the owner of a publicly held company?"

"Of course." She smiled. "That's why we're here. We do need some sort of identification—driving licence, credit card . . ."

"Certainly." She took my licence and locked it away in a drawer, then came out from behind the worktop.

"I'll just get you started." I followed her to an empty terminal, and she motioned for me to sit down in the chair. "Now, then. What company was it you wanted?"

"Hanford Banner. Hanford Banner Publishing Co Ltd, UK. Though it's just changed hands—twice."

"Not to worry; we'll have all the records here. They have to be in place before the purchase is official." She showed me how to find out not only who owned which companies, but who sat on the boards of directors. Now that would be interesting, I thought.

When she left me, however, having brought up Hanford Banner's official information, I saw no great surprise. It was already in the system that Wellbrook's owned Hanford Banner. The surprise came when I typed in Wellbrook's name. They were registered, of course, to do business in the UK, and so their records were available. But it seemed that as of last week Wellbrook's itself had been purchased by yet another firm, and not by one of the recognisable media conglomerates we'd grown so used to in the books world, either. Just the name "Petrus." Okay, I thought . . . and who's behind Petrus? Was it a holding company trying to hide its identity? It couldn't be just any old operation, if it had the funds to purchase Wellbrook's. I scrolled to its list of board members; stranger still. Of the eight names listed, I recognised not a single one from the book or any other industry. Fascinating. A mysterious, faceless organisation now owned two of Britain's preeminent publishing-related firms.

"Thanks very much," I said, returning to the front desk, and received my collateral back with a smile. In a private fog I walked back to Tottenham Court Road. Yet again, I pulled out my phone and tried Matt and Nate . . . still nothing. Where on earth were they?

Somehow, what troubled me most was that Hanford Banner's and Wellbrook's ownership by Petrus was not widely known. Not that I was a business wheeler-and-dealer—admittedly, I left the legal and financial end of things to our lawyers and accountants. But I was one of eight people on the board of the Publishers Association, and certainly kept track of changes of ownership in the industry. If I didn't know, no one knew . . . except for those, perhaps, who didn't *want* anyone to know.

Where had Petrus come from? When? So much had changed so fast . . . was it all so that the proud owners could announce their new purchases and pre-eminence at the Frankfurt Book Fair? Was this what Nate had meant when he'd said "it was starting"?

Especially when taken with the recent deaths and threats in the publishing and bookselling world, the secrecy of it all seemed sinister to me.

I vowed I would find out what on earth was happening to my industry—before it was too late. But I was afraid. A great deal was at stake, and too many people were running about with guns who didn't hesitate to use them. I felt very much like Beowulf, out to slay Grendel . . . alone.

CHAPTER 6

. . . for it was strange unto them that she was come . . .

—JUDITH 13:13

A horn blared; I looked out at Tottenham Court Road. There was a woman walking towards the tube station—a woman I knew and loved better than any other.

"Sarah!" I cried after the tall figure in the long coat. *"Saraaahhhh!"* I ran after her as if my life depended on it, struggling through the crowd of late-morning pedestrians. But half a street away in the thunderous traffic, she either ignored or didn't hear me. I was still in hot pursuit when she disappeared into a taxi and was gone.

The second Sarah-bearing taxi, just out of reach, in two days? *Was* I going mad? I began to seriously consider the possibility.

This taxi had got away before I could see a number plate. But I couldn't believe this was all coincidence. I hailed a taxi, told him the address, and brought the mobile to life.

"Hello, Jonathan? Alex Plumtree here." Jonathan Metcalf, at the Foreign Office, had worked with me to get Sarah back.

"Yes, Alex. What can I do for you?"

"Sorry for barging in like this, but I wondered if you could spare me a moment."

He hesitated. I knew what he was thinking: *The Sarah Townsend file is closed. What more does he want from me, and when will he stop wasting my time?* "I suppose so, but . . . well, when?"

"Er, ten minutes—if you can manage it? I'm on my way now. I know it's an imposition, but I would be grateful. Something rather strange has come up."

Again, his hesitation reminded me how severely I was taxing his goodwill. He'd been very kind through the thick of it all, but now he had other bereaved people to help; other British citizens to rescue. I could practically hear him thinking it was time I wiped my own nose.

"Yes, all right—come on in, then. See you in ten minutes."

I rang off and turned to the cab driver. "Pardon me," I began, leaning forward and speaking through the slit in his Plexiglas shield. He lowered his radio and slid the screen farther to one side, cocking his head towards me. I noted that he bore quite a strong resemblance to Stanley Holloway the actor who played Eliza Doolittle's father in *My Fair Lady*—ruddy face, determinedly pleasant expression, perhaps fifty-five or sixty.

"If I wanted to speak to the cab driver who drove a certain someone yesterday, could I do it? I only know that it was a T reg., but it did have something sparkly hanging from its rearview mirror."

"Girlfriend where she wasn't supposed to be?" To my surprise, even his voice and accent were reminiscent of old Alf Doolittle.

"Something like that."

"Well, this is your lucky day, i'n' it? My mate Lenny has one o' vem crystal wotsits danglin' from 'is rearview. 'E's the only mate of mine as drives wiv' one. 'E's ashamed to have the bleedin' thing swingin' back and forf in his taxi, mind you, but 'is trouble-and-strife insists. Says it gets 'is energy balanced, some sort of New Age fing. It might not be Lenny, of course—a lot o' vem crystal fings hanging about these days—but ven again it might. I can try 'im on the radio, if you like."

Somewhat taken aback by this miraculous good fortune, I managed a "Yes, please. Thanks."

My driver went through his radio-calling mumbo jumbo, and we waited. He repeated the call, and the next thing I knew the radio had crackled to life. My driver answered, "Oy, Len! Got someone 'ere who needs to talk to ya. Yeah, urgent business regardin' one o' your passengers yesterday." He passed the handset back to me, stretching the curling cord.

"Yes—hello, Lenny. Thanks for this . . . I was just wondering if you remembered driving a tall, good-looking, dark-haired woman in a tan mackintosh yesterday afternoon. It would have been just before two o'clock. You picked her up in King Street."

He laughed. "You don't 'alf remember your particulars, do you? I can tell what this is concerning." A pregnant, teasing pause. "Yeah, I remember her right enough. She's a looker, mate—I'd get back in 'er good graces, I would. Took 'er to near Cadogan Square. But it was odd . . . while I waited in traffic—dreadful, it was—she walked over to this very posh 'ouse in the Square. It had these perfect little potted trees in front, all sculpted-like into those little round balls, you know 'ow they do. I wondered why she didn't just 'ave me take 'er right to the door."

I'd gone cold. Cadogan Square? More coincidence? I didn't think so. But I wouldn't know for certain until one o'clock, when I traipsed up to 21 Cadogan

Square and kept an eye out for some rather attractive topiaries.

A squawk from the radio brought me back to the moment. "That 'elp you, then?"

"Yes, Lenny—thanks ever so much. Spectacular memory you've got. I'll leave your friend here a little something by way of thanks—for both of you."

"Ta, then—best o' luck, sir."

My driver pulled over to the kerb in Whitehall and I was aware of his eyes assessing me via the rearview mirror. "Bad news, then."

"Puzzling, at best." I climbed out and passed more than was necessary for my five-pound ride through his window. "Thanks for your help."

"All the best to you, sir."

I waved and trotted up the steps to Jonathan's lair in the Foreign Office. At the security desk I gave my name and was promptly escorted through the maze to his door. I'd been through this routine so many times before, but always, until now, in a fog of loss. Now I found myself feeling the cold, hard clarity of suspicion and doubt. In fact, I wasn't entirely certain that I wanted to know if Sarah was back in the country. If somehow she'd managed to save herself and get out, but hadn't come to me, what did that mean?

In the three seconds I stood with the guard at Jonathan's door, dozens of unpleasant possibilities flashed through my mind. She'd been brainwashed, a modern-day Patty Hearst . . . She'd been so psychologically damaged, emotionally scarred, she was no longer able to feel . . . She'd come back a different person altogether . . . She didn't remember me . . . She despised me, blamed me for what had happened to her.

"Alex." Jonathan looked harried. Just to make sure

I was fully aware of how much I was inconveniencing him, he glanced at his watch before shaking my hand.

"Thanks for seeing me, Jonathan. I won't take much of your time."

He indicated that I should take my usual chair opposite him in his sterile, spartan little sardine tin.

"I think I've seen Sarah. Twice. Here, in London."

"Alex, I know you've been through a lot, but *really*. There's simply no way you could have seen Sarah Townsend in London." There was a coldness behind his words that had never been there in our earlier meetings; he was keeping me at a distance now. As I studied him, I told myself I shouldn't have been surprised. As far as he was concerned, Sarah was dead. He actually began to shuffle papers on his desk, almost *guiltily*, I thought. Was he hiding something?

I could take a hint, but I wasn't through yet. "I could swear it's Sarah, Jonathan. I know the way she moves. . . ."

He blew air out through his lips, the very picture of scepticism and irritation. Colour rose in his cheeks as he said, "Look, Plumtree. I'm sorry for all you've been through. But I think it's high time you paid a visit to a good psychiatrist. For God's sake, man, pull your socks up and get on."

This was so unlike the calm, reasonable civil servant I'd come to know that I couldn't help but stare for a moment in surprise. He avoided my eyes.

"At least tell me this: have there been any changes in the situation where she was held? Movement by the dissident group, or even a rumour?"

He shook his head, still not meeting my gaze.

"Jonathan—is there any way she might have been brought back, but you've asked her to keep quiet about it?"

He slowed in his reached for the file drawer, and I wondered if I'd happened on the truth. *"Jonathan!"*

"Look." His eyes snapped as he threw the papers down, whirled away from his desk and stood, glowering down at me with intensity.

I rose to face him.

"There's nothing more I can do to help you, Alex. I wish I could, but I can't." His eyes might have been two blue ice cubes. Definitely something there . . . I'd hit on something.

"Well. Thanks for your time." I turned on my heel and left.

What was he hiding, and why?

I walked back towards Maggs, out of habit trying Matt and Nate on my cell phone. This time I left a message with the receptionist for Matt, instead of leaving it on his voice mail. I also asked for the receptionist at the *Bookseller*, who told me that Nate hadn't fallen off the face of the earth but *was* out of town for a few days. I left another message for him anyway.

It was becoming clear that things in all aspects of my life were changing at a frightening pace. I had to map out a course of action. Should I sell the Press? Get out while I could and be done with it all?

As far as Sarah was concerned, I knew that only one course of action was open to me: to wait. *If* she was alive and in London, and I wasn't having hallucinations of Sarah lock-alikes, she would get in touch with me . . . if she wanted to. If for some reason she no longer cared for me, she wouldn't get in touch . . . and I would have to let her go.

Regardless of her feelings for me, I would be a very happy man indeed just to know that she was alive.

My mobile rang just as I'd put it away again; it was

Lisette. "Alex. Matt Ireland rang for you just now—he said it was urgent. Can you ring him back?"

"At last! Okay. How are things there?"

"Everything is in 'and. Don't worry about a thing. Oh—I got your message from last night; I've rung Neville at the solicitors'. 'E says 'e will contact the duke's business agent personally. Today."

"Great. Anything else?"

"Ah, yes—Nick met the insurance investigator at Botkin's. 'E is not back yet. But Alex . . . I am worried about you. You sound—tired. Overwhelmed. Can I 'elp?"

"You're a love, Lisette—but I'm afraid I'm in publishing purgatory again. And I'm not about to endanger you or the others by coming in to the Press." *Or even telling you about it,* I thought. Before she could find more to worry about, I said, "I've got to go—I'll stay in touch," and punched the phone off.

Back at Maggs, I went in through the back door to my basement headquarters. There were not even forty-five minutes left before I was due at Cadogan Square . . . but I was eager to sort through the bizarre collection of information I was gathering.

Grudgingly grateful for the invention of mobile phones, I entered Matt Ireland's number, reached his receptionist, and this time was put through to the esteemed publisher himself.

"Matt. Alex Plumtree here. I've been trying to reach you for days—didn't you get my messages?"

"Yes, I did. I can explain—but just one moment, please, Plumtree."

I looked round my unusually bookish domain and saw, just opposite my room, a set of Johnson's dictionaries. *The* Johnson's dictionaries, some of the greatest treasures in the rare book world, just sitting on a shelf like any other book. The sight of the calf brown folio-sized volumes, a complete set of them, made me shake my head.

"Sorry to keep you waiting, Plumtree. I wanted to be certain that we could speak in privacy. Are you alone?"

As alone as any human being has ever been, I thought. "Yes. I am."

His voice was hushed as he said, "You know that Knotty and I were old friends. And you know that my father was a bookseller. In fact, I find in my old age that most of my friends are booksellers rather than publishers. Anyway . . . no doubt you remember my outburst at the PA meeting."

"Yes, I wanted to ask you about—"

"I was quite serious, you know, Plumtree," he interrupted. I'd got used to his brusque manner; I respected his wisdom and experience enormously, and hardly minded.

"I haven't wanted to get you involved, my dear boy. God knows you've enough on your plate. But my friends have told me of a great evil in our midst."

"A *great evil*? What sort of—"

"Not one or two, but *six* of my respected friends in the trade have told me they've been—well, threatened— blackmailed—into selling their shops."

"Selling to—"

"In every case, Plumtree—mind you, *every case*— an unpleasant fact has been brought to light about the bookseller personally, or about irregular accounting practices. It doesn't matter if it's true or false, the poor fellow is made to sell."

"Like Botkin," I murmured, recalling the letter I'd found accusing him of a breach of ethics. It no longer seemed coincidental that he'd lost his lease. Only Plumtree Press had snatched up his shop before . . . *Whitticombe!*

"You see," Matt was saying, "Botkin had no family to be used as a lever. My associates who've been forced to sell aren't allowed to say who's buying them. The purchasers threaten the families of the owners. In Knotty's case, they were afraid he'd talk—they expected him to talk to you, for some reason. But Botkin told me he wasn't going to put you in that sort of danger, though he'd make the information available to you if you needed it. Before this is over, Plumtree, I'm going to prove that they killed him."

Was that why Botkin hadn't met with me again at all, even to tell me about the hidden Cotton Collection books? Had he felt he was being watched? "What information, Matt? And who is *they*?"

He ignored the question.

"The others—there are only a handful of independents left, as you know—can't fight it. They've all agreed to sell, Plumtree, all of them. But secretly. And for very handsome sums, I might add, paid out in monthly instalments so as not to look too questionable to the bank. If anything goes wrong, they'll stop getting paid."

I tried again. "Matt, what information was Botkin going to leave for me? To whom are the bookshops selling? And why all the secrecy? It's nothing unusual for the big chains to swallow up the others, though at this point I can't quite see why they'd bother—"

"Botkin was extremely secretive about whatever it

was he was leaving you. We don't know who. It's all done without revealing identities ... and every holding company name is different. Unrecognisable."

Like Petrus, I thought.

"Each independent bookshop's been sold to a *different* buyer, you see. And they're not chains at all." His voice went down to a whisper. "*They're publishers.*"

We shared the tremendous unlikeliness of this in silence for a moment. I had the fleeting impression that I was in the midst of a very bad dream. I'd only just got my mind round the fact that Wellbrook's had bought Hanford Banner—a book chain buying a publishing house. But now Matt was saying that publishers—a variety of them, from the sound of things—were buying up the independent bookshops. What if Whitticombe had killed Botkin for selling to me instead of him? Whitticombe was a publisher, too ... his family's Perseverance Press.

"When you bought Botkin's," Ireland went on, interrupting these unsavoury reflections, "I wondered if you were part of the scheme. Botkin and I always felt you could be trusted, but I'm getting jumpy these days ... too much happening too fast. I'm sorry I didn't return your calls. You can see how carefully I must tread. At any rate, Plumtree, now we need your help. Someone is taking over the book business from the inside out."

I didn't want to mention it to him, but it wasn't just the bookselling business that had become a jelly elephant. As a publisher, I'd received those two very impressive offers, with our sin in signing Julia Northrup's *Her Flight* expunged in the bargain. As far as I knew, though, Hanford Banner/Wellbrook's and Spitze-Verlag were in no way associated. And then there was the *Bookseller*, also bought this week by a foreign concern, a book publisher . . .

"The secrecy is what puzzles me, Matt. What are they trying to hide?"

"What if it's all *one* entity, trying to buy all the bookshops, by hiding behind other companies? It would be illegal—a monopoly—so they'd have to conceal it. Think of the discounts, Plumtree—and of the power to dictate what would be published."

Ireland had founded and headed the PA's Freedom to Publish Committee for years now. Perhaps his suspicious and defensive nature had been sadly prescient.

"Why now, do you think? Why is it all happening the week of the Frankfurt Book Fair?" I squirmed a bit at the thought, remembering with discomfort that Henning Kruse had asked me to get back to him in the next few days. Trevor, too, for that matter.

"I don't understand, either, why the Book Fair should be at the centre of all of this." His voice was grave. "If it's all so desperately secret, they can't be planning to make any sort of announcement."

I tried to come to grips with what Montague's death might mean in all of this. Had that somehow kicked off the rest of the deadly "it" Nate had told me was starting early? And why had someone tried to kill *me* as well? If Nate *had* been telling the truth about Hanford Banner murdering Montague, might they be trying to silence me? And could it have something to do with Botkin and this oh-so-secret "information" he had left for me? Far too many unknowns for my taste.

"Matt, I must run, but I'll be in touch." I had twenty minutes to reach Sam's house in Cadogan Square. "Perhaps a bit of baiting would do the trick."

"Plumtree, no—remember Botkin. I swear they

killed him. He told me someone had been watching his shop, intimidating him with hang-up phone calls. I meant to tell you about my suspicions that he was pushed. Don't—"

For once, it was I who cut off my old friend, and not the other way round. "Don't worry. And keep your head down. I hate to say it, but have you thought that you might be in danger? You know as much about what's happened as anyone; someone might be afraid you'll put it all together. Why don't you go to the country for a while, until this blows over?"

He agreed that he might do just that, and we rang off. Running a hand over my chin, I felt a healthy crop of stubble. Well, Sam Stone would just have to take me as I was.

As I stepped out of the service entrance to Maggs, the sky was an unusually vivid blue, the grass in Berkeley Square a shocking emerald green, and all the trees still fully clothed in their autumn colours. A mild breeze stirred their leaves and carried a hint of fortifying chill. By any standard, it was a perfect day. But it was with trepidation that I made my way to Number Twenty-one Cadogan Square. And it was with a rush of fear and anger that I saw that the Stone home, a large, respectable, rather intimidating white Georgian house with a glossy black door, indeed had two potted topiaries, as the taxi driver had said.

What would Sarah—if indeed the woman I'd seen *was* Sarah—have been doing at Sam Stone's house? There had to be a way to find out.

Before I reached the door, Sam opened it with a flourish. Her golden hair shone in contrast to a relatively ordinary navy blue suit, albeit of slubby silk. Her bright smile faded a bit as she looked me up and down, but she put a hand on my shoulder and said, "Come in, come in."

I'd half expected to see a stripped-down overseas commuter rental, temporarily kitted out with hired furniture or ultramodern junk. However, it was obviously a very personal place to the Stone family, with group photographs of all manner of Stones—it wasn't difficult to tell, with their stubborn, outward-jutting jaw line and drooping eyes—gracing the walls.

For just an instant, I associated the Stone face with a famous one I'd often seen in books, but perhaps it was lack of sleep that clouded my brain. I couldn't think who . . . I looked at Sam intently for a moment, trying to work it out, but without success.

She cocked her head at me, frowned, and closed the door behind us. "What is it? Are you all right?"

"Of course. I suppose I'm a little taken aback by how at home you are here. I didn't expect it, that's all."

She smiled. "You'd be surprised; I can pass myself off pretty well as an Englishwoman to people who don't know me." Her eyes stayed on me for a millisecond more than necessary.

"What?" I asked.

"Sorry . . . I do love a man who doesn't shave every day. You didn't give that impression at first. I thought you were more . . . well, the buttoned-down type." She shrugged, arched her eyebrows daringly, and showed me through a spacious central hall, past an extravagant flower arrangement. A uniformed maid emerged and nodded at us in greeting. "We'll have drinks in the library, Marie."

Marie nodded again deferentially and went about her business in silence.

Sam looped her arm through mine, encouraged, it

seemed, by my stubble. I began to feel uncomfortable. "Alex, I'm glad you could spare the time to come today. I've been so eager to really get acquainted. I don't know if you realise it, but even in America, people are coming to think of you as a sort of bookish James Bond. I'm pleased to be able to do something for *you* for a change. In fact, I hope to do quite a bit more, very shortly."

I tried not to think too much about exactly what she meant. "Full of surprises, aren't you?"

"You have no idea."

Despite the presence of Marie as chaperone, it seemed to me that now my worst fears about being alone with Sam in her home were being realised. Things were not going at all as I'd intended. Sam was, however, clad in that very professional, unsuggestive navy blue suit, and had given off no danger signals other than the shaving comment.

"Here we are," she announced, turning in to a room on our left.

I have seen a good many impressive libraries in my time, and the Stones' was right up there with the best of them. It wasn't just the books; it was their surroundings. Carved fruitwood bookshelves covered every wall of the room, and even surrounded the four large windows along one wall. Velvet curtains hung to the floor, and sheer fabric shielded the room from damaging light. At one end of the room was an eight-foot grand piano of the same wood and finish as the shelves, on a light-toned Oriental rug. At the other end of the room was a group of chintz-covered overstuffed chairs in front of a fireplace.

After taking the measure of the library, as Sam clearly intended, I nodded my approval—giving her a brief smile—and went to the piano. I played several chords; the touch was easy, the sound mellow, and the keys were made of real ivory—nicely yellowed with age. There was nothing new in the entire house, besides the flowers.

"Rachmaninoff, Prelude in C-sharp Minor."

I looked up, startled. I hadn't taken her for a musician.

She shook her head and crossed her arms where she stood. "A Renaissance man besides. I'm not sure I can cope, Alex."

"I'm afraid the piano chapter of my life has long since closed," I admitted. I left the temporary diversion of the piano and went to have a closer look at the books, aware that Sam was watching me.

Clearly, this collection of books was—*had* to be— the extended family's main library. People didn't have *two* such collections of books, one on each side of the Atlantic. "What a magnificent room," I murmured, going directly to a complete set of the very first printings of Dickens's novels. "And a stunning collection."

Marie entered with a tray that held, to my dismay, two martini glasses and a crystal jug filled with clear liquid. Inwardly I groaned; there was a sort of retro martini-cocktail craze on at the moment in England as elsewhere, but it was beginning to seem quite a long time since my last meal—the partially finished ham croissant of seven this morning. Still, it wouldn't do to offend her.

She handed me a glass. "Cheers," she said, raising her drink.

"Cheers indeed," I echoed. "To your year in London. May it be a beneficial one for you."

She grinned and clinked her glass against mine,

took one sip, and instantly became all business. Fascinating.

"So," she said. "Tell me who's shooting at you. And why."

As I followed my hostess over to the sofas, it was impossible to ignore the fact that her heels made the outline of her calf muscles stand out in sharp contrast to the rest of her leg. With a pang I recalled that Sarah's muscles had been equally sculpted, but more elongated because of her height. Everything about Sam was more concentrated, intense, obvious. Sam's muscles, as with everything else about her, blatantly suggested power and aggressiveness. True enough, Sam Stone was no milquetoast.

"Ah . . . it's a long story." If she thought I was going to trust her after meeting her barely twenty-four hours before, and after I'd been told that Sarah (or someone who looked very much like her) had been dropped at her front door, she needed to think again.

"Well, let's start somewhere else then. I'll bet this is related, anyway: What was *really* going on at that incredible PA meeting yesterday?" She made a face. "All that about people dying—being killed—whatever. It was awfully dramatic." She took another sip as I came to sit across the antique coffee table from her. "Don't you like it?" She indicated my drink.

"Oh, no—I mean yes, of course. Lovely." I took a small sip to please her and almost immediately was reminded of the reason I never touched the nasty little things. But how to sidestep her earnest questions? Perhaps send a signal that I didn't really want to talk about it. She was clever; she'd work out what I meant and could interpret it any way she liked.

"Well, Sam, Matt Ireland *has* been known to be a

bit on the dramatic side—but he knows his business. You just have to realise that you've come to us at an extraordinary time for British publishing." I decided to eat my olive for a bit of sustenance, but the instant I'd popped it into my mouth I found that the benign-looking fruit was a veritable alcohol bomb—a so-called "tipsy olive."

I smiled. "I trust you saw the papers this morning."

"Indeed I did. Not just one, but two British institutions gone in a single day. And both to foreigners." She *tsk-tsk*ed. "I think I chose the right time to come."

Her implication that she'd controlled the Godwin Fellow selection process by some sort of telekinesis from New York amused me. Perhaps she had; power bred power. I took another sip and felt myself sink more deeply into the sofa. It did feel good to relax.

"You know, things have changed a lot in American publishing recently, too. The day I left, another consolidation. Boom. Now there are four major players instead of five. It just doesn't stop."

Boom indeed, I thought. Boom the way Nottingham Botkin's head had smashed against his cellar floor.

"What are you thinking when you look like that?" she asked, almost gently. "Oops—sorry." She held up both hands in a "stop" gesture. "Too personal. Tell me, Alex: Is it true, the rumours about what's happened to you since you've taken charge of Plumtree Press? I'd like to believe it all, but . . . Pierce Brosnan look-alike aside, are you really the James Bond of book publishers?"

I sighed. "I *have* had a number of very unusual experiences, and they certainly have involved danger and books in equal proportions. But these things tend to be overblown. And frankly, I wish my days in extremis would come to an end."

Sam was watching me carefully. "Well, anyway, I think I have something that will take your mind off your problems. In fact, something that will virtually eliminate your problems."

"Oh, really." I smiled. *If only,* I thought. If only someone *could* bring Sarah back, I'd let the rest of it go.

"Really." She leant forward, cheeks glowing, her glass slanted at such an angle that it came perilously close to sloshing out its last tablespoon of vodka all over the oversized Toulouse-Lautrec book on the table.

"Careful," I said, my hand touching hers as I righted the glass.

"Oh! Thanks." She reached for the jug and topped up my drink without asking, then her own. "All right. How would you like to receive eighteen million pounds to have Stone and Stone take care of all your problems—you keep your own imprint—with a New York flat thrown in to the bargain?"

"I love an American who talks in pounds." I'd meant it as a joke, but it came out sounding like a pass. "Sam, we were just bemoaning all the consolidation in the industry. You can't be serious. Besides, you're low," I teased. I let my words hang in the air as I took another sip of my martini. "Another firm offered me more just yesterday. Still, I suppose I should adjust for the New York flat."

Come to think of it, how much was Plumtree Press worth? Until the last two days, the possibility of selling had never come up. I actually thought all three offers were somewhere in the ball park, as Sam might say . . . *all three offers*! This was craziness.

Her eyes narrowed. Too late, she tried to look unconcerned. "Oh? Who offered you more?"

I shook my head slightly. "Seriously, I'm not at all comfortable with this, Sam. I almost feel—well, *hounded* to sell the Press. As if there's a sort of frenzy on. You'll have to give me time to think about it. In fact, may I ask *why* you want Plumtree Press?"

Marie appeared in the doorway.

Sam put down her glass. "Ah, are we ready?"

Marie nodded.

"Good. Alex?"

"Wonderful," I said, and followed her as she led the way in to lunch. As we passed out of the room into a wood-panelled passageway, I stopped in front of another collection of oil portraits. These, too, looked familiar. . . . Where had I seen those close-set, downward-slanting eyes, that long, aquiline nose, and the markedly oval-shaped face with the jutting jaw before? I'd been reading something fairly recently . . .

My *Beowulf* author', Hammonds's, proposed *History of English Printing*! The portrait was of Christopher Barker, the Cambridge printer who'd had the licence to print the Bible for the Crown in the 1600's! Surely *he* wasn't in the deep past of the Stone clan . . . though the family did seem to have books instead of blood in its veins.

Sam had been chattering on about the food. ". . . caught the salmon in Vermont and insisted upon flying it over here—" She suddenly realised I wasn't with her and stopped short.

"Sorry," I told her. "I couldn't help but notice these portraits. I just caught a glimpse of this gentleman in a manuscript we were thinking of publishing on the history of printing. Is he a Stone ancestor?"

A smile spread across Sam's face as she came to stand beside me before the portraits. "Trust you to know about anything to do with books and printing." She shook her head. "Somewhere in the very distant past, yes. My father's side. It's frightening, how perceptive you are." Her gaze moved from the rather stern visage in the painting to my own face. The frank look of assessment blended with approval implied that she'd revised her estimate of me, and my stock had gone up several points. I also saw something a little like caution, or worry, and wondered for the thousandth time why people always underestimated a quiet, mild-mannered man of books.

We went in then to the exceedingly well-travelled salmon. But my trustworthy intuition told me something alarming that I'd rather not have acknowledged: I was quite sure I'd just seen Sam decide it would be a bit more difficult than she'd thought to pull the wool over my eyes.

CHAPTER 7

... 'May God Almighty prosper your venture
And hold you safe!' He wheeled about on his horse
And galloped away to the shore.

—BEOWULF

After lunch I shook my head when Sam suggested we share a taxi to the Press. Two cups of strong coffee had ameliorated the effects of the prelunch martinis, and I'd only pretended to drink the wine at lunch.

"Thanks," I said, making my way back to the spectacular floral arrangement near the door, "but I can't just now. National Book Week events to announce, authors to see, books to sign."

"Come on. What's really happening here?" Once again I heard the plaintive *you're-never-available-to-spend-time-with-me-and-I'm-important* routine in her tone.

I shrugged. "Okay—I've already told you there are people looking for me so they can put a few bullets through me. I'd rather those bullets not stray into my colleagues at the Press, including you. I can't go to the Press, Sam. The only reason I could come here is that people would never expect me to."

Her eyes widened and her mouth opened, ready to utter an exclamation that never came. It was, perhaps, the first time I'd seen her at a loss. I quite enjoyed it.

"You—and your family—know the perils of book publishing," I continued. "Don't tell me your father hasn't had threats of his own in New York."

"Yes, but . . ." For once the unflappable Sam Stone had no response.

I decided to push my advantage while I had it. "Never fear, I'll be in touch. And Sam, don't forget: You're with a small publisher over here. Just because I'm not in the office for a few days doesn't mean you're not important to us. You're a vital part of Plumtree Press for this year. In fact, we're counting on you."

She nodded.

"Bye, then," I said and left her standing at her front door. "Thanks again for lunch." Feeling her eyes on my back, I began the trek back to Maggs where I still planned to quietly chronicle the extraordinary events of the past few days and make some sense of them. I still had an hour or two before the next event in my calendar . . . which slipped my mind at the moment. Oh, well—I'd check when I got back to my Filofax.

But as if to remind me that my life was not under my own control, my mobile rang. I knew that it would be yet another diversion from my already blind, stumbling course.

"Alex Plumtree here."

"Plumtree. Gabriel Hammonds, again—I wondered if I might pop round to the Press to see you before I leave for this *Beowulf* conference in Cambridge. I've decided I can't cower in the dark with my scholarship; I'm going ahead with the conference. There are some things I'd quite like to discuss with you—but not over the phone."

What now? I was silent for a beat longer than

normal, and Hammonds must have interpreted this as reluctance. "I hope it's not too inconvenient," he continued. "I know I've already caused you enough trouble. It won't take long."

"No, of course not—but let's not meet at the Press. Where are you now?"

"I'm up at the Library."

Because Hammonds was Hammonds, I knew he meant the British Library, near St Pancras. He'd told me, before disaster struck, that he occasionally went to commune with the copy of *Beowulf* on display in the special collections room. "Why don't I meet you there?"

"All right. . . ." He sounded surprised at my willingness to travel to him. "Yes. Meet you in the Ritblat Gallery, then. In the far corner, by the *Beowulf* manuscript in Cotton Vitellius A.fifteen. You've been there before?"

"To the Library, yes," I said, "but I'm ashamed to admit this will be my first glimpse of *the Beowulf*. Give me half an hour." I struck out onto Cadogan Gate, crossed Sloane Street, and trotted down into the Underground station.

At Victoria I changed for the Victoria Line, and rode it all the way up to King's Cross St Pancras, mulling the Hammonds situation over as the train whined. His serious, determined voice had brought back the violence and immediacy of the threat made to him. How could it possibly matter *that* much to anyone when an Anglo-Saxon epic had been penned? Who would benefit from the book staying firmly rooted in the seventh century instead of the tenth? A competing scholar, desperate to cling to the theory that had made his name?

Another publisher, who doesn't want its famous texts to become obsolete? An Anglo-Saxon poetry fanatic? None seemed particularly likely.

As I passed the remarkably ornate structure of the St Pancras train station, currently awaiting renovation, the puffy, dark-bottomed clouds suggested nothing more than a distant threat.

Every time I came to the British Library I was struck by the same feeling: It was eerily quiet, as if all the knowledge in the books massed inside presented too great a force for mere mortals to face. The expansive courtyard was always deserted, too, a sort of buffer zone for the sanctity of the library. This was in obvious contrast to the designers' intention of providing a gathering place for outdoor lunches and social occasions that might eventually end up with a visit to the library. Ah, well . . . the best-laid plans.

I went to the front desk and asked about the Ritblat Gallery. "Up those steps, sir; take the stairway to the first floor and follow the signs."

I nodded my thanks and passed beneath a white marble bust of Sir Robert Bruce Cotton, with whom I now felt quite an intimate connection. Wasn't it odd, I mused, that once you learned a bit about a subject, suddenly everything you saw and heard seemed to relate to it?

The library was hushed; I followed a tastefully lettered sign that led me into the Ritblat Gallery. I felt I should know who this Ritblat was, given my close association with the world of books. But all I knew was that he must have given a stunning amount of money to the cause.

The large room, lit with tasteful reserve, was deserted but for two people bent over a display case directly ahead. Small spotlights at the ends of half-inch-thick cords within the glass display cases focussed subtle illumination on the masterpieces. As I admired the cases that lined the walls of the room and stood round the floor at well-spaced intervals, an elderly guide-cum–security guard rose and asked if he could be of help.

"Er, yes—I'm looking for the *Beowulf*. In the Cotton Vitellius volume?"

"Follow me, sir." He led the way to the far end of the room and indicated a case with a pillar in front of it. *Number 23*, the sign said. It seemed strange to me that there was a pillar so close to the *Beowulf* window as to hamper crowds from viewing it. As I came closer, I saw that the pillar did indeed have a purpose, at least on that particular day: It hid Hammonds from view until I was practically upon him. Even the guard looked startled to see the rumpled academic there.

As Hammonds nodded a greeting, leaning rakishly (as rakishly as a chubby, sixtyish scholar in rumpled tweeds and scuffed shoes can) against the side of the pillar that hid him from casual observers, I thanked the guard. The old man backed off, eyeing us curiously before returning to his post near the main entrance.

"Thank you for coming, Alex." It always surprised me how deep Hammonds's voice was; he wasn't a particularly large or prepossessing man.

"It's my pleasure. I'm eager to hear what you have to say. Can you tell me who coerced you into claiming your research was false?"

Hammonds stepped away from his refuge towards the glass case. "I've no idea; it was done anonymously. It wasn't until some time had passed—and oddly, after that fellow I'd helped with *Beowulf* references, Montague, died—that I decided I didn't want to be remembered for being a fraud. Because I'm *not,* Alex. You *must* believe me. I have never compromised myself ethically, not even when little white lies might have made all the difference to my career. My reputation, academically and personally, is solid; always has been. I'm going to that conference in Cambridge today—if they'll still have me—and tell them exactly what happened."

He flushed angrily. "The only way I can win now is to make sure my theory, my research, is publicised and shown to be authentic. I wish I'd never let their threats of violence influence me . . . but I was frightened. You see, nothing like this had ever happened to me before." His lower lip trembled.

"I do understand—and I can't blame you. I admire you for standing up to them, Gabriel, whoever they are."

"Here it is . . . the source of it all." He turned, as if for comfort, to the display case. "The most important poem in Old English, the first great English literary masterpiece."

I gazed inside case number 23 and saw four volumes, each open to what must have been two of its most attractive or representative pages. In the lower left-hand corner I saw the labelled *"Beowulf."* The quarto book of rumpled vellum pages would have been approximately four inches thick had it been closed. The calf leather that had been processed into vellum for the pages looked thick and off-white, not to mention much mistreated in its eleven or fourteen centuries— depending upon which theory one subscribed to. Considering it had been through fire, plague, and pestilence, it hadn't done too badly. A black line surrounded each page on all four sides; I didn't know enough to understand whether this had been done by restorers, or was the original state of the codex from the days of the monks.

Hammonds was studying me. "I'm going to push to have it removed for further study, Alex; that's the other reason I asked to meet with you today. You've heard about the latest techniques for inspecting these ancient codices under ultraviolet light." When I nodded, he drew a deep breath. "I believe that not only will we discover the true date of the *Beowulf* manuscript's origin, but we might discover who made the changes in the poem and why. In fact, we might learn a great deal about the other bits and pieces in Cotton Vitellius A.fifteen as well. It would all be a worthy subject for another book from Plumtree Press, don't you think?"

"Mmm. I was wondering, Hammonds . . . Why do you think Cotton—or was it Nowell?—*whoever* bound the Nowell Codex with the Southwick Codex, put *Beowulf* and Judith in together? Just because they're Anglo-Saxon poetry?"

Hammonds gave me a weary, infinitely patient smile. "Aside from being ripping good yarns, they do have something else in common, and with the other bits and pieces in the codex as well. The unifying element of the Nowell Codex—which makes up half of Cotton Vitellius A.fifteen—is lore about mirabilia and wonders, and so monsters and wonder-workers. The lesser known elements include a fragment of an *English Life of St Christopher*—interestingly, the English thought St Christopher a monster, *healf hundisces menncynnes*. There is also a document entitled *Wonders of the East*, and an English translation of Alexander's spurious letter to Aristotle regarding his wondrous adventures in the East.

"*Beowulf*'s inclusion in this collection is obvious

enough, because of the hideous monster Grendel and the 'wonder-worker' Beowulf. Where Judith is concerned, it depends on your outlook, whether it's a story of a performer of miracles or of a monstrous woman! On the one hand, she saved her people; on the other, she murdered the king. But this particular poem based on Judith in Cotton Vitellius A.fifteen is of special interest to Biblical scholars, because it is the sole version whose details conform to the oldest Greek version extant. . . . Sorry, more detail than you wanted, I'm sure."

"It's fascinating, Hammonds. You never told me you're a Bible scholar as well."

"Goes hand in hand with studying ancient manuscripts. Antiquities and Orientalia are frequently related to holy writings of one culture or another."

"While we're on the subject, if you don't mind, what's the gist of Judith? I'm afraid I'm frightfully ignorant about it."

"Briefly, Judith was an Israelite widow who single-handedly slew Holofernes, the Maccabean general. She was a model of courage and intelligence, and won the respect of all Israel for saving her people from bondage. But Judith was no longer allowed in the Old Testament after the Protestant Reformation, and in fact this fragment was probably removed from a book around 1537. King Henry the Eighth wasn't too understanding of people who didn't follow his edicts. Biblical scholars agree that Judith contains blatant inaccuracies, and lacks certain details that would make it a *believable* historical record instead of merely an inspiring story. For instance, the name of the town in which the story takes place, Bethulia, is not a known name in Samaria. So the story was relegated to the Apocrypha. But we're getting off track."

"I suppose ... but I do see why you enjoy your work. Fiction can't begin to compete with history, can it?"

The benign scholar, however, seemed centuries away; he stared at the ancient codex as if he could read something between the lines. And I soon learned that this was exactly what he intended to do.

"What I really need, Alex, is for you to support me when I request that the codex be made available for further study. Obviously, someone doesn't like my theories ... and it'll take some pull to get it out of here and under the ultraviolet lamps. Any strings you can pull—well, I'd be grateful. And I could write you one hell of a book about it—though I certainly couldn't blame you if you wanted nothing further to do with me. You've been most understanding, Alex."

He pulled up the sleeve of his oversized tweed jacket to check his watch. "I really must be on my way to the conference—it opens in just four hours, and I mustn't be late if I'm going to request such favours. Especially since I'm now out of grace because of caving in to those threats, and will have to reconvince them of my scholarly integrity. My colleagues at Cambridge might just be willing to help get *Beowulf* removed for study, if I whisper enticingly about Biblical issues—especially the Cotton Vitellius A.fifteen's Judith."

Hammonds's comment was oblique, but as an old Cantabrigian myself—though only as a postgraduate—I thought I understood what he meant. Cambridge University had been given a patent to print "all manner of books" by King Henry VIII in 1534, which the university press interpreted to mean Bibles as well. The royal printer didn't much like it, nor did the Guild of London Stationers, as they both thought *they* had the monopoly on the Bible. Fascinating conflicts followed, but Cambridge University Press had over time emerged as one of the preeminent scholarly authorities on the Bible and the history thereof, as well as all manner of antiquities and Orientalia.

"Best of luck," I told him, and meant it. "And Hammonds, do be careful. I don't want to alarm you, but after we were cut off last night, I was attacked by some very serious people—the sort who carry guns and actually use them."

His eyes flashed, showing his distress and anger on my behalf. "What happened? Did you find out who they were?"

I shook my head. "I don't know whether it's related to the original threat you received; like you, I have no idea who they were. The police came charging in and saved me, though only through a very strange—well, *coincidence,* I suppose you'd say. But I did think I should mention it."

"Someone must feel very threatened indeed by our project, Alex, though why I can't imagine. It's utterly baffling. I've considered this from every angle, and still can't work it out." Grimly, he cast one more look at the *Beowulf* pages displayed behind the glass. "I'd best get on. Good-bye, Alex—I'll be in touch after the conference."

With an air of stealth, he galumphed off in his squeaky-soled Clarks towards an industrial-looking door marked EXIT not far behind me. I admired the man tremendously for standing up for his research and its honest revelation.

I stayed for a few moments to inspect the other treasures of the Ritblat Gallery, among them Magna Carta, the earliest Chaucer volumes, and illuminated books of hours. It was an embarrassment of riches.

Aware of too much to work out and not enough time in which to do it, I reluctantly left the room, nodding good-bye to the guard, and descended the steps again to the ground floor. But as I was walking towards the main exit, I spotted piles of books about books in clear view, just through the door of the library shop. I was lost.

Twenty minutes later I emerged with a more technical scholarly volume on *Beowulf* than Hammonds's, *Beowulf and the Beowulf Manuscript* by Kevin Kiernan, an American. When I glanced inside, I saw that it had a full explanation of the binding of *Beowulf* with Judith in Cotton Vitellius A.xv, down to paginations and re-paginations. I thought it might come in handy if I were to begin to understand what Hammonds was talking about in his quest for literary justice. Another work, entitled *Treasures of the British Library,* featured a beautiful four-colour reproduction of the opening page of the Book of Matthew from The Lindisfarne Gospels on its cover and had proved equally irresistible.

I left the holy hush of the library. Outside, I found myself momentarily stunned by the blinding, irreverent sunlight. As I made my way across the sea of red bricks, I plucked out my mobile and entered the number of the Press, followed by Lisette's extension number.

"Lisette Stoneham—Can I 'elp you?"

"You certainly *may,*" I said. How it was that she had failed to master the finer points of English after all these years and marriage to a blue-blood besides, I could never understand. I earned a cross, coarse epithet every time I tried to correct her, so a casual comment was as far as I went these days. "What's the news from Neville about our eviction?"

" 'Allo, you. The news is not good. 'E reviewed the

agreement from 1915, when your great-grandfather undertook the lease from the duke. The duke *does* 'ave the right to evict us. Neville suggests that you try for a meeting with 'Is Grace." Her voice dripped with irony. "But not through 'is business agent. Neville—who as you know represents many bookselling and publishing clients—'as some interesting scuttlebutt on this agent. 'E tells me the duke's business agent shares offices with the same gent that is booting 'alf of Charing Cross out of its digs. The bas—sorry, the *bloke's* meanness is contagious, it seems. So Neville recommends the personal approach: see 'Is Grace one on one. Neville advises you to invoke the images of the duke's father and your grandfather."

"Not a bad idea. Perhaps it's a case of the business agent being a bit more businesslike than the duke might like, or even realises. I'll see what I can do. Is everything in hand for Frankfurt?"

"Actually, it's all going quite well this year. No last-minute crises—yet." She lowered her voice. "And our Godwin Fellow is getting 'er 'ands dirty even as I speak, 'elping to prepare the literature packets. Maybe she will not be so bad after all," she said with a sniff.

"Hmm. Good. Remember, be nice."

"I am offended that you think you 'ave to tell me! I treat 'er like everyone else, don't I?"

I smiled. Lisette wasn't known for treating others with kid gloves, especially if she suspected they had a tendency towards snootiness.

"Where are *you*, may I ask, and what are *you* doing?" she demanded.

"Doing my best to stay out of trouble, thank you. I've had two very interesting meetings—first with Sam, over lunch." I took a quick decision not to pass on the breathtaking information that Sam Stone was related to Christopher Barker, the King's printer, as it would only earn Sam harsher treatment from Lisette. Of course I avoided the discovery of the Cotton Collection remnant entirely. "And second, with Gabriel Hammonds." I took a moment to fill her in on what had transpired with our beleaguered *Beowulf* scholar. "I think we'll have another book out of Hammonds on a discovery he feels is imminent with Cotton Vitellius A.fifteen, the book in which *Beowulf* is bound. It might even turn into a series, or we could repackage it as one."

"You never stop, do you? You'll need a 'oliday after next week. I do 'ope you are planning to take one, or I shall 'ave to take measures."

The truth was, until the bizarre sightings of Sarah had begun, I'd been leaning towards accepting Nicola's offer of the sailing holiday. Just because we did a bit of sailing together didn't mean we had to become romantically involved. But I wasn't about to tell Lisette any of that. "We'll see."

"Hmmph." A short pause, during which I knew she would be sipping the inky liquid she called coffee, which she consumed constantly throughout the day. "By the way," she said with exaggerated casualness. " 'Ave you noticed the time, by any chance? I 'ope you are near Charing Cross Road."

I hurriedly consulted my watch and uttered a cry of anguish. National Book Week; my first author lecture to facilitate was beginning in just seventeen minutes—and it wasn't just any author: it was Baroness Thatcher, the ex-prime-minister-turned-novelist.

"Thanks, Lisette! Bye!" I disconnected and broke into a trot. The only way I could possibly make it would be on my own two feet, given the traffic. How could I have let this happen? Of all the authors I might insult by being late, Baroness Thatcher was the most unthinkable.

No one crossed Baroness Thatcher. No one.

It flashed through my mind that it was most unlike me to forget such a commitment, even for an hour. What was happening to me?

With gratitude to Threepwood for helping me to stay reasonably fit, I alternately ran and walked through the web of streets surrounding the University of London just north of the Press, past Bedford Square, and finally to Charing Cross Road via New Oxford Street. I managed it in fifteen minutes—which gave me two minutes to mop my brow and catch my breath outside the back door of the huge new Frontiers shop hosting the event.

Although I saw Baroness Thatcher raise her eyebrows at my corduroys, turtleneck, stubble, and flushed cheeks as we greeted one another near the podium, I told myself she knew how Bohemian the literary world could be. She shook my hand cordially nonetheless as I introduced myself and told her how delighted I was to have this honour.

It wasn't until she had taken her seat at my left, waiting to be introduced, that I remembered: Whoever was trying to eliminate me from the face of British publishing would know that I would be here, announcing Baroness Thatcher, at that very moment. It had been in the *Times,* the *Guardian, Time Out, What's On,* and every other possible avenue for publication. I doubted they would shoot at me as I spoke—though it was certainly possible. If I were they, I'd wait to catch me alone afterwards.

And so it was that during Baroness Thatcher's remarks, as I sat inwardly gnawing my fingernails, I hatched a plan to preserve my life over the next few hours.

When her speech, this year about the adventure of writing fiction, and question time were over, I thanked Baroness Thatcher for having honoured us all with her presence. Then, instead of allowing her to make a graceful exit with her security people, I attached myself to her entourage. "Do you mind, Baroness, if I ask you a question of my own?"

Very graciously, if curtly, she agreed with a nod as her three security men—one of whom had been guarding the rear exit throughout her speech—hurried her out the back way. I followed, talking fast.

"What is your favourite part of the fiction-writing process: coming up with the idea, researching the subject, or actually doing the writing?" By the time I finished, we were nearly at her car—a large black Rolls-Royce, in which a driver was waiting with the engine running. I could see that the men were not going to let her dilly-dally long enough to answer my question. But I'd succeeded in putting myself under her protection for the few moments I needed to get out of the shop.

Glancing about, I saw him immediately: a man watching us, trying to blend in with his surroundings. He was badly camouflaged; his black leather jacket, even the narrow rectangle sticking out from behind the rubbish wheelie-bin, contrasted garishly with the tan-coloured bin. Watching him out of the corner of my eye, I stayed at Baroness Thatcher's side and listened attentively for her answer.

Succinctly, with a polite smile, she said, "The writing," and disappeared into her car.

"Thank you so much," I said with as much dignity as I could muster, waving as if we were friends. As the car pulled away, I was already moving, pelting down the narrow alley to the next street. I emerged onto the pavement and whipped through the door of a dark, smoky Ladbrokes bookmakers. My sudden entrance earned me astonished looks from several older men who appeared to be in a daze.

"Please," I said, finger to lips, and ran down the hallway to a small office on the right. I knew they kept one for holding difficult customers, private conversations, and large deals. As I bolted the door shut, a memory, painful as anything my pursuer could possibly do to me, flashed through my mind: Sarah had wanted to come into a Ladbrokes once, assuming that "bookmakers" meant that books were assembled there. I'd played along, managing to keep a smile off my face, and brought her inside. Her face fell when she saw the televisions showing horse races, the thick smoke in the air, and the shabby room full of hopeless men. Understanding had dawned swiftly and we'd hurried out, Sarah laughing uproariously at her misinterpretation of this frequent London landmark. But in the meantime I'd seen the way it was all laid out.

As I pushed the door shut and silently bolted the lock, I heard the front door open and close again. I imagined my pursuer eyeing the sad, dazed men and wondering if they'd seen me come through. But no one spoke—at least that I could hear. With growing anxiety I peered round one corner of a dark curtain that blocked most of the daylight from the single window into the office, hoping to see the black leather jacket emerge. When it didn't after a moment or two, I knew something was wrong.

Half-expecting bullets to come flying through the hollow wooden door, I plucked the phone off its cradle on the desk, punched 999, and whispered my location and difficulty. Then I waited . . . and waited. Perhaps it was only five minutes; it seemed an hour. I sensed his presence outside the door in the grubby hall, heard the occasional shift of a foot—even heard an obnoxious nasal-passage-clearing habit—and soon realised that my opponent was playing a waiting game. Perhaps one of the dozy men had given me away after all, hoping for a reward of more money to wager. But why wait? The men with the guns hadn't waited.

Still expecting the unknown antagonist to tire of this and burst through the door at any moment, it was with great relief that I heard a police car pull up with a screech in front of the betting shop. Two constables leapt out and raced towards the entrance at the same time I heard a hissed four-letter word just outside my door. I heard footsteps down the hallway beyond my door, then glass breaking. The poor black-leather bloke had, I soon learned, found his way out the loo window.

The two policemen were quite understanding, considering. I explained to them that the accused had first threatened me outside a Frontiers bookshop on Charing Cross Road, and I'd fled to the nearest refuge. Though one of the constables knew my face from the newspapers, they both looked at me askance. A Ladbrokes?

"Look." I laughed. "I've only been in this sort of place once before." Since I couldn't explain why people with guns were trying to track me down, I didn't try to explain it. In fact, I didn't mention it. I gave them as full a description as I could manage—medium height, fair hair (I thought) under a black cap, black leather jacket, and a high forehead.

When I mentioned the latter, the two constables

looked at me. "A 'igh for'ead?" the beefy one echoed with a strong London accent. "A 'igh for'ead, 'e says," he told his colleague.

"Yes, a high forehead." I grinned, aware that they were having a bit of fun with me. "Long thought to be an indication of intelligence—though in this case I'm not so sure."

They smiled grudgingly at that and I was temporarily off the hook. They didn't like me though, and didn't much like it that I seemed to be mixed up with the seamy sort. "Anything else you'd like to tell us?"

They watched me; clearly they thought that I'd done something to deserve such trouble. "I wish there *were* something I could tell you . . . I've no idea who or why. It just happened."

"You're quite a busy man, Mr. Plumtree. Keeping us busy, too, aren't you?"

After the pair left, it was painfully apparent that they didn't care where I went, *I* didn't care where I went, *no one* cared where I went. I was well and truly alone. I didn't believe in indulging in self-pity; my loneliness was just a fact that was impossible to ignore.

I placed one phone call to Mick, asking him to meet me at the Orchard at seven o'clock to make sure it was safe. It was asking a lot, I knew, but I did it anyway. Then I took the tube to Green Park, picked up the Passat from near Baggs, and began the nearly hour-long, thought-filled drive to Chorleywood.

While the rest of my world tried to convince me that life must go on without Sarah, I had a secret. I'd got in touch with a Dartmouth friend of mine, one Moose (Mandeville Alonzo) Fox, whose uncle had been a prisoner of war in North Vietnam. His uncle had made it back in the end—not undamaged by the experience, of course. But because of my situation with Sarah, Moose had put me in touch with his uncle's wife, Paula. Via E-mail, Paula and I had had weekly chats ever since Sarah's disappearance two months ago. She told me, before I'd ever confided in her about my feelings that Sarah was still alive, that she'd had similar feelings about her husband. She could *feel* he was alive, she said, and she'd been right.

Personally, I was appalled that anyone would write off someone they loved as much as I loved Sarah after a mere two months. But you can't imagine how people tried to persuade me that I was insane not to carry on with my life and forget about her. As if I *could* forget about her . . . or carry on without her.

When I got off the motorway and sped along the narrow lane towards my home, I rolled down my window. The smells of night in Chorleywood, the sight of my breath in the air, and the quiet of the countryside were balm to my soul. Balm that, like so many forms of comfort, brought tears to my eyes.

At the point where the ancient and rural Old Shire Lane departed from the well-travelled Stag Lane, I left all lights and civilisation and drove slowly down the lane to the Orchard and peace.

Mick was there, cheerful and conscientious, and agreed to stay for a cup of tea. I told him what had happened after Baroness Thatcher's National Book Week lecture, and about my run-in with the London police. He urged me not to hesitate to call if I needed anything.

When he'd gone, I forsook the kitchen for the library . . . and found what I had been hoping for all along.

CHAPTER 8

*But enquire not ye of mine act; for I will not declare it
unto you, till the things be finished that I do.*

—JUDITH 8:34

In the refuge of the library, free from marauding in-
terlopers, I lit a fire. Then I threw myself into a chair
and massaged my burning eyes with thumb and forefinger. Merely being in the room helped me to feel that
things would come right in the end, if I could just stay
the course.

As I sat in the quiet gloom, with only the flickering
fire for light and heat, the chaotic mess of the last two
days—could it be only two days?—sorted itself out into
discrete bits. In times like these, I found comfort in sepa-
rating the entire disaster into components, so it wasn't
quite so overwhelming. Here were the pebbles—no,
boulders—in my shoe:

Sarah—and Sarah's perfume—kept drifting in and
out of my presence, never close enough to reach out
and touch. Was I losing my mind? Was she in London?
If so, why hadn't she come to me, or at least told me?
And why had a taxi driver dropped her at Sam Stone's
house? What did Sam know that she wasn't telling me?

Gabriel Hammonds had been threatened if he told
the truth about his *Beowulf* findings. Why? And by
whom?

Nottingham Botkin, to hear Matt Ireland tell it, had

been murdered; before that, he'd been maligned, discredited, and evicted from his leasehold in what appeared to be a deliberate campaign to wear him down. Why? And what had he really expected of me as the keeper of the secret library-within-a-library behind his shelves? Who had come searching in Botkin's, apparently for the Cotton Collection remnant? Had Whitticombe tried to force the old bookseller to sell as part of an industry-wide conspiracy?

Who had told Nate to call and tell me that McKinley Montague's publisher had murdered him to sell more books? Why?

Why were men of varying degrees of skill trying to kill me, and who was behind it all? Was it related to the threat made to Hammonds, or the bookselling/publishing conspiracy Matt Ireland so feared?

Why did three different major publishing firms suddenly want to buy my little company?

I revised my estimation: this time things really were overwhelming, even taken one horrible, confusing bit at a time.

When my mobile began to ring on the table next to me—the house line was still cut, courtesy of the gunmen—I studied it for a long moment before picking it up. Phone calls had become synonymous with bad news. "Alex Plumtree." My voice sounded exhausted, even to me.

"Alex. Thank God I've reached you." It was Ian, his voice grave.

"Ian—are you all right? What is it?"

He let out a breath. "Alex, Gabriel Hammonds is dead. It happened just before his lecture—the lecture the society had unanimously encouraged him to give after all."

"Ian, I just saw him this afternoon. How—how did he die?"

"That's a very good question. You know—knew—Hammonds . . . not exactly athletic, but certainly competent. Not at all delicate, or awkward on his feet."

I thought of his squeaky rubber-soled Clark shoes.

"When he didn't show up to deliver his lecture, they sent someone looking for him. He'd fallen down the stairwell and hit his head."

A chill gripped me; *he'd fallen down the stairwell . . . hit his head*. All too similar to Botkin's demise—and there *were* no coincidences.

"I don't think he fell, Alex. I think he was killed by the people who threatened him."

I tried to take this in. "Ian, have you rung the police?"

"Mm. They don't see any signs that he was pushed—but then what signs could there be? I told them about the threat. They listened, but obviously it doesn't prove anything."

I closed my eyes, gritting my teeth in frustration. "What do you think we should do, Ian? And who on earth would *kill* Hammonds for his *Beowulf* theory?"

"I don't know. I've wondered if it could be a competing scholar, but I've never known any of my academic colleagues—all the people I've worked with over the years—to resort to something like this over a scholarly squabble. And I simply can't think who else would care."

"When I talked to him this afternoon, he was eager to have the British Library's *Beowulf* taken off display and made available for ultraviolet study."

At first Ian was silent. Then he said, rather darkly, "Cotton Vitellius A.fifteen."

"Precisely," I said, ever amazed at his perspicacity. "Ian, how is it possible that you know everything?"

"If only it were so, Alex." He sighed. "Tell me more about what Gabriel said to you before he left for Cambridge."

I told him all I could recall . . . even about mentioning to his friends from the Cantabrigian Press—Cambridge University's Press—that there might be something to be gleaned from further study of *Judith* as well as *Beowulf*. "How long does the conference go on?"

"Until the day after tomorrow, supposedly—I was going to have to leave before the conclusion to get to Frankfurt. But I don't know if they'll carry on now . . . everyone's pretty upset. Hammonds was the best-liked, most respected of them all."

"Ian, if the police aren't going to check into this, I'd like to talk to Hammonds's colleagues. Even if one of his *Beowulf*-obsessed friends isn't responsible, and I can't imagine they are, they're our only chance for shedding light on this."

"I agree."

"I have to be in London tomorrow for another blasted National Book Week event, but I'll zip up to Cambridge in the afternoon—should be there by about four. Where will I find you?"

"Didn't I tell you? The conference is being held at the Pepys Library, in your old college."

Magdalene, site of my postgraduate studies in Literature. At least I'd know my way around. We rang off, and I could tell Ian felt as wretched as I did about our author.

Hammonds was dead. Slain by a modern Grendel. This *Beowulf* business had gone much too far—the poem was nearly a millennium old, even under Hammonds's new—

Beowulf! I groaned; how could I not have seen it before? First Botkin, then Montague, and now Hammonds: all *three* had shared a connection to *Beowulf.* Botkin had owned the *Beowulf* that was now mine, and was related to the one-time owner of the Cotton Vitellius version; Montague wrote his thriller involving Beowulf and put the name in the title, even calling Hammonds for references; and Hammonds, of course, had practically dedicated his life to the epic.

What else did Montague and Hammonds share? I considered what I knew about them both: Montague was a reclusive, best-selling commercial novelist; Hammonds was an academic scholar of obscure subjects. Montague was published by Hanford Banner, Hammonds by us; Hammonds was directly threatened by someone, but I didn't know if Montague had been threatened or died an honest death.

What was *Beowulf*'s deadly secret?

I switched on the table lamp and went in search of the book I'd bought on *Beowulf* at the British Library. I found it in the kitchen. While I was there, I flipped the switch on the electric kettle before sitting to peruse the book at the scarred refectory table. One unquestionable benefit of being a book publisher was that I had learned to scan virtually anything in print and get its gist in a satisfyingly short time.

The cup of tea was never made. I found two things that completely distracted me—*and* drove me to distraction.

First, any theory I might have had about a competing scholar wanting to kill Hammonds was quashed by the fact that Kevin Kiernan, the American scholar who'd written the tome in my hands, had *himself* implied that *Beowulf* scholars would do well to question the date of authorship. I felt I could safely assume this daring assertion hadn't got Kiernan killed, because the book had been updated by Kiernan five years after its first printing.

Second, I found a fascinating reproduction of a page of *Beowulf,* very much like the pages I'd seen in the open codex at the library. The scholar had taken some pains to describe an *X* made by the scribe, and how very characteristic it was of that particular scribe. His point was that the same scribe had not penned the entire poem; one part had been added later—possibly even after the fire at Ashburnham House where the Cotton Collection had been stored. This peculiar *X* was found both in parts of Judith and parts of *Beowulf.*

A strange feeling came over me as I turned back to the reproduction page to look at the *X* described by Kiernan. I knew that *X* . . . that particular scribe's *X.* I had seen it before. . . .

I pushed back from the table in such a hurry that I knocked over my chair. Still carrying the *Beowulf* book, I rushed back into the library and went directly to the most precious volumes in the Plumtree collection: the Malconbury Chronicles. In these beautifully illuminated books the monks had chronicled life in Malconbury Priory, on the coast in East Anglia, from the tenth to the fifteenth centuries.

With shaking hand, I reached above and behind the first volume of vellum-encased monastery records and tipped the book forward. Then I grasped it between thumb and forefinger and pulled it towards me, supporting the heavy volume with my other hand as it left the shelf. I set it down on the library table and carefully opened it to the page I always turned to first: the recto (right-hand page) that described the operations of the scriptorium. What the monks set down with their quill pens and how it was determined that they should do so, which roots they used to dye their inks, et cetera.

But my eyes widened as I looked down at the page with its brilliant blues and reds, for a small square of fine stationery had been inserted there. For a moment I heard blood rushing in my ears; my surroundings receded. The note was in Sarah's half-European, half-American semicursive handwriting.

> *My dearest Alex—I will always love you. No matter what happens, you have made my life complete. To have been your one love for a time is more than I could have asked for. One of the many things I have always treasured about your most generous love is that you never restrained my freedom to live my life as I saw fit. I want you to know that I give you the same freedom.*
> *God bless you always, my love*
> *Sarah*

I sat down, trembling, at the library table, reading and rereading the note, seeking to read volumes between the sparse yet deeply meaningful lines. How long had it been there? When I'd smelled Sarah's scent in the library the other night—the same day I'd seen her on the street—*had she been here*? Perhaps I wasn't losing my mind after all—perhaps she was alive, and well . . . and avoiding me.

With intense concentration I inspected the words yet again for a hint: Had she written it before her disappearance or after? It was impossible to tell. I felt a hint of the irrational anger I'd sometimes felt toward Sarah return—except if she'd written this note since her disappearance, perhaps it wasn't so irrational. Wasn't anger a normal, healthy reaction to loss?

But whereas in the past my anger had always made me feel guilty, if I found out she'd been in my house and was telling me good-bye, I'd simply be furious. And absolutely guilt-free. Why would she—*how* could she—do such a thing?

As I stared at the paper—the sort of textured linen Sarah liked to use—my vision moved past it to the vellum page on which the note sat. Though it didn't matter half as much as it had five minutes ago, the *X* of the Malconbury monk was unmistakably the same as that of the *Beowulf* scribe. The obvious conclusion was that the same scribe had written both of them . . . and therefore *Beowulf* dated from the same time as the Malconbury Chronicles. The particular volume I was looking at was from the tenth century.

I had just confirmed Gabriel Hammonds's theory. What a shame he wasn't alive to know it.

I picked up Sarah's note and the Malconbury volume and took them back to my favourite chair, along with Kiernan's *Beowulf* book. When I finally tired of rereading the note, I shook my head, set it on the table next to me, and took up the two books. When I had the *X*'s side by side, it was indeed obvious that the same scribe had written both of them. Placing the Chronicles volume gently on the rug, I leafed through the Kiernan *Beowulf* book until I came to the part about the unusual strokes of the scribe that identified him.

His *X* is consistently formed of three separate strokes: the main stroke is a heavy diagonal from upper left to lower right; usually the cross is made with two additional strokes—a heavy hook in the upper right of the main stroke, and a long, thin tail, extending well below the minim line at the lower left. Sometimes the cross is made with a single stroke, but the style is unchanged, particularly with respect to the long, thin tail.

Then something caught my eye, one of those seemingly worthless bits of trivia that one always seems to latch on to. The scholar was making the point that Judith had been ripped from another codex—presumably a collection of religious writings, at the time of the English Reformation in the 1530's—and bound into the new one with *Beowulf.* He postulated this because the hand responsible for the Judith page numbers and the *X*'s in the later sections of *Beowulf* was identical—that of this scribe with the unusual technique.

If an air-raid siren had gone off, it could not possibly have astounded me more than the gentle *bong* of my own doorbell. My first thought was to switch off the lamp on the table next to me; I'd turned out all the lights behind me elsewhere.

Who knew that I was here? Surely someone wishing me harm would not be so obvious as to ring my doorbell, but I was twice shy. Cautiously, I went to the front of the house and nudged aside a corner of the curtain, in order to see the step.

Ian. But he was supposed to be in Cambridge, at the conference. . . . I'd only spoken to him less than three hours ago. He looked distraught. I ran to the door.

"Ian! Are you all right? What—"

"I had to come right away, Alex. I know I'm supposed to be in Cambridge, but I had to come down immediately to tell you."

Ian, who had never, I was sure, interrupted anyone in his life before, stepped inside. Then came the second shocker: He gave me a hug. Not just any hug: an unqualified bear hug. I'd known him for more than three decades; he'd been my surrogate father for five years. This was our first awkward hug. He was uneasy with it, and pulled back—though we still gripped one another's arms. "I had to come and tell you. I *know* she's alive, Alex."

His expression was odd: There was no joy or relief in it.

"I—I just know, Alex. That's all I can tell you. But I had to tell you as soon as possible. Obviously, as I've come all the way from Cambridge."

Was there something guilty about his expression? The very thought of Ian lying was so foreign as to be laughable. But he had hidden the truth when necessary in the past . . . when it was for my own good. Why would he keep what he knew about Sarah from me? There was something not quite right about this sudden appearance.

I looked into his eyes.

He looked away.

Then I knew for certain. But in the spirit of the sort of kindness and mercy he'd always shown me, I decided to play along. Whatever had happened, he could not be held to blame. Ian was as close to perfection as human beings came.

I wanted to ask him a great many questions, but

was so astonished by this new and very different Ian that I didn't quite know how to respond. "I'm sorry—come in, come in. Would you like a coffee? Herb tea?"

"No, thanks. I am *very* glad to see you, Alex. Very glad indeed. Do you think we might sit in the library? By the fire?"

"Let's do." I led the way, offered him the chair next to my father's—the massive Lawson-armed leather monster I'd grown up seeing him in. I watched him relax, settling in and taking in the room around him like a soothing tonic. Only then did I broach the subject. I didn't ask him to put himself in my shoes—false hope was the last thing I wanted—because I knew he almost *was* in my shoes. He, too, cared about Sarah very deeply.

"What—exactly—do you mean, that you know she's alive? I mean, how did you become convinced of this?"

"Would you mind if I took you up on that herb tea after all?"

"Ian, you know how much this means to me—" I caught myself just in time. He needed me to give him a moment. "Of course I don't mind. Excellent idea. Back in a moment." As I stood, I reflected that I'd never seen Ian put anything harmful into his body. The amount of tofu, rice, fruit juice, and herb tea he consumed were enough to send anyone else running to the corner store for a packet of salt-and-vinegar crisps and a can of beer.

In the kitchen, I filled the kettle with fresh water and set it boiling. I threw several dessertspoonfuls of his favourite chamomile tea leaves into the pot, prepared a plate of his favourite natural biscuits (kept in the freezer for just such visits), and set out the bulky brown mugs made by my mother during her early pot-throwing years. Ian claimed nothing held the heat—and the tea—like those mugs. But I think he liked them because they reminded him of my mother.

I was staring at the mugs as the kettle switched off, wondering if I'd ever be married to Sarah . . . or, in fact, anyone. Ever. Somehow the definite click of the kettle switch seemed to tell me that I was a fool to think so; I stood and filled the pot, then picked up the tray. What on earth could have happened to Ian? I was more than a little worried about him.

I set the tray down on the ottoman between us. We were waiting for the tea to steep when I broke the silence—mercifully, I thought.

"Ian, tonight I found a note from Sarah."

"A note?" Ian's voice was sharp. "You found a note from Sarah? What do you mean?"

"I can't tell if she wrote it before or after she disappeared. Sometimes I think I'm losing my mind—I've glimpsed her twice in London in the last thirty-six hours, but she's always got away before I could reach her. Even more strangely, I've smelled her scent . . . her perfume. The strangest thing is that I tracked down the cab driver who drove her on one of those occasions. He dropped her in Cadogan Square—at Sam Stone's."

"No." Ian was shaking his head. "You couldn't have really seen her . . ."

"I think I know my own fiancée, Ian."

"I didn't mean that—of course you do. Sorry, Alex. It's just . . ."

"I know, I know. How can it possibly be?"

"May I see the note, please—"

"Yes, of course." I took it to him, watched as his eyes consumed it greedily.

"Ian, if there's something you know that I don't, you

would tell me, wouldn't you." I made it a statement, not a question. Surely *Ian* . . .

"Alex, you know I would—if I could." He looked me squarely in the eye. He *did* know something else. "I've already told you all I can—I know that she's alive. Hold to that, Alex. I wouldn't lie to you."

I felt anger blossom as it had towards Sarah just moments ago. This game of cat and mouse with the truth was absurd amongst family, which we very nearly were. I came a breath away from berating him for treachery, and saved myself only by focussing on pouring the tea.

"Thank you, Alex," he said, accepting the mug. His tone told me it was a thank-you for not blowing up at him, for trying to trust him.

"May I ask," I said, regretting the snottiness of it as soon as it left my mouth, "if Sarah is alive, do you think I will see her soon?"

"I'm sorry, I don't know."

I could see that Ian was struggling, that he wanted to say more. Still, I had to close my eyes for a moment to control myself. "Okay. Let's talk about the other life-or-death issues before us, then. Why did you say on the phone, hours ago, 'Cotton Vitellius A.fifteen' in your most tragic voice? What aren't you telling me about *that*?"

He caught my velvet-knifed comment, but to his credit replied in a neutral tone.

"It's just that Cotton Vitellius A.fifteen is a very special bit of calf's leather." He took a sip of tea. "Beyond containing the oldest known copy of *Beowulf*, its Anglo-Saxon Judith poem is unique. It's the only ancient version of Judith that matches new paleographical evidence about the book that's come to light—the scroll that uses a different name for the site of the story, and refers to King Nebuchadnezzar as the slain leader instead of the general Holofernes."

"You know about all that?"

He nodded. "Obviously you do, too. There might even be more to it." Taking another sip of tea, he gazed off towards the fireplace and mused, "Too bad old Botkin is gone. He might understand what people think Hammonds was on to."

Knowing Ian, he might have been telling me at that very moment that there was something there, behind those carefully arranged books, that would reveal why Hammonds was murdered. Sometimes I almost wished Ian weren't so honourable, so that he could betray others by telling their secrets . . . at least I would have a clue what was going on.

"Well. Thanks for the tea, Alex." He set his mug on the tray and stood. "I wish I had something more to tell you about Sarah, but I couldn't resist telling you what I *do* know. Thank you for accepting it as best you could. I know it's hard for you."

I followed him to the door; he picked up the waxed jacket he'd hung on the rack as he came in. "Thanks for coming all the way out, Ian. I should tell you, I'm not going to be staying here much these days—after my visitors last night. They must think I know what Hammonds had discovered . . . or Botkin, or perhaps even Montague." I ran a hand through my hair as I let out a sigh. "I only came here tonight because I—well, I needed to be home."

Concern radiated from his eyes. "Don't take chances, Alex. You know how serious they are, after what happened to Hammonds." As an afterthought he added, "And Botkin. And Montague." As he slipped on his jacket, I noticed that he refrained from asking me where I would go, where I was staying. "If I need to get in touch with you, then, I'll ring you on your mobile."

I nodded and said good night, then ran upstairs to fill a bag with enough clothes and toiletries to see me through a few days. Then I closed up the house, got in my car, and drove to Botkin's as fast as I could.

CHAPTER 9

That fiend from hell, foul enemy of God, [came]
Toward Heorot. He beheld it from afar, the gleaming roof
Towering high to heaven. His tremendous hands
Struck the studded door, wrenched it from the hinges
Till the wood splintered and the bolts burst apart.

— BEOWULF

I'd taken every care to ensure that no one followed me. Still, I had a crawling feeling at the back of my neck as I unlocked the rear door at Botkin's and slipped inside without turning the lights on. I'd brought the torch from the car—one of the inch-wide, superfocussed variety.

Feeling very much like a cat burglar, if an awkward one, I skulked over to the wall where Ed had shown me the wondrous hidden library. The books still lay strewn on the floor; it would be up to me to carefully gather the volumes needing repair, and also to replace the intact ones. It gave me pleasure to think of organising them once again according to the arcane symbolism that only the most obsessed British bibliomaniacs could decipher. Most of the time we were a happy lot, delighted to thumb our noses at A.E. Housman, who had once labelled us—as a category of people—idiots. Poor fellow had never known what he was missing.

As I began picking up the books one by one and setting them in their rightful places, torch between my teeth, the responsibility of owning such a collection bore down heavily on my shoulders. I would have to safeguard the hidden collection somehow. Or perhaps these treasures belonged in the British Library, with the rest of the Cotton Collection.

But why had Botkin kept them such a secret? Ed had said something about Botkin feeling the need to protect them . . . but from whom? A half-formed thought that I might find something in his collection that would tell me the great and deadly secret of the *Beowulf* had brought me there, but I had no idea, really, what I was looking for. Anything about *Beowulf* would almost certainly be located behind the section corresponding with Little Britain or Paternoster Row on the map of old booksellers ∴ in other words, in the upper left-hand quadrant of the bookcase.

Reaching for the shelf, torch in teeth, I heard a distinct *click* at the back door. I spun round and switched off the light—happily, I had not yet opened the secret case, as I'd only replaced one shelf of books—then went quietly to the door and listened. After several seconds I grasped the latch and whipped open the door. No one.

Shaking my head at my paranoia, I nevertheless placed a metal wastepaper basket against the door so I'd hear it rasp if anyone so much as jiggled the door. I locked it again and returned to my cleanup task. As tenderly as if they were babies I picked up and replaced books on the history of every aspect of the books business—from binding to forging contracts with authors—grieving quietly for the split and broken volumes. These I placed on Botkin's library table.

I'd sorted and replaced all but the last dozen books when I heard the unmistakable sound of the metal wastepaper basket scraping against the wooden floor. Hurriedly I twisted the top of the torch until it went dark. Backing against an adjoining shelf, I waited. The intruder entered the shop; came quietly, but not exactly stealthily, towards me. When his footfalls told me he was just three feet away, I switched on my light.

Ed Maggs looked as if he might knock my block off—blinded or not. He swung one giant fist with remarkable speed, before I could move out of his way. I felt and heard his fist connect with my skull and reeled, the sheer force of it knocking me sideways and down. The torch flew against the opposite bookcase and bounced to the floor, pretty much following my trajectory. It was a measure of my priorities that I worried more about the books as I fell against them than about possible injury. With visions of damaged dust jackets dancing in my head, I saw the light moving and soon found the torch shining in my own face.

"God! Plummers." Another oath. "I'm so sorry—Are you all right?" He was solicitously helping me up before I'd thought of anything clever to say.

"I'm glad it's you, Maggs, whether you've assaulted me or not. And if you don't get your hands off me this instant, I'm calling the police." He was fingering my hairline, inspecting my head for injuries.

At that he chuckled. "All right, then. I don't think there's been any permanent damage. If you can still insult me, you must be reasonably intact."

We stood there for an instant, both relieved, I suppose, that we hadn't had to fight an unknown assailant. I was beginning to wonder just how many keys Botkin had given out. "Er, Ed—you never told me you had a key."

"Didn't I?" He took it out and proffered it in his open palm. "Want it back?"

"No—no. Well. As long as we're having a party, we might as well announce we're here." I stumbled over to the light switch and illuminated the seedy glory of our surroundings. We blinked in the sudden light. "Bring any friends with you? The famous Maggs poltergeist, perhaps?"

"Very funny." His eye fell on the nearly intact front shelf of books, and the stack of injured ones on the table. "Ah! You've been getting down to business. I've been worried—you haven't been in my basement, and you haven't been here. Just checking up on you. I'm surprised you could resist opening the wall."

"That's exactly what I came here to do, but these poor things needed to be taken care of first. Besides, a giant, ham-handed oaf nearly decapitated me just as I was about to get to the fun part."

He laughed. "Get on with it, then. I'll help you."

I picked up a worn volume on type design, inspected it, and replaced it on the shelf. "I'm afraid things are going downhill fast in the *Beowulf* department, Ed." I told him about Gabriel Hammonds's unlikely "accidental" demise, so similar to Botkin's, the former threat to him, his theory about *Beowulf*'s time of authorship, and his desire to have the book removed from the library for ultraviolet study. I also imparted the realisation, now so obvious to me, that Montague, Botkin, and Hammonds all shared an interest in *Beowulf*—for very different reasons. And I explained to Ed that I couldn't help but think Botkin must have something *secret* in his secret library . . . perhaps something pertaining to the *Beowulf* issue. Otherwise why keep the library hidden, and why all the sudden deaths surrounding *Beowulf* aficionados?

"Ian seems to think that Botkin knew a great deal

about Cotton Vitellius A.fifteen—the book containing both *Beowulf* and the Judith poem. He even said there were rumours, long ago, that Botkin might have had his own collection pertaining to the codex."

"That's true," Ed affirmed. "I'd heard that, too. I'm just trying to remember what's back there that might be related to the codex . . . but we'll see soon enough."

At last the tidying up was done. With a nod to Ed, I went round to the end of the book arts wall and together we rolled it away to reveal the hidden cases. Again, I was overwhelmed by the riches that humble old Botkin had owned so quietly through the decades.

"This could rival your basement," I teased.

"I'm not worried," Ed countered. "By the way, you must have wondered by now if there's a catalogue of these books. When Botkin showed me his little secret, I asked him whether he kept a list to gloat over. 'It's all up here,' he told me, tapping a finger to his head. 'Don't need a list.' " A nostalgic smile came over his face at the thought of the old bookseller.

"I think I'd better keep a record, for the safe deposit box if nothing else. I will have to insure these. I'd like to keep a record, too, of the order in which Botkin arranged them, considering his proclivity to symbolism in such things." The thought of all that painstaking recording with paper and pen was enough to make me want to yawn. "What we really need is a photograph of all the spines, at least for now. I'll have to find a camera—don't want to use a flash on these, though—and come back."

"I've got a camera back at the shop. We take photos of all our acquisitions for insurance purposes. I'll run over and get it."

"Are you sure? You have time?"

He started for the door, grinning over his shoulder. "All night, if necessary. Sandra's at her book group, and the nanny's with Ben. Anyway, I wouldn't miss this for the world!"

I rubbed my head, which had begun to ache a bit, and surveyed the shelves, allowing my eyes to leap from one section to another. In the shelf corresponding to the Temple Bar area, where booksellers specialising in history, plays, and law used to ply their trade, my wondering eyes took in Shakespeare's quarto edition of *Hamlet,* of 1603, in original calf. Only two copies are known, and one is imperfect. After a quick look, I saw that I now possessed the perfect one.

On the area of shelving corresponding to the north side of St Paul's, where classics were sold, I found a copy of Virgil's works, printed on vellum by Aldus in italic type in 1501. This was the first "pocket-book," and was bound in Italian green morocco leather.

In the Paternoster Row area, I found the priceless Caxton printing of Chaucer's works in a "pecking crow" binding. Caxton was the first English printer, and so was much revered and eminently collectible.

Good heavens. It was nearly impossible to believe that these fabled treasures were still in existence—let alone mine to look after for the rest of my life. When I died . . .

Was that the reason people were trying to put me six feet under? And purchase Plumtree Press? I groaned. *Of course.* If I died, whoever owned the Press would own Botkin's.

I glimpsed a small volume, whose spine enticingly read *Cottonia,* and took it down. The one-word title was inscribed on the spine of untreated and otherwise unadorned vellum. It was tied with crumbling cream-coloured cloth tape, I saw, on the fore-edge side. I'd gently started to undo it when I heard a knock at the back door.

"Ed?"

"Yeah."

I put the book down and went to open the door for him, and only then realised he would've had his key. Something wasn't right. "Hang on—one minute!" I called, and hurried to the front of the shop. Because the shops in Curzon Street were terraced, I had to go round the end of the street to get to the rear entrance. I ran until I got to the edge of the building, then heard loud thudding round the back. Was someone—it sounded as though someone was trying to break the door down. I only hoped it wasn't Ed who was being broken down.

Hugging the masonry, I edged round until I was at last behind Botkin's building. Two squat, beefy thugs were ramming the door with their bodies, but the solid old door was holding up admirably. Though I hated to judge a book by its cover, these boys didn't look like the bookish type . . . wouldn't know a first edition from a book club printing. If they were after Botkin's library, if someone had hired them who knew about it . . . was that person watching, waiting for the chance to enter? I turned and surveyed the darkness of the narrow alley behind the Curzon Street shops. Nothing.

As I turned back to the spectacle at Botkin's door, dread came over me as a physical sensation: *What had they done with Ed?*

Then I saw motion in the dark behind the battering rams: He was coming up behind them, swinging a heavy piece of wood towards their backs. I cringed; heard the impact, saw the intruders fall, watched as Ed banged them again, but over the head this time. I ran the five yards to where they lay; Ed was inspecting them as an angler might inspect his catch. "Yep," he pronounced with satisfaction, evidently having detected signs of life. "Not permanently out of commission—yet."

I heard the echo of running footsteps down the alley and pursued the sound, hoping I wouldn't fall over something in the dark and break my neck. I was running virtually blind. But once I'd gone beyond the source of the sound, I could hear or see nothing more. I stood still for a moment, listening, feeling very vulnerable indeed. But there was nothing at all to be heard.

I retraced my steps back to Ed. "I suppose you'd better ring the police after all," he joked.

"This is getting ugly," I replied as I entered the number on my cell phone. "First Hammonds, now this. What did you do, spot them at the door?"

"Yeah. I'm glad you had the sense not to open it for them. But I'll bet they're sorry now. Let's see who our muscle-bound little friends are."

While Ed searched the two men for driving licences or anything that might tell us who they were and where they'd come from, I told the police where we were and what had happened. And I looked at Ed, bent over the now-moaning bodies, through new eyes. Had he really been taken by surprise, by strangers? Or had he become a stranger—one with a key to Botkin's treasure trove?

We gave the police a cursory look at the inside of Botkin's, but we kept them at the rear of the shop and out of the alcove with its bookcase wall moved out of place. The secret collection would have been too difficult to explain, and we didn't want the police to know about it, anyway—they were human, too. Ed and I presented the encounter with the would-be intruders as a simple (!) assault and attempted break-in, which was certainly believable even where Botkin's *ordinary* collection was concerned.

"Ooh, that's a nasty bump coming up on your head, sir—I'd put some ice on that," one of the constables suggested helpfully.

"Thanks, I will," I said, and shot a look at Ed. He beamed, and I decided it was impossible that he had been working against me. Not only did we have a history of utterly guileless friendship and trust, but he didn't act guilty.

Once the police had gone—after I'd requested that they let me know the identities of the two men when they found out—we took our photos of the secret shelves. Afterwards, I tucked the spent roll of film into my carryall and trotted back with him to Maggs. Ed saw me inside the back door safely and rolled away in his father's Bentley; I rolled gratefully into his basement bed. I was too tired to worry much about whether I was still safe there.

I sighed as my eyelids slid over what felt like deep beds of gravel. Somehow I felt that these few hours would be a sort of calm before the storm . . . not that the last two days hadn't been fairly heavy weather. It wasn't only because tomorrow was another National Book Week event, this time featuring Julia Northrup, our extremely costly literary experiment . . .

Nor was it because in the afternoon I would go to Cambridge to talk to Hammonds's colleagues from the *Beowulf* conference.

The fact that someone was trying to kill me, and

that two authors and one bookseller had already died, *did* contribute.

But even that wasn't all. A very real feeling of apprehension came from the approach of the massive and unavoidable behemoth of the book world: the Frankfurt Book Fair. Nate had told me, in our last rushed phone call, that the Fair was where "it" was all supposed to happen.

Tomorrow, Wednesday, was the last day before the publishing community left en masse for Frankfurt, Germany, where agents, publishers, and booksellers would drink unconscionable amounts of beer, seal book deals for outrageous amounts of money, and merge giant corporations into small nations. What better place for Matt Ireland's suspicion of a massive conspiracy in the book world to be proved out? Everybody in one place, ready and eager to sign contracts that would make them obscenely wealthy. The way events had snowballed in the past week gave me a feeling that this year's fair would be quite extraordinary, and not necessarily pleasant.

Thank God, I thought as I drifted off, that I wasn't going this year. . . .

Seconds after my alarm went off, my brain was still burning through the residual fog of a dense sleep when I heard a knock at the door. Before I could raise my head from the pillow, someone burst into the room. I grabbed my glasses and shoved them onto my face: It was Ed, bearing gifts. In one hand he held an enormous cup of Starbucks coffee, and in the other he flourished a promising little white paper bag—the sort that might contain scones or croissants.

Every time I thought of the Starbucks on what had

formerly been the most notorious street for brothels, I enjoyed a private joke: In the nineteenth century, women had pandered openly to men's desires on that street corner. In the twenty-first century, a trendy American coffee vendor pandered to their caffeine addictions. Had people grown more innocent, or had they merely learned to bury their secrets more deeply?

"Rise and shine, book boy." Ed tossed me the bag; it was a scone. "Hope you like cinnamon chip." He delivered the coffee in a more civilised manner.

"Who'd have thought that a full-service bed-and-breakfast lurked in the depths of Maggs Bros?"

He chuckled. "Don't let on—the Americans will never leave me alone if they find *that* out."

"Thanks," I said, taking a sip of what I soon learned was a double-shot latte. "Extremely considerate of you."

"Not at all. May I ask what sordid thrills and chills you have planned for today?"

"Mmm." I closed my eyes at the thought and took another sip of the coffee before answering. "First, I'm going over to Botkin's for another look. But not for too long, because I have to introduce Julia Northrup"— Ed groaned—"at the lecture at eleven. Then it's up to Cambridge to see if I can find out anything about Hammonds's death."

I didn't tell him where I planned to go after that . . . it would be a sort of mythical quest of my own. It only seemed reasonable, since I would be in East Anglia anyway.

He shook his head. "Sorry. Doesn't sound like the most delightful of days. You're going to have to come over for an evening of relaxation when things settle down. Perhaps with Nicola?"

I smiled. "Thanks, Ed. Yes, perhaps with Nicola." I half wanted to tell him about the note from Sarah and Ian's odd revelation, but he would only give me the horrible look of pity he reserved for the times when I'd confided in him about Sarah. Then he'd tut-tut and ring the shrink he'd long threatened to put on my case.

"Good." He clapped me on the back as he stood. "Call if you need me."

My mouth full of scone, I mumbled my gratitude as he retreated. Then I lost no time getting ready for the day—on this particular day no suit was required, fortunately—and slipped out the back door to Botkin's. With me I took the carryall containing the John Murray book, and the films from the night before.

As I went out through the locked gate onto Berkeley Square, the elderly employee polishing the brass on the front door of Maggs looked up with surprise. I raised a hand in greeting, but he bent his head back to his work as if he'd seen something he shouldn't have—perhaps his eyesight was as bad as mine, and he thought he'd glimpsed the legendary Maggs basement poltergeist. The old man's reaction brought home the point that I was currently living in a sort of netherworld, hiding in a basement from killers, while at the same time secretly seeking them. It wasn't at all where I thought I'd be this October.

It was a grim morning; London was firmly in the grip of a dreary grey chill. As I walked round the corner into Curzon Street, I was actually grateful. This weather matched my mood.

It was just before nine, and many of the shops were sliding up their metal grilles to open for business. As I let myself in to Botkin's, daring even to use the front

door in broad daylight, a dramatic arrangement of
white tulips on the circular table in the conversation
area by the fire blazed light into the dreary room like a
beacon. I stopped in the doorway and stared. Tulips—
Sarah's favourite flower.

The arrangement hadn't been on the table last
night . . . and how could anyone have got in to put it
there? Ed had a key, and so did Nick Khasnouri, our
accountant. But why would either of them do this to
me?

My mind was just suspicious and convoluted enough
to conceive of the idea that one of my enemies was
trying to persuade me that Sarah was in London.
The Sarah-like women I'd seen, the hints of Ysatis, the
note—all of it.

It would be positively psychopathic, but it was possible.

The flowers seemed a very feminine touch . . . and I
couldn't help but think of the taxi driver saying he'd
seen the Sarah-like woman walk up to Sam's house.
What if Sam had got the key from Nick's office on the
sly, had a copy made, and was using it to torture me?
Did she think that if I were driven mad by hints of
Sarah I would lose my mind, and Plumtree Press would
have to be sold? Perhaps she was the one after Botkin's
precious library—knew about it somehow through her
illustrious publishing ancestors, the Barkers. Again, it
was possible . . . but difficult to credit.

I tried to drag my eyes away from the spectacular
flowers, so evocative of the woman I loved. When my
phone rang, I was grateful for the distraction.

" 'Ello, you." Lisette's voice came down the line.
"What 'ave you been doing—lounging in bed?"

I felt myself relax upon hearing her easy insolence; it was such a relief I smiled. "You didn't want that pay rise, then, at the end of the year."

"Mmm . . . We seem to have forgotten that I am now the managing director."

"Undeniably true." I sighed. "No hope of getting you out, either." We both knew it would be a disaster for the Press—and for me personally—if she ever left. "Ah, well. What's up?"

" 'Is Grace will see you, Mr Plumtree, at ten o'clock this morning. 'E will receive you in his private rooms in Moulton Street."

"Good heavens, you must be joking."

"The duke's personal secretary doesn't know a thing about this meeting . . . nor does 'is business manager." She sounded quite proud of this accomplishment.

"How on earth do you do it, Lisette?"

"You know that I 'ave my own ways of getting things done, Alex," she said mysteriously. "Just be there, yes?"

"Oh, I'll be there. You're absolutely amazing, Lisette. You'd better give yourself that rise."

"Men are so easily persuaded. Well, I am sure you 'ave things to do. . . . Bye." Abruptly, she was gone. Thus the Queen of Plumtree Press dismissed her subjects when she was busy.

It was ten past nine. I wouldn't need to leave for the duke's until just before ten; time to get down to business with Botkin's books. I wanted to look at the ribbon-tied *Cottonia* volume straightaway this morning.

I went directly to the wall that we'd rolled back into place, moved it out again, and carefully pulled out the book. I took it to one of the comfortable chairs—unfortunately in close proximity to the distracting tulips—and untied the ribbon. I wondered when it had last been opened, and by whom. The volume was not exactly a book, but a collection of letters, tightly packed between the flexible covers.

Perhaps ten letters were inside; all the folded pages were the same size, all the same dirty cream colour. These missives obviously predated the use of envelopes. As I opened the cover, my eyes fell on the name of the addressee of the top letter:

Daniel Plumtree, Lord Sarratt
Plumtree Manor
Churl's Wood
Hertfordshire

Was there no end to the Plumtree family's exploits when it came to books? I had certainly never heard any family lore pertaining to Cotton. Perhaps this was why Botkin had made sure I was the one to purchase his shop, so that I would learn of it and take a personal interest in protecting the collection.

A small scrap of notepaper was tucked just inside the cover. The paper was much rougher and darker; its wood pulp had not aged as well as the creamy rag of the older letters. Scrawled on the bit of paper, un-headed and unsigned, were the words *Botkin, Found these at a sale in Cambridge and thought you'd better have them.*

Odd . . .

I picked up the first letter. It had been sealed in red wax, stamped with the crest from the Cotton family arms—but the seal had been broken.

When I unfolded the several sheets of paper inside, my question was answered immediately. In a large, attractive script, the date was given at the upper right-hand corner: 17 October, 1742. I froze; 17 October was today's date. The feeling that I was a player in an ancient drama that had taken centuries to unfold swept over me once again.

My Dear Sir,

    I wiſh to offer moſt sincere thanks for your great kindneſs in preſenting the volume you sent to me yesterday. Your Servant fully comprehends the generoſity of this gift, and I fear I am at an utter loſs as to how to repay you. It has long been a moſt diſtreſsing thorn in my side that the portion of my eſteemed relation's book collection which was to have come to me has been neglected, then later traded for profit and otherwiſe careleſsly diminiſhed by self-serving relations, heedleſs of its true import. The entire collection is now, to my utter deſpair, fallen completely out of my hands. But I ſhall paſs over the remainder of my thoughts on that ſubject in ſilence. To have returned to me one volume of that eſteemed collection, which you had intended to houſe in your own eſtimable library, means more to me than money ever might. In an effort to recompenſe your generoſity, I ſhall relate to you a ſtory that has been told in our family for theſe many decades, and which cauſes me no ſmall amuſement (though I suppose this does not caſt me in a favourable light considering the tragedy that has befallen my family's collection). As you, My Good Sir, will know, one of the moſt prized volumes in our

*family collection was Cotton Vitellius A.XV, beft
known for its uniquenefs in containing the
earlieft known verfion of Beowulf, which many
hold to be the firft Englifh poem. Few are aware
that the good nuns of the Priory of St Mary, in
Southwick, Hampshire, placed a curfe on
anyone who dared remove a certain book—now
known as the Southwick Codex and bound
together early in the laft century (moft likely by
my anceftor, Sir Robert Bruce Cotton) with the
Nowell Codex, containing both Beowulf and
Judith.*

Thefe holy words of the curfe follow:

Hic liber est Ecclesie beate Marie de
Suwika. Quem qui ab eadem abstulerit. Vel
Titulum istum dolose deleuerit nisi eidem
Ecclesie dondigne satisfecerit.' Sit Anathema.
Maranatha. Fiat. Fiat'. Amen'. Amen.

I took a moment to attempt to translate this from the
remnants of my school Latin. To the best of my knowledge, it read, "This book belongs to the Church of
Blessed Mary from Southwick; whoever takes it away
from there or through guile removes that title, if he
does not give worthy satisfaction to that same church,
let there be a curse. Come the Lord! Let it be. Let it be.
Amen. Amen.

The letter continued:

*I cannot but afk myself if God did not in fact
perform a miracle to satisfy the holy women's
wifhes, for as you know the Cotton collection
was all but destroyed in a fire in Afhburnham*

*Houfe, in Weftminfter, in the Year of our Lord
1731. Our family has endured great hardfhip
ever fince. It has been faid that Cotton Vitellius
A.XV was tofsed from a window and thus faved
from certain annihilation. Its burnt edges may
ftill be feen to this day, I am told.*

I hope this will amufe you.

*I am, Sir, much obliged to you for your
kindnefs and generofity,*

Baxter Botkin

Fascinating. Surely there was time for another. . . . I saw
as I carefully replaced the letter and extracted the next
that I still had twenty-five minutes. The next letter
in the stack was also addressed to my ancestor, and
bore the same seal.

Moft generous Sir,

*Do permit me to exprefs my unbounded
thanks for your generofity in presenting me with
the volume your fervant delivered to me
yefterday. My deepeft gratitude is yours.*

*In the nature of what has become a delightful
tradition of mutually fatisfying exchanges, and
in partial thanks for your lateft gift, I should
like to pafs on to you another bookifh fecret
from my family's paft. Knowing that we both
share in the fervice of our Lord and Saviour,
and believe in the Sanctity of His Word, I am
convinced that you will be interefted in a great
and terrible fecret pertaining to the stewardship
of God's word as we know it in England.*

*My father's great-grandfather, as you may
perchance know, was afsiftant to the King's*

Printer, Chriftopher Barker. In thofe days, work
on the King James Version of the Bible had
commenced. The King was moft concerned that
the monarchy—indeed, any monarchy—not be
denounced in Holy Scripture. (His concern for
this feems oddly prescient, coming as it did not
so very long in advance of Cromwell's reign.)
Certain pafsages were particularly vexing to His
Majesty, but none more so than the Book of
Judith, which, though it had been relegated to
the Apocrypha by St Jerome in the Vulgate, was
ftill read by many. As you will know, the book
tells the ftory of a widow who flays Holofernes, a
general of the King of Assyria, and thereby faves
her people.

But in truth, this is NOT the subftance of
the original Book of Judith. King James, ufing
no fmall durefs forced my anceftor, his printer,
to alter the original words of the poem—
which said that the King of Afsyria himself—
Nebuchadnezzar—was in truth beheaded by
Judith, and not his general, Holofernes. With an
Englifh-language tranflation thus approved by
the Crown, and deftined for use by Royal Order
in every Church in England, the King believed
that changes had to be made . . . although even
His Majefty, according to His printer, was
Himself very moved by the pafsage in the
Revelation which declares a curfe on the man
who should make fo bold as to alter "one jot or
tittle" of God's Holy Word (The Revelation of St
John, 22:18–19).

Does this then offer explanation of the fortunes
of the Stuarts, and of royal families fince?

> *I hope that I have amufed you once more.*
> *I remain, Sir, your devoted Servant,*
> *Baxter Botkin*

How very interesting that Botkin's ancestor had been the assistant to the King's Printer under Christopher Barker. I hurried to replace that letter and get on to the next. Same addressee, same seal.

> *My Deareft, Moft Efteemed Sir,*
> *You cannot imagine what delight this lateft Tome from the Cotton Collection has brought me. I enjoy our exchanges immenfely, and am pleased to further our correfpondence.*
> *Another book, another bibliophile's fecret: and another Curfe. I can scarcely believe I have not related this to you before now, as it is of no fmall importance to me perfonally. King James placed a most onerous and violent threat of punifhment on my anceftor the printer and his defcendants, if any word was ever fpoken of thefe alterations to Holy Scripture. Perhaps His Majefty believed he might be succefsful in avoiding the gaze of the Almighty? Suffice it to say that I entreat you to keep thefe fecrets as carefully as I have for thefe laft forty years.*
> *Perhaps it would entertain you to further your knowledge of the Judith debacle. I mentioned that King James required that my anceftor render the flaughtered King Nebuchadnezzar a mere general by the name of Holofernes. He did alfo—very cleverly, I think—change the name of the location from the well-known city of Schechem to Bethulia,*

which is a fictional name. In this way he
intended for the holy book to be seen as a poem
only, and not Holy Scripture. By discrediting it
in this way, he sought to further diminish its
importance in the Bible and eventually have it
drift into complete obscurity.

As I am aware of your fascination with all
things pertaining to ancient books and the
writing thereof, I know that you will be
interested to learn in what way this was
accomplished: ink is quite easily scratched off
vellum, which may be inscribed once again with
little trace of anything having previously existed
on the spot. (How very unfortunate, my Dear
Father used to say, that all the writings ever lost
in this manner might not be replaced, and I
confess that I do agree with Him most heartily.
O to see these original writings in their first
state!) The King's Printer bore away Cotton
Vitellius A.XV to a little-known priory in East
Anglia near Malconbury, where the alterations
were performed by a scribe of no small renown,
one Brother Petrus. The Holy Monk was loathe
to do the work, but Mr Barker described the dire
consequences of disobeying His Majesty's Royal
Order. After he finished these alterations to the
Codex, Brother Petrus corrected several folio
numbers in the Beowulf, which had not been
altered after rebinding.

King James went to no small lengths, even
despatching His emissaries to the Middle East
to "discover" the oldest copy of Judith known to
man. One of these, said to date from the second
century, was touted abroad with all possible

> *authority, brought back to England, and ufed to*
> *refute the hundreds of thoufands of reafonable*
> *people who will point out how unufual it is that*
> *only the King James Verfion of the Bible*
> *contains thofe alterations.*
>
> > *I remain, Sir, your devoted,*
> > *Baxter Botkin*

This brought me up short: Not long ago, a scroll containing Greek text had been found during some construction work beneath one of the royal residences in London. It had been shipped for display to the genizah in Cairo, a sort of manuscript repository where many such antiquities were displayed. At that time I hadn't known the first thing about Judith and I hadn't made much of it. Was this the same scroll Baxter Botkin was talking about?

What if the secret of Cotton Vitellius A.xv had *nothing* to do with *Beowulf,* but instead concerned these changes to Judith? It bore consideration, I supposed; though who would care about a couple of relatively minor changes made to one version of the Bible as late as 1611? Of course, it was still one of the most widely used translations in existence, and until the mid–twentieth century had dominated. Perhaps King James thought that, as the head of the Church of England, he could simply bend the Bible to suit his purposes.

But if Judith were the real thorn in someone's side, only Botkin's and Hammonds's deaths were tied. Montague's appeared unrelated. I didn't actually know for a fact that Montague had been killed, either.

I thanked my Plumtree ancestor with all my heart

for having been generous enough with his books to cause Botkin's ancestor to part with his literary secrets. If only Baxter could have known that one day there *would* be a way to tell what the scribes had written first on palimpsests: ultraviolet light. And King James wasn't around to prevent the original words coming to light, so to speak . . .

I replaced the letters exactly as they had been in the *Cottonia* cover and tied them with the ribbon. After putting the volume back in the hidden shelf, I locked up and for the moment tried to put the mysteries of *Beowulf,* Judith, and Cotton Vitellius A.xv out of my mind. It was time to embark upon a more mundane, but no less significant, battle than Beowulf's: that of hanging on to my leasehold.

CHAPTER 10

Then Hrothgar stretched out his arms in welcome
And took him by the hand and said, "Beowulf,
I knew you as a child, and who has not exulted
In your fame as a fighter? It is a triumph song
That ocean thunders to her farthest shore,
It is a whisper in the frailest sea-shell.
Now, like your princely father long ago,
In the brimming kindness of your heart you have come
To deliver us."

— BEOWULF

When the duke's daughter greeted me at the door, her blond hair just brushing the top of the Hermès scarf knotted round her neck, I thought she must have mistaken me for someone else.

"Alex! What a delightful surprise." The fortyish Hilary all but threw her arms around me, beaming and reaching out for my hand in a most uncharacteristic display of warmth.

"Lovely to see you, Hilary. How are you?" I'd seen her last at New Year's, when the prime minister had hosted a lively do. But I'd met her fifteen years ago, at a succession of hunt balls everyone attended. She'd been a wild thing then, but had found her aristocratic destiny in helping to organise charity events. I read about her in the *Times* constantly.

"I'm very happy—delighted, actually—because

you've made Daddy so happy. He's ever so chuffed about your publishing his memoirs—the *stories* he could tell! That wonderful Frenchwoman in your office was absolutely charming. Wasn't she clever to know that Daddy would be here today? Do come in and sit down." She gestured towards a masculine-looking study. "I'll tell him you've arrived."

God bless Lisette, I thought. I'd once told her the story of my grandfather's friendship with the duke, and the code phrase they'd had for getting past one another's servants and family members when they needed to gossip over a drink at the club. "Publishing memoirs" had been their phrase of choice. It had been a bit risky on Lisette's part, I had to say, but fortunately the story must have been handed down through the duke's family as it had through mine.

"My dear boy," he said, tottering into the room. He looked just the same, if a bit more stooped, than he had twenty years ago. Intelligent, dancing eyes smiled for his mouth, which never, *ever* smiled. I knew, however, that this was his front—his sense of humour was alive and well. "Goodness me, you're all grown up, Plumtree. My, but you look like your father. Gave me quite a start. How is your brother?"

And so we were launched onto a comfortable tuffet of small talk that took us straight through to coffee ten minutes later, and so to business. "Now, then, Plumtree. What was it you came to see me about?"

"Well, sir, I wondered . . . it seemed most unlike you to send us a rather terse letter the other day, evicting us from Fifty-eight Bedford Square." I tried to word the next sentence carefully. "I wondered whether we had done something to displease you, or if you might at least tell us what prompted such a sudden departure from our cheerful little agreement of almost ninety years."

"Evicted? Plumtree Press? From *my* building? My dear boy, there must be some mistake. I would *never* . . . of course you'll stay. Your Press is an institution; I wouldn't have Bedford Square without it . . . it'd ruin the whole damn place. Whatever letter you received, I hereby declare it invalid." He shook his head in exasperation. "What on earth . . . it's not the first cock-up Sloane's made like this. Sometimes I wonder. Well, that's not your problem, is it? I do apologise, Plumtree. What a ghastly mistake."

"Thank you, sir. That's very kind of you indeed. I can't tell you how relieved I am, and how pleased everyone at the Press will be."

"Good, good. How's Ian Higginbotham these days?"

"He's very well, thank you. I'll tell him you asked." I asked him about his pet charity, the Theatre Fund, while we finished our coffees. As he saw me to the door, he blustered about "finding out what on earth that blasted letter Sloane sent was all about. Have to put an end to this sort of thing, you know. Won't do to have the Plumtrees out on their ear," et cetera.

As I left, Hilary came to say good-bye. Walking down the street I heard the duke say kindly, "I'll tell you all about it, my dear. Yes, I'll have to begin work soon . . . most generous offer, really . . . don't know how I'll find the time . . ."

Smiling at the duke's lively sense of humour, I hailed a taxi to meet Nicola—on time—at the Frontiers bookstore for the Northrup event. According to the agreement with the organisers of the Book Week, I was to take the podium first as the more publicly recognisable figure. But they had agreed to let me hand over the microphone to Nicola to introduce her author. After all, she had signed the famous—or should I say infamous—Northrup, and had the most to say about her.

Northrup did have a reputation for being a fascinating speaker, and for being what my American college friends used to call "relevant." Every word had deep meaning and emotion, and her voice quavered as she delivered her innermost thoughts without regard for structure, taste, or convention. Exactly like her books, I thought. At least she was a purist.

Nicola seemed relieved to see me as I climbed out of the taxi, twenty minutes early. "Hullo! Julia's not here yet, but we can hope—" Nicola's face went white and utterly blank. Gazing at something just beyond me, she whispered, "Alex," lifting a finger to point. "It's—it's—"

I followed her frozen stare, her lifted finger. Behind us, I saw the long, dark hair of a woman in the backseat of a taxi, once again just pulling out of my reach. This time I wasn't going to lose her. Thrusting my briefcase into Nicola's arms, I dashed after the cab and reached its rear wing, banging on it for the driver to stop, before it picked up speed. Staying in the road, I pursued the vehicle like a madman, bellowing at it to stop all the way. We had travelled perhaps one hundred yards in this outlandish fashion when a giant hand of steel slapped me flat on the pavement.

Even as it happened, I heard the squeal of brakes, then a momentary hush before multiple car doors slammed and footsteps came running. Somewhere very near, a car reversed and then roared away. Voices cried after the retreating car; someone yelled, "That was it—that was the car that hit him!" Another voice said resolutely, "I've got the plate number. Silver—Audi, isn't it . . ." A woman's voice said, "Hello? Yes, I'm calling to report an accident—a man hit by a car. Charing Cross Road, at . . ."

My head pounded; I smelled the damp oil on the tarmac against my face. A firm masculine hand came, rested gently on my arm. "Are you all right? Can you hear me?"

I heard him, but couldn't seem to answer.

The sound of heels running, stopping, then Nicola's voice right next to me, with a quiet "Dear God."

"Do you know him?"

"Yes! I—*Alex*. Alex, can you hear me?"

I could hear everything perfectly, but for some reason couldn't give voice to my words.

A cry of anguish came from Nicola. I opened my eyes, and there she was, down on the street next to me. She looked so worried, I wanted to tell her that I was all right—I could still think and see. Her look of despair became a tearful smile as I looked at her. "Can you hear me, Alex?" She gently stroked my hair.

I tried to nod; the small motion hurt my head desperately. I closed my eyes again.

"Help is coming," she said, and continued to stay next to me.

Thoughts about where I was and what had happened began drifting into my awareness . . . a car had hit me and then driven off. Another attempt to finish off Plumtree Press, I assumed—or at least me for whatever I knew, or was suspected of knowing, about *Beowulf* or Cotton Vitellius A.xv. I opened my eyes again; Nicola's bright, tear-filled ones looked into mine.

This time everything worked. "Hi," I said, and smiled.

Her face lit up. "Hi. How do you feel?"

"Monstrous headache," I admitted. Everything was already sore, as if I'd worked out the day before with punishing weights in every muscle group. I couldn't wait till later.

But everything seemed to work. Slowly, I gathered myself up into a sitting position. The crowd around me backed off as if they'd just seen someone rise from the dead. It was really very embarrassing, being the cause of such a fuss.

The raucous sirens approached then. One of the ambulance men joked with me about having caused all the trouble, and Nicola told them what had happened as they loaded me on their rolling stretcher. I insisted that I could walk, but they insisted more forcefully that we'd see what was what in a few minutes. As they hoisted me inside, I realised they needed to get me out of traffic's way as much as anything else. Nicola climbed in, too, then said, "I'll come find you after." She tapped her watch and I realised it had to be time for her to introduce Julia Northrup and *Her Flight*.

"Great," I said, taking in her smudged face and oil-smeared knit suit. "Knock 'em dead." At that moment I realised how utterly capable she was of taking over the entire editorial duties of Plumtree Press—functional, ceremonial, and editorial—and was greatly relieved by it.

She smiled back at me, then grew serious again. "Alex, it *was* Sarah, wasn't it?"

"I think so. This isn't the first time I've spotted her . . . that's why I ran. I had to know."

"Excuse me, miss," the ambulance man said.

Nicola waved a good-bye and ran off to say her piece on behalf of Julia.

Shortly after she left, a constable came to stand at the door of the ambulance. Evidently the witnesses had already given their information to the constable; the Met had been notified to watch for a silver Audi, he said; they had its plate number. One of the witnesses had even given a fairly clear description of the driver: an older man, grey hair, hardly high enough in the seat to see. I didn't mention to the constable that someone might have deliberately tried to hit me; how could someone orchestrate a crime like that in the middle of traffic, even with Sarah as bait? It may well have been an accident, after all. I filled out the report form, told him thank you, and he promised to be in touch when and if they found the hit-and-run driver.

With the police out of the way, the ambulance men began to close the doors. "Wait!" I called. "There's nothing wrong with me—I don't need to go to hospital."

They looked at each other askance. "Sorry, it's the rules," one of them said, and slammed the doors. We were off.

It was all a ridiculous waste of time. After nearly an hour in Accident and Emergency, by the time I returned to stand at the back of the crowded shop for Julia's lecture, half of it was over. Nicola saw me come in and widened her eyes at me briefly, with a little smile. I noted that the disastrous reviews from the *Bookseller* and major papers hadn't diminished our author's crowd appeal; from the looks of it, Julia was at least as popular as Baroness Thatcher. The ground floor was filled to overflowing with Northrup devotees standing, leaning, and perching on whatever they could. I found it most gratifying, as her publisher. If the reviewers had been bought to try to put still more pressure on me to give up and sell the Press, whoever paid them had failed dismally.

"So for me," Julia intoned in her characteristic monotone, waiflike with honey-coloured dreadlocks, "the butterfly in *Her Flight* symbolises the tragic constancy yet inconstancy, the meaninglessness yet all-meaning, short-lived but *eternal wholeness* of our being." I observed the crowd in amazement; they were taking this in with rapt attention. Not a sound could be heard in the sea of people. Julia's style of self-expression had never been my own, but I was grateful that Nicola had seen what she had to offer. At least we would never be called a prosaic, staid publishing house after taking *her* on.

"I love you. I love you all," were the last intensely serious words of Julia's, er, speech, and then it was question time. Later, as the crowd trailed out, chattering amongst themselves, I drifted up towards Nicola and Julia.

"Wasn't she *marvellous*?"

"What talent!"

". . . a gift for saying what no one has ever said . . ."

"Positively radiant . . ."

I also couldn't help but notice that they were snatching up multiple copies of her work. Displays consisting of stacks of the book were being dismantled to supply the heavy demand. The Frontiers events manager began to look worried at the rapidity with which she was running out of books.

"Congratulations," I said when I'd reached the

front of the room. "It looks as though *Her Flight* is another sensation, Julia."

She turned expressionless eyes on me. "I write books to be true to myself, true to humanity. I don't write books for commercial success."

"Of course you don't," Nicola said matter-of-factly, and escorted her away to a waiting car without further comment. The National Book Week organisers had insisted that all authors be taken away by car from the rear entrance, for purposes of crowd control. Nicola had told me the week before about the huge struggle it had been to persuade Julia to ride in a fuel-consuming, polluting vehicle just this once.

When Nicola returned, looking satisfied, I said, "Nice work. You never know when something like this will happen, do you? When the author's personality alone can carry the work, or when it will strike a chord with the public."

"How do you feel?" she asked, a charming and considerate little furrow between her brows.

"Not bad," I answered, assessing the state of my earthly vessel, as Julia Northrup might have referred to my battered body. "D'you have time for lunch? There are a few things we should catch up on."

"Lovely," she said, brightening. "You were beginning to seem a stranger." As we left by the rear entrance, waving to the manager who was far too busy with the teeming crowd of book-buyers to exchange pleasantries, Nicola chuckled. "It's hard to believe that you could be walking alongside me after having been hit by a car. You must be made of steel."

"Just very fortunate. I could do with a bit less excitement, I must say."

"Alex, what were you saying earlier about having

seen Sarah before? I thought I must have been imagining things—seeing things—"

"Indeed. I know just how you feel. But if you knew Sarah as I do, you'd know that she would never do something like this."

"Mm. I see what you mean. If you love someone, you don't hurt him."

"Exactly."

Nicola always understood me as if she were inside my head. When she first started working for the Press, we would sometimes complete sentences for one another; now we just looked at each other and nodded. Julia Northrup might say we were spiritual twins. The siblinglike nature of our relationship had always been very pleasant; not for us, worries about attraction in the workplace. Convenient, too. Without asking, I knew where she would most like to go to lunch.

I steered us in that direction and she gave a distant smile; she was aware of my intentions. "Do you think she has a double, then?"

"Who constantly shows up where I am and allows herself to be seen before rushing off each time? Who, incidentally, for your ears only, has been dropped off at Sam Stone's house on occasion?"

Nicola stopped and looked at me. "Not seriously," she said.

I nodded and carried on towards Monmouth Street.

She didn't go through the motions of asking me what I made of it all; she knew. The usual heavily-French-accented young woman showed us to a table at Mon Plaisir, gave us menus, and took our orders for a glass of red wine each and their plat du jour—coq au vin today, always heavenly at that Francophile's paradise.

Leaning towards Nicola, I said, "Someone is trying to discredit me and drive me out of my mind, as they tried to do to Botkin. Someone's also trying to kill me—as they did Botkin. And Montague. And Hammonds." I told her about Botkin's questionable death, and the letters I'd found in his office, but saved the secret library for later.

I did, however, call her attention to the *Beowulf* connection between the three deaths, and told her about the three offers to buy the Press, including Matt Ireland's conspiracy theory. By way of conclusion, I told her about the attack at the Orchard and Sarah's favourite flowers on Botkin's coffee table. Having been through one such episode with me already during her short tenure at the Press, Nicola accepted it all with an impressive lack of drama.

The food came then, and we turned our attention to the tender, steaming fowl, heaped with onions and potatoes. She buttered a piece of warm baguette and asked, "Do you know what it is they want?"

"I have a couple of ideas—mmm. Wonderful." I felt as though I hadn't eaten in days. "Sorry. First, though I'm not very clear on any of this, it seems there might be two different factions: one trying to discredit me and put me in the nuthouse, and the other trying to dispatch me."

Nicola shot me a look, full of dark humour at the frank nastiness of what I'd just said.

"Yes, delightful people, I'm sure. I think each faction wants something different: one wants to buy Plumtree Press—and the other wants to get rid of me for knowing something Hammonds might have passed along."

"*Beowulf* again?"

"Yes." I stopped short of telling her about Judith, and the ancestral correspondence I'd found that morning. Perhaps it was an instinct to protect her; the more she knew, the more she might be in danger, too. She sensed my sudden reticence but didn't press.

"At any rate, I thought you should know what's happening before I dash off to Cambridge, and you shoot off to the Fair. When does your plane leave, by the way?"

"Sevenish. Everything's at the Press, ready to go."

"Are you staying at the Frankfurterhof?" She nodded, and we were off, discussing her wild schedule of acquisition and bartering during the Fair.

"Good luck." It was the stuff of legend, the way the long, grueling days and nights of the Frankfurt Book Fair could grind down the hardiest of souls. "And be careful. If Sam Stone is somehow working against me to further her family publishing interests, she could be dangerous for you, too . . . though when you do happen to be around her, I'd appreciate your keeping an eye out. Feel free to chat her up, see what you can find out—if you're not in an isolated setting. And remember: Frankfurt is where Nate claimed that something momentous was about to happen. If that's true, and if Matt Ireland's right about this conspiracy thing, who knows *what* might transpire over there?" The more I thought about it, the more fearful I became. "Just promise me you won't take chances; stay with others when you go to and from the hotel, that sort of thing. All right?"

"All right, but frankly I'm much more worried about you."

Instead of admitting my own fears, I lifted my wineglass. "To our health."

Nicola smiled. "Hear, hear."

•   •   •

In the car on the motorway up to Cambridge, my thoughts turned to the possible significance of Judith in my current troubles, given Baxter Botkin's letter. I rang someone who was likely to know a little something about Judith. "Martyn Blakely," a familiar voice answered.

Disguising my voice, I said, "Hello? I'd like to register a complaint about the vicar of Christ Church Chenies." I proceeded to describe at length some rather unvicarlike antics I purported to have seen on the lawn of the church. When he said nothing, I asked, "Is this the correct number?"

Martyn hesitated only a moment before saying, "Very funny, Plumtree. Exceedingly droll. Dare I ask what you're up to, besides harassing your vicar and possibly your oldest friend?"

"You'll be pleased to know that I have need of your unparalleled skill in Biblical summary and exegesis, Martyn. What do you know about Judith?"

"Judith Nicolson of the altar guild? Or Judith as in Holofernes?"

"Very good . . . I see you're in fine fettle. You and Amanda must be getting on well today."

He actually sighed. "Marvellously well. And to think I owe it all to you and those nasty messes you get yourself into at the Press. To think we'd never have met if—"

"Yes . . . well, about Judith."

"Right. You're in luck, you know, because I did a paper at theological college on Judith and its battles for canonicity."

"My, it *is* my lucky day."

"But you do come up with some odd topics, Alex. On Sunday it was *Beowulf*, now Judith. Of all the obscure . . . well, anyway. What exactly would you like to know?"

"Mostly why it was relegated to the Apocrypha; what's so questionable about it."

"Hmm. All right. Let me get my Oxford Annotated here to refresh my memory, it includes the Apocrypha . . ."

I heard pages crinkling in the vicarage study, a rather pleasant room I'd helped Martyn clear out and redecorate when he'd moved in. "Ah: Judith." A pause. "Oh, you'll like this—quintessentially an *ironic* book, it says. The book's religious ideas are neither unusual nor objectionable. . . . The atmosphere of the tale is entirely realistic. . . . Judith 'bristles' with problems, though. . . . Despite the fact that the book declares itself to be an historical account, evidently it has serious problems in the area of history and geography.

"Yes, I remember now . . . this Samaritan town of Bethulia, where the whole story was meant to have taken place, doesn't exist. Evidently that's the greatest mark against its being believable. Others point to Judith's behaviour—lying to get into Holofernes's inner circle, lying with him in his bed (love these euphemisms, don't you?), beheading the poor blighter, et cetera—as being less than exemplary.

"Here it says that the book was probably written during the reign of John Hyrcanus the First, 135 to 105 B.C. Don't recall hearing of *him* before. . . . There are four slightly different Greek versions recorded, in addition to two Latin ones and a Syriac. Even an Anglo-Saxon epic, if you can imagine. But—this is odd—evidently there has been an epidemic of vandalism against the original, physical copies of the poem, or novel—all destroyed over the years, except for the Anglo-Saxon epic, and one scroll containing what is believed to be the oldest copy of the book, donated to the genizah in Cairo by the Queen just a couple of years ago. How very odd . . ."

Yes, strange indeed . . . and remarkably in line with my developing theory.

"Good heavens, listen to this: all the Bibles that predate the King James Version—Douay, Geneva, et cetera—contain the name of an actual Samarian city, Schechem. *And* those earlier versions say that it was King Nebuchadnezzar himself who was slain by Judith! Not Holofernes. It's only the King James Version of the Bible, the relatively newly discovered scroll in the Cairo genizah, and the Anglo-Saxon poem of Judith in the British Library that contain the fictional name Bethulia, and say that Holofernes was killed instead of the king."

"Martyn, you're brilliant. It's more than I could have hoped to learn."

"Wait! I haven't even told you my thesis, the one for my paper. I received top marks, *and* was called before the dean, who seemed to take a special interest in it. I've always thought, you see, that perhaps Judith *is* historical, and therefore valid—only embroidered a bit in the details. If it weren't for the name of the town— and the newly discovered scroll which confirms it—the book might have been considered entirely valid.

"Ha!" I jumped at his loud outburst, holding the phone away from my ear and marvelling at its capacity for amplification. "Here's a real kicker, Alex: Nebuchadnezzar did actually die in that era, though it's not recorded how. Did you know old Nebs was mad as a hatter? He often had spells when he thought he was an ox, and went out into the hills to eat grass. What do you think of that? There's a titillating little morsel for your next drinks party."

"How right you are—fascinating, all of it, Martyn. Do me a favour, though: keep this quiet for now . . . I think our academic series on Sacred Writings is about to expand. Your friendly local publisher needs you."

"D'you mean it? You shouldn't joke about things like that, Alex. I—"

"Have I ever lied to you?"

"No."

"All right, then."

"One more question. Since you've never lied to me, I obviously expect the truth: are you in the midst of one of your quests for the Holy Grail, with utter disregard for mortal danger again?"

"Well, yes—if you must know. Such an inventive turn of phrase!"

"Just don't let yourself be done in—I rather fancy the idea of being published. I'll put in a word for you."

On that note we rang off, and I finished the grim drive to Cambridge. I might, I reflected, just need Martyn's word with The Guv.

CHAPTER 11

For now is the time to help thine inheritance, and
to execute mine enterprises to the destruction
of the enemies which are risen against us.

—JUDITH 13:5

The steely grey cold front still held all of England in its grip; Cambridge was never as beautiful as in this sort of weather, I thought. But the cold and damp penetrated right through to the bone. It was actually a relief, after checking for the attendees at the site of the *Beowulf* conference—the chilly Pepys Library in my old college, Magdalene—and finding it deserted, to be directed to the cosy pub over the road. Half past four seemed a bit early to nip to the boozer, but as an academic publisher I knew all too well that the academic lifestyle had its cherished perks. Besides, the *Beowulf* scholars had had a very nasty shock.

I observed the group as I picked up a whisky mac from the bar; their table was liberally littered with empty KP peanut packets and wet rings from pint glasses, indicating that they'd already been there for some time. Those who remained of Hammonds's colleagues—nine of them, not counting Ian—were almost comically recognisable: all wore a uniform of academia, a hard-to-define down-at-the-heel, highly individual mélange of comfortable shoes, baggy jackets, and overlong hair.

Another quality set them apart from the run-of-the-mill Cantabrigian punter: all were supremely confident, wearing their professorial air as obviously as their clothing. And very, very subdued—morose, even. I certainly understood why.

Ian caught sight of me and stood. "Alex, come join our little group."

Startled, and not very pleased, several of them looked at me askance. "Gentlemen," Ian began, "this is Alex Plumtree. My employer, and Hammonds's publisher." They perked up at this; I was after all, someone who might publish *them* one day. "Alex, this is Desmond Wilcox, Francis Peters, Thomas Kather, Richard Dunstan . . ."

The group made room for me with a great scuffling of stools and shifting about. "You must forgive us," the man Ian had introduced as Desmond Wilcox apologised. "I'm afraid we're not at our best. Hammonds's death has hit us all rather hard."

"I can imagine. Hammonds was a fine scholar. A good man."

"There were more of us at the conference, but we've broken up a bit early, as you see. There was to be dinner tonight, but we don't seem to have the heart for it."

"We—er—rather talked things to death last night, I'm afraid," Wilcox admitted. "But Ian said you wanted to speak with us."

"Yes, thanks. Did you arrive at a consensus last night?" I asked. "I must say, I find it difficult to believe that he fell—accidentally—down the stairs."

"So did we," Wilcox said. The long faces round the table nodded.

"It was no accident," Peters said.

"But who would do such a thing?" I asked. "Who would want Hammonds dead?"

Looks passed among the various members of this group; they were deciding whether to tell me what they thought.

"I know who," Dunstan said.

"Dunstan, you *can't*—"

"I can and I will. Mr Plumtree—"

"Alex," I said.

"All right, then, Alex. There was one member of the conference who'd fought with Hammonds for years about the date of the epic's composition."

"The seventh-century crowd, then," I said.

"Exactly," he said, regarding me with new respect. "Well, until a certain American scholar came along, and then Hammonds, no one questioned the dating. But our friend Michaels was so wedded to this idea that *Beowulf* was *early* Anglo-Saxon that he's been rude to Hammonds for two years or so now, ever since Hammonds proposed this tenth-century theory. I think it's this formal proposal to remove the manuscript for study that has Michaels scared. He's built his career on the early-dating theory: How'll it make him look if it's thrown out now?"

"Yes, I see what you mean," I said, trying for diplomacy. "Was Michaels the only person openly hostile to Hammonds?"

A quick, exasperated explosion of breath came from a man to my left. "What Dunstan here forgot to tell you is that Michaels was so broken up about Hammonds's death, he couldn't even stay at the conference. Went straight home, shaking like a leaf. There's no way that man could've hurt—let alone killed—Hammonds. I can't believe you've publicly accused him, Dunstan. You'd do well to watch yourself."

"I'm entitled to my opinion. Why don't you tell Alex *your* theory, then?"

"Yes, all right." He squared his shoulders. "What if the curators at the British Library have something to hide? What if they don't want that codex removed for study . . . because they've lost it, or allowed it to be damaged or something? What if the *Beowulf* manuscript in the Ritblat is a fake?" He shrugged as several of his colleagues shook their heads, rolled their eyes, or otherwise indicated their disbelief. "I know it sounds outlandish, but Dunstan's idea is twenty times more far-fetched than mine."

"May I propose my theory?"

I tallied the response: four nods, three surprised looks, two blasé.

"I don't know nearly as much as you do about the Cotton Codex, of course. But I do know that there are other bits and pieces bound in with the *Beowulf* manuscript. The Judith poem, for instance."

"Right . . ." Desmond Wilcox's tentative agreement implied, *but what does that have to do with anything?*

"I've wondered . . . what if there were an issue—similar to Michaels's with Hammonds, about dating or whatever—concerning Judith, or one of the other bits and pieces in that codex?"

"I suppose it's possible, but I don't know of any current debates—public ones, anyway—about other works in the codex. Peters? You studied the entire Cotton Vitellius A.fifteen a decade or so ago, didn't you?"

Peters, a sallow-skinned man, shrugged as he drew heavily on his cigarette. He blew out a huge cloud of evil-smelling smoke before answering. "I haven't heard of any debates on the others."

Did the man always look so uneasy, I wondered?

Perhaps he wasn't saying all he might. I was, I knew, grasping at straws . . . but straws were all I had. These men were my only hope for getting some insight into the reason for Hammonds's death—always assuming it hadn't been accidental.

"I do know," Peters surprised me by persisting, "that the Cotton Codex now contains the only surviving ancient copy of the Judith Anglo-Saxon poem. All the others have had the most appalling luck—vandals, thieves, fire . . . But I don't know if that means anything. Gabriel mentioned—not long before he, er, fell—that you were interested in a book he might write about findings from an ultraviolet study. It obviously meant a lot to Hammonds. I thought you might like to know."

I thanked him, but noticed that the group sat as if ossified, the most morose assemblage I'd seen in recent history. *Good heavens, this is tragic,* I thought. *Better do something.* "I'd quite like to know what you're all working on," I said. "But first, who needs another pint?"

When I'd bought a round of drinks and Ian had helped me deliver them, I sat again and asked, "What's your speciality, then, Peters?"

As expected, the entire group was most forthcoming about their subareas of interest. These ranged from the symbolism inherent in Grendel's mother—a rich and fruitful theme—to the evolution of Anglo-Saxon storytelling. By the time we'd got round the table, they seemed more themselves again—or was that just the effect of the drink?

I almost dreaded leaving the pub; it was warm and snug, and at least gave the illusion of safety, which was quite attractive to me at the moment. But after a look at Ian, I pushed back from the table, saying I wanted to have a look at the staircase where Hammonds had perished. Ian also stood, and we said our thanks and good-byes to the group.

"Well?" I asked him, out in the misty air once again.

Ian sighed heavily. "I don't know what to think. And I feel so wretched about old Hammonds—there I was in the very next room, chatting to Desmond, when he . . . went out."

"There's no way you could have prevented this, Ian. You mustn't take it upon yourself."

"What did you do to your head, by the way?" He glanced at the flesh-coloured bandage on my forehead, courtesy of my Accident and Emergency friends.

"Another Sarah sighting, Ian, just before Julia Northrup's National Book Week lecture. Someone ran me down as I chased after Sarah in yet another blasted taxi. If it is in fact Sarah. When are you going to tell me what you know about her?"

Even I was surprised by this sudden angry outburst. Ian turned to look at me. "I'm very sorry. You know that if I hadn't promised—"

"Promised *Sarah*? Not to tell her own fiancé, practically your own family, Ian? And promised not to tell me what? That she is alive and well, but wants nothing to do with me? I can't believe this. I really can't."

Several steps in silence. "I am sorry, Alex. I gave my word. She's been through a lot."

I wheeled and faced him. "You think I don't know that?! Why isn't she letting *me* help her? You're not marrying her, Ian, *I* am!"

He looked around to see who was near us; I had raised my voice. I always sounded like an adolescent when I got angry with Ian, but this time I didn't care. I thought it was reprehensible that he was keeping information about Sarah from me.

As we walked the few steps remaining to the porter's lodge, I tried to calm myself. In the past, Ian had kept things from me . . . but it had usually turned out to be for my own good. Every time, in fact. He had even saved my life by keeping secrets from me. But this was *Sarah* we were talking about. . . .

At the porter's lodge we asked permission to enter the Pepys Library, but a Cambridge CID detective was just showing his warrant card to the porter. This young man had the most unfortunate luck in resembling Rowan Atkinson's constable in *The Thin Blue Line,* though I was certain he had to be much more competent.

"Sorry, we're not letting anyone in—the area's under investigation." But when we told him who we were and why we were there, we seemed to pass some sort of litmus test. His name, he said, was Detective Inspector Stratton. He said we could come with him if we kept off the staircase.

As we trod the gravel path to the rear courtyard of the college and the Pepys Library in the dusk, the detective inspector spoke quietly. "We've actually just had news on this case; that's why I'm here. Your calls persuaded us to perform an autopsy, and forensic found an injury on the back of the victim's head that appears *not* to have been caused by an accidental crack on the edge of a step. So we're now treating this case as a suspicious death."

"I was there," Ian said. "I was just on the other side of the door when he must have been—er—struck? Pushed?"

Stratton looked at him with interest. "Had you seen anyone that day who didn't seem to belong at the conference? Did you hear anything at all around the time it happened?"

"No," he replied. "And I've racked my brain before now, I can tell you. No one at all. Everything seemed in order. But you've heard that he was threatened . . . ?"

"*Threatened?*" Obviously, D.I. Stratton had not.

Ian replied, "Gabriel Hammonds had come up with a theory that the Anglo-Saxon poem *Beowulf* was written much later than previously thought. He'd just finished a book for us about it when he received an anonymous phone call, telling him to recant his theory through a letter to the *Times,* or face the consequences. He did so, without a word to us about it. We had egg on our faces at Plumtree Press when all this came out; we had to cancel the book, of course."

I spoke up. "Then Hammonds rang me, just a couple of days ago, to say that the theory *hadn't* been a lie. He told me about the threat, but explained that he wasn't going to play along anymore. He'd spent his life on *Beowulf,* he said, and had to tell the truth. So he was going public with all of this here at the conference— threat and all, to explain why he'd retracted his theory. He was going to speak here, as you must already know."

Stratton nodded at me.

"There is a group of conference attendees still over at the Quill and Leaf," I added. "Do you plan to speak with everyone who was at the conference yesterday?"

"Yes, I'll need to do that . . . I understand that the conference continues tomorrow."

"It was meant to," Ian answered, "but it's broken up now. A number of the attendees have already left. It wasn't the most conducive atmosphere, after . . ."

"I can imagine," D.I. Stratton said, slowing. "I'd better go across to the pub now, while some of them are still there. Go ahead and have a look at the staircase—tell the constable that Dickie said it was okay."

He set off for the pub at a jog as we thanked him and continued on towards the pale yellow jewel of a library. It seemed to glow in the misty dusk.

The constable looked at us dubiously until we repeated D.I. Stratton's message; he smirked and took us through the spartan rooms lined with priceless books until we came to the interior staircase. He opened the door and we gazed inside. The light was on, and revealed absolutely nothing but several dark, downward-slanting scuffs on the wall's pale yellow paint that might have come from anything at any time.

But there was a feeling about the place; I couldn't avoid the brief scenario that played itself out in my head. Had Hammonds heard someone coming and turned, surprised, only to be hit over the head? If he was still conscious, had he struggled for his footing on the steep, narrow stairs before tumbling to his death?

"It's surprising no one heard anything," I said to Ian. "With these noisy wooden stairs . . ."

"But the conference was about to get under way in the far room, and we were all chatting. There was quite a bit of noise."

"No one was missing, besides Hammonds, who perhaps should have been there?" I asked.

"I've thought and thought," he said, looking distraught. "No, I can't think of a soul missing from the conference—but then I didn't notice Hammonds was gone, did I?"

We thanked the constable and made our way out of the library.

"I don't suppose you'd care to have dinner with me?" Ian asked quietly.

"You're not going to tell me anything more about Sarah, are you?"

He shook his head.

"Then I'm sticking to my plan to make a little jaunt to the coast this evening in search of some information. It's a long shot, but a necessary one."

"You're driving to the coast *tonight*?" He didn't add, *in the dark, on a foggy night like this, with your eyesight?*

"Mm."

"I see." He considered. "In that case, I imagine I know where you're going . . . and perhaps it is best done alone."

"Safer for *you* if I go alone, anyway."

"Off you go, then, Alex. But for goodness' sake, look after yourself. And try to have a bit of faith."

I climbed into the car and set off on the journey to the east coast, and so to Malconbury. I knew that the priory had long since crumbled into dust, except for its foundations of rock, several stone staircases, and two towers. But when I'd gone to the tiny village once before with my father, on a quest to discover the heritage of the Malconbury Chronicles, he'd introduced me to a retired priest named Father Mike. Now that I thought of it, I never had known his surname. Father Mike had known as much as anyone living about the minute details of the Malconbury Chronicles. It was he who had told us about the special blue dye used in the illumination of the books, made by the monks from a plant that had grown in that region alone. I was hoping the priest would still be there.

Was I a fool to drive all the way out to Malconbury on this particular night, with the sword of Damocles already hanging over my head, on what amounted to a whim? Perhaps . . . but I'd learned to trust my intuition. And intuition told me there was a link between Cotton Vitellius A.xv and the Malconbury Chronicles that reached beyond the scribe with the distinctive *X*. I needed to know what it was.

Inland, this part of the country was exceedingly flat, as I knew from previous trips. It was a pity that in the dark I would not be able to see the coast.

Seven o'clock passed, then eight. I drove eastward through Bury St Edmunds, Stowmarket, then slightly northeast on the A1120. Eventually I reached the sort of single track road I loved. Now the rural hamlets of Darsham and Westleton, where a Wall's sign seemed the height of civilisation, were all that lay between me and Malconbury. I'd brought my AA road atlas, and the Passat had an excellent map light . . . but even thus equipped, in those last twenty minutes I eventually began to wonder where on earth I was.

And then it happened, just as it had on that long-ago summer holiday with my father. Suddenly the stone farmhouse appeared, barely off the side of the road.

I glanced at my watch and got stiffly out of the car. My head ached from earlier in the day, but the smell of the sea air carried on a fresh breeze—closer to an actual gale—was rejuvenating. It made me wonder why I spent so much time in London. What would it be like to live in a place as remote as this? I studied the charming, minute house, a square stone edifice perhaps fifteen by fifteen feet, and wondered again what it would be like to live there—a sort of East-Anglian Walden, perhaps, for someone like me.

Eight forty-five. Was it too late to trouble the now elderly man—if indeed he still lived here? It would almost be a miracle if he did, I knew. . . .

Perhaps it wasn't too late; a light shone in the front window. And I couldn't exactly get back to this isolated place on a whim.

Gathering all my courage, and feeling a bit of a rascal for troubling the man, I dared to walk the few steps from the road to the door. I knocked.

What was I going to say? *Hello, I've stumbled upon a remarkable plot to alter the King James Version of the Bible. Yes—I do realise that was 1611, but it might still be of some importance.* . . .

Just as I was anguishing over the twin issues of troubling the man and wondering if he would think I'd gone round the bend, I heard a noise at the door. Shuffling, a key at the lock—a lock!—and the door drifted open, almost on its own. Then a face, kindly and wrinkled, peered round. "May I help you, young man?"

I hardly dared to hope. "Father Mike?"

"Er—yes?" A beatific smile.

"You'll never remember me, but I was here once before, to meet you with my father. I'm—"

"You're Alex Plumtree, or I'm not Michael McGonagle. Thank God you've come. I always hoped . . . Do come in, my boy, do come in." Father Mike had aged considerably in the nearly twenty years since I'd seen him; he'd gone from a brisk sixty to an unmistakable eighty. His face was as wrinkled as an old apple, and he walked with a stick. But he did seem to be spry of spirit. "Please, do sit. May I offer you a wee dram?"

What I really needed more than liquid refreshment at this point was a wee bite of food, but I didn't see how I could refuse. "That's very kind. Yes, thank you."

Looking round me, I saw that Father Mike lived in this one room, aside from a small curtained area where I imagined he slept and dressed. The minuscule place was maintained to perfection; every last spot was white-washed, and his dark bits of furniture, mostly ecclesi-astical in origin, I suspected, stood out in contrast like the valuable antiques they probably were.

A cheerful fire burned in the grate, almost as if he'd been expecting company. Ancient wooden chairs, high-backed ones, almost like settles, with pointed tops—clearly from a church—were placed on either side of the fire and decorated with tapestry pads to make them comfortable. I imagined he was very happy here.

"You'll be noticing the furniture," he said, having finished pouring two small tumblers half-full of whisky with great exactitude. "Some of these pieces were actu-ally rescued from the priory by my predecessors through the years, and presented as gifts. The scribe's table is particularly precious to me." My eyes went to the table; I envisioned the scribe of the Malconbury Chronicles himself bent over it with a quill pen.

He turned with an amber-filled glass, and I stood to accept it. "Thank you."

Father Michael smiled at me, a smile that implied we'd known each other for a very long time. It seemed to say, *Everything will be all right, don't worry . . . you're here now.*

"I've read about your fiancée in the papers," he said, settling into a chair. "Don't give up hope. There is always hope, you know, until the very end. Don't ever let anyone persuade you otherwise."

I was utterly amazed. How could he have known about me . . . about Sarah? How desperately I'd longed to hear someone say those very words. Perhaps he saw in my face that this was the opposite of what the rest of the world said—except for Ian, of course. "You can't imagine how much it means to hear you say that," I breathed. "Thank you again."

He closed his eyes briefly; he understood. "What brings you here, Alex Plumtree?"

"Somehow I think you'll understand, Father. You already know that my father brought me here to teach me the wonders of the Malconbury Chronicles."

He only smiled. He knew, all right.

In that moment I had the feeling that something in the books themselves had ordained our meeting those many years ago, to pass the knowledge along to the next generation. And something in the books—something, Someone?—had ensured that we met again on this night. Perhaps meeting Father Mike . . . the very acquisition of the Malconbury Chronicles by a long-ago Plumtree . . . hadn't all been by accident, as my father had always made it seem.

Astonishing . . . but no time to think about all that now.

Struggling back to the present, I said, "Recently, I've had cause to learn a bit about Cotton Vitellius A.fifteen. We have an author—"

"Yes. I've read all about him in the *Times*."

"Ah." I found myself continually having to adjust to the fact that this man, whom I'd expected to be—if alive at all—barely able to impart a few gems on scribes at Malconbury Priory, knew everything there was to know about me and my life. "I'm sorry to tell you, Father, he died yesterday."

"Oh, no. I *am* sorry." The old man shook his head,

but almost gave the impression that Hammonds's death had been inevitable. "I hadn't heard."

"His death wasn't an accident, either . . . which is, in part, why I'm here." I put my glass down on a stool-cum-table next to my chair and leaned towards the old man. "A friend of mine sold me his bookshop, and since I bought it, I've learned a number of things. My friend was a descendant of Sir Robert Bruce Cotton, and possessed certain extremely valuable volumes—all cleverly hidden where no one would ever think to look for them. Those . . . er . . . volumes have led me to understand that—and this might come as a shock—"

He could throw you right out, Alex . . .

"—it seems that at the time of the publication of the King James Version of the Bible, Judith might have been altered to accommodate the view of the times."

Closing his eyes again briefly, the priest nodded. "You know. I see that. And you've noticed, since you're an intelligent, well-educated Plumtree with a love for books—God bless you—that the scribe's *X*'s match. You needn't agonise, my boy. I do understand. You see, I've been waiting for you to come to me."

He took in my look of amazement, but didn't make light of it.

"Nottingham Botkin and I weren't strangers."

My mouth dropped open.

"He was in my theological class. But it seems God had other plans for him. He saw the need to preserve the part of the Cotton Collection that his branch of the family had kept. He also understood that the time would come to set the record straight, and he very much hoped that you might do that."

"Father . . . what is it that I don't know yet?"

He laughed out loud. "I like that. No time to waste, is there? Quite right, too. What you don't know is that your own Malconbury Chronicles hold the key to everything. They've been waiting for you, in the safety of your own home, to discover their secret."

"But—what is that secret?"

Father Mike was enjoying himself. "Look carefully in the illuminated initial capitals. It's all there."

"The initial capitals? That's it?"

"That's it . . . unless you're interested in the how and why."

Now it was my turn to smile. "I think it's safe to say I'm fascinated."

"Good. Another wee dram, then. This is a night I've anticipated for years."

"Allow me." I was on my feet, wanting to help him avoid the physical struggle of rising.

I saw that he was about to refuse, but then changed his mind. "Yes, it's time. It's time for you to take over, young man. Thank you." I took up his glass and crossed to the small table. "When Christopher Barker was forced to obey King James in the years leading up to 1611— and he might have had his opinions on the matter, as a man of words—he came to Brother Petrus at Malconbury. Petrus was the scribe whose X's you now know so well . . . but each generation of friars had a Petrus, so that it was still possible to find someone who knew their tradition in the early seventeenth century. Barker, of course, knew exactly where to come—the only place in England where something was still done exactly as it had been in the tenth century. That script; that X."

"I don't understand. Then how did the initial capitals acquire the—er—"

"In the seventeenth century, the Chronicles were still housed at the parish church. King Henry VIII, of course, had dissolved all of the monasteries. The Petrus of the time simply drew them out and continued to record what he'd done to Judith, and to other parts of Scripture, in his own hidden designs within the illuminations of the initial capitals."

Other parts of Scripture. There was more, then, that the monarch had changed to suit his view of the way things should be. It took a moment for it all to fall in to place, and then I saw. "The King's Printer came to Malconbury to have the Judith epic altered because he knew it would look just as though the tenth-century Petrus had done it! Then it wouldn't be questioned in future."

"Exactly," Father Mike confirmed. "But you see we all knew—"

We? I wondered. Who exactly was—were—*we*?

"—that the truth would come out in the end. And so it has."

"Well, almost. It's not out yet."

"No. Not yet. But we know the Plumtrees. Plumtrees have a way of getting things done."

There was little more to say, but time seemed to stand still within the tiny house. We were at peace. Father Mike and I sat and sipped our whisky, a quiet celebration of things having come right. A triumph of right over wrong; divine plan over man.

Despite the tide of disaster consuming me and, it seemed, everyone I loved, cared about, or even knew—including the industry I loved so well—I felt the first stirrings of genuine optimism. Perhaps things really would be all right . . . for all of us.

But as I hurried to my car through the crescendo-ing gale, I received a phone call that would plunge me still deeper into the darkness that had suffused the world of books—past and present. Strangely enough, it would also save my life.

CHAPTER 12

*"Noble Beowulf . . . one word
Of warning."*

—BEOWULF

I'd got to the point where I dreaded answering a telephone the way other people dreaded earthquakes, plagues, and famines. So I agonised as I slid into the car to get out of the wind and slammed the door shut. But ever a slave to responsibility, I pulled the blasted thing from my jacket. "Alex Plumtree."

"Alex! It's Nicola. You're never going to believe what's happened. I've just got off this *jammed* flight to Frankfurt—everyone and his grandmother on board— and all the journalists were talking about it. *McKinley Montague is alive!*"

"Alive? How can he be, possibly? It's been seven days since he first disappeared."

"I know—it's incredible. A boat rescued him, but then *they* had motor trouble *and* radio failure, and were stuck out at sea. Quite a story."

"Indeed. Nate must be licking his chops over it." But privately, I wondered again where Nate was, and again whether he'd been trying to mislead me by calling and taking back what he'd said about Trevor having killed Montague. There was no way to avoid noticing the similarity between his and Hammonds's retraction of their disastrous claims. Now that Montague was alive, he, too, had refuted the announcement of his death.

Thinking of Nate again brought to mind a new angle on his calls to me: what if someone had hired Nate to call me with the accusation that Trevor had had Montague murdered, just to turn me against Trevor ... so that I'd sell Plumtree Press to someone else? Whether it was to acquire Botkin's library or not, I didn't know—but if there was anything to this idea, either Sam Stone and company or Henning Kruse would be the guilty party.

Personally, I voted for Sam Stone.

"Alex?"

"I'm here." I glanced at the lonely house and saw Father Mike pull back the curtains for a look. No doubt he wondered what I was doing, still outside in my car. The curtains slid back into place. Tucking the phone between my ear and shoulder, I brought the Passat to life, turned round, and set out on the three-hour drive to Chorleywood and the Malconbury Chronicles.

"You don't sound overjoyed at McKinley's miraculous return to life."

"No ... I must say, it all seems a bit unlikely to me. The boat accident, the rescue—I smell a publicity stunt. I hate it when big business manipulates the public like that."

"I see. You know, you're nearly becoming a cynic, Alex." Her voice sounded bemused.

"You can't tell me the people on your flight didn't say the same thing."

"I never said they didn't. But I wanted to hear your reaction."

"I see. You know, you're nearly becoming cagey, Nicola."

"Fair enough." She laughed. "Where are you?"

"You'd never believe it if I told you. Someday I will. But earlier I met Ian in Cambridge. We learned that there *was* someone else involved in Hammonds's death; the police are treating it as a murder." I longed to confide in her about the Judith—and other—alterations; the uncanny encounter with Father Mike at this forlorn, wind-blasted edge of the earth; so many things.

"I see . . . poor man." She heard all that I wasn't saying—I could practically hear the cogs whirring. With typical restraint, she confined herself to the topic at hand. "Any ideas?"

"Yes. I'm on my way back to Chorleywood now to check one of them out."

She sighed. "Please be careful, Alex. I know you'd never see it this way, but if it's your life against saving Plumtree Press—or the entire publishing industry, for that matter—choose your life. I do understand how discouraged you must feel, about Sarah and everything, but time does heal." She paused for a moment. "How are you feeling, by the way?"

"The truth? Physically, everything's still working. Otherwise, beastly."

"Get some sleep. You're not actually sleeping at the Orchard, are you?"

"I can't even go home properly at the moment. No, when I get back I'll go to—well, the place I've been staying. After I pick up a few things at home. I'd better let you get on, too. Good night, Nicola. And thanks."

" 'Night, Alex. Take care of yourself."

I'd been so caught up in our conversation and my thoughts that it was only after I'd switched off the phone that I noticed an odd odour in the car. Nothing I could put my finger on, but the smell of—well, of *not me* . . .

In the same instant that I finally twigged to what was happening, I heard a sudden rustling in the backseat that made my blood run cold. I braked violently, throwing myself against the seat belt and throwing my attacker, I prayed, momentarily off balance. The tyres squealed against the road as the car lost speed; I jerked the steering wheel back and forth to further thwart him. I fumbled for the seat belt release but couldn't find the irritatingly small button, felt him pull against my seat for balance as he tried to get a footing in the lurching car. His proximity to me was revolting, horrifying. Still struggling with the seat belt, I threw my door open and prepared to launch myself . . .

Too late! A pair of cold, weedy hands locked round my neck, squeezing with remarkable strength, obviously determined to wring every last bit of life out of me. I reached up to prise them off, but they were attached like tentacles. The car was still rolling. I jammed my foot on the brake, felt his body press forward with disgusting closeness, smelled his acrid sweat. I kept working at his wretched, frigid hands, but they wouldn't disengage. I left off with them and reached behind my head, grasping his hair and pulling with all my strength, yanking his head back and forth against the seat. He grunted but held firm.

As I fought to loosen his grip, the car started to roll. I felt a giddy sensation as the car tipped nose downward, started to roll faster . . . then I was on the rollercoaster ride of my life as the Passat bumped wildly down a steep incline. As the car's speed increased, I felt my attacker's hands loosen—then I was weightless, suspended in midair.

A hard impact, a bounce and another, harder, more final landing. I heard a loud *whoosh* and felt the air bag against my face. Another rollover onto the roof, and the car rocked slowly to a stop, upside down. It was deathly quiet.

I hung upside down, held to the seat by the safety restraint. It took a second or two to get my bearings, and to realise that the man who'd been trying to kill me moments before was still in my car. With a resurgence of panic I reached to unfasten the seat belt, only to exclaim as my still-tender head plonked down onto the roof of the car. With what seemed a very great effort, I shoved the car door open and half fell, half rolled out. My backside was horribly cold and wet; we were in a shallow waterway, presumably just in from the coast. Though it was dark, I half-saw, half-sensed steep but not tall cliffs rising on both sides.

I scrambled to my feet and saw that very little moon shone through the thick clouds to help me find my attacker. The torch . . . the glovebox. I waded through the ankle-deep water and wrestled with the passenger-side door. It refused to open; jammed in the accident, perhaps. Reluctantly, I stumbled back around to the driver's side and listened for some sound from inside before making myself vulnerable again. Hearing nothing but the eeriness of absolute silence, I got on my knees at the edge of the car's roof and reached across for the glovebox. I lifted the catch and got it open, reached for the torch.

"Aaargh!" I screamed as a blow fell on my back. I lashed out at my attacker, flailing at him with the torch and my other hand. But there was no response: Had I knocked him out so quickly? Still kneeling on the inside of the roof of my tragically ruined Passat, certain that my attacker was waiting to sandbag me once again, I flicked on the torch and shone it fearfully into the backseat.

With revulsion I saw that what had once been my assailant could not possibly still be alive. My movements, combined with the force of gravity, had caused his hand to fall onto my back. I clenched my jaw and turned away, knowing that if I hadn't failed to unfasten my seat belt the first time round, I could well be in the same condition.

Now if only my mobile still worked . . . I pulled it out and saw its green display glowing encouragingly. I entered the emergency number and told them what sort of nasty job they had on that cold, dark, and windy night, then sank down onto a rock to keep my bum out of the river and sat with my teeth chattering, clutching the torch, until I felt more human. I'd only just made it up the bank to the road when I saw the flashing lights of the ambulance coming along.

The gents from the Norfolk Constabulary who accompanied the ambulance listened carefully as I described the attack from the unwelcome passenger in the back of the car. No, I didn't know him. But there had been other attacks lately . . . I told them briefly about the siege at the Orchard, the man in the bookmakers', the hit-and-run accident, and the two burglars at Botkin's. They listened a bit incredulously, but at least they knew I hadn't killed the poor bloke the ambulance men were removing and putting in a bag. They'd checked with their office by radio, and the officers there had looked at the computer and reported that my unlikely tales were true.

The police were kind enough to deposit me at the nearest bed-and-breakfast; I requested, as with the thugs at Botkin's, that they inform me of the identity of the man when they learned it. Again, there had been no identification on the body.

There was no one I could call to come and fetch me; my closest friends and colleagues were in Frankfurt, except for Ed, and I didn't want to take him away from his family. Ian would gladly have chased out to the middle of nowhere in the middle of the night. But even if I'd wanted to bother him late on the eve of the Fair, I was too angry with him to do him the favour. In the morning I'd hire a car and get back to the Orchard to see what secrets the Malconbury Chronicles held.

It was ten A.M. before I roused myself from the sleep of the dead—and sleep of any sort was an amazing feat, considering the matted-down mattress and microscopic, creaking bed. By noon I had breakfasted and got to Cambridge via local car service, but on the way I recalled my talk with . . . *Father Mike.* Perhaps the bump on the head had dulled my mind more than I'd realised. If someone had known I was on the road to Malconbury, and had hidden in my car outside his house, then someone knew about Father Mike.

I rang the Norfolk Constabulary and told them who I was and what I wanted. The constable took my cell phone number and the location of the priest's little house, and said they'd get back to me.

In Cambridge I hired a car and set off for Chorley-wood, where some time later I approached my own home with trepidation. Shaking my head, I stopped along Old Shire Lane and rang Mick Parsons at the constabulary. Within ten minutes he was there, ready

and willing to check out the house for me—even to remain while I got what I wanted and left again.

"No sign of trouble," he reported shortly thereafter. "But I'll stay with you just the same."

Together we went into the library, where I plucked
out the three Malconbury volumes from the shelves. I
tucked them into my carryall and reset the alarm. Then,
thanking Parsons profusely, I made for my bunker in
Berkeley Square. It was a supreme effort of will not to
stop by the side of the road and open the books, but it
didn't seem right to subject the ancient volumes to
such flippant treatment. As I eyed them on the seat
next to me, I wondered what "Petrus" could possibly
have hidden in the initial capital designs. Would I find
drawings? Symbols? Father Mike hadn't been specific.

Reaching Mayfair at nearly half past two on Thursday, I locked the basement door carefully after me,
took my bag to the bed, plopped down, and pulled out
the three heavy, folio-sized volumes.

Gingerly I lifted the padded leather cover of Volume One and inhaled. The Chronicles always made me
feel that the past had come calling; I never ceased to
marvel that after all these years, the dank-stone smell
of the ancient monastery survived. But in many ways
paper was like a sponge; aside from the stories in the
ink it absorbed, it stored up scent, food residue, smoke,
and damp from the air. All together this gave the effect
of producing a puff of the past when the leaves of an
old book were freshly opened.

On page five I found the first initial capital. I knew it
well: Framed by the letter *O* was a portrait of the priory's
first prior. Inscribed in a circular pattern, round the portrait but still inside the *O*, were the words, in Latin: HE

SERVES THE LORD IN A HARD PLACE, IN THE PLACE OF
THE ENEMY, LIKE UNTO SCHECHEM. Schechem . . . the
name Martyn had told me predated the fictional
Bethulia. Was it possible that Petrus was trying to tell
the future that this was the actual name of the city in
which the story of Judith had taken place? I needed
Martyn's expertise. I would make a list and call him to
find out.

Taking out my notebook, I recorded the sentence.
Then I turned to the next initial capital. Putting my
face close to the vellum, I made out the nearly microscopic sentence, in graceful script encircling the *I* in a
sort of outline. THE KING WAS SLAIN SO THAT ALL
MIGHT LIVE.

Yes; this was making sense, as far as the Judith
theory was concerned. I was searching for the next illuminated capital when my mobile made its obnoxious
sound. I snatched it up. "Alex Plumtree."

"Mr Plumtree?" A woman's voice, with a Norfolk
accent. "Constable Tiffin here, from the Norfolk Constabulary. I understand you rang about Father Michael
McGonagle, of the stone house on the Malconbury
Road?"

"Yes—is he all right?"

"Mr Plumtree, the house you described—in the
location you described—hasn't been occupied in a
decade. No one lives there, sir. Are you certain—"

"Of course I'm certain! Did you check inside? Did
you look? It was perfectly cared for, decorated—and
most definitely occupied."

"We looked in through the windows, and saw
that it was unoccupied. The door was ajar, so we did go
inside—it was freshly whitewashed, which none of us

can explain. But I assure you sir, no one has lived there for—oh, ten years now."

"I don't mean to be awkward, but you simply can't have found the right house. Was the house you were in made of stone, roughly twelve feet from the road, with a black-painted door?"

"Yes, sir. I've lived here all my life, not far from the stone house. Father Mike did live there for many years, but he's been dead now for ten years, as I said. I assure you, we know our own neighbours here." This last was said with a bit of pique.

"I'm sure you do." *What on earth?* "I'm sorry, but it's a bit puzzling to me that I could have just been there and seen . . ."

"Well, there's only one house on the Malconbury Road . . . it was Father Mike's, and it's well known round here."

"Look, Constable . . . did you happen to notice the furniture? The tapestry pads on the chairs?"

"You know, I'm really very sorry, Mr Plumtree—I'm telling you, the house is deserted. There's just nothing like that there. Come see for yourself, if you like."

I didn't know what to say. I thanked her and shut off the phone, utterly perplexed. Maybe my brain was playing tricks on me . . . but if Father Mike hadn't been there, how could I have learned about the encoded initial capitals? Or was I reading too much meaning into the tiny script? I stared down at the sentences recorded in my notebook:

He serves the Lord in a hard place, in the place of the enemy, like unto Schechem.
The King was slain so that all might live.

They didn't *necessarily* have anything to do with Judith ... and could very easily mean exactly what they said, and that alone.

An uncomfortable feeling about the attack on the road from Malconbury grew into a definite and horrible thought: What if someone had suspected I might make a pilgrimage to the stone house, and had installed a "Father Mike" for the sole purpose of misleading me? Because if the old man wasn't there, and the attacker knew *I* would be there ...

But who? And *why*?

I thought of the way the old man had pulled back the curtains and looked out at me as I drove away. Nicola's call about McKinley Montague had only just come in; I'd taken it while unlocking and getting into my car. Had her call, and the fact that it kept me outside Father Mike's where the attacker couldn't risk being seen by the old man, saved my life?

On the other hand, what if Father Mike was in league with the attacker? Put in that light, "Father Mike's" glimpse out of the window took on a decidedly sinister cast. Had everything he said been a lie?

Where in heaven's name do I go from here? Everything that had gone wrong, everything that was a mystery to me, was *still* wrong, *still* a mystery. Worse yet, just as I'd begun to care whether I lived or died, someone had decided to wipe me off the face of the earth. The publishing industry was mutating, before my eyes, into a Grendel-like monster that would leave no trace of the healthy, diverse, *normal* variety of publishers England had come to enjoy. What had first seemed an academic scuffle over dating *Beowulf* had turned into a murder over altered Scripture.

On top of it all, I felt utterly helpless: What could I

possibly do to change any one of those recent disasters? Unlike Beowulf, I couldn't slay Grendel alone, with my bare hands. I didn't even know who he was.

I heard the door from the upper reaches of Maggs Bros open, heard a footfall on the creaky stair. "Ed?"

"Yes—yes, it's me." Something about his voice sounded peculiar . . . shades of the night of the thugs at Botkin's. I jumped to my feet, thrust the Malconbury Chronicles (gently) into my bag and wedged it under the day bed with my foot, then went to meet him. Ed emerged from behind the bookcase at the bottom of the stairs, looking very stiff; behind him came the black-leather-jacketed man from the giant wheelie-bin behind Frontiers in Charing Cross Road. There was no mistaking the short, muscular physique and the jacket. Too bad Baroness Thatcher wasn't here to save me—or Ed—this time.

"What do you want?" My voice was terse.

"I want *you*, that's all. Your friend is certainly on edge." An eerie calm suffused the London-accented voice; a violent calm. "Won't you come with me, please, Mr Plumtree?"

Ed blurted out in a rush, "Alex, I'm sorry, he—"

"I'd keep quiet if I were you," the leather-clad man interrupted, a threat implicit in his voice.

Ed stumbled, pretended to nearly fall. But I saw the look on his face; saw him whirl and lunge for the man's knees. But the smaller man was quicker. I winced even before the boot hit Ed in the face and knocked him backwards. For his small size, Black Leather was strong. Quick, too. He walked quickly over to Ed, who was holding his nose and groaning on the floor, apparently intending to do him more damage.

"Don't," I said. "If it's me you want, here I am."

A smile spread over his face; he snorted a laugh. "That's more like it. Now come quickly." He gestured for me to come and walk in front of him. I crossed the room and obeyed, exchanging a regretful glance with Ed as I went.

On the street, a limousine sat idling. A uniformed chauffeur waited in the driver's seat while a second man got out and opened the door for me. Black Leather propelled me down into the backseat, where a fourth man already sat. There wasn't much hope of getting out, I saw. Where were they taking me? Would I now meet the end my assailant on the Malconbury Road had meant for me?

Black Leather didn't come with us; evidently his work had ended with merely delivering me to my doom. We took off southward in uncomfortable silence. As we rode I took note of my captors: they wore reasonably civilised suits, and while they were clearly present for their brawn as much as for their brains, they didn't seem too eager to rip my head off.

From the very start I didn't try any posturing, blurting out ridiculous demands such as "Let me out at once!" or blatant untruths along the lines of "You can't do this to me." From hard-won experience I knew that they jolly well could do it—and would and had.

In the end I was glad I hadn't made a fool of myself, for to my infinite surprise—and relief—the driver manoeuvred the car to none other than Whitehall itself, where he pulled into an underground garage. The car slid gracefully into a parking place marked prestigiously, if prosaically, "3." The gent on my right climbed out and nodded at me to follow. When the three of us stood next to the car, Suit Number Two gestured that I should follow Suit Number One. I did.

My two new friends and I negotiated a maze of white corridors that would be the envy of any lab rat. At long last Suit Number One knocked briefly and opened the door to an unmarked office. "If you would step inside, please."

I barely had time to register who it was behind the desk before he'd come round and was reaching out to me with both hands.

"Plumtree! My good fellow! So pleased you could join us. Good heavens, but you're a difficult man to get hold of. I had to employ my specialists." He smiled the dazzling smile. "Most impressive, actually."

"Jones-Harris! For heaven's sake—why didn't you just ask me to come see you? I thought these men were taking me to my death. Your, er, persuasion specialist badly injured my friend."

As Colin Jones-Harris and I regarded each other curiously, I recalled what he'd told me the last time we'd met. I'd been on a weekend—er, retreat—with fellow bibliophiles, and Colin had pretended quite convincingly to be a drunken lout. At the end of it all, I learned he actually did terribly secret things for the government . . . and was a decent individual besides.

"Thank you," he said to the Suits. "I don't think Mr Plumtree will elude us any longer." With the utmost respect they smiled dryly and went out.

"Colin, what on earth . . ."

"Please. Alex. Sit down. I am sorry I had to bring you here this way. But believe me, it's for the best—we don't want anyone suspecting . . . Can I get you something while we talk? Time's a bit of an issue, I'm afraid."

"Why didn't you just ring, for heaven's sake? A coffee would be nice, yes. Please. And an explanation. It was Ed Maggs your friend roughed up, you know."

He winced. "Right." He went to flip the switch on a kettle in the corner of his small domain. "The coffee's instant, I'm afraid. Or, of course, there's tea."

I knew what this meant. Jones-Harris was heir to Britain's—the world's—most formidable tea fortune. The name "Jones" was synonymous with tea. "Ah. Tea, then. Thanks."

He smiled with satisfaction and scooped some loose tea from a primitive-looking wooden box into a humble blue teapot. "Wise choice. Now," he said, seating himself opposite me, behind his desk. "I'm afraid we've some serious business to attend to. I know you weren't planning on going to the Frankfurt Book Fair, but—well, we'd appreciate it very much if you'd reconsider."

"Oh?"

"Alex, since you're in the publishing industry yourself, you must have seen hints of this. Someone has been very careful about how it's been done, but we've received alarming reports from your fellow publishers about a sudden and unnatural consolidation in the industry."

"It's true, but I hardly think it's a cause for government—"

"Publishing is, as you know, not only a vital industry for our nation but one of some considerable prestige. It's in the best interest of the government to have a number of diverse *British* publishers. Our indigenous publishing industry is not something we can afford to lose."

"Colin, are you joking? The government would go out on a limb to preserve the likes of Plumtree Press?"

As he looked at me in mock reprimand, he reminded

me of no one so much as Bertie Wooster, discussing a food fight at the Drones. "Really, Alex, I'm surprised you don't have a higher opinion of your profession. What's published shapes the nation—shapes the *world*," he added decisively.

With a pang, I remembered when I'd shared that conviction . . . but publishing books, at least at Plumtree Press, had a way of wearing one down. Especially when people were murdered, abducted, beaten, and—

"But you're right," he continued. "There is more to it than that. Quite a bit more. It's very unhealthy for too much power to be focussed in the hands of one company, especially if it's a non-British company. Such a situation would give this company leverage over us—the government—in some areas, not to mention influence over legislators. And an extraordinary amount of money could change hands. Again, if the money's flowing out of Britain, that's something we'd prefer to avoid. Obviously."

I sighed. "All right. Point taken. What do you want me to do?"

Jones-Harris grinned and rubbed his hands together with glee. "Lovely. Tea first, old boy. Tea first."

CHAPTER 13

'I am no weakling.
With my trusty blade I have slain a monster brood
And blindly at night many a foul sea-beast
That writhed and twisted in the bounding wave.
. . . I shall not fail.'

After I'd ensured that a rather large basket of speciality tea products and an official apology would be sent to Ed Maggs on Jones-Harris's behalf, and lectured him sternly on his methods, I set off for the Orchard to gather my things for the Fair. This time I had an escort of two capable fellows, Suits One and Two, who drove me in their own government vehicle. It was their job to ensure that no one like their own Black Leather terrorised or otherwise waylaid me on my mission.

My home was mysteriously devoid of muggers, sackers, and killers as we entered and I disarmed the alarm system. I put the kettle on for my two friends and told them to make themselves comfortable while I went upstairs to pack. They had been instructed to give me a ride to Heathrow, where a first-class seat had been arranged on the next flight out. But on the way upstairs, I glimpsed the library door and thought of Sarah's note. I couldn't resist nipping in to the library to look at it again.

It was gone. Flummoxed, I stared at the empty surface of the mantel, where I'd left the note after showing it to Ian. Was she here, in England, flitting in and out of my house? Or was someone else just doing a fairly decent job of driving me out of my mind?

I gave up and took myself upstairs. The house was acquiring that slightly damp, unfamiliar smell of the disused home. It hadn't taken long for it to happen. . . . How simple my dreams of Sarah and children—even perhaps a pony or two—had seemed, as recently as three months ago.

No use dwelling on it, Alex.

I gathered my own suits and other supplies and stuffed them into a bag. As I took one last look round my bedroom, I saw something that made me stop cold. Sarah and I had had a running joke about the leaf of a table in my room. It had a spring mechanism, and a small support under the leaf could be slid over to allow the leaf to fold down. Every time she came into the room, Sarah put the leaf up. Every time I came into the room, I put it down—at first because I thought it made the room too crowded, but eventually just to play along.

The leaf had been down since she'd disappeared. It was now up.

The note, the flowers, the table . . . ? Who else could possibly know about that table? Even Ian had never known about our silly little game. I felt certain that if Sarah were here—*Please, God, let her be alive and well*—she would have got in touch with me. What Ian had told me about her being alive didn't make sense; the Sarah I knew wouldn't leave me in the dark. And she would never, never, speed away in taxicabs, leaving me to be run down in the road behind her.

But what, I thought, if something had happened to her? What if she were in some way . . . not the same?

Or what, I thought with nearly equal dismay, if something had happened to my mind? Could I be imagining all of these apparent manifestations of Sarah—and perhaps even Ian's assurances?

On a whim, I slid the lever aside and lowered the leaf, drawing my hand over it fondly. "I love you," I said to the air.

"Sir? Are you all right, sir?" The voice came from the bottom of the staircase.

"Yes, sorry—only talking to myself." Chagrined, I hoisted my bag and went down to meet them.

Ah, Frankfurt again. I sighed as my taxi left the Frankfurt am Main airport, heading for the hotel. Frankfurt was one of those cities that never ceased to remind its visitors of the not-so-long-ago war that had raged in its skies and through its streets. It wasn't that wartime rubble sat about, but the architecture was such a mix of new and old that it was impossible not to realise that much of it had been rebuilt.

Aside from its most prestigious addresses, Frankfurt exuded decay and disrepair, and stark bleakness. On previous visits I'd found it difficult to believe that it was the financial centre of Germany, and even the site of the European Bank. One of those fascinating accidents of human migration also meant that it had become the home of tens of thousands of immigrants. Signs in Turkish on the walls of buildings gave it an exotic foreign feeling.

As I absorbed all of this for the fourth year in a row, I reflected on the unfortunate circumstances that made it necessary to lodge with Nicola in her suite at the

Frankfurterhof. In the first place, lodging in Frankfurt—
or anywhere within a hundred miles—was a night-
mare during the Book Fair. Getting any hotel room at
all during that period was akin to finding a Kelmscott
Chaucer. Many people stayed with families in the sub-
urbs as bed-and-breakfast guests, and travelled on
trains an hour or more to get into the city.

Lisette and George, who would otherwise have
made a party out of my staying with them, were using
this time as a couple's getaway. George was studying
German on an intensive course during the days while
Lisette was working, and the nights were theirs alone.
They'd left the children with the nanny; it was the first
holiday they'd taken alone together in years. There was
no way I was going to insert myself into that equation.

Ian was staying with an academic friend, a professor he knew from scholarly publishing circles. It
wouldn't do to invite myself into that gentleman's home,
either.

And as for Sam Stone . . . I wouldn't have been surprised if her family kept a pied-à-terre in Frankfurt
just for the Fair. Wherever Sam was staying, I was *not*.

But my friendship with Nicola was such that I
knew we could share accommodation without fuss; I'd
take the sofa, she could keep the bedroom. When I'd
asked apologetically about sharing her suite over the
phone from Heathrow, she laughed. "Stop! It's no problem at all—in fact it'll be useful to have a chance to go
over the day's meetings. But I must warn you—I'm not
the tidy sort."

The least of my worries, I assured her. I only hoped
someone wouldn't get wind of our cohabitation and
blow it all out of proportion.

As the taxi zoomed along the motorway, I reviewed why in fact I was there. My duties were clear, as dictated by Jones-Harris: Find Henning Kruse, Trevor Gravesend, Samuel Stone—Sam Stone's father, the Bill Gates of US publishing—and insist upon a tête-à-tête with each as soon as possible. When Colin Jones-Harris and I had had our forced little chat, I was stunned by the people he named for me to interview. But he was even more taken aback to learn that they were the same three who had pursued me in the last week with offers to purchase Plumtree Press.

"You're joking!" he'd exclaimed. He looked at me across his desk with laughing eyes and a half-moon mouth; he might have been a six-year-old at a birthday party. I often had the feeling this was all a game to him. "Unbelievable," he said. "Well. It couldn't be better, then. You're to ask them—no, *demand*—that they tell you the future of Plumtree Press, if they want to buy it. How many other companies would be involved, who they are . . . see what you can find out for us about what they have planned."

Um, perhaps, I'd answered. But privately I hoped it wouldn't get too nasty along the way. Jones-Harris's mouth twitched as he admonished me to lose no time in getting to these men. He possessed such an extraordinary degree of self-control that this small aberration told me he suspected something vitally important was about to happen.

The taxi driver delivered me to the Frankfurterhof. Nicola had arranged for a key to be left for me at reception, so I took my bag to the room. I put on one of the suits I'd brought and donned a tie. Best battle dress, I thought, for marching as to war.

It was a gorgeous day in Frankfurt, picture-perfect blue sky and breathtaking autumn leaves, so I set out on the walk to the Messe—the fairgrounds—without an overcoat. Hordes of obvious book-business types overflowed from the pavements into the busy streets. The small gangs of Gastarbeiter who normally roamed the *strassen* of Frankfurt ignored our week-long invasion of their territory.

As I crossed the Baselerstrasse, taking care not to be one of the Fair attendees run down each year by the active tram system, I saw the huge moving sculpture that was intended to represent the working man. The giant steel workman lifted a sledgehammer and brought it down endlessly, up and down, on and on . . . forever. Personally, I thought it was a bit of a negative message to the workers of Frankfurt instead of the intended tribute. But I wasn't there to criticise the public art.

Inside the hall, registered and now formally part of the Fair, I opened the information book provided in my packet and consulted the map. Henning Kruse's company, Spitze-Verlag, had taken the equivalent of six stand spaces, so it was not difficult to find on the plan. I went directly there, past the usual displays of young and voluptuous girls in unbelievably short skirts, and pulsating music coordinated with rhythmically flashing coloured lights. Moving walkways transported pedestrians down the endless aisles.

When I presented myself at the Spitze-Verlag booth and asked for Henning Kruse, the receptionist enquired, "You have an appointment?"

"No," I replied. "But if you would please tell him that Alex Plumtree would like to speak with him."

Her eyes snapped, *Who the hell do you think you*

are? Publishers' calendars were notoriously crowded at the Fair. But she did my bidding, and moments later Henning ducked out of a meeting space in the middle of the booth. "Alex, I'm delighted. Delighted." I saw him searching my face for confirmation that my sudden appearance meant I had agreed to sell, but I remained noncommittal. Behind him, I saw a minion come out of the room with the rejected meeting partner—who shot daggers at me—and dispose of him courteously.

Business was cruel. Perhaps I was about to learn just *how* cruel.

"Sorry to barge in like this, Henning. When can you spare a few minutes? I have some questions."

Clearly he was not used to having others stop by to request meetings with him. At the head of the Spitze empire at such an early age, everyone bowed and scraped as if he were King. But Henning seemed amused by my boldness. "Of course." He smiled, glancing at his watch. "Would right now do? Katrina, if you would please reschedule my next appointment."

He ushered me into a remarkably well appointed conference room, complete with twelve-foot-long mahogany table surrounded by twelve leather chairs. I considered this opulence remarkable, knowing that a hire company had transported it there by lorry just forty-eight hours ago, and it had been assembled by the hammer-wielding Frankfurt workers just twelve hours earlier, in the manner of all trade fairs.

"Please." He gestured that I should sit. "Coffee? Tea? Something else?"

"No, thank you. I—well, to be blunt, I have some reservations about an agreement between our two firms."

"Oh?" He frowned. "I'm sorry to hear that. Perhaps

if you tell me . . ." He picked up a pencil from the smooth, highly polished table and began bouncing the eraser off its surface. The set of his mouth and a sudden coldness in his eyes made it clear that he was no longer cheery, breezy. Perhaps he expected me to bargain for more money. Perhaps I had misjudged him.

"Henning, you know how much I admire your publishing house. But I'm concerned about all the consolidation sweeping little independents like me from the deck. And I feel that if I'm going to sell to you," I continued, "I need to know what direction you're going to take with Spitze's acquisitions. For instance: Do you plan to keep the separate companies intact, allowing them to retain their personalities? If Plumtree publishes to your criteria instead of mine, who will publish the more eccentric authors in our line—like Julia Northrup, who looks to be a winner after all? Will you require copublishing agreements between Plumtree Press and other firms that might be to Plumtree's detriment? And, will you collect more and more companies, until mine is competing with six others in exactly the same areas? Can you give me any sort of promise that you won't?"

He closed his eyes briefly and the pencil stopped. From the ensuing silence I knew that I'd overdone it . . . but I needed to push him, to get him off balance. It was quite unpleasant to make an enemy of a man I admired so much—and an oarsman besides.

"I think I see where this is going. And, Alex, I am deeply offended. I thought we understood one another. I very much resent this sort of insinuation." With that, he reached inside his coat and drew out a folded newspaper clipping. "The *Herald Tribune,* yesterday. The French, also, continually assume that we Germans are trying to take over: in finance, in publishing, in anything you can name. It's ridiculous. Absurd. When will it end?" It seemed to me he only narrowly avoided saying, *I'm extremely disappointed in you.* He stood, glowering.

I'd really done it now.

I glanced at the scrap of newsprint he'd tossed onto the table. Its headline shouted, *French Scholars Write Book Accusing Germans of Plot to Control European Bank.* His wrath and sense of injury were obviously genuine, but at the same time I couldn't help but notice that he'd brilliantly sidestepped my question.

"Henning, please. You misunderstand me. I'm not suggesting a political plot . . . certainly not a *German* plot. I'm only concerned that there seems to be a great deal of consolidation going on. I'm worried about where it will all end. If I sell Plumtree Press, I don't want it to be part of some buying frenzy that locks up a lot of publishers under one name and then emasculates them. If you can't trust me enough to share your plans with me, then I don't trust you enough to sell you my Press."

I was glad that my work did not normally consist of posturing and giving offence in order to gain information. I really wasn't much good at it.

Henning was no fool, or he would not be leader of one of the world's largest publishing companies. He must have sensed something in my voice. He leaned over the table toward me, his eyes boring into mine with disturbing intensity. "It sounds as though you know something I don't." I felt as though he could read my mind. "What is going on, Alex?" Here he sat down again, crossed his arms, and waited . . . still watching me.

I'd have given anything for the floor to open up

and swallow me. This man was much too smart—*and* sensitive. But I still couldn't be sure I could trust him. I would have to try a different tack. *Go closer to the truth; see how he reacts.* I felt myself begin to sweat. Deception was so exhausting.

"All right, Henning." With a rueful smile and a quick shake of the head, I tried to tell him, *You've got me.* "A friend of mine watches the industry closely. He told me that he feels the very ground shifting; that a consolidation is under way in our industry of such magnitude that British publishing—indeed, *all* publishing—will never be the same. As you know, once these consolidations occur, they are rarely undone. What's more, he thinks the deal will be finalised here at the Fair so it can be announced to the world."

Henning shot me a sceptical look. "But surely this can be easily found out, who is buying whom?"

I thought of the network of unknown names shrouding the existing firms on record at Companies House. "I only know what my friend tells me," I replied. "No doubt you can see why I'm afraid to throw my family's pride and joy into that sort of black hole. And surely you might forgive me for thinking you could be involved, considering Spitze's position . . . and yours. When you said you needed to know by tomorrow, I jumped to conclusions."

Henning still scrutinised me warily. Unfortunately, my interview of him had turned rather into an interview of me. I had the impression he'd sussed out exactly what was happening: I'd told him part, but not all, of the truth. But he seemed intrigued; he wanted to know more. I found myself believing that he wasn't involved.

He nodded. "I am going to talk to my own friends

about this, Alex. Obviously, it would affect me, too. Don't worry; I will be discreet. I won't mention your name."

I sensed that he was keen to get on with it, and we'd said all we were going to say. I pulled a business card from my pocket and scrawled my mobile number on it. "In case. Thanks for seeing me, Henning."

In turn, he pulled a card from his pocket and handed it to me, saying only, "My private number. Let me know what you find out." He escorted me from the room and shook my hand next to the stand's reception desk.

I left feeling that more than my hand had been shaken. Drawing a deep breath, I started walking down the aisle. As I drew near to the edge of the Fair exhibits, I heard the buzz of one of the bar areas—where all the *real* business took place in Frankfurt—and saw the crowd spilling over into the aisle. It didn't matter what the hour—the bars were always busy. But now, at nearly closing time, they were chock-a-block.

A small, balding young man came reeling backwards towards me, stumbling away from the bar. "Hey, careful!" I said, laughing, and put out my hands to steady him before he ran into me. The man turned round and I stared, disbelieving, at his face. It was Nate—but so dissipated, shrunken, and hollow beneath the eyes that I could scarcely believe it was the same man I'd chatted to over coffee—and bullets—only five days ago.

"Nate!" With an effort, I ignored the distress his appearance caused and pretended everything was fine. I didn't want to scare him off.

He gazed back at me with the glassy eyes of the very drunk, then burst into tears. Deep, silent sobs consumed him as his face collapsed into a mask of anguish. He teetered towards me as I caught hold under his arms and pushed him to a standing position. But without my assistance, I knew, he'd slide to the floor, drunk off his feet. He wasn't far from losing it entirely, and I badly needed a conversation with him.

"Nate—I've wanted to talk to you for ages. How about a coffee? I really don't think anyone will shoot at us this time." I ushered the troubled journalist, still shaking with silent sobs, out a side door and to a taxi. "*Zum Marriott, bitte.*" Nate always stayed at the Marriott just across from the Messe, and I thought we'd better go to his hotel, given his precarious state. I didn't fancy carrying him across half of Frankfurt.

I won't describe the ordeal of getting to his room. I got him sitting in a chair and threw the prepackaged coffee filter and some water into the coffeemaker. He gasped a shuddering breath and spoke to the floor in a high, unnatural voice. "You're——too——good, Alex."

"I don't think so, Nate."

He shook his head, rocking his whole body as he did so, like a child. "Too good. They'll finish you. They'll——" He began to list, and I caught him before he rolled off the chair altogether. I got him sitting up again and drinking a glass of water. The coffee machine had only just begun to drip.

"Nate, please. I'm up to my eyeballs in alligators. People are trying to kill me. You know why; I really think you do. Please tell me what you know."

"They'll finish . . . you . . ." A horrified look came over his tear-stained face, and the sobs began again. I hurried to the coffee and poured him what there was of it.

"Nate. Who rang you and told you to tell me Hanford Banner/Megacom had killed Montague? Doesn't it make you angry, now we know he's alive? Who lied to us?"

I couldn't even get him to sip at the coffee. I was actually worried about whether he would be all right. Still, I had to press him. "Nate. Please . . . what did you mean about the Frankfurt Fair being the start of it all? Did you mean the consolidation conspiracy?"

At that his eyes filled with tears again and seemed to search for mine. "Damned . . . clever . . ." The massive effort required of him to hold his head up was pitiful. I felt I was taking advantage of him; he should be allowed to sleep for a very long time.

But I had to persist. "Who shot at us, Nate?"

He moved his lips as if he were about to answer. But a grimace turned his face into a study of misery. He shook his head slowly, but it set him on his way off the chair and onto the carpet. I ran to catch him, called his name. He looked up at me once, through half-closed eyes. After that, there was no rousing him.

I became so worried at his grey pallor that I called hotel reception and asked for a doctor. It wouldn't be possible for me to baby-sit him for the next three days—I had to get on to Stone and Gravesend. While I waited, I looked around his room. It was an ungodly mess; clothes and bedclothes were strewn everywhere. But what I was really looking for was Nate's legendary notebook. He always had it with him, though not always in full view. I'd seen it when he interviewed me for the Plumtree Press feature in the *Bookseller*; he'd used it to take some sort of unintelligible notes. I was certain he'd taken equally unintelligible notes about whatever it was he thought would happen at Frankfurt.

But the notebook was nowhere to be seen . . .

perhaps it was in his pockets somewhere. I looked over at the poor unconscious boy and couldn't imagine rummaging through his pockets for it. What a shame I hadn't learned anything before he passed out. I knelt beside his inert form and checked; no notebook.

A knock sounded at the door, and I opened it to find a man there of roughly my own age. "I am the doctor," he said, displaying his willingness to speak English.

"Hello," I said, "please come in. I'm afraid my friend had far too much to drink; I'm quite worried about him."

The doctor gave me a knowing look. "This is not unusual at this time of the year." He went to Nate and assessed his condition, opening his eyelids and taking his pulse. With a quick shake of the head, he said, "I will need your permission to take him to the hospital, to be certain he does not suffer from alcohol poisoning."

Poor Nate. I consented and waited while the doctor called transport. Then I had a difficult decision to make: Did I have to stay with him and hold his hand at the hospital, or would it be all right to go back to the Fair and carry on? I decided I wasn't going to be much help to Nate for the next few hours. I sent a note with the doctor to leave with Nate at the hospital, reminding him of my mobile number.

Feeling a bit guilty, once they'd carted Nate off I headed back to the Messe to get on to the almighty Stone and Gravesend. It was dark now, just after half past six, and while I could see that the Fair was still open, a constant stream of people flowed out of the convention center. If I lost this entire evening, I would be disappointed indeed. Sighing, I pulled out my guide book for its map and located the Stone & Stone stand. It was huge, even larger than Spitze-Verlag's. Trust the Americans, I thought.

Bells chimed over the sound system, and a silky female voice announced, *"Meine Damen und Herren, die Messe wird um sieben Uhr schliessen. Vielen Dank.* Ladies and gentlemen, the Hall will close at seven P.M. Thank you." Twenty minutes left, then. The Stone & Stone stand was as far away as it could possibly be, and I set off at a brisk pace to get there before I was thrown out of the hall. Perhaps I'd be able to sound out Gravesend later tonight. The restaurants used by the British contingent in Frankfurt for entertaining authors and their agents were the same from year to year; if nothing else I'd track him down at one of the old standbys.

This late in the day, most of the senior staff had gone on to social functions, or to prepare for dinner with authors and other notables, leaving junior staff at the stands. I doubted I could still catch Samuel Stone ...

As I hurried along, I caught sight of Nicola coming towards me. She looked sublimely elated. It always amazed me that the sort of knot she put in her hair could still look as perfectly elegant at the end of a grueling day as it had at the start. "Alex, we've done it. I daresay a celebration is in order."

"What's this all about? You certainly look as if you've just swallowed the proverbial canary—but do you mind walking with me? I've got to reach Stone and Stone before it's too late."

She picked up the pace by my side. "I signed a deal memo with McKinley Montague, Alex! Nothing final, of course, until you approve it—but it'll be the talk of the Fair tomorrow. He said he wanted the name of a real literary publisher like Plumtree behind him, and turned down Hanford Banner's option. Can you imagine? I even found Nate before he was too sloshed, and told him as well. We've *done* it!!" She made a light-hearted little skip as she said this last.

A deal memo was used at the Fair to take a book negotiation one step beyond an oral agreement. But strictly speaking, it wasn't a contract. Contracts were rarely signed at the Fair, without lawyers and corporate bigwigs there to vet every last detail . . . fortunately.

But with *Montague*?! I was put out with Montague for going along with what I felt sure was a massively manipulative act of being lost—presumed perished—at sea. There were other ways to win the public's heart, preferably by writing a truly worthy book. And how on earth had she got a meeting with Montague? Why would he be interested in talking to us, when he was a top best-seller with Hanford Banner as it was? Why on earth wouldn't he accept the generous offer he'd have been contractually obliged to consider from Hanford Banner? I thought back to Nicola's and my lunch at Mon Plaisir, and realised that I'd said nothing about staying away from signing anything that had to do with Hanford Banner, Spitze, and Stone & Stone, in view of Matt Ireland's conspiracy theory and Nate's warning about the Fair. I just hadn't envisioned what methods they might use.

Nate had been right: "It" was all happening at the Fair . . . though I knew now with sickening certainty that I'd glimpsed only the tip of the iceberg.

"I didn't know you had a meeting with Montague."

"Oh, I didn't—*he* came to *us*." She noticed that I wasn't jumping up and down beside her, and wilted a bit. "But he came running onto the stand this morning and wanted to do business. His agent was with him, of course—asked me to initial an odd little memo about rights, too." She wrinkled her nose.

"But you didn't, did you," I said with conviction. "Good on, Nicola. Always beware those—"

"Well, actually . . ." Her step had slowed. I turned to look at her. She was utterly crestfallen.

"Oh, no." We both stopped. She seemed stunned that I had transformed her remarkable success into a disaster. It was obvious what had happened: unaware of the conspiracy, Nicola had seen the contract with Montague as an irresistible opportunity for Plumtree Press. And under normal circumstances, she'd have been absolutely right. Nicola's judgement had always been impeccable; it wasn't her fault that this creeping infection had been brought in proximity to the Press. I felt time ticking away. Until I knew exactly what these memos said, I wouldn't know whether I was overreacting, or if Hanford Banner really had—in accordance with my worst fears—managed to put us at a disadvantage that might force us to capitulate. Gravesend might already have his hooks in us, but I had to reach Stone before he, too, sneaked in through the back door of my busy little firm. Come to think of it, his daughter already had—under the guise of the Godwin Fellowship.

I felt ill at the sudden realisation of the way Hanford Banner/Wellbrook's had used my employee and circumstances to insinuate its way into our firm. Stone & Stone, too, now had access to our innermost thoughts and machinations via Sam—though I supposed I could always abruptly terminate her Fellowship. It would certainly make news . . . not to mention waves.

"Nicola, I'll see you back at the room later. I know you did your best. They were only deal memos. We'll

see if Neville can put it right." As I left she was still
standing in the middle of the aisle.

You're too good, Alex. They'll finish you. . . . Nate's
warning burned in my memory.

I made it to Stone & Stone's at ten minutes to
seven. Samuel Stone himself was striding round the
side of the stand as I approached, and I slowed, a bit in
awe of the man. Good heavens, I thought, but he's big.
Not overweight, but massive in a well-proportioned
way. He was a good example of the sort of sixtyish
American I saw more and more among the wealthy
and well-educated, who seemed to keep aging at bay
through regular workouts and healthy habits.

Was this the man responsible for hiring a Sarah
impostor to drive me out of my mind, so I'd put up
less of a fight to keep my company? He, and his daughter, were certainly the most likely candidates, since the
woman had been seen at their house. I felt anger rising
but reminded myself I had to stay cool. I was supposed
to be honoured, flattered, delighted to know them.

The kingpin of American—er, world—publishing
was at least as tall as I was, and perhaps half again as
heavy. Stone had a full head of grey-white hair, and was
the very picture of a successful American executive in
his navy blue suit, black wing tips, and red foulard tie.
When he turned, I could see that he indeed had the
Stone family jaw, jutting out like the prow of a ship,
and the eyes that drooped down at the outside edge.

He had an easy, athletic way of moving that made
all that mass quite impressive, with a booming voice to
match. Something about his confident, good-natured,
casual way suggested American football in his past. Yet
he managed to give an air of refinement at the same

time. He reminded me of a congressman in America who had been a professional football player and then gone on to run for president several years ago. That was it: Samuel Stone was *presidential*.

He was larking about with his staff, joking with them about something, the very life of the party when he caught sight of me. Excusing himself from the adoring young women surrounding him, he came towards me with a half-smile, one arm already outstretched to shake my hand.

"Alex Plumtree," he said heartily, pumping my hand. I gave him as good as I got, which clearly surprised him, coming from a British publisher.

"Delighted to meet you, Mr Stone," I said. *And I'll thank you to keep your rather large hands off my publishing company.*

"Please! Call me Sam. We're practically family now, after all, now that Sammy's over here with you." He leaned closer. "You've impressed the hell out of her, Plumtree. She never stops talking about you." At that he raised his eyebrows. "I don't know what you have in mind, but if you said jump . . ." Then he told me she'd kill him if she knew what he'd just said.

I'd already learned one thing about him: He enjoyed sharing man-to-man secrets, with an astonishing disregard for his daughter's feelings.

Unable to laugh or otherwise condone this breach of ethics, I did not give him the good-old-boy response he expected. But he seemed undaunted. Glancing at his enormous brushed-gold watch, he said—again in a confiding tone intended to make me feel one of the inner circle—"You know, this works out perfectly. I don't know if you're free for dinner, but my appointment just cancelled a few minutes ago. What do you say we

talk about things over dinner? I'll give Sammy a ring—
she'll want to join us." He beamed at me with the force
of a blowtorch.

I felt its heat.

"I'd love to," I answered, and wondered if I'd make
it through the evening without getting burned.

CHAPTER 14

Then fear shall fall upon them, and they shall flee
before your face.

—JUDITH 14:3C

S ammy" appeared flushed—whether from alcohol
or pleasure, I wasn't sure—when she got to us from
the bar. She indulged in a double-cheek European kiss.
When in Rome, I thought, use custom to your advantage.

"Alex, what're you doing here? I thought you
weren't coming to Frankfurt!"

I stammered around a bit and finally came up with
the excuse that Nicola had some fairly large deals to
handle all on her own. Which had certainly proved to
be true. Sam Senior, I noticed, was pacing while talking
on his mobile, with his back to us.

"Ah, you mean Montague. Quite a coup for her.
She was pretty impressive, cutting that deal."

I refrained from comment. "And how are you enjoying your first fair with Plumtree Press?"

"Loving it. Nicola let me sit in on some of her meetings. Your meetings have a very different tone from
ours. I've learned a lot already about why and how
publishing is different in Britain. It all comes down to
the fact that you have a superior culture—though ours
has its practical advantages." She smiled from beneath
her lashes. "As you know, I'd love it if our companies

worked together more closely. But I suppose we can talk about that over dinner."

Sam the Elder joined us again and put an affectionate arm round his daughter. "Shall we?" They said good night to their staff on the stand and we began the long march to the exit—or so I thought. "This way, Alex." They led me in the opposite direction from the exit, to a fire door. "We have a special arrangement with the fair organisers," he said. "Security can be a concern."

"Ah. I see," I murmured, and stepped through the door that a guard, nodding curtly, held open for us. A Mercedes limousine waited several yards away, its motor running. It all seemed carefully choreographed when Sam Senior walked round to get in on the far side, while Sam Junior climbed in on my side, showing a good bit of leg in the process. She scooted over into the middle seat and I folded myself in next to her.

It suddenly occurred to me: Here I was, riding with two of the most well placed, successful book publishers in the world, but I felt as if I were riding in the backseat with Suits One and Two.

"We use the home of friends when we come to Frankfurt," Sam Senior confided, sliding an arm around his daughter. "They prefer to travel when the Fair descends on Frankfurt, so we trade them one of our homes for theirs during this week. We can discuss our business in private, without a lot of curious ears around."

The Stones' temporary home was, it turned out, on Mendelssohnstrasse, home to Frankfurt's privileged. Entering the centuries-old, beautifully decorated jewel of a house was like walking into a small palace. A staff saw to our every need, including a paper-thin Wiener schnitzel with countless accompaniments. Two and a half hours later, replete, we retired to the sitting room, having discussed the current trends in literary fiction and the future of the novel. "That was magnificent," I said, referring to the four-course meal. "I haven't eaten so well in ages." Knowing that the real discussion always came after the meal, I braced myself.

"Good, good. We'll have coffee in here." We settled into comfortable white down-stuffed chairs. Before dinner "Sammy" had changed into what I'm sure was meant to be a provocative little dress, a slinky, clingy scrap of fabric in off-white. As she sank onto a white chair, she reminded me of a kitten—graceful, pampered, soft, and ferociously smart.

It occurred to me that many men would dream of the opportunity to cement a relationship with the heir to the world's greatest publishing family. In fact, many people would say it only made sense for two publishing dynasties to unite, rather like marriages between royal families. It was clear that Sam saw things in this light. But even if she and her father weren't the top suspects for trying to break me down with Sarah sightings—and perhaps even hit-and-run accidents—I couldn't help it: She in no way attracted me. Not her business, not her wealth, not her status, not her personality, not even her body.

This, I realised as the coffees were delivered by the maid, gave me a definite advantage. Even Sam Senior seemed to be playing up to me in an effort to win me for her. If he wasn't the one amassing companies to sinister purpose, I wondered for the first time if they were offering to buy Plumtree Press just to curry favour. Stone & Stone and all its ancillary corporations certainly didn't need my little company . . . but this wouldn't be

the first time an American woman of means had preferred to acquire a husband with an English accent.
Now that I had a title—though I hadn't exactly broadcast the fact—it was possible that my value as an acquisition had risen significantly. For people who thought
like that.

". . . know it's a consideration for you," Sam the father was saying.

"Sorry—I was miles away there for a moment.
What were you saying?"

He smiled indulgently. "That's OK. You do look a
bit tired, Alex, if you don't mind my saying so. We'll be
sure not to keep you too late. But we did want to talk
about Plumtree Press joining us at Stone and Stone. I
was just saying that the family tradition must be a consideration for you, thinking of selling Plumtree Press
after so many years."

"Indeed." Perfect opportunity, I thought. "You can
imagine, as the head of a family firm yourself, what it
would feel like to sell Stone and Stone. You'd want to
ensure that the qualities that made it unique would
carry on; that it wouldn't become just one more pearl
on a very long string. I am worried about this sudden
shifting of—"

Samantha slammed her cup and saucer down on a
priceless table and rose in agitation. "You see, Father? I
told you. . . . Alex, in the bar at the Fair I overheard a
conversation. It all sounded a bit wild, and the poor
man was clearly three sheets to the wind, but he was
babbling about one publisher buying all three of the
main British book distributors, in addition to secretly
acquiring other publishers using hidden companies.
Now we've *all* seen a lot of consolidation—in fact,

Stone and Stone has been responsible for its share. But this goes beyond that. It's sinister—and if it's true, one publisher is calling all the shots."

The poor drunken sot she'd overheard could well have been Nate. What a tortured soul he'd become. I didn't know if he was able any longer to differentiate between the genuine rumours he heard, the false ones he was meant to hear, and the truth. But he did have a lot of sources. . . .

The distributors, too? Could it be?

Whatever the truth, the Stones had turned the game round on me. I couldn't ignore the possibility that this was all an act on their part; that they might in fact be the ones taking over the publishing world as we knew it, and doing it so swiftly that no one could prevent it. Right here, at the Fair. I recalled what Colin Jones-Harris had said: it was not merely a matter of massive profits. It was power as well, political and industrial power.

I chose my words like footsteps through a mine field. "A friend in the industry is convinced that one publisher, or one group, intends a rather unhealthy monopoly in the British publishing industry. He seems to have received information about it, but is reluctant to share anything more. Naturally, this would be disturbing to me even if I weren't thinking of selling . . ." *and I'm not.* "Like you, I care about the world of books and don't particularly want to see Big Brother running the show."

Samuel Stone cleared his throat and set down his coffee. "I think it's time I confided in you two. Alex, normally, I'd keep something like this in the family—and in the company—but I feel I can trust you."

I knew this ploy; saw the illusion that this oh-so-smooth man was trying to create. He wanted me to feel he was doing me a great favour; that I had been drawn into a special position of trust and privilege. I vowed not to be flattered or compromised by it.

It was impossible to miss the fact that Sam was irritated by her father's statement; she glared at him without bothering to hide her pique. I wondered if this happened often, that she felt she was kept in the dark, or rather *protected* from the darker corners of her father's world. Or perhaps it was merely that he had outmanoeuvred her in my presence. Whatever the issue, I sensed a bone of contention between them. Sam senior seemed not to notice her baleful stare, or else pretended that he didn't.

"I've heard similar rumours, Alex, and of course there is a certain responsibility that comes with my position. I've been looking into this supposed industry takeover; I have people asking around. It must be done subtly, otherwise uncovering anything will become doubly difficult." He met my eyes; the bland look could have meant any number of things. Was *he* Big Brother, telling me he knew what I was up to and that I had blundered into it? Or was he merely saying that I'd been too obvious?

I was cautious about reading too much between the lines, especially with Americans, because they could be oblivious to the subtleties of word choice. With Stone, I honestly didn't know which way to lean.

My frustration mounted like a chemical reaction run amok; I struggled to contain it.

"If we don't learn something in the next day or so, I think it'll be too late," I replied. "Whoever it is, if in fact there is someone hatching such a takeover plot, they'd be fools not to wrap it up at the Fair. I just wonder if we'll even know when it's happened—they might choose to hide their accomplishment for a while. It wouldn't be hard to do, using holding company names so that no one knows who's who."

We all reflected on this for a moment. Even Sam seemed subdued at the thought. But then I saw her visibly regain control, rearrange her face into its customary cool expression, and turn to me. "Let's agree to tell one another anything we learn. Frankly, it doesn't sound as if anyone knows much of anything for certain. But let's move on to something we *do* know in the meantime."

She was taking charge now. "Alex, Stone and Stone needs a presence in the UK. We want that presence to be Plumtree Press. We like your size, your diversity, the solidity of your academic base, your bibliophile's book club, your blossoming genius for picking literary winners. In fact, we don't feel we could design a better publishing house ourselves."

Well, thank you very much. Her unintentional condescension was revealing. So in the end, for all her flattery about the positive side of British publishing, she was of the bigger-is-better school. How amazing that a *small* publisher like Plumtree had so much taste! Better than theirs, in fact, I thought—then realised how childish I was being. The antipathy for Americans waltzing in and thinking they could take whatever pleased them with their pots of money ran deep in the British soul; even a half-American British soul. I hated to be patronised.

I didn't say a word. Naturally, she misinterpreted this as a positive sign.

"We would like to leave Plumtree Press intact; keep all the employees, the building, the character of your lists—all of it just as it is. Except we could afford to do more, of course. *More* books of the sort you want. Better publicity, promotion, and distribution."

Now she was speaking as if Stone & Stone had already sucked Plumtree Press into its gaping maw. I was amazed that she had managed to miss any signals I'd given off about the unlikelihood of such an acquisition.

"I hardly know what to say," I said honestly. "Such flattery. . . ."

Sam shook her head. "No. We also have more favourable terms to offer you."

I almost felt I should put her out of her misery; she'd taken seriously the lighthearted quip I'd made at our Cadogan Square lunch about having been offered twice the price. But I didn't; I listened with a carefully impassive face.

With something approaching a flourish, she leaned forward in her slinky dress and said, "Thirty million pounds."

"And . . ." Her father spoke as Sam spun round, surprised at this trespass on her territory. ". . . voting rights on the Stone and Stone board."

Voting rights?!

I saw Sam's jaw drop before she recovered herself and pretended this had been the plan all along. She smiled at me with . . . what was it? *Rapaciousness.*

"I'm astounded," I said truthfully. "I'll need to give this some thought. You're not in any hurry—or are you?"

Sam hesitated. Sam senior shrugged. "No hurry, but it does seem that since we're all here—I don't get over to this side of the pond every week. But then

Sammy can take care of it; she's going to be in charge of our UK publishing, we've decided, instead of starting her own imprint."

In the awkward silence that followed, both seemed offended that I hadn't jumped at their incredibly generous offer. But I wasn't worried about their feelings; it was possible that they were out to destroy me.

I looked at my watch as though to imply worry about overstaying my welcome. Actually, it *was* quite late—past eleven o'clock. "I promise to give it serious thought," I told them, rising. "I should leave you to get some rest. Thank you so much for the lovely dinner and conversation—and of course your offer."

Both graciously saw me to the door, and insisted that their driver had expected all along to take me to my hotel. *No*, I told them, rather forcefully in the end: I would walk.

And how I needed that walk. Lord, what a lot to take in, all in one day. The rumour of all the major English distributors being purchased by one entity . . . the consequences of such a purchase . . . if the distributors were owned by the same publisher, that publisher would have control of which books were available throughout Britain . . . and of course would make only *its* books easily available—on the most favourable of financial terms, one could only presume.

A similar issue had reared its ugly head in America several years ago, when a leading bookshop chain had purchased the nation's largest distributor. Eventually government regulators had got involved and retroactively forbidden the purchase, but it had been a near thing. I remembered reading that it had taken a surprisingly long, tedious court process to reverse the deal once it had been quickly and privately sealed.

On my way to the Frankfurterhof I passed Borsestrasse and the statue of Gutenberg. The Judith/*Beowulf* affair came flooding back—why, I wondered, did these monumental crises never come one at a time? It couldn't be the veracity of the Bible *or* the British publishing industry: it had to be both, in the same week.

Fatigue and the sheer immensity of the issues at hand had dulled my mind by the time I reached the hotel. I was halfway through the seating area near reception when I noticed the tall, dark-haired woman with Sarah's posture and gait. She was just disappearing through the side door. *Always just out of my reach . . .*

This time I was furious. Sarah would never torture me like this; I was confident that the woman was a hired look-alike. And there was a good reason, probably, why I'd never been able to catch a glimpse of her face. I wasn't about to let this woman get away with it again.

Nearly knocking over a dignified older gentleman on his way to the lifts, I dashed after her. She must have heard my footsteps behind her, or my "Sorry!" to the gentleman I'd nearly sent sprawling. By the time I got through the door, she was running—was that Sarah's run?—through the dark side street next to the hotel. The doorman who attended the hotel's taxi rank down that street saw her flight, and decided to tackle me.

"*No!*" I bellowed, grabbing him by the shoulders and pushing him away. No one was going to get in my way this time. "*Freund—ich bin freund des Mädchens!*" I shouted this defence over my shoulder as I took off after the fleeing form in the mackintosh. Fury propelled me. I was catching up to her, but I was still at least a street away. She kept running fast, disappearing round a corner. Determined to keep her in my sight, I pursued her with all the tenacity of the lead hound of hell. Through sheer blind exertion I reduced the space between us to perhaps ten yards, then seven. When I was just five yards away, amazed at her speed and stamina, I heard the tram's bell. I saw her turn, still running, and look at the tram, then back at me—*was it Sarah?*—and saw her decide to try to beat the fast-approaching vehicle.

With horror I saw that she wasn't going to make it. I galvanised the last of the power I had in my legs and sprinted the last two yards. The tram's brakes screeched as I flung myself against her. We slammed into the gravel-strewn ground on the other side of the tramline.

For an instant we were stunned, lying breathless as the tram screamed past, still trying to stop. Then I felt her struggle to move beneath me. She was all right. I smelled Sarah's scent; her shampoo, her perfume. I pulled myself up, braced myself, and forced her to turn over. The shock jolted through me.

It wasn't Sarah's face. This woman's face was wider, plainer . . . less fine in every way. And her eyes were bigger and more closely set; they weren't almond-shaped and didn't tilt upward like Sarah's, either.

She began to whimper. I realised that she must have thought I would hurt her, and as I looked at her I felt myself begin to shake. When I spoke, even my voice shook. "Who—who *are* you? Have you any idea what you've *done*?"

Sobbing miserably, she said nothing. I couldn't help but notice what a remarkable double she was of Sarah, aside from her face. Even her running stride had seemed spot on. For just a moment the insane thought occurred to me that perhaps it *was* Sarah, with a different face . . . but I realised how absurd that was.

"It's all right," I said, embarrassed at how uncontrollably I was shaking. "I'm not going to hurt you. I only want to know who hired you to do this to me."

She turned her head to the side and closed her eyes, either too miserable or too afraid to look at me.

I felt consumed—sick—with frustration and anger. *"Answer me!!"*

The tram had stopped, and the conductor was running over to see what had happened. *"Mein Gott! Mein Gott! Sind Sie verletzt?"*

I got to my feet and tried to appear in command of my faculties. "Okay," I said, still breathing hard, not knowing a better answer in German.

"Englisch? You are okay?"

I nodded. I could feel cool air through the knees of my suit trousers, and was certain both of us *appeared* far from okay. But he wanted to believe. And he had a tram to run.

"Und die Fraulein? Okay?"

I nodded again. The conductor left us, glancing back uncertainly over his shoulder, but in the end the temptation to maintain his schedule won out. I got on my knees and gripped her arm. My questions came in a furious rush. "Who are you and who do you work for? Why were you at Cadogan Square? Why are you *doing this to me*?"

But I couldn't get anything out of her. I couldn't even persuade her to let me escort her back to the hotel taxi rank. I didn't wait for permission to search through her handbag—my second such invasion of privacy that day. But I found no hints of her identity or associations—No passport, no credit cards, no driving licence. In the end I threw the bag down on the gravel, pulled out my mobile, and eventually got through to the taxi firm I'd used earlier. We waited in silence until the car came, at which point she refused to get in with me. Exasperated, I set off on foot and let her take the taxi.

Anger alone gave me the energy to get back to the hotel. The manager eyed me askance as I walked through the elegant lobby in my tattered, filthy clothes to the lift, but I met his stern gaze with insouciance. I got out at Nicola's floor, trudged to her door, and let myself in. She was sitting at the rather ornate desk, pen in hand, wearing pyjamas and robe.

"What happened to you?" she asked instantly, putting down her pen and coming to see.

I collapsed on the sofa. "This is what dinner with the Stones will do to you."

"My God!"

Surprised at my own ability to joke at this point, I let Nicola slip my shoes off and ease my feet onto the cushions. Everything hurt: my head, my knees, my ribs, my heart. "No, actually . . ."

Actually, I was so exhausted that I couldn't even finish the sentence. I was aware of Nicola hurrying off; felt her come back shortly with a warm flannel. Through a fog I felt her wash my face and hands. The last thing I felt was the warmth of a coverlet placed gently over me.

But the last thing I heard was Nicola's muffled voice speaking to someone over the phone . . . I just had time to wonder who she was calling and why before I slipped into oblivion.

●   ●   ●

When I woke, sunlight streamed through the window. In a rush, my aching body reminded me of what had happened the night before: Every joint seemed to creak, every muscle had frozen into unyielding stiffness, every available inch of skin felt torn or bruised.

And on top of it, I felt absolutely wretched about the way everything was going.

Nicola, tiptoeing through the room in one of her sleekly sophisticated black suits, her hair already swept back in what Lisette had once called "The Beauchamp Knot," must have seen me stir.

"How are you today?" she asked gently, perching on the edge of the coffee table. A wave of her complicated perfume washed over me.

Here I thought a blatant lie was in order. "Fine."

"Right," she said, studying my face. "I thought I might need to call for help last night. You still look pretty awful, actually."

"Thanks. I'm afraid I can't say the same for you."

She laughed.

I tried to sit up; it was a disastrous idea.

"Let me get you some aspirins. Breakfast is on its way."

"You're an angel. Thanks, Nicola."

When she returned with a tumbler of water and two pills, she said, "Are you going to tell me what happened to you last night? I have news for you, but only after you tell me." She eyed the shredded knees of my trousers, the dried blood beneath, and the ripped elbows of my suit. Something black was smeared, I also noticed, all down the front of my suit and tie. A shame about the tie . . . Sarah had given it to me last year. Maybe it could be salvaged.

I swallowed the medicine down and gave her a brief

rundown of dinner at the Stones'. I also shared Sam's rumour about the distributors being snatched up.

"Snatched up by whom?!" she exclaimed.

"Haven't the foggiest." Breakfast arrived, and we talked between bites. The coffee went a long way towards making me feel human again.

Nicola again demanded a recounting of the previous night's exploits. I sighed. "Remember the woman you saw in Charing Cross Road who looked exactly like Sarah?"

"How could I forget?"

"Right. Well, I saw her again last night."

Her eyes widened.

"And this time I caught her. It wasn't Sarah. But the similarity was incredible. No wonder I was fooled time and again."

"Who on earth *is* she?! Did she explain?"

"Wouldn't say a word. In the end I just called a taxi for her there by the tramline, where she was curled up in the dark. She wouldn't move. I chased her all the way from the hotel—we must've run nearly a mile, maybe more—at top speed. Then I had to push her out of the way; she would have been run down by the tram, she was so desperate to get away from me. That's how all this happened." I gestured at my torn clothing.

I sipped my coffee. "It's a very strange way to try to get someone to sell a company—*darkly* strange. You know, I even considered that it might have been Sarah for a moment last night, looking at her. But no one's face could change that much."

"Only in films," Nicola agreed, and tackled a slice of ham.

But her comment gave me pause. I remembered a

film from several years before that had—rather disgustingly, at times—shown two men completely changing faces. Aside from making even the nonsqueamish squirm, it had seemed ridiculously unbelievable. Besides, I would know Sarah *anywhere,* altered face or not. There were her eyes, of course, and mannerisms. I laughed at myself for even considering it again . . . all the same, I couldn't get it out of my mind.

"All right." Nicola put down her knife and fork and folded her hands on one knee, looking quite perky. "Now I have some news for you. I took McKinley Montague out for dinner last night . . . a very extravagant one, I might add, but all for the good of Plumtree Press."

I gave her a stern schoolmaster look, but she could tell it was tongue-in-cheek.

"Good. Well. McKinley had far too much Riesling. I'll confess that I was instrumental in plying him with it. We had some Spätlese with the sweet, and a nightcap afterwards here in the hotel bar."

"Mm, you *were* extravagant. You must genuinely enjoy his company."

"Not particularly. He's a bit hung up on himself." She wrinkled her nose. "Massive ego. Anyway." Her eyes sparkled. "Something he said in our meeting yesterday morning came back to me . . . and in view of the unfortunate deal I've got us into, I thought I'd better see what I could do to make it up to you."

"And . . . ?"

"First, I don't quite know how to explain how I let it happen. If anything, I thought getting McKinley Montague in our stable was pretty much worth whatever it took."

I started to make comforting noises, but she shushed me with a raised hand. "I did, however, learn something that might support our anonymous monopoly suspicions. I commented about the clause granting Hanford Banner foreign rights having put the squeeze on us, and he leaned close and said something interesting. 'Lots of new ways Hanford's goin' t' be exerting its influence, Nikki,' " she slurred, doing a decent imitation of an inebriated author. " 'This is just the beginning. 'S'going to be the biggest, most amazing publisher in the world—all the biggest books'll be Hanford's. You wait 'n see.' He all but touched the side of his nose, Alex."

"But why would they have told—ah. Of course. The really outrageous advance-earners get a share of profits, not a royalty."

"Sorry—you've lost me." Nicola put down her knife and fork.

"When someone gets as much as McKinley Montague for a single book, the publishers are concerned that, for whatever reason, they might never get those millions back from sales of the book. Mind you, this has happened only once or twice, and only in America—but the author might agree to take a percentage of the company's entire profit, instead of royalties. That's why Hanford would have reason to share news of their expected profits with Montague."

"I see." She winced. "You'd probably like to see the memo I signed for McKinley's new 'literary' novel."

"Yes, as a matter of fact, I would." I appreciated it that she understood she'd really made a huge mistake, and didn't expect me to tiptoe around that ugly reality. She also hadn't wallowed in self-pity for having committed such an egregious sin; she'd just got on with helping to fix it in any way she could.

I watched her walk away to fetch the copies of the deal memo, then come back again.

"What?" she asked, noticing the way I was looking at her. "Did I drip bacon grease down my front?" She looked down to see.

"No, nothing like that. Sorry, I was miles away." But in actual fact I was thinking—and hated myself for doing it—wouldn't I be the fool of the century if her little slip with Hanford Banner/Wellbrook's over McKinley hadn't been an accident?

CHAPTER 15

Loud loud he laughed . . .
. . . his gross appetite still unslaked.

—BEOWULF

As soon as Nicola had rushed out of the door to her first meeting, I bent over the Montague deal memo with great anxiety . . . and found that my fears were justified. My trade list acquisitions editor had—unwittingly, I hoped—made the deal not with Montague himself, but with Hanford Banner/Wellbrook's. There were two very big problems with this. First, in the attempt to snare Montague for Plumtree Press she had signed away foreign rights to the Montague "literary" masterpiece. And that led to the second problem. She had, in exchange for this opportunity to publish McKinley's probably rubbishy prose, made us essentially co-publishing partners with them.

It was incredible to me that an intelligent woman like Nicola could have signed anything remotely resembling this agreement, but at the same time I understood she'd felt she couldn't let a chance to sign McKinley Montague slip through her fingers. Trevor Gravesend's signature, just beneath McKinley's, his agent's, and Nicola's, was like a slap in my face.

That unethical, two-faced, *supposed* upholder of ethics in the publishing industry . . . the president of the Publishers Association.

I let my head fall forward into my hands. Was all of this worth the angst? Why did I care so much?

The devil of it was that if someone could take over British publishing without anyone realising they had done it, through shadowy holding companies, they'd stand to make several million dump-bins full of cold, hard cash. Even if they were caught by Jones-Harris and his merry band afterwards, and made to spin off their acquisitions, someone would be several billions richer. I remembered reading about the American Ted Turner, who'd netted a cool billion when America Online and Time Warner merged. Turner had sold his empire to Time Warner some time earlier . . . so the mind boggled at what the large shareholders in AOL and Time Warner might have received.

But greed, though probably the prime motivator, was not the whole story. With massive infusions of cash came massive infusions of influence, most notably in the political arena. Politicians *did* need to serve the interests of their constituents, so . . . what the huge firm wanted was what they got. Legislation to order, specifically written to support the monopoly and hurt the independents, all cloaked in benign verbiage or shunted through with a load of other, apparently more important, issues, of course.

And there was yet another grave concern. Always, pulsating beneath the sometimes shabby surface of book publishing, was the awareness of the power in our profession. What we published, the world read. The normal, healthy publishing industry ensured that a wide range of opinions was expressed and considered. Everyone had a chance to advance his point of view, to grind her axe.

But what if all that changed? What if there was one

dominant force in publishing claiming all that power for itself? The dominator's point of view would be forced onto the world's psyche. What's more, though one could argue that small presses are springing up all the time, and people are publishing on-line, *distribution* is the key. What people read is what's printed in the greatest quantities by the huge publishers who can afford to do that, and sent out through the most highly efficient distribution channels. I couldn't forget what Sam Stone told me she'd heard Nate say about Britain's top three distributors—the ones that really mattered— having been acquired.

A monopoly could always beat the others in distribution, even in the E-age . . . and what's to say this monopoly hadn't already snatched up a healthy portion of the Internet? Okay, now I was beginning to sound as paranoid as Nate. But the thought was a horrible one, and it had happened in other industries— with Microsoft, for instance, in America. By the time people started making a fuss about it and getting the legal system involved, it was nearly too late. Much of the viable competition had been either acquired or smothered.

It could happen . . . it *was* happening.

Call me idealistic—or perhaps *Ishmael* would be more appropriate in the circumstances—but yes, okay, it was worth it. I'd soldier on.

Underneath all of this energy and optimism about keeping the world safe for publishing, however, I was keenly aware that the underpinnings of my life were eroding. If Sarah no longer wanted me, all the publishing intrigue in the world, and all the early lectionary readings at Christ Church Chenies in the world, would be a poor excuse for the mutually satisfying life of marriage and

family that I had imagined . . . the opportunity to contribute as much as I received, or perhaps more.

I got into the shower, turned on the hot water, and
stood under it until I felt better. Eventually I even cleaned
my teeth, donned my other suit, and drew out a fresh
tie. Resolutely positive, knowing it was the only way
forward, I ensured that my socks matched, gathered up
my briefcase, and left the hotel for what could only
prove to be an *encounter* with Trevor Gravesend.

And then, crossing the major street called Baselerstrasse, I saw one of those Piccadilly Circus–type signs
that flashed messages in continuously changing patterns of multicoloured lights. There was no mistaking
the message of this one:

> REUTERS.
> THE TRUTH.
> DEAL WITH IT.

Right, Alex, I told myself. Take heed.

It was a good thing I'd seen the sign, because in the
next moment I saw something I might have listed under a heading: *Things I will never see in my lifetime.* A
limousine remarkably like the Stones'—large, black,
Mercedes—purred to a stop at the intersection opposite me, its rear window open to the warm autumn air.
I was forced to wait for traffic to cross, and had plenty
of time to think of what to say should they pull up next
to me. But I needn't have worried; as the car accelerated past me and I stepped forward to cross the street
myself, I saw Sam Stone senior, Henning Kruse, and
Trevor Gravesend all in the car together.

Jones-Harris's suspect three. The three who had
offered obscene amounts of money to buy my little

family publishing company. The three who'd ended up knowing everything *I* knew about what was going on.

This was it; I needed my top gun. I pulled out the mobile and entered Ian's number. It rang more than four times; he was busy or not within reach of his phone. When invited, I left a message. "Ian. It's Alex. I need to talk to you. Ring me back as soon as you can. Please."

It was the most urgent message I'd ever left him. After the way I'd treated him in Cambridge, I hoped he would still answer it.

I flagged down a taxi immediately—thank God for small favours—and had it follow the cross-street the Mercedes limo had taken. But I couldn't see it ahead of us. I craned my neck down each side street, looking for the black behemoth. On the third street, there it was . . . outside a coffee house.

I asked the driver to stop one street away; I didn't want the Stone driver to spot me. Then I sat in the taxi for a moment and thought, listening to the meter tick. At this point, what could I lose by barging in and confronting them?

Nothing.

I paid the driver and climbed out, making a beeline for the coffee house. This establishment was based on the Viennese model of lace tablecloths, low light, quiet, and privacy. Some people, it was rumoured, stayed here all day . . . reading books, writing books, talking about books, or—this being Frankfurt—talking about deutsche marks and dollars. The place actually had a special spot in my memory, because once, several years ago, I'd spent nearly half a day here sketching out a novel. I'd eventually abandoned the project as being too time-intensive, considering my other responsibilities. But I still remembered the joy of it, and the place.

What an absurdity the entire business of publishing was coming to seem. I drew a deep breath before pushing open the door; God only knew what I would find when I was face to face with them.

Little did I expect what happened when I advanced upon their table. "Kruse! Stone! What did I tell you? Plumtree's one of us." Gravesend was on his feet, welcoming me. My new archenemy was now apparently also my champion.

"Alex—we were just talking about you," Stone added jovially. "Here, pull up a chair."

Henning Kruse greeted me with a formal nod.

"I am amazed to find you all here together," I said, ignoring their friendly greetings. Before they could ask, I offered, "Do you know why?"

Stone glanced at Kruse; Gravesend glanced at Stone. Interesting. All remained silent.

Without waiting for their assent, I said, "Each of you offered outrageous sums for my small firm. Each of you is at the head of a quite remarkable empire. And each of you—sorry, we actually never got the chance, Trevor, though you did manage to get my trade editor to sign something—wanted to talk about a giant monopolising the industry. I'm intensely curious about the subject of your meeting."

"Alex, please. Sit down." Henning's eyes drilled into mine. "Please."

I found a chair and sat. The others were staring at me as if I'd become a homicidal maniac, but Henning spoke again, in such a low voice that we were all forced to lean forward to hear. "You might be gratified to know that we are discussing the very thing you are so concerned about: the buyout of the great British publishing industry, perhaps even publishing worldwide."

My laughter began with a snigger, exploded in a bark, then mushroomed into a full-blown attack of silent, rocking hysteria.

They—were—meeting—to—talk—about—*themselves*. It was too much.

"Get him a coffee, why don't you," Gravesend suggested in a worried voice.

"*Noch eine Kaffee, bitte,*" I heard Henning say to the waitress.

But now that I sat there, I saw I'd get nowhere with all of them together. The hilarity I'd felt was rapidly turning to anger, and it didn't take much pretending to stalk angrily out to the street.

I heard the door to the coffee house close again, just as I'd hoped, and Henning's voice came from behind me. "Plumtree, you *must* get hold of yourself. This is no time to lose your composure. Can't you see? We need a power ten now. You must be at your strongest."

When he put it all in terms of rowing—ten full-power strokes—it snapped me right back to reality. There was no time to waste; it was win or lose. Now.

I wiped the tears of laughter from my cheeks and shook my head. "Right. *Right.* Okay. But I need some answers from you."

"Sure. Let's walk."

We met no others coming towards us. "What, exactly, were the three of you talking about in there?"

He glanced back towards the coffee house before answering. "We have all noticed the same phenomenon that you talked to us about. Each of us is highly enough placed in our group to influence the outcome of a major merger, and each of us swears it is not our firm that is trying to take over. We were comparing notes, that's all." He hesitated, but I felt there was more. I waited and was rewarded for my patience. "In the last two days, each of us has received a notice from one of the many firms that orchestrate mergers, stating that efforts are under way to acquire us. Our legal people are going mad trying to work out who is behind it, and it is the same firm behind all of the takeover notices. A name none of us has ever heard."

"What is it?"

"Petrus."

The unknown name at Companies House that was listed as the owner of Wellbrook's . . . and the name of the timeless Malconbury monk. I would have to ring Jones-Harris with Henning's nugget as soon as possible.

"But there is something else you should know, Alex. While I was making enquiries into our other matter, a close friend in Spitze told me about a conference taking place in the countryside just outside Frankfurt tomorrow. If you ask me, what you should really be worrying about, given your interests, is that conference. A group of scholarly publishers is forming a consortium. It's your sort of stuff: antiquities, Orientalia, Middle- and Near-Eastern studies, the Bible. Cantabrigian Press is one of the leading proponents of this."

He stopped and turned to me. "Alex, it's more consolidation; less independent thought on an extremely important subject. And new discoveries are coming to light all the time about ancient texts; I read about your scholar, Hammonds. I know what's bound in with the *Beowulf* epic."

I, too, stopped in my tracks. "I have my beliefs, also," he continued. "I watch these things. It is of great concern to me that our ancient writings are treated with the greatest respect and caution. If someone tries to keep new discoveries from coming to light, I want to know why, and I want to stop them. This consortium would make it too easy for the already small world of religious and other antiquities to be led around by the nose, and led by one influential shaper of opinion. We need more opinions, not fewer—particularly in this area. It is because I admire your scholarly biblical and antiquities publications that I wanted to buy Plumtree Press, though I certainly see now why you don't want to sell. I wouldn't, either, if I were you. Let's just be friends, Alex, and forget the business deal. I think we are worth more to each other this way. Yes?"

All I could manage was a nod.

"Where is this conference?"

"Half an hour south of here, in Worms." With his German pronunciation, it sounded like "Vorms." He looked at me to see if I caught the significance.

"You must be joking. Not *that* Worms . . . ?"

"Exactly."

The Diet of Worms was a 1521 meeting of the imperial emperor, German princes, and noblemen, which had the effect of changing the shape of Christianity, and the use of the Bible, forever. A troublesome monk named Martin Luther had been brought before the Diet, judged a heretic, and thrown into prison—where he had plenty of time to translate the Bible into German, thereby bringing it to the masses. Revisionists later dubbed this event and its consequences the Reformation.

"Events do have their own poetry, don't they?" I said.

"Indeed. I've gradually come to believe these things can't all be put down to coincidence. We should go back. Are you all right now?"

"Fine. But I don't think I'll join you for coffee."

"Yes, I understand. I want you to take my car to Worms, Alex. You might as well; I won't be using it all day." He reached into his wallet for a ticket and handed it to me. "It's in the valet parking at the Messe. Don't worry about when you get it back; I have other transport."

"Thanks, Henning. I'm sorry about—"

He dismissed my apology with a wave. "Please. Leave this other issue to Stone, Gravesend, and me. We are well placed to handle it."

He was right. Who did I think I was, that I could single-handedly root out and slay this beast? They were the powerhouses of the publishing world. If anyone knew what was going on behind the scenes—or could find out—it was they. But—

"Henning, you know that either one of them could be . . . something they pretend not to be. You will be careful . . ."

"Surely you do not think that I am unaware of this, Alex." He gave me the knowing smile an uncle might give his nephew during a discussion about the facts of life. "I, too, was not born yesterday."

We lifted a hand in farewell as I turned back towards the Messe to claim his car. I had confidence in the tall, athletic German. Glancing back at him as he pulled open the door to the coffee house, he looked strong and capable, confident and intelligent. I only hoped he was strong and capable *enough* . . . and had integrity enough.

Such was my faith in him that it wasn't until I was sitting in his sporty blue BMW, working out the route to Worms from the map book in his seat pocket, that doubt began to creep in. What if he—they—merely wanted me out of the way? What if the day in Worms was nothing more than a wild goose chase?

Ian. I'd told him all about the biblical alteration issue; besides, the Plumtree Press books on religious antiquities were his bailiwick. He would surely know about the conference, would know the people involved. I frowned as I recalled, pulling out my mobile, that he'd never rung me back. And I'd made it clear that it was a fairly desperate plea for help. Was he perhaps giving me a taste of my own medicine, since I'd been rather difficult? But it was so unlike him.

This time, I got an answer . . . but it wasn't Ian's voice. "*Guten Tag?* Hello?" a tentative feminine voice answered.

I looked at the number displayed on my phone's tiny screen, thinking I must have pressed a wrong button somewhere. But it was Ian's number—I knew it well. "Er—*guten Tag.* Hello—*auf Englisch bitte?* I'm trying to reach Ian Higginbotham. Have I got the wrong—"

"No, no! We have been hoping someone would ring. There was a young woman here, but she left quite abruptly. Are you a relative of Mr Higginbotham?"

I felt the first tingle of alarm. "Yes—I'm his son." How easily that popped out. "Is something wrong? Where is he?"

"Please don't worry—he is fine. He is here in our hospital. His appendix decided it was time to come out. But he kept it for a quite long time, yes?" The woman chuckled at her own joke, but I didn't find an appendectomy for a seventy-six-year-old—or anyone—amusing. "He'll be able to speak to you shortly. We do like to have a family member help for a few days when our older patients leave. Can you come?"

"Yes, of course. Where is he?"

"Here in Worms, of course . . ."

Worms. It had to be the religious conference; Ian had got on to it before I had. Or perhaps he'd planned long ago to attend, and simply hadn't mentioned it. Still, I found it odd that it had never come up.

"I'll be right there." I got directions from Frankfurt and pressed the accelerator to the floor, thankful for the rule that I'd learned in my one and only year of German: *Es gibt keine Geschwindigkeitsbegrenzung auf der Autobahn.* There is no speed limit on the autobahn. Strictly speaking, it's not true, but in practice . . .

As I drove the growling, overpowered sports car at death-defying speed down the wrong side of the road, I wondered about the young woman the nurse had mentioned. Impossible not to imagine it was Sarah. She was extremely devoted to her grandfather. If somehow she was in touch with him by phone, she could have found out where he was and gone to him. As I drove, I caught up on my phone correspondence. I left a message for Jones-Harris about what Henning had told me about the three takeover bids, then one for Matt Ireland. He deserved to know, too. Finally, I rang Nate, feeling guilty that I hadn't got back to him earlier. He wasn't in hospital, nor in his room at the hotel, so I left a message for him to ring me on the mobile.

I was at the door of the hospital in forty minutes, at the door of Ian's room in four more. When I peered round the door he appeared to be asleep. I went to the chair at the foot of his bed and sat, watching him. Even in hospital, he looked almost ridiculously healthy, as if he were about to bound out of the bed and toss off a round of calisthenics. But I couldn't ignore the fact that this operation might have been very dangerous for him. To lose Ian . . .

Perhaps he sensed me there; he opened his eyes as easily as if he'd been pretending to sleep, and saw me.

"Alex!" His face lit up.

I stood and went to him, smiling to see his look of delight at seeing me. Tears of affection welled up.

"How did you—"

"The wonder of mobile phones. How are you feeling?"

"Much less awful than you might expect. They tell me I'll be out of here the day after tomorrow at the latest."

"That's wonderful. When did all of this happen, Ian?"

"Yesterday. I suppose you're wondering what in heaven's name I'm doing in Worms."

"I am rather curious," I said, deciding to let him tell me in his own words.

"You'd better sit down, Alex. It's going to take a moment." I pulled the chair from the foot of the bed to the head, and sat. "You mustn't think I was trying to hide anything from you, Alex. It's just that you had so much on your plate, between Hammonds and—I say, what *are* you doing here in Germany?"

"Mine's a long story, too." As I tried to think how best to tell him—and whether I should include Jones-Harris in the bargain—I heard a noise behind me at the door. Ian looked just past me and widened his eyes dramatically. There was another small noise, but by the time I turned round to see, the doorway was empty. I hurried to the entry, hardly daring to hope that it might have been Sarah . . . but a strong-looking middle-aged nurse pushing a trolley down the corridor was the only person to be seen.

I told Ian everything, and when I'd finished, he

frowned. "Odd that I hadn't picked up any of this. I believe you, of course—I hate to think it, but perhaps I'm a bit out of touch. Mind you, I might be a bit *overly* perceptive when it comes to this Worms conference, but I think it's absolutely vital that it be stopped. Thank God you're here, Alex. Someone simply must point out to them the dangers of such a consortium. In fact, what would you think of actually *telling* them about what's happened with the changes to Judith, and the letters Botkin's relative exchanged with your ancestor? But I'll warn you: now they've come this far, they want to make it happen. Old Beattie at Cantabrigian has pumped up excitement to the point where they're all desperate to consolidate." He shook his head with something that might have been interpreted as anger, if it hadn't been Ian. "I just don't understand it."

"Perhaps someone has a reason for wanting to railroad this through," I mused. "Have you thought that whoever is behind it might have had something to do with Hammonds's death?"

"Yes, of course—especially if the goal is to suppress further study that might reveal changes to the only remaining ancient sample of the book. Perhaps those changes would reveal other obvious changes, the ones your letter-writer claimed were commissioned by King James."

As our minds raced down that line of thought, I heard my phone's trill. The caller ID displayed Matt Ireland's London business number. "This is Alex—is that you, Matt?"

"Alex!" My old friend's voice was intensity itself. "You'll never believe what I've found. It's not at all what we thought! Not at all. We had the wrong end of the stick. It's not the publishers, it's the—"

An ungodly crash made me instinctively jerk the phone away from my ear.

"Matt? Matt! Are you there?"

I had the impression that someone had heard me speak those words, then calmly disconnected the phone.

"Damn!" First I rang the Met, told them I thought there was a problem at Matt's address. But I also rang Ed Maggs, feeling I couldn't just leave my friend to the police.

Ed was clearly relieved to get a call from me. "Alex! Where the hell are you?"

"Near Frankfurt, Germany. I've been at the Book Fair. But Ed, I think something awful's happened. I hate to ask this of you now, but it's important . . . you remember Matt Ireland, don't you?"

"Of course! Founded the Independent Publishers Association, right?"

"Exactly. I think he's in trouble. We were talking on the phone, and I heard a loud noise—I'm afraid he was attacked. I've rung the police; do you think you might run over to his office in King Street and see if he's all right?"

"Of course. I'll ring your mobile as soon as I get there."

"Thanks, Ed. I appreciate it."

Ian had heard all that I'd said to Ed, but not what Matt had said just before he was cut off. "He said, 'It wasn't the publishers, it was the—'?" We shared a look of deep disquiet. Ian's friends, colleagues, and authors were being taken from him one by one: Nottingham Botkin, Gabriel Hammonds, and now perhaps even Matt Ireland. I could see that Ian and I were probably asking the same question: What did these older gentlemen know that made them so dangerous? And whatever it was, did Ian, for so long a friend and colleague of those men, also know it?

God willing, we'd sort this out before they got him, too.

"Alex, there is one more thing we need to discuss. I've been keeping something from you. Something very important."

I waited. It had to be Sarah.

Ian gripped my hand. "First, please try to understand my position. She made me promise not to tell you, but I can't bear to have you go on like this. And this person . . . this impostor in London . . . it's been so cruel, when Sarah's really alive."

"I finally confronted the impostor last night, Ian. She was running from me again, and I tackled her. It's over now; I don't think she'll try it again."

"I'm talking about the *real* Sarah! Alex, they got her out by pretending she was killed in the American raid. You need to know that—well, things have changed since you last saw her."

I wanted to go to her immediately, of course—as I had ever since Ian told me she was alive. But now I was desperate to see her—and desperately worried about her.

Ian seemed to sense my desperation. "She saw you with Nicola, Alex, a week ago at the Wellbrook's signing for Montague. The—um—changes in her life made her hesitate to come to you in the first place, and when she saw you with Nicola . . . I tried to tell her it was nothing, but it was too much for her just then. She's been in quite a state."

"Where is she now? What kind of changes?"

"Let her approach you, Alex. I think you need to hear it from her. She has—well, she has quite a bit to tell you."

"But if she doesn't want to see me—how could she—" I leapt to my feet and paced around the room, trying to bear the news that the woman who was to have been my wife . . .

"Try to think of *her,* Alex. What she might have been through. I know it's horrid for you, too, but focus on Sarah."

I heard his words, knew he was trying to give me a strategy to cope. But it didn't work. "I've got to get out of here," I choked. I banged through the door, raced down the corridor, and took the stairs down four flights, three at a time. Outside in the golden afternoon, I went round the side of the building, leaned against the warm brick wall of the hospital, and just breathed. Scents of pine and dry grass emanated from the meadow facing me. It was quiet, very quiet, there.

I felt numb. I don't know how long I stood there, but at some point I became aware of a strange and deeply peaceful sensation: Time stood still. Regardless of how Sarah had been changed by her treatment as a hostage, I would—of course—stand by her for the rest of her life. Perhaps she would need me now more than ever . . .

I was more than ready to face her—if she was ready to face me—and to offer her more love than ever before. I climbed the stairs back up to Ian. The sun, low in the sky now, cast a golden shaft of light across the room. "Ian, please. Tell her—if you talk to her—tell her I've a cup of water for her every day of her life."

He knew that we talked of acts of selfless, determined love as "cups of water in the middle of the night," from a book we'd read. In *A Severe Mercy*, the couple were as wildly in love as we were, and had made a beautiful art of being devoted to each other. But the wife had died . . . saving her husband's life, in a way, in the end. This was the first time I'd thought of how nearly the story matched mine and Sarah's . . . until now. Sarah had literally saved my life many times in the past.

"I promise." He smiled back at me, looking weary. "Let me tell you about this conference tomorrow, then. It begins tonight with a dinner, but that's all fluff . . ."

I listened carefully, but every now and then a grin spread across my face. I felt that this latest crisis in the world of books wasn't going to be the end of the world: Sarah was back.

CHAPTER 16

'Beowulf, dearest youth . . .
. . . In the farthest corners
Of the earth your name shall be known. Wherever
the ocean
Laps the windy shore and the wave-worn headland,
Your praise shall be sung.'

—BEOWULF

I spent the night in Ian's hospital room. It wasn't entirely unselfish, though of course I did want to be with him. But I also wanted to be there if Sarah returned. In retrospect I knew that the little noise at the door, when Ian's eyes had widened but no one had come in, had been Sarah.

She was here; I knew it. I would wait.

I did battle with my mobile in the hallway during the evening while Ian dozed. The news from London was most disturbing: When Ed got to King Street, he found the ambulance men packing Matt Ireland off to hospital, evidently unconscious after a nasty blow to the head. The police, Ed reported, had been most interested in exactly who *he*, Ed, was and why he was there. They also wanted to talk to me. Ed said, "I don't like this, you know, Plumtree. Botkin, your scholar, and now Matt . . . At least Matt has a chance of pulling through."

I rang Jones-Harris with another progress report. He was puzzled to hear that I was in Worms. *"Where?"*

he'd asked, dripping irony. His surprise was due not so much to fear that I'd deserted my mission in Frankfurt as to the fact that he'd never outgrown the remarkable provinciality of the truly aristocratic. I explained what was happening at Worms, with as little supporting information about Judith and *Beowulf* and Hammonds as I could get away with.

"Good heavens," he said. "One major cultural-industrial crisis is not enough, eh?"

"But things are progressing nicely back in Frankfurt . . . ," at which point we backtracked to the message I'd left him the day before about the Big Three having themselves been under assault by corporate marauders. If they could be believed, that is. I backtracked still further to tell him about dinner with the Stones and their outrageous offer.

"*Voting rights!*" he exclaimed. "Maybe you're a fool not to—"

"Very funny." I also explained that we had a real ally in Kruse, and that I would not have left the Fair had I not thought so.

When I told Jones-Harris about the assault on Matt Ireland, and the breakthrough he'd been trying to share with me when he was bashed over the head, my friend astounded me by saying, "Good, good."

"Jones-Harris!" I reprimanded him, shocked. "The man nearly gave up the ghost, and you mumble, 'Good'?"

"Sorry, sorry. I only mean that it tells us Ireland was on the right track. Of course I'm awfully sorry for the old fellow. Stay in touch with the hospital, won't you? The minute he's conscious I want you to find out what he was trying to tell you."

Finally, I told Jones-Harris about Nicola's dinner with McKinley Montague, and his prediction about

Hanford Banner being the biggest, best, most dominant, et cetera, et cetera.

"Most intriguing," he said.

"Yes, isn't it." I told him I'd be back from Worms by tomorrow evening to pursue things with Kruse and the others. Generally there was big news by the Friday of the Frankfurt Fair; that was today. If there were earthshaking deals, they were nearly always made before Sunday.

During the night, I woke frequently. A jealous and protective fiancé's imagination devises horrible things in the wee hours. What had happened to Sarah during her captivity? Were the "changes" Ian had mentioned physical, or worse? Something about the way Ian had said it hinted at the latter.

Early in the morning I said good-bye to Ian and set off for the castle where the religious scholarly publishers' meeting was to be held. Ian had a bona fide invitation to the meeting; I took it with me as his replacement.

Kastell Treu sat at the edge of the town of Worms. One of the stone masterpieces of perhaps the twelfth or thirteenth century, it was breathtaking in its massive grandeur and simplicity. I couldn't help but wonder if perhaps it was in that very castle, nearly five hundred years ago, that people had met to discuss even more crucial matters of faith.

As I rolled through the wooded parkland that preceded the castle for perhaps a mile, I was bathed in the golden glow of millions of amber leaves. It was a gorgeous site for industrial intrigue, I thought cynically, as well as for the seventeenth annual conference of the catchily named Society of Publishers of Near- and

Middle-Eastern Studies, Antiquities, Orientalia, and Judeo-Christian Scholarship.

I parked and made my way to the well-marked registration area. As I presented Ian's membership and registration papers to the secretary, I peered into the room where proceedings had already begun. I knew perhaps half of the three dozen attendees; many had been to Plumtree Press or even the Orchard over the years. I certainly recognised the speaker. Vladimir Beattie was president of the Society and second only to God at Cantabrigian Press, one of England's oldest and most prestigious publishers. He was already droning on in his pompous monotone, so I quietly took my conference packet from the secretary and went to sit at the back.

Beattie had not been especially blessed in the looks department, and I always wondered if that was what made him so defensive. A slender, yet large-boned, man of perhaps fifty-five with abysmal posture, he uncannily resembled a vulture. To my knowledge, no one had ever seen him without greasy hair, dandruff, and a stained tie.

Beattie stuttered a bit over his speech when he saw me. I couldn't think why, unless he still resented Ian's having taken an author he'd wanted for his biblical scholarship line two years ago. The sad fact was, big, prestigious scholarly publishers sometimes got lazy—and increasingly profit-oriented. Little guys like us could sometimes dash in and snatch some very large crumbs from beneath their tables. I supposed that Plumtree Press was a bit of a thorn in Beattie's side.

". . . and so today we meet to perhaps change for the better our long and rich tradition of furthering human knowledge. As you know from the communications of our Society, the board has decided this year to propose a joining of our resources, a much closer cooperation than in the past. Through joint publication of our titles, we can publish more books and monographs, more collections of conference papers, in a coordinated and financially beneficial fashion."

He went on to explain the details of this copublishing consortium, but all I could think about was the single filter all the publications would have to go through. It would utterly change scholarship in the Society's domain by preventing alternate views from being published by the English press. The only hope for dissenting views on such issues as the Dead Sea Scrolls, the significance of new archaeological findings, et cetera, would come from other countries—thereby eliminating England's premier position in scholarship of antiquities and Orientalia, including the Bible.

As I considered his proposition, a creeping, sinking feeling came over me. Who ultimately owned the seven major presses represented there today? There were, of course, a number of smaller presses that as far as I knew were still independently owned. But the largest ones were almost certainly part of a collection of firms owned by one of the big boys. Who was behind this? Why?

Beattie was still presenting a very one-sided view of the advantages of such a consortium when I jumped to my feet. "Sorry—excuse me—may I?" The entire assemblage rotated in their seats to see who had spoken.

"Mr Plumtree?" Beattie asked, his tone indicating that this was highly irregular. "If you would be so kind as to wait for the discussion following—"

"Dr Beattie, ordinarily I would, but it seems to me that this discussion has already been more than a little one-sided. So I would like to point out the other side—the one you have neglected to present." I addressed the group at large. "I'm here not only for myself, but for Ian Higginbotham. He sends his regrets, by the way, but his appendix wasn't able to make it to the meeting." A hum erupted, sprinkled with chuckles. "Ian and I want to tell you about a recent occurrence in the world of biblical scholarship. I think you'll find, Dr Beattie—ladies and gentlemen—that it has quite a bit of relevance to this idea of a consortium . . ."

As I unravelled the yarn about recently discovered letters having exposed King James's alterations to Judith and the rest of the King James Version, and the very distinct possibility that Gabriel Hammonds had been murdered to prevent such discoveries, Beattie flushed as noticeably as the others paled.

"But it's *impossible* that such things could have escaped discovery—" he broke in.

"New information—even new Gospels—are coming to light all the time," I persisted. A scattering of the audience nodded. "I have a copy of one in my collection, published by the British Library. And you remember the scroll found quite recently under St James's Palace, when the renovations were being made. What if someone wanted to prevent, for whatever reason, one of these new bits of history coming to light? We've just seen that it can happen. In the seventeenth century it was King James; who would it be today? I propose not only that the seven major publishers of religious scholarship in this country continue to work independently; I invite you to step forward in the name of ethical,

responsible scholarship and demand that Cotton Vitellius A.fifteen be removed from the British Library
gallery for ultraviolet study!"

The group burst into a dozen animated private conversations. Beattie looked completely stunned by the
direction his meeting had taken. I sat, regretting ever
so slightly that I'd thrown such a sizeable spanner into
The Vulture's conference, but considerably relieved. At
least perhaps *this* crisis could be held at bay for the
moment . . . though I wondered if it didn't have something to do with the larger crisis of general monopoly.

Beattie was, clearly, extremely irritated by my inter-
ruption. "Mr Plumtree, I would suggest in future that
you and Mr Higginbotham approach the committee
with items for the agenda well in advance, as the rest of
your fellows have done. This is hardly the time or place
for such a radical departure. Moreover, I hardly feel you
are qualified to call for Cotton Vitellius A.fifteen to be
removed from safekeeping at the British Library.

"But more important, I would like to speak to the issue you have raised of cooperation in the scholarly publishing community. I wonder if you realise how many
more books could be undertaken if we consolidated the
relatively similar projects we all produce separately. *More*
new discoveries could be addressed, not fewer. The absurd insinuation that somehow secrets might be kept—
and what sort of secrets I can't imagine—is not only
absurd, but—well, *unintelligent.*"

A stocky, goateed man in the row in front of me
stood. "Isn't it true, though, that you would head the
committee, Vladimir? I think we should talk about the
means of dissent . . ."

Beattie spoke imperiously—and far too loudly—
into his microphone. "This conference is disintegrating

into a free-for-all, ladies and gentlemen. I call for a fifteen-minute recess, after which we will present the proposal for a consortium and discuss it in an orderly fashion. *As planned*." He glared at me. "We will reconvene at ten o'clock."

I was immediately surrounded by friends of Ian's wishing him well, and by publishers who said they agreed with me and weren't quite certain how the consortium idea had come to dominate this meeting. Six months ago it had been a puff of smoke on the horizon, but Beattie had fanned it into a forest fire.

The most intriguing bit of information came from a man who drew close and spoke quietly, his lips almost brushing my ear. "Were you aware that the various publishers involved in this agreement were offered incentives if they would support it?"

"Fascinating," I said. "What sort of incentives?"

"Financial. I took an informal poll, and was most disturbed by the results: most of us were offered larger amounts for the books we copublish with the big presses if we voted for the consortium. But for those who don't copublish, an outright payment was promised—if they voted in favour of the consortium. It was presented as savings from the consolidation of their efforts, of course . . . but there's no denying that it was money promised in exchange for a vote."

Just as that suspicious gentleman finished, the cluster of concerned scholarly publishers parted like the Red Sea to make way for the dreaded Beattie, who was fast approaching.

"I'd like a word with you, Plumtree. In private."

He stalked off, expecting me to follow. It escaped no one's notice that his was an edict, not an invitation.

"Er—excuse me," I said lightheartedly to the others,

and went after him. They smiled after me; Beattie had already lost.

We'd barely made it to the small anteroom of the Kastell Treu when Beattie exploded. "Good God, Plumtree, but you're a loose cannon. Couldn't you have found a way to present your point of view without making me look like a—a *criminal*? I'm stunned that you would stoop this low to enhance the visibility of your own publishing company."

I replied calmly, "I think we both know that's not why I'm here."

He snorted sarcastically. "You've no idea what you're up against. Let me give you a word of advice: Stay out."

"You're not threatening me, are you, Dr Beattie?"

"No, Mr Plumtree—" He spat my name like an insult. "I can't threaten you. But there's no telling what sort of mess you might find yourself in if you carry on like this."

His words could be taken in any number of ways, from political advice to physical threat. No one could threaten me any more than I already had been, so I listened . . . but couldn't let it stop me.

"Thank you, Beattie. Very kind of you to warn me."

The battle raged all day, as Beattie and several henchmen fought with fevered brow—the stakes were extremely high for them, obviously—to staunch the flow of blood from their doomed scheme. I almost felt sorry for the old Vulture; in the end, the only people to vote in favour of the consortium were those who would otherwise have lost their jobs, plus several obsequious hangers-on of Beattie's (God help them). Moreover, several publishers had contacts with people in high places in the universities who could see that Cotton Vitellius A.xv was brought out for further study.

The main meeting room of the Kastell Treu was, at the end of the day, strewn with what remained of the battered and beaten losing party.

As I walked out into the late afternoon sun, I half expected Beattie and his cohorts to hurry up to the ramparts and tip cauldrons of boiling oil onto me. As soon as I was clear of the castle keep, I rang Ian, eager to tell him of our victory over the forces of darkness. No answer. Perhaps he was walking about a bit as he regained his strength. I drove on, knowing I'd speak to him soon enough.

But when Henning's BMW had purred safely into the hospital car park and I'd pounded up the steps to share our triumph, I found Ian's room eerily deserted. Before panicking, I forced myself to look round the floor. No Ian. I stepped over to the nurses' station and asked in halting German where he was.

"He is in his room," the nurse replied in perfect English, looking perplexed. She came with me to see for herself, only to stare wide-eyed at the intravenous tubes hanging unattached.

Then I panicked. "Listen," I said. "There are some very unscrupulous business people about—it's all to do with the Frankfurt Book Fair."

She nodded; Worms was well within range for housing Fair attendees. She knew what I meant.

"I'm concerned that they've done something with him. Please—call your police, tell them there's been an abduction from the hospital." Then, thinking of poor Matt Ireland, I added, "These people are highly dangerous, extremely violent. Tell the authorities they'll have to be careful."

She ran from the room without another word to get help. As she did, I saw a small white square of paper folded and placed above the door moulding. My heart missed a beat; this was another of Sarah's and my secrets. When she'd wanted to leave a note for me that she didn't want others to read—either in her London flat or in my home when my brother had also lived there—she would sometimes tuck it up above the door, where I alone would see it because of my height.

I hurried over and snatched it down, my fingers fumbling in their rush to unfold it. The scrap was so small that in my excitement I lost hold of it. The tiny white square fluttered to the floor. I knelt and picked up the paper.

Sarah's handwriting. Her script, her graceful, Sarah-like looping together of letters, had obviously been scrawled in a very great hurry. The letters slanted forward in a rush, nearly falling over one another with haste.

Alex—don't follow—all OK—I've got him. Talk soon, Sarah
P.S. You're needed in Frankfurt.

I stared at the note for several seconds, torn between utter relief and incredulity that this tiny, cold scrap of nothing should be proof of Sarah's—*Sarah's!*—return.

Wasn't it all too typical of our lives that Sarah's return should be overshadowed by the latest crisis in the world of books?

Now I knew beyond a doubt that she was alive and in this part of the world.

Reading between the lines, I thought that Sarah had perhaps been with Ian when they became aware of a threat. She'd taken him off to safety—somehow. Somewhere. Where could she have been waiting? Had she been watching until I left?

I groaned aloud, my stiff upper lip failing me in this endless torture of delayed gratification. Was this *fair*? Would my life ever be *normal*? When would it all be over?

I went to the nurses' station and told her Ian had gone with a friend after all. I left my name and number, just in case.

"Henning," I spoke into the hated phone again, flying down the motorway back to Frankfurt. "You were right about the Society consortium. Vladimir Beattie wanted to rip my heart out, but I forestalled his scheme for now. I couldn't help but wonder, though, who ultimately owns them all. I've a bad feeling about it . . ."

"Exactly what I want to tell you, Alex. Trevor Gravesend's just asked to see us in his German affiliate's stand. You know, Dreessen. Gravesend claims to have important news for us. Can you meet us there?"

Back at the Frankfurt Messe valet parking, I was disturbed to see a man in the glass parking booth pick up a phone as soon as I'd driven up. I wouldn't have assumed he was talking about me except that he was watching me, still speaking into the phone as I walked away.

Someone might be waiting for me, then . . .

I picked up my pace. As soon as I'd rounded the corner and was out of his sight, I broke into a run. I ran back towards the rear of the temporary metal buildings put up to accommodate the Fair. The security guard who'd seen me with the Stones might remember me and let me through. I paused once I'd made it round the rear corner, huffing a bit, but saw a cluster of uniformed security personnel there. One caught a glimpse of me and pointed; they started purposefully in my direction.

Complaining under my breath at this profusion of pursuers, I was incredibly fortunate to catch a taxi. *"Schnell, bitte—fahren Sie irgendwo hin!"* Anywhere. Fast. I had the poor man drive round Frankfurt until there was not the ghost of a chance that anyone had followed us. As I passed Nate's hotel, wondering how the poor man was getting on and promising myself to find him after this meeting, I decided to resort to a very simple plan. Perhaps if I had the driver pull up to the front entrance of the Fair, and lost myself in a crowd of Nordic giants long enough to get inside, I could reach Dreessen's stand unnoticed and unpursued.

Near the Perpetual Hammerer, I attached myself to a laughing cluster of Dutch men who were tall enough to camouflage me. Once in the front door, it was easy as *ebelskiver* to slide in to the heart of the Fair unnoticed and find the Dreessen booth. I asked for Trevor Gravesend at the stand's reception area, and was shown into a conference room much like Spitze's. The secretary closed the door behind me.

"Alex." I was greeted by the worried faces of Henning, Gravesend, Stone, and a man I didn't know. I assumed this was Gravesend's associate at Dreessen. Trevor stood and invited me to sit in a chair at the end of the table. "Georg Dreessen, Alex Plumtree."

Dreessen nodded a greeting, frowned, and spoke. "Mr Plumtree, I have just told your colleagues some very disturbing news. Trevor confided in me about your suspicions of an attempt at monopoly in British publishing. I'm afraid that upon looking into the records of various European firms, I have found that this problem exists throughout the West." He paused to let this sink in. "Just yesterday, I had my managing director check the public ownership records of the major firms in Europe. Not one, not two, but *every last one* of them had changed the name under which it is registered."

"That's what I found in England," I said. "Were these names unrecognisable companies, their addresses post office boxes?"

He nodded. "Very cleverly done."

Frighteningly so, I thought. "Hang on. Have the names of *your* companies changed?"

"Yes," Henning answered, bouncing the rubber of his pencil against the conference table again. "We have our legal people working on it right now. We have no idea how this has happened. I have approved no such change."

I wanted to say, *But this could be a clever ruse . . .*

Don't let on, I cautioned myself. *Pretend you believe they're pure as the driven snow.* "But who could make all this happen? How would any one company be able to ensure the silence of the entire European publishing industry?"

Gravesend pursed his lips. "Remember there are perhaps a dozen major players at most in Europe. These are the ones that matter—who have entire stables of smaller firms belonging to them. We've each sent our most trusted people to meet, with appointments made by us, with the managing directors of each of these firms."

"Excuse me." Sam Stone the Younger appeared at the door of the conference room.

"Come in, Sam, come in," her father said. It was

hardly surprising that he'd chosen his own daughter to gather the information for him.

She stepped inside and closed the door behind her. I stood to give her my chair, but she shook her head and gave me a subdued little smile before addressing the group. "In the case of Turnbaugh and Pickering, it was their banker who recommended *and executed* a change of name only; not of actual ownership. Something to do with a new European Union law. Or so they say." She narrowed her eyes at this last, effectively communicating that she didn't necessarily believe them. "They seemed quite affronted to be asked."

"Sounds believable enough," her father said. "But why all at the *same time*? It's almost as if the bankers' efforts are coordinated." Sam Stone senior sounded truly baffled. If he wasn't innocent, he was a superb actor.

"I think we are obliged to get the European Union trade authorities involved now," Henning said. "This is serious. We cannot possibly deal with it ourselves. Shall I contact Brussels?"

Heads nodded all round the table. "Whatever has happened, and *however* it happened, it did happen by the Friday of the Frankfurt Fair," Sam junior said quietly.

She was right. The scheme had succeeded. I stood first, keenly aware of the need to ring Jones-Harris, and the group followed suit. Everyone was much subdued.

"Let's stay in touch," Gravesend said as we drifted towards the door. "It might be a good idea if we didn't broadcast what we've learned. For a number of reasons."

I saw the wisdom of this. Not only might we create a panic in the publishing and business worlds, but someone might act to silence the broadcasters. Sam stayed behind to confer with her father as I left the stand. It was nearly half past six; it occurred to me that my own stand would be a logical place to take refuge from all the people who seemed to be so eager to find me. But if it seemed logical to me to hide there, it would seem logical to them to look there.

Sighing, I travelled instead in a crowded vein of tired, slow-moving Frankfurt survivors (by the end of the third day, the Fair always began to take its toll) towards the front exit. I waited for a taxi in a clump of American journalists, and reflected that it was just as well the room at the Frankfurterhof was registered in Nicola's name, otherwise I wouldn't be able to take refuge there, either. By the time my turn for a taxi had come, however, my thoughts had turned to Nate again. I desperately needed to talk to him. True, it was a long shot that I'd find him at his hotel instead of a bar; aside from the publicity warriors tripping all over themselves trying to befriend journalists, Nate was obviously afraid for his life.

I asked the taxi driver to take me to Nate's hotel. On the way I rang the hospital treating Matt Ireland. He was still unconscious. My heart went out to him; I only hoped that Ian and Sarah were all right.

I then rang Jones-Harris to tell him what had happened at the meeting with Dreessen—he said he'd raise the issue with his superiors, who could take it through to Brussels—and also told him about Matt.

At Nate's hotel, I asked the front desk to ring his room. No answer. "We have a large number of messages for him. He is—perhaps—staying somewhere else?" I hoped he'd recovered from his dangerous episode of overindulgence. From a hotel phone, I called the hospital to which they'd taken him to make sure he hadn't returned. He hadn't, they assured me. So where on earth was he?

The terrible thought occurred to me that he might be lying ill in his room, unable to ask for help. His dire state the last time I'd seen him made this seem entirely possible.

I returned to the desk. "Now that I think of it, I'm a bit worried about my friend. It isn't at all like him to leave so many messages unanswered. Do you think we might check in his room?"

"Of course." The very soul of professionalism, the desk clerk rang for someone to take me up. "I do hope everything is all right, sir."

The bellboy and I discovered only a perfectly orderly, uninhabited room. But I saw one very strange thing: Nate's notebook, which I'd wanted to find so desperately on my last visit, now lay utterly exposed on the table next to his bed.

I'll be the first to admit that my imagination is on the overactive side, but my image of what might have prompted Nate to leave his notebook behind was a grim one indeed.

"Well, it looks as though everything is all right after all. I'll just write him a note, in case he comes back."

The bellboy shrugged his approval and went to the window for a look outside.

I scrawled on the hotel notepad, *"I've taken your book. A bookshop owner."* I could only hope he'd make the connection with Botkin's. I slid the notebook into my pocket.

"Thanks very much," I said, and the bellboy turned away from the window. I slid him a tip for his trouble and retired to the Frankfurterhof with my prize. Nicola was not in the room. I sank onto the sofa, grateful for a safe, quiet place. After a moment I took off my shoes, went to the minibar and poured myself a whisky that cost the equivalent of seven and a half pounds, then opened a five-quid packet of peanuts to go with it.

Then, propping my feet up on the coffee table opposite the sofa, I opened the notebook and groaned aloud.

Code. Nathan had written the whole damned thing in code. Paranoia was one thing, but Nate's case had advanced far beyond that. But I knew him, knew what was important to him. Surely I could work it out.

I applied myself to the task, first studying the sort of notes he'd made. Snippets of crowded lettering, two lines long at most, made up the bulk of the entries. He always left one blank line between one chunk of lettering and the next. The letters looked like a cross between Russian and Czechoslovakian, not that I knew either of those languages.

Two hours, another whisky, and two packets of crisps later, I was at my wits' end. None of the tried-and-true schoolboy methods of code-breaking worked: not the *E*-as-the-most-frequent-letter ploy; not even trying each different letter of the alphabet as *A*. In frustration, I threw my head back and said to Nate in absentia, "This is as bad as your *Star Trek* language."

At that I sat up straight. His *Star Trek* language! I couldn't remember what he called it, but he'd attended all of the sci-fi and *Star Trek*–specific conferences for years. It was his first and truest love. He'd told me that an entire language had been developed based on the words used in *Star Trek* episodes, and once he'd even taken two weeks of his holiday to travel to America for an intensive language camp to learn the entire thing.

I searched for my mobile and rang Ed Maggs at

home. It was only half past six in England—half past eight here—but on Saturdays he frequently stayed at home.

His gruff voice answered with an abrupt "Hello."

"Ed! Alex here. Is Ben home?"

"Er, yeah. May I ask why?"

"I need his expertise to save the world."

"Have you been drinking?"

I laughed. "Well, yes—a bit. Seriously, Ed, I need his knowledge of that *Star Trek* language. Doesn't he even have a lexicon for it?"

"Yes. I'm sorry to say he does. Klingon, it's called. Why don't you let *me* help you with it—he's playing Harry Potter with an overnight friend. Besides, I don't want him to start speaking in that horrific language again."

We started through the notebook in reverse order. I assumed any discoveries Nate had made about recent events would be towards the rear. I learned a lot in a hurry, including that *"much"* meant "publisher" in Klingon, and that one of the most noteworthy publishers in Britain was having an affair with one of the most noteworthy politicians in London. Most of Nate's notes had more to do with peoples' private foibles than with the book business. No doubt he knew they'd make him more money in the end.

It was slow going. "Conspiracy?"

"QuS."

"Bookseller?"

"Paq ngev."

But we struck gold short of one page into the notebook. It was very like Nate not to have called particular attention to the earthshaking entry with exclamation marks, stars, underlining, capital letters, or anything so obvious. As a result I didn't realise I was looking at the Main Event until we'd translated the whole nine-word sentence:

It is not the publishers, it is the booksellers.

"That's it, Ed," I said, drawing a deep breath. "That's exactly what Matt Ireland started to tell me when he was cracked over the head."

"Holy bloody hell," he replied.

As indeed it proved to be.

CHAPTER 17

Straightway Beowulf stripped off his armour, his
  mailcoat,
His shining helmet. His shield and precious sword
Gave he to his servant, and . . .
Lay down to rest. But spent as they were—
For tumult of Grendel and his havoc, like runaway hooves
Making riot in their brains—they could not sleep.
Under their fleeces in terror they sweated and trembled
Wide-awake, till at last, outworn with weariness,
Heavy-lidded they slept—all but Beowulf.
Alone, he watched.

—BEOWULF

Ed and I gleaned nothing more of significance from Nate's notebook, even after three hours on the phone, aside from the most remarkable—and scandalous—notes about people and their private behaviour. I'd hoped for a few notes on the Montague publicity trick: who'd hired Nate to ring me and lie about Montague's death and Trevor's involvement in it (and *why*); who shot at us the night of the signing. But there was nothing.

Of one thing I was certain, as I stared at the lights of Frankfurt through the hotel room window. We had failed; the Euromerger was a fait accompli.

What more could I hope to achieve in Germany? I wrote a note to Nicola, stuffed everything into my bag—including Nate's notebook—and took a taxi to the airport. In London, I could find out what Nate and Matt meant about the booksellers. Companies House would be closed for the weekend, of course, but I did know the booksellers in London. They would help me. Sabera would be my first visit in the morning, and many booksellers were open on Sunday.

Because it was a Saturday night, once I reached the airport, the flights home were jam-packed. There was space on the last flight of the evening at eleven-twenty, the ticket agent told me, but I could stand by for an earlier flight if I liked. I found an out-of-the-way corner and rang Jones-Harris again to tell him about Nate's notebook. Of course at that hour I reached his answering machine; he had a life.

I also tried Sabera's home number, but received no answer. I left a message that I hoped we could have a chat in the morning, but didn't dare leave more than that on the tape.

No space opened up on the earlier flights. As I waited to hear my name called, through first ten o'clock and then eleven, I did my best to separate the jumble of bizarre events into some sort of order.

First, there was the issue of the strange woman masquerading as Sarah. Did the impostor have something to do with breaking me down enough to sell the Press, or was she some psychopath torturing me for sport? And why had the impostor disappeared into the Stones' house? It didn't make sense, because Sam appeared to have designs on me. Why would it be to her advantage to have me go mental?

Second, were the separate events of violence of this week related? Was Hammonds killed by the same person who murdered Nottingham Botkin and attacked

Matt Ireland? And if so, did that mean that Matt Ireland had something to do with hiding the changes that had been made to Judith, and/or *Beowulf*?

I couldn't imagine.

My brain hurt—not just from hard rights to the jaw, car accidents, and plunges across tramlines. Here was yet another possibility, which I preferred to ignore but couldn't. Did the changes made to Cotton Vitellius A.xv have anything at all to do with the plot to have all the publishers owned by one mega-firm?

Surely not.

I buried my head in my hands.

The last flight out of Frankfurt did have a seat with my name on it. I staggered in to Ed's basement at half past one in the morning, very grateful for his bed. Along the way, I'd noted that Her Majesty's government did not provide the same prompt airport service on the way *in to* Britain, after the job, as it had on the way out. How I did long to live out the James Bond experience, which would have Sarah and me happily lounging somewhere when Jones-Harris rang to enquire about the outcome of the mission. We would ignore him and roll over in our bubble in the ocean, or private jet, or . . . but then, James Bond never failed.

I might have slept at Ed's safely, had I been able, and that was what really mattered.

By four o'clock, I was exhausted from twisting and turning alone. How to *not* imagine a reunion with Sarah . . . Would she be all right? How had she changed? What would she say? What would she do? How would she look?

·   ·   ·

When I woke, I'd received a blessed reprieve. It was ten A.M. True, I'd missed the early bird's jump on the day. But I was rested, and things never looked quite so bleak after a bit of sleep.

Sarah was alive! What else could possibly matter?

I stepped into the shower feeling quite cheerful, but as the hot water rained down, reality came home to roost. Sarah had not yet got in touch with me. The English—sorry, *European*—publishing industry was in a "parlous state." But what a joke: The publishing industry was, always had been, and always would be in a parlous state. It was the nature of the beast, the beast I loved so well. Second to Sarah, of course.

I went to the phone and rang Sabera again; his answering machine greeted me.

I left my name and number again, but considering the message of the night before, I was well aware that unless my friend was out of town, he was avoiding me. Although Sabera had been my first choice, I had other friends in the bookselling world . . . but would they know about the Machiavellian machinations at the pinnacle of their industry?

I stopped to indulge in a coffee at the caffeine brothel and gave myself a moment to consider. The colourful characters I knew from the book world of old were not the ones calling the shots now. I hated like Hades to do it, but I would have to go to the very top. I knew that the head of Wellbrook's would see me— we moved in the same circles, and he'd suggested me for the Thatcher and Northrup events of National Book Week. But publishers and booksellers kept a certain healthy distance; our relationship was a curious one. Utterly dependent on one another, we pretended a cavalier disregard when it came to business matters.

And then there were always historical resentments: So-and-so failed to get us shipments on time three months in a row, or so-and-so didn't display a book in the proper section nationwide, sentencing a book that could have made the lists to remainders hell.

Still, there was no getting round the fact that we were in the same business; after all, publishers and booksellers had been one and the same as recently as two hundred years ago. I did hate to use up my reserves of goodwill, as it were, with the top few bookselling industry magnates. But I also hated to see the business of books take a turn for the worse.

Tom Wellbrook, David Greenberg, and Max Young were the men I needed to see. As I finished my coffee and pulled out my phone to ring Tom first, it struck me that once again, this industry's future came down to just three individuals. But before I could enter Tom Wellbrook's number, the miserable thing rang.

I pressed *talk.* "Alex Plumtree."

"Alex. Sabera here. I have much to tell you. In confidence. Can we meet to talk?"

"Of course. Where are you?"

"In Piccadilly, just half a street from the store. But things have got complicated, Alex. It would be best if we met somewhere else."

"All right . . ." I nearly suggested the Maggs basement, but at the last moment decided it would be safer if even Sabera didn't know where I was staying. "How about Green Park, then?"

"Excellent. Near the tube station entrance."

I trotted over and as I approached saw Sabera giving a superb imitation of carrying the weight of the world on his shoulders. When he saw me he brightened and came to meet me. "I am very sorry, my friend; I have bad news for you. But I think it is better that you know."

We turned down the path into the park. "Thank you, Sabera. I've always appreciated your honesty."

"And I have appreciated all you've done for me. This is the least I can do." He took a deep breath. "Alex, the first thing I must tell you is that—I am Bookworm."

I stopped and flashed him an amused smile. Bookworm was the columnist who wrote the half-gossip, half-hold-industry-figures-responsible-for-their-actions page at the back of the *Bookseller* each week. His caustic wit had brought more than one eminent book figure to his or her knees.

He gave me a sad, half-apologetic little shrug.

"People assume that a quiet foreigner could not possibly be such a busybody, have such contacts. But partly because of you, Alex, it has happened. People seem to confide in me—perhaps because they think it won't matter if they tell me. Who would I tell?"

He glanced round the park and then lowered his eyes again to the footpath ahead. "Alex, I was walking in Covent Garden yesterday, and saw Tom Wellbrook and David Greenberg just leaving Terra, where they'd obviously had lunch. It was Tom who hired me to be manager of the Piccadilly flagship, as you well know. He asked to walk me back to the store. He warned me that more changes were coming. What sort? I asked him, but he shook his head.

" 'Can't say just yet, old boy. But this makes all the rest of it look like child's play. You'll be close to the very top of this business, my friend, with one hell of a lot of power to say what's published and what's not. The way it *should* be. Who knows better than we booksellers what'll move, eh? For heaven's sake, though, don't breathe a word to your old friend Plumtree. Evidently he's got wind of it somehow and plans to put the brakes on us all. You know that I'm fond of Alex, but we can't have him getting in the way at this point.' "

Sabera looked at me for a reaction, and when I didn't respond, continued. " 'Can you tell me anything at all?' I asked Tom. He smiled at me as if he were about to *give* me the Piccadilly store. 'Let's put it this way, Sabera. Imagine if the whole industry were turned upside down—or inside out. You're in for the ride of your life—strap in and hang on.' Then, very smug, he looked at his watch and said he had to get on. And then he winked."

Again Sabera glanced at me to gauge my reaction. I was thinking that Wellbrook's comments fit all too well with what Nate and Matt had passed on: *It was the bookshops who were buying the publishers, and not the other way round.*

My mind clicked through the ramifications of such a takeover, and how they'd brought it about. Why, then, had Stone and Gravesend tried to buy *me*? At least Kruse had explained his own interest.

Did those men *know* what was happening? How could they be bought without knowing and agreeing? There seemed too many impossibilities . . .

"Alex?" Sabera's gentle accent brought me back to Green Park.

"Sorry—sorry, just trying to work all this out. Sabera, the reason Tom said I was on to the whole thing is that I've become aware that someone has been gathering most of British publishing under one roof. The ownership of all the major firms has changed recently, and in the same week *three* huge companies offered to buy little Plumtree Press—for outrageous sums.

"Three of the biggest publishers in Europe—four, actually—are totally flummoxed by what's going on . . . even they are being swallowed up. And even the big four have changed the names under which they're registered. They claim it's a move by their banks, for financial reasons, but I don't know whether to believe them."

Sabera stopped and turned to face me. A boy, perhaps ten or eleven, darted between us, chasing after a black Labrador on a lead. We both stared after him, longing to be so carefree again.

"Alex, this is all very serious. You know I love selling books—but I love it because of the variety of works I can recommend to people with diverse interests. If booksellers became publishers—if *one* bookseller becomes the *one* publisher—you know what will happen. The only books out there will be best-seller clones. It's all right to say that the smaller presses will compensate, but good authors can't be expected to write for pennies if they can get more. They're not stupid. They'll go to American publishers. We'll be left with the rest. We already know there are no territorial rights. What will happen to the quality of fiction? Who will win the Booker Prize? People like Orangutan will be put right out of business . . . because of course the One Publisher will only stock and push its own books!"

He realised he was shouting and went silent, glancing round to see if anyone had heard. A mother pushing a pram gave him a slightly fearful look. "What can we do?" he asked plaintively.

"If it's all been done legally, there might not be anything we can do. But if things are happening quietly behind the scenes that ought not to be, we could reveal them and cause such a huge outcry—"

"And who better than Bookworm for a job like that?" He grinned. "The *Bookseller* lets me have until Sunday evening for my column—I'm the last bit in, because they want the latest rubbish."

"Good. *Good.*" Quickly, I filled him in on the failed consortium of scholarly publishers.

His eyes gleamed. "This is going to be a particularly fun piece to write," he said, rubbing his hands together in anticipation. I was thinking how cheerful he looked when a cloud passed in front of the sun, as if we needed a reminder that things could take a turn for the worse.

"I'd better get back," he said, glancing up. "Oh! By the way, I just read that new Northrup. That's the sort of thing they wouldn't publish. And I'll bet she wins the Orange Prize for it, too. Women's book clubs all over the world will be clamouring for it, for years to come. Well done. Don't forget to read your *Bookseller*," he said dryly, and hurried off to his shop.

I found a quiet street and rang Jones-Harris at home with a progress report. Then I tried Ian; I knew he might be under siege. But he picked up on the second ring, sounding quite perky.

"Ian. Hi, it's me. How are you getting on?"

"Very nicely, Alex, thanks—but I would imagine things are pretty dicey for you. What's happening?"

"Is she there with you?"

"Mm-hmm."

Yet another young couple—they were ubiquitous—strolled past me hand in hand, as if to rub salt in the wound. I gritted my teeth and told Ian what I'd learned.

Ian reacted with puzzlement to my news and immediately posed the same questions that I had. How could any one bookseller purchase all the publishers without them knowing it? We knew about Wellbrook's, but . . .

And were Stone, Gravesend, and Kruse part of it, or honestly unaware?

He gave a short, nostalgic laugh. "You'd think old Barker was back with us. He always used to say—quite seriously, mind you—that booksellers and publishers should never have gone their separate ways."

"Old *who*?"

"Barker. Way back in the seventeenth century, Christopher Barker was the King's Printer, you know. But the name died out in the 1930's, when that generation produced no male heirs. One of the Barker women married a Stone, of American publishing fame. Samantha's grandparents."

I thought of the portrait in Sam's house that I'd recognised as being of the King's Printer. "What an extremely small world."

"Indeed. You know, now that I think of it, a number of the people who were in that group still have descendants in publishing. Gravesend, too."

I felt a chill that came from something much more substantial than a cloud eclipsing the sun. "What group, Ian?"

"Good heavens. Is it possible that we've never discussed the old group that used to meet at Botkin's? This would have been Botkin's—let me see—*grandfather*. It was a collection of people in the bookselling business in the 1920's who got together for "cocoa" and buns— euphemistically speaking—every now and again. Your father told me once that *his* grandfather had kept a little book of the things they discussed—rather the way Haslewood did for the Dibdin Club a century before. He never publicised the record, of course. It was more of a personal diary."

"Do you know where it is?" I was already on the way back to my car.

"The little book? No idea at all, I'm afraid. Don't believe I ever saw it at the Orchard. But it wouldn't hurt to check Botkin's. It would have been like him to find it and preserve it." Rather like the book of letters from Baxter Botkin, I thought.

"Right. Um, can you think of anyone else who would have been in this group of bookmen?"

"Oh, let's see. Besides your grandfather, Botkin, old Gravesend, and the last Barker . . . ah, yes. Maggs and Gerhard Quaritch and—"

I nearly dropped the phone. A Stone relative, a Gravesend, and a German? It couldn't be . . . and a Maggs, too . . . "You don't happen to know if the Quaritch line carried on, do you? Perhaps with a name change?"

"No—I don't know about that."

"Ian, you're a veritable wellspring of information. You can't imagine how grateful I am for what you've just told me."

He sounded taken aback by my enthusiasm. "If I'd known you were so interested . . . but then, you know there's more history in our business than there is time to tell it."

"Just one more thing, Ian. Does she hate me?"

"Most definitely not, Alex. Please try to remember what I told you."

Be patient . . . think of all she's been through. I didn't have any trouble with the latter, but the former was nearly impossible. "Right. I'll be in touch. Thanks again, Ian."

I hurried back towards Berkeley Square with three goals: first, find the book Ian had mentioned at Botkin's. Second, consult the page at the back of my diary for confirmation of one of those awful suspicions—one that had started with Ian's mention of Gravesend's name as part of the group. And finally, somehow, somewhere, find out who had descended from the noble line of Gerhard Quaritch.

Ed! He would know. Again I felt that disquieting suspicion. . . . What if Ed was in on this? I thought back to the night at Botkin's, then the mysterious appearance of Jones-Harris's leather-clad goon in the Maggs basement. Ed was the only one who'd known where I was. But then, Jones-Harris was on the *good* side, and no one else had come round.

As I walked I rang Ed at home and got his wry brand of humour. "Not back from Frankfurt already?!"

"I'm afraid so."

He groaned. "I forgot to put away the Klingon lexicon and Ben found it. We've heard nothing but *'jegh qoj Hegh!'* since."

"What's *'jegh qoj Hegh!'*?"

" 'Surrender or die.' "

I couldn't help but smile, though I always felt a pang of longing at the irresistible charm and appeal of other people's children. I wanted a little girl or boy racing about and shouting at me in Klingon, too.

"Ed, I know this might seem an odd question, but . . . did Gerhard Quaritch have children?"

"You do crawl down the most obscure ratholes, Plummers . . . Let's see. Yes, what's-his-name, Gerhard, had four girls. Two of them married here, one a vicar and the other a professor of some sort—religion, I think. The other two ended up going back to Germany, and married there. One of them married a young man named Wilhelm Kruse, who founded the Kruse empire— what do they call it?"

"Spitze-Verlag?"

"Exactly. As for the other daughter, I have no idea. But why the sudden interest in Quaritch and his progeny?"

"Tell you later, I hope."

"Ah. Well, your secret's safe with me."

I sincerely hoped so. We said good-bye.

As I made my way to Botkin's, I thought of the extraordinary link that had survived in spite of time—and even death—amongst the men who'd met in Botkin's so long ago. Suddenly Botkin's comment, always oddly phrased, I thought, that it was "good to see me there" when I stopped in to the bookshop, had new significance—as did the way he would stand back and regard me thoughtfully before saying it.

My family history, it seemed, held more secrets than the average . . . but then Plumtrees had dealt in books for centuries. And books were in no way the average family business.

Back in my grotto at Maggs, I pulled out my diary and hurriedly consulted the chart I had sketched of who owned whom in publishing, now absurdly crowded with crossed-out names and hastily scribbled new ones. To make matters worse, lines crisscrossed the page to join newly merged companies. Still, it was accurate.

And it told me that my niggling suspicion in Worms had been there for a reason: Stone, Gravesend, and Kruse each owned a small, scholarly, religious publisher as part of their empires—and ones that just happened to belong to the Society of Publishers of

Near- and Middle-Eastern Studies, Antiquities, Orientalia, and Judeo-Christian Scholarship. Stone's was Ecumenical, Gravesend's the famous Cantabrigian, and Kruse's Festburg. Each was a gem with an unimpeachable reputation, but Cantabrigian was the leader and had been for centuries, with numerous recent biblical translations and study volumes to its credit.

Again, I wondered: Why had Stone, Gravesend, and Kruse been interested in buying me—I mean my Press? If they already owned scholarly religious lines, why did they need mine?

I was still staring at my amazing chart, thinking how drastically it would be simplified by the Big Takeover, when I jumped at the sound of my own phone in the absolute quiet.

"Alex Plumtree? Dr Vladimir Beattie here." I rolled my eyes. The Vulture was the only person I knew who was conceited enough to use his academic title in everyday parlance.

"Yes, hello." I must have sounded as surprised to hear from him as I felt.

"After your—er—call to arms, as it were, at our conference, I received so many calls about Cotton Vitellius A.fifteen that I decided to do what I could. You'll be glad to know that I have managed to have the codex removed from exhibit, and that I have called upon the most eminent of scholars to conduct an investigation."

"Brilliant!" I exclaimed. Was it possible that I'd misjudged Beattie? No, on second thought, I didn't think so. "Might I ask you to inform me of the results? Please?"

"That's one of the reasons I'm calling you, *Mr* Plumtree." His irritation at being preempted was audible; anything I said or did seemed to irritate the man beyond belief. *Dr Difficult,* I thought, and the childish thought afforded me some joy.

"The study will take months, of course, but the scholar conducting the study realises that everyone is most eager for a preliminary report on his findings. Now that the journalists have been informed"—It sounded as if he held me responsible for this, too— "he's offering to hold a small meeting tomorrow to disclose his early findings. If a statement isn't made soon, this thing will be blown all out of proportion. You are, of course, invited." Without actually saying it, he managed to tack on the thought, *though you certainly don't deserve to be.* "Ten A.M., the library conference room."

"Thank you, Dr Beattie. Thank you very much. May I ask who the lucky scholar is?"

He hesitated, worried, perhaps, that I might second-guess his choice of scholar.

"Dr Desmond Wilcox, of Cambridge. By far the most qualified man for the job." He said it defensively.

"I've no doubt," I replied, remembering the chairman of the *Beowulf* conference from the pub in Cambridge. "Is he at work on it now, then?"

"Yes. He started first thing this morning and plans to keep at it all day."

"Ah. Well. See you tomorrow morning, then."

I rang off with a feeling of shock that the Vulture had leapt into action on behalf of the Cotton Codex, and that he had actually *told* me about it besides. Still, better not to look a gift horse in the mouth.

On to Botkin's in search of my grandfather's book, though I knew chances of finding it were slim. I was encouraged, as I left the basement just after noon, that information seemed to be flying in my direction faster than I could assimilate it—a definite improvement over banging against closed and locked doors. I practically jogged to Botkin's, went round the back way, and listened for a moment at the door before going in.

Oddly, all was well. I told myself to remember to take the flowers out when I left; they'd begun to pong a bit. Recalling the booksellers' map system, I rolled out the wall and went first to the part of the secret bookshelf that represented Paternoster Row, where I knew my grandfather had kept a shop for a time. Nothing.

I searched through St. Paul's Churchyard, Westminster, even Covent Garden—eventually every section of the wall, without success. Though I reminded myself I'd known Botkin might not have had the book—indeed, it might have been lost or destroyed—I was disappointed.

When I'd carefully rolled back the wall, I sank into one of the chairs—a chair that might once have held my grandfather . . . or Gravesend's, or Stone's, or Kruse's. The only thing to do was to go back to the Orchard to look for the book—though I knew every volume in our family library and had for decades. Still, perhaps it had always been there and I hadn't recognised it. Now that I knew what I was looking for, I might spot it.

I gazed at the "front" wall that hid the secret collection: What if Botkin hadn't hidden the volume about the old bookmen? Perhaps it had even been for sale. Feeling foolish, I got up again and inspected the book-arts wall from top to bottom. Nothing. Was there anywhere else the old man might have kept such a book?

His office. I trotted in there and turned on the light. There were, indeed, a dozen books perched on the single shelf over the desk, among them an octavo-sized volume that caught my eye.

I snatched the book off the shelf, rearranging the

others so they wouldn't slide off, and blew the thick dust off my chosen volume. I hurried to one of the comfortable chairs in Botkin's seating alcove and sat, switching on one of the good reading lamps over my shoulder.

A smile spread over my face.

CHAPTER 18

Then the minstrel sang
Of rousing deeds of old. Like flames in the firelight
The heart leapt to hear them.

— BEOWULF

I cradled the small book of soft red calfskin in my hands. The spine had been embellished in black ink by a calligrapher: *Reminiscences of Several Book-Men*. Eagerly I inspected the front cover. The artist, presumably my grandfather, had drawn an engagingly rough sketch of five men sitting in Botkin's alcove, fire in the grate, "cocoa" cups in hand. He'd then impressed this design into the leather and blacked in the recessed areas with ink. The result was charming. Enjoying the yellowed paper and the musty smell of a long-lived book, I turned a page, looking for an inscription, and found it in a spidery hand: "*To Maggs from Plumtree. Never forget . . .*"

It was a journal with a difference; my grandfather had gone to the trouble to set his reminiscences in type and print them, out in the barn-cum-printshop.

In Bembo, though that had never been one of my favourite typefaces, he chronicled the meetings of the bookmen for more than eight years—from 1918 to 1926. They seemed to have met once a month, always on a Thursday night, from half past nine until past one sometimes. My grandfather had not taken great pains with the writing; indeed, both the writing and the typographical errors were appalling. But I'd seen that in many older books; they simply hadn't been as careful. I told myself that one day I would have to look into why that was so, perhaps for the book arts series. Had they been less well educated than we modern bookmen? Or had the *way* they wrote it been less important than what they wrote, and the fact that they wrote it at all?

In 1921, I found something very interesting indeed. In that year, it seemed, the Barker of the day had made a pact with the other bookmen. *"We will,"* he had written, *"if we are so blessed as to be successful in our work, and to carry on our lines, together undertake to purchase such publishing companies as will restore the bookseller's preeminence as the man of books. We do solemnly declare to perpetuate this agreement through our children, grandchildren, and beyond, be it necessary. We also solemnly declare that whosoever shall fall out of this pact, through slothfulness or deliberate choice, will sacrifice his greatest book-possession to all the others."* My grandfather described a document that they had made and signed at that very moment, to be kept by Barker for the foreseeable future.

The more I read, the more fascinated I became. It was like stepping into history—an unknown chapter. The men in the bookmen's group believed that bookmen (booksellers) knew more about literature than the relatively recent breed who called themselves "publishers." The bookmen wanted to take back their position in the book world; they wanted to sell books that they themselves had printed. They honestly believed it was a better way.

Well, why hadn't they simply done it? Why all the

folderol of a formal document, when they might have simply opened up their own houses and *done* it? Perhaps there was something that I didn't understand. No doubt there was a great deal that I didn't understand.

I sighed and folded the book closed for a moment. Okay, I had found it. I'd got what I'd hoped for. But what did this old gentlemen's agreement have to do with anything? Probably nothing. I read on.

The book, to be honest, was not very compelling reading. Yes, true enough, it was fascinating to think of one's ancestors hanging about and chatting with famous people's ancestors.

To a certain point. But after more than one hundred pages, the sort of bun they had one night (with *sultanas*! and not currants!; with *sugared orange rind*! instead of currants!), the revelations of their business affairs (and other more tawdry ones), gave way after an hour or so to somnolence. I prided myself on never having knowingly fallen asleep on a book, but . . .

Startled, I became aware of someone hovering over me. I jumped off the chair and faced the intruder. He cringed in abject fear, his hands up to protect his face.

"Alex! *Don't!* It's me! Martyn!"

"Martyn, for heaven's sake!" I shouted, my heart still threatening to beat out of my chest. "Why did you have to—"

He gaped at me, then his cheeks flushed. "I was doing a bit of shopping on Bond Street for Amanda's wedding ring. Since you've been having such a rough time of it, I thought I'd stop in to see you—you did urge me to visit Botkin's, after all. You haven't been at the Orchard, and I wondered if perhaps you were spending some time here. But I'm sorry I bothered.

I've been to hell and back with you, Plumtree, and this is how you—" He raised his hands again, palms ahead, as if to remind himself to stop talking. The tongue as flame, and all that sort of thing. "Sorry. Sorry. Never mind." He was nearly at the door before I gathered my wits and went after him.

"Martyn! I'm sorry. Please. It's just that I was asleep, and you startled me . . . *please.* I'm really very sorry."

He stopped, then turned slowly round to face me. "You fell asleep over a book," he said deliberately, a slow smile starting across his face. "Look! It's still in your hand! You told me you never, ever . . ."

I looked at the book in my hand guiltily. "All right, all right."

He was pointing at me, laughing.

"Oh, stop it, will you, and come in. Is Amanda unable to be with you this afternoon?"

"I resent that," he said, drawing himself up to his full height of five foot four. "You assume that the only reason I would come to visit you is that Amanda isn't here to occupy me? But yes, as it happens, she is at a friend's in Sussex this very weekend. Remind me not to check in on you again, will you?"

"I'm sorry. Come in." I looked at my watch to determine the appropriate refreshment; any proper Englishman knew that this decision was solely time-dependent. At the moment, we were just straddling the tea-or-tipple line. "Tea or whisky?"

"Hmm, as it's Sunday night . . ."

"Right. Please, sit down."

I told him about the booksellers who had made a pact so many years ago.

"May I see the book?" he asked, all ears because the book had been hand-printed, the very trade of Amanda, his fiancée. He was the saddest case of a smitten male I'd seen in years, but I was very happy for them both. I'd been told I would be invited to the wedding planned for April; Martyn, however, was careful not to talk too much about it in view of my own delayed nuptials.

When we'd fully dealt with how fascinating it was to have discovered this book after so many years, I dropped the real bomb. "Martyn, Sarah's back in London. She's staying with Ian somewhere."

He stared at me blankly for a moment, obviously trying to think what to say. He couldn't say, "Wonderful!" because she clearly wasn't here with me. He couldn't say, "I'm sorry," because the very fact that she was alive was earth-shattering.

"Alex—what's happened?" Trust Martyn to find the perfect way to react to awkward news. Empathetic, but acknowledging that all was not well.

"I don't really know. Ian—who had his appendix out in Worms—"

"In Germany? *Worms?* As in Martin Luther? Is he all right?"

"He's right as rain. Anyway, he told me that Sarah has been 'changed' by her experiences. What would you make of that?"

"Well, it could mean that she's temporarily *not herself* in some way. It would be difficult to go from being a terrorist's victim for *months,* expected to obey at the slightest command with the constant threat of immediate death, to being a free person again. Maybe she wants to be more herself before she sees you again, Alex."

There was so much conviction in his voice that I found myself latching on to what he said. In any case, it was far better than all the alternatives I'd come up with. "Yes, that could be. Of course . . ."

Silence overtook us for a moment. "Are you hungry?" I asked.

"Yes. You?"

"Mmm. Let's have dinner somewhere."

"I know—come to the Vicarage, Alex. I've *loads* of food. There was a wedding last weekend—sorry." He closed his eyes in self-reprimand for having said the taboo word. He smiled apologetically and carried on. "Rachel Bartlett did the food, but she made far too much and brought it all over to me. Wasn't that kind of her? It's been in the freezer since last Saturday. Please come and help me finish it. It's not good stewardship otherwise . . ."

So at my vicar's urging I went, tucking the little book in my jacket pocket. It wasn't until after the admittedly glorious meal that Martyn admitted he had a small DIY project he'd undertaken as a surprise for Amanda while she was away. "It's an office for her printing business, while she's in the country. Don't suppose you'd like to help me put the wallboard up?" he asked hopefully. So after dinner we worked like fiends on the new room for Amanda.

It was late when Martyn said through the nails between his teeth, "Can you imagine how embarrassing it would be for Ecumenical Publishers Ltd, which prides itself on being so painfully accurate, to have to admit that their illustrious founder, Barker, altered the words of Scripture because King James asked him to?"

"Well, the King was head of the Church, after all. I'd

imagine Barker would be in the clear, ethically speaking. He'd probably have been beheaded if he'd refused."

"Ha." Martyn, his hair white with wallboard dust, dissented. "I think if the news came out today Ecumenical would be pilloried by all the other publishers. The Catholics would drag him through the mud! A book of their Bible, now shown to be a fraud? And it would be his fault. I'm glad I'm not in his shoes."

I thought about what my friend had to say. True enough, it wouldn't be at all good for Ecumenical, Stone's religious arm, if word got out.

Vagabond that I had become, I spent what remained of the night on the vicarage sofa. Before I knew it, it was Monday morning: time to dash to London for the ten o'clock meeting at the British Library.

I took the train in to King's Cross and walked to the library, desperately curious about what Desmond Wilcox would have to say about changes made to the codex.

When I stepped in to the conference room, I saw that only four people were present besides Desmond Wilcox and *Dr* Vladimir Beattie. Certainly an intimate group, I thought. The assembled included the library's curator of ancient manuscripts, a journalist from the *Times,* and two others who were introduced as ultraviolet testing specialists who were helping Wilcox with his study.

After the introductions were made, Wilcox took the floor. He was wearing a pair of white cotton gloves, as he was handling the actual Cotton Vitellius A.xv volume. I had trouble dragging my eyes away from the book, which had the Cotton family crest stamped on the front in gold.

"I have good news and bad news today, depending

on what you think about Cotton Vitellius A.fifteen. The good news, if you choose, is that the codex has not been altered, aside from folio numbers that were evidently changed when Sir Robert Bruce Cotton—or a predecessor—obtained the fragments and bound them all together.

"The bad news," he continued, "is that this rather demolishes our late friend Dr Gabriel Hammonds's theory about *Beowulf* having been written in the tenth century rather than the seventh."

"Did you look at anything besides *Beowulf*?" I asked. Beattie threw me a black look.

"I inspected the entire codex, page by page. Here, let me show you the slides I made from different sections of the book. These are samples, you understand, because in the time I had it was impossible to make a slide of every page—nor would you care to see them." Smiling at his little joke, he turned on an overhead projector and slid a foil on to it. Large black script in a rounded style covered the page from top to bottom; I recognised it as a leaf from the *Beowulf* manuscript I'd seen with Hammonds in the library.

In the upper right-hand corner of the page, two folio numbers were visible: a shadowy 49, and a much darker 17. "This is *Beowulf*. You can clearly see that the folio number has been changed. The forty-nine is the earlier number, much earlier. The seventeen was added over the existing, scratched-off folio number in the seventeenth or eighteenth century."

Wilcox took the foil off and slid another one into its place. The page looked much the same; again, only the folio number appeared to have two different versions. "This is Judith. Again, only the folio number has been changed.

"The page containing the curse, originating from Southwick Priory," he said, putting up another new foil. "Change in folio number only."

"How is the test performed?" the *Times* journalist wanted to know.

"Come and see," Wilcox urged. He picked up the precious volume in his gloved hands and led us out of the room and down the hall. He opened a door and we entered a rather industrial-looking room containing a sink with accompanying work area. But the main feature of the room was a long, sturdy, Formica-topped work table right down the centre. Storage shelves covered the walls, and a cardboard box filled with white cotton gloves sat on the table. Wilcox took us to an apparatus at the far end of the table that resembled a light table—the sort you might use at the photo developer's to inspect negatives, or slides. A strip light was suspended over the light table. "Ultraviolet light is extremely damaging to the eyes," Wilcox explained. "I don't mean to sound dire, but under no circumstances look *directly at* the lamp. All right?"

He received nods from his audience, then switched on the lamp. It emitted a purplish glow that made me think of "black light," the sort that had been popular for illuminating psychedelic glow-in-the-dark posters in the seventies. Wilcox opened the codex to a page of *Beowulf,* placed it reverently on a cotton cloth already spread over the light table, which remained unilluminated, and pointed with one cotton-encased finger to the folio number on the recto.

"Can you see this shadowy image beneath the dark number?"

I strained to see it; there was something there, but only just.

The journalist asked Wilcox to switch the light off, so he could see the difference in how the changed number stood out. Wilcox turned it on again for a final comparison.

"Would it be possible to look at a specific word in the Judith text?" I asked.

Cold stares from Beattie and Wilcox, until Beattie spluttered, "I hardly think we have time to plough through word by word, Plumtree . . ."

"It's just one reference—the name Bethulia. Please." I smiled pleasantly.

Wilcox stood erect and said, "I've told you. I studied the codex with great care. I resent your suggestion that I have missed anything at all. Furthermore, I was unaware that you yourself were an expert in the examination of palimpsests by ultraviolet light, or on the subject of the Nowell Codex."

"Well, then. I'll just say thank you. Thank you very much," I said, shaking hands with both Beattie and Wilcox.

I felt dissatisfied in the extreme about Wilcox's study as I left the library. Why would Botkin's ancestor have lied, and wouldn't *my* ancestor have been clever enough to spot a liar and stop giving him precious books in exchange for information? I vowed to learn the truth about Judith, one way or another.

As I walked down Gower Street towards Companies House—I could hardly wait to see if there had been any changes filed since last week—I rang the skeleton staff left at the Press. "Shuna!" I shouted over the rumble and roar of buses and lorries. "I hope to be back before too much longer. I know, absolute craziness. Listen, I need you to do something for me." I paused to allow an unconscionably deafening lorry to pass.

"Sorry, obviously I'm on the road. Would you please consult your on-line listing of academic books in print and tell me what's been published by a Desmond Wilcox? The subject would be *Beowulf*, or Anglo-Saxon poetry. Great, yes, if you can do it right now . . ."

I imagined her tapping away at her keyboard in her quiet office. After no more than five seconds she said, "Here he is . . . Let's see. Five books . . . looks like one every five years, from 1976 on. *Beowulf: A New Translation; Beowulf: Story for Our Time; Anglo-Saxon Poetry of the Seventh Century; A New Look at Cotton Vitellius A.fifteen;* and *Judith: An Anglo-Saxon Epic.* All published in the US by Stone and Stone Scholars Library, except for the last, which was published here by Ecumenical."

Which was, of course, part of Stone & Stone. Wilcox would jolly well say whatever his publisher told him to about whether changes had been made to Judith; would pretend not to see those changes if they did exist. Ecumenical's reputation was on the line.

I thanked Shuna and carried on, skirting round the Press through the University of London passages, and coming out again below the Companies House Information Centre. I hurried in and got a smile from the woman who'd helped me the week before.

"You're back," she said.

I handed over my driving licence. "With more questions. How long does it take for changes to be registered on your public database?"

"Oh, if the company is registered, or ownership changes, the record is immediately updated. It happens automatically, you see."

I sat down at a terminal and checked the ownership of the book chains; nothing had changed from what I already knew to be the case. But as I checked the board of directors for Frontiers, and then for Wellbrook's, and then for Books &, I noticed something curious. A Francis J. McDonald sat on the board of each giant chain. It was very, very unusual for competing chains to share a common board member.

And another thing was odd: In all my days of living and breathing the world of publishing in England, I had never, ever heard or seen the name Francis J. McDonald before. And the people on these boards were never "unknowns"; I could point to the names of all of the others and tell you exactly who they were, how they'd made their names in the industry, and which company they were affiliated with now.

Who *was* he? I pulled out my phone and entered the number for directory enquiries. Scores of McDonalds, but no Francis J. McDonald in London or vicinity. Hmm.

Next I looked again at the records for Hanford Banner/Wellbrook's and the other major UK publishers. No changes from the dog-eared chart in my Filofax. Just because I was there, and I could, I looked up Ecumenical.

Eureka. There, on the board of directors, sat one Francis J. McDonald . . . along with one Trevor Gravesend, and a Samuel Stone III who headed the list. *Samuel Stone had taken over the British book business?!* Even as I saw the link I had long sought between one of my target three publishers and the rest of the industry, I knew I was grasping at straws. After all, a common board member did not a monopoly make. But it was the first shade of the sort of proof I'd been seeking that *some*thing was going on.

My fingers flew over the keyboard . . . Cantabrigian, Board of Directors. Among others, including Beattie, of course, were Gravesend, McDonald, and Stone. Wow.

Not only was it strange that they were all in one another's beds, but one rarely found such busy, powerful, eminent men on the boards of tiny religious scholarly presses. But did the fact that these men served on the religious publishers' boards of directors have anything to do with Stone's takeover of the bookshop chains? If indeed Stone *had* taken over the bookshop chains?

I retrieved my driving licence, thanked my friend behind the desk, and rang Jones-Harris as soon as I got outside. "I've been waiting to hear from you," he said. "Where have you been? What have you been doing?"

I told him, beginning with the questionable Cotton Vitellius A.xv ultraviolet study results, and finishing with my visit to the Companies House Information Centre.

"Better and better," he said.

"Jones-Harris, I don't know if this small-religious-press cooperation is directly related to the book business coup. But I really do feel I must oppose the deliberate altering of scientific test results for personal reasons . . . and I think that's what Beattie and Wilcox have done. I think Barker, Stone's ancestor, did alter Judith according to King James's wishes. No one can really blame him, of course. But I think the truth should come out now. It could even result in a change in Judith's status in the Bible. Don't tell anyone, but I'm going to find a way to have that test redone while the book's still out of the gallery."

Jones-Harris sighed. "That's the reason I asked you to be our eyes and ears on this project . . . I knew you'd do the right thing. But Alex, is it worth it risking everything you've got—including your life, and your life with Sarah—to set a dry old historical record straight?"

Sarah? What did he mean, "your life with Sarah"? I felt the world around me recede, the noise deadened as my brain applied itself to sorting out how he could have just said what he'd said.

"Er, Jones-Harris, old boy. You've just made a rather shocking blunder. *I never told you that Sarah was back.*"

Silence. Then a weak, "Look, I only meant to be hopeful—that *if* and *when* she does return, you would have a life to live with her. Unless I'm mistaken, you've been giving off quite strong signals that you believe her to be alive. Don't go all hypersensitive on me, Plumtree." Another pause. "At any rate, when all this is settled, you must come for lunch at my club. We have a great deal to discuss."

I must have answered before I rang off, but I can't think how. I felt physically ill. How could Jones-Harris have known about Sarah? Was *anyone* who he seemed? Had *anyone* been honest with me?

Ian. He could not tell a lie. I pressed in his mobile number and set out for Diana Boillot's new office space in Gordon Square, cleverly located almost exactly halfway between the British Museum and the British Library. Diana and I had embarked on manuscript adventures before. She was the museum's, and now the library's, expert of choice for study and restoration. I felt certain she could help me.

When Ian answered, I asked immediately, "How many people has Sarah been in touch with—other than *me*, of course—since she's been back?"

No answer.

"Does the name Colin Jones-Harris sound familiar to you? Or perhaps to Sarah?"

I knew Jones-Harris was unmarried; naturally, I imagined the worst. And Jones-Harris had played a beastly joke on me that had involved Sarah the previous summer, during my initiation into the Dibdin Club. But what had I done? How had I failed Sarah since she'd been gone? There was the misunderstanding over Nicola, but that hardly—

Ian sighed, bringing me back to the here and now. "Alex, you're overreacting to something that's really very logical and simple. If you can only hang on until the time is right, you'll see."

"Is she there?"

"Yes."

"Are you at the flat?"

"No."

"Do you know why she won't talk to me?"

"Er, yes and no."

I wanted to dash the phone onto the pavement and make it explode into twenty thousand little black plastic pieces.

"Please, Alex. I'm not trying to be difficult. There are just some things that I cannot tell you, for quite awkward reasons. But it's only temporary. Please try to understand."

For the second time in my life, I hung up on Ian. It took only two minutes to feel ashamed, but I didn't have it in me to ring him back. I carried on to Diana's.

"Alex!" She greeted me with a warm hug, and invited me in to her office. "It's wonderful to see you. Tell me, how is everything?"

"I'm delighted to see you, too, Diana. Sorry if I

seem a bit—abrupt—but it's been a difficult day. And I'm afraid I need your help again."

I told her about the suspected changes to Judith, revealed in the letters from a Cotton relative to an earlier Plumtree, and my suspicions that the results of an ultraviolet test on the codex had been rigged. She reacted exactly as I thought she might: fascinated by the new light shed on old books; indignant that anyone should falsify history-making test results.

She gazed at me seriously across her desk. "You want me to redo the tests, don't you?"

"Yes."

"I have had extensive training in ultraviolet testing, but little practice. Still, I know what I'm doing . . . what about access to the codex, though?"

"That's a bit of a problem. But I'm hoping you're willing to, er, come up with another of your creative solutions."

"Leave it to me. No one will question what I'm doing at the library at any time of the day or night, and I have access to the necessary rooms. When do you need this done?"

She knew me too well. She laughed at the look on my face and said, "All right, then. Tonight. For heaven's sake, don't tell anyone, or we'll be cooked."

We spent the next forty-five minutes talking about exactly what she was looking for. Her eyes widened when I told her about what Petrus had written in the Malconbury Chronicles about the changes, and that the Anglo-Saxon epic was now the only ancient relic of the Judith story because of thefts, fires, and vandals round the world.

"Extremely suspicious," she said. "I can hardly wait to get to it!"

I agreed to come to her office again at half past seven that night, at which point we would fortify ourselves with dinner before setting off for the library. She didn't feel comfortable going after ten—thought it might raise suspicions—but didn't want to go *before* ten, either. "Desmond Wilcox might still be there, if he's even pretending to do a proper study," she said. "But I've never seen *anyone* there past ten, other than cleaning staff."

So at nine forty-five, I accompanied Diana from the restaurant to the British Library. The place was even more eerie in the black of night; our footsteps echoed across the deserted courtyard. The subtle lighting gave rise to all sorts of frightening images in the shadows for anyone possessing any imagination at all.

When we reached the main entrance, I had no choice but to stay outside. The guards knew Diana but not me, and she didn't want to attract undue attention. As the door closed behind her, I waved good-bye and turned to leave. No point in standing about in the cold for several hours. Traipsing across the courtyard alone, I found myself missing the congeniality of her companionship.

I heard a car stop just behind me on the road; heard its doors open. The next thing I knew, something dark was pulled over my head. Strong hands manhandled me in the direction of the car. I fought like an animal, kicking, flailing, until an iron fist flew into my solar plexus with enormous force.

I collapsed into a ball, unable to breathe, and hazily realised I was being trundled into a car. In the several moments it took me to get my breath back, I fought hard to think. The car had reversed direction via a fast U-turn, and was heading back west on Euston Road. No one knew where I was; no one could help me but me. How had they known I would be here? Who was passing along these bits of information?

CHAPTER 19

*Then the children of Israel cried unto the Lord their
God, because their heart failed, for all their enemies had
compassed them round about, and there was no way to
escape out from among them.*

—JUDITH 7:19

They opened the car door and shoved me out. The
area was very quiet, but I couldn't hear anything
that would identify the neighbourhood and confirm
my theory of where I'd been taken. It was a mistake
to yell and struggle as they tried to unload me. All I
got for my trouble was another bang in the chest; this
time the intense pain and fight for breath put me in a
daze. Three or four of them, it seemed, half carried,
half shoved me through a door. As they did, I smelled
old ashes and musty books . . . and knew where we
were.

Botkin's. This was a relief, because from the direction we'd been going, I'd been concerned it would be
Maggs. I didn't want to lose any more friends.

I was shoved down some steep steps; I kept my
footing at the top, but they let me tumble down the last
bit. I didn't give them the satisfaction of moaning
as I gathered myself on all fours at the bottom. This
was where Botkin had met his end. I felt it was safe to
assume that whoever had killed Botkin here was about
to do the same to me.

"Good evening, Mr Plumtree."

I shuddered at the grotesque sound that boomed at deafening volume from one side of the room. My hands flew up to cover my ears; but powerful hands wrenched them down to my sides again. The small portion of my conscious mind that was still functioning knew that a distortion device was being used to slow the sound of the speech. The panic-stricken, irrational side of my mind was simply terrorised. After a moment I turned to face the voice, blinded by the black hood still firmly in place.

"You will notice that we are doing everything in our power to keep our identity secret. That way we can let you live. Do you understand?"

I nodded.

"You have two choices. You can either cooperate with us or make things difficult. If you cooperate, you may leave alive. It will all be over then, without further unpleasantness. If you decide to go against us, it will not be easy for you. You might never be the same again."

Something about the way he said it left me in no doubt that this was true. But what did they want?

I needn't have worried. In the next instant he told me.

"We need you to sign your name to this piece of paper, Mr Plumtree. I'm afraid we must insist."

Paper? All this, to get me to sign *a piece of paper*? It took me several beats to work out what piece of paper could be so important, and so repugnant to me, that I would have to be threatened with physical torture to sign it.

It had to be an agreement to sell Plumtree Press.

Given that we were in Botkin's basement, I thought it likely that this was all about someone wanting the Cotton Collection remnant that now belonged to the Press.

But if I died, the Press could be purchased easily by the highest bidder, along with Botkin's and any books therein . . . unless my death was sudden and unnatural. In that case, my will—

My will! I'd been a fool to tell Nate about the provision I'd made some time ago, in the midst of another book-related intrigue, that Plumtree Press could not be sold immediately in the event of my sudden or unnatural death. The idea had been to prevent me from being killed by an unscrupulous purchaser, but it seemed only to have resulted in spawning new and unusual methods to achieve the same end.

Nate had written this up in his Plumtree feature in the *Bookseller,* so it wasn't necessarily my journalistic friend behind the voice machine—and I had my doubts about whether Nate was still alive. It could be anyone who read the *Bookseller* . . . and that was everyone in our business.

After removing my mobile from my jacket, they left me for some time. It might have been two hours or twenty minutes. Breathing cautiously to prevent spasms of tooth-grinding pain in my rib cage, I tried to work out exactly who might be behind this. Given what I'd learned about the relationship among Stone, Gravesend, and Kruse, could it be the three of them working together?

Somehow I just couldn't imagine Kruse in on it, but I'd been fooled by people before now.

Besides the dilemma causing my current distress, I

felt betrayed and left in the dark by nearly everyone. Even Ian and Sarah seemed to have secrets from me. It was impossible to imagine being brought any lower.

I heard the shuffling of feet as they came back in to the room. No one spoke. I estimated four people in the room besides myself. This time I vowed to try to concentrate on speech patterns. If it was Stone behind the voice-changer, perhaps I would recognise some Americanisms. "Mr Plumtree. We have given you time to consider our proposal. What is your answer?"

I couldn't do it. I *couldn't* say yes. I shook my head.

Rough hands grabbed me then, forced me onto my back on some sort of long, hard table. To my dismay, they fastened me down with straps, and tied my hands to the table. I felt the first waves of panic rising, but tried to keep them under control. I didn't do well when restrained or pinned down.

Stay calm. Just stay calm.

I felt the hood coming off; saw one man in a black ski mask and goggles—did they think we were on the piste at Verbier, for heaven's sake?—bring a strap down across my forehead, then another across my chin. He stretched them tight; now my head was fastened down hard against the table. A second man in full regalia held my left eye open.

Dear God in heaven, not my eyes!

But it was all too clear that's exactly what they intended. The mad skier who'd strapped me down approached my eye with a pair of tweezers. It was all I could do to keep myself from begging him not to . . . what was he *doing*? He lifted the contact lens out of my eye and tossed it aside; they moved to the other eye and did the same thing. A cold sweat covered my body.

How could they possibly have known my worst

fear? The rats in George Orwell's *1984* couldn't hold a candle to this. Nearly as awful as the threat of what they might do was the unavoidable fact that once again, someone quite close—someone who knew my worst fear—had betrayed me.

I thought of Sam Stone in my office on her first day, asking if I had trouble with my eyes. Perhaps she'd even sniffed around my colleagues at the Press on the subject.

While the two men continued to hold my now lens-less eyes open, the contact-removing man came into view again; he seemed to be holding an eyedropper.

Anything but my eyes!

"Mr Plumtree." I jumped as the awful voice filled the room. "The liquid we are about to put in to your eyes is an acid solution. With each drop, your vision will degrade until you can no longer see at all. We know exactly how many drops this will take in each eye. If you change your mind at any point, we can wash the drops out. The sooner they are washed out, the better chance you have of retaining what is left of your eyesight. Now. Before we put in the first drop, will you change your mind?"

I couldn't bear the thought of losing more eyesight. . . . My eye doctor had already told me that I had an inherited rare eye disorder that might stop destroying my eyes at any point, or carry on until I was blind. Our hope was that some treatment would be found, or surgery, before that happened.

"Mr Plumtree?"

I couldn't answer. The man with the vial looked towards the Voice in silent query, then brought the eyedropper down just above my eye. I strained against the straps with every ounce of strength I had. Even the crushing pain in my chest didn't matter anymore, compared to my eyes. But it was no use. The drop fell with awful slowness, and that was the end of my self-control.

I screamed. Never in my life had I felt such excruciating pain; the drop seemed to burn right into the centre of my brain and radiate agony through every cell of my body.

They let my eye close.

"We will be back, Mr Plumtree. Do think carefully."

There was no need to think; besides, I was consumed with agony. My eye felt like an atomic fireball as it grated against my eyelid. But at a level deeper than thought I knew that to sell the Press was to sell myself— and what was my life worth if I sold myself? It did occur to me that I could sign the ridiculous scrap of paper and later declare it invalid. But once they had it, why should they let me live?

I wondered briefly why they didn't just forge my signature. But handwriting analysis was such a sophisticated art these days that they knew better. No magic way out of the situation presented itself. I simply couldn't free myself from the damned straps and the table; couldn't even get my hands loose. The grim course of the night seemed very apparent; torture past blindness, and then they'd kill me anyway.

And then . . . were those voices? I thought I heard female voices, muffled by distance and my depth below ground. The rear door seemed to explode; I heard rapid footsteps on the floor above me. At the same time I heard loud shouting . . . what sounded like an elderly man, indignant, and authoritative voices over his. More scrabbling on the floor as several sets of feet tried to escape out of the front door. More loud shouts, and the crack of a gunshot.

Had someone come to help me, or was this the beginning of the end?

Light footsteps descended the steep staircase, hurrying, followed by heavier male ones. A sharp intake of breath, a favourite American swear word.

"It's all right, Alex," Sam Stone said. "We're here. What's—what have they done to you?"

"Get him out of here as fast as you can," a man's voice commanded. "Can you manage it?"

"Yes." It was Sarah's voice; there was a hand on my shoulder. "Alex . . ."

I opened my eyes and instantly regretted it. During the second before I slammed them shut again and tried hard not to cry out with the searing pain, I saw that everything was milky . . . I couldn't see her face. She began to unfasten the straps that bound me, hands first.

The moment was so far from anything I'd imagined in the way of a reunion. But I was exceedingly grateful for these two strong, intelligent women, and whatever had brought them to me.

"We've got to get you to the eye doctor. Can you walk?"

I nodded. "But first, water for my eyes—is there any down here?"

Sam rushed to one side of the room. I heard a tap running, heard her hurry back to my side. "Just pour it . . . ?"

I nodded as best I could, leaned my head back, and

felt the cold water coursing over my face. I struggled to open my eyes to let it in, but gasped at the unbelievable agony it caused. I gripped the edges of the table hard, concentrating on that so I could stay quiet. "More," I whispered.

Sam hesitated.

"Please. Sarah—hold my eyes open! Quickly. Please." They immediately did as I asked.

"You'll be all right now." Sarah's voice sounded just as I'd always known it, calm as ever in a crisis. She touched my hair with one hand, gripped my shoulder with the other. "I'm so sorry, Alex. We'll take you straight to Knightsbridge Eye Hospital. Let's go now, okay?"

Sam loosed the final strap round my chest. I tried to sit up, but what they'd done to my chest made it impossible and I fell back onto the table. The two women each hooked an arm under one of mine, but my dignity couldn't bear it. I shrugged them off, painfully, and rolled off of the table.

But in the next moment I realised that my dignity was to be shattered completely anyway. I couldn't see. Opening my eyes was like inserting hot pokers into them. Sarah and Sam would have to lead me wherever I went.

I went with Sarah towards the steps I'd tumbled down on the way in. Sam uttered her favourite colourful curse again, and I heard a paper rattle behind us. "I've found your mobile . . . and look at this! A contract to sell Plumtree Press and Botkin's Books. Unsigned, fortunately."

"Make sure you've got that with the evidence." Sarah again. I didn't know who she was talking to, but her voice was authoritative.

"Got it. Go!"

When we reached the top of the stairs, Sarah and Sam hurried me out the back door. Judging from the voices, a small knot of people waited against the back of Botkin's; a vehicle was just driving off, its siren wailing.

Sarah helped me get into a car; Sam climbed into the back and Sarah ran round and started it up. My beloved fiancée drove away fast; I was keenly aware of the awkwardness in the car. After three months of longing for this moment with Sarah, I now could think of not one single word to say. And Sam was there, not exactly the way I'd imagined it. And I was all but sightless. *Definitely* not the way I'd planned it.

I had so many questions. Who had been behind the torture? Why did they want Plumtree Press so very badly?

Before I could begin, Sam plunged in. "Can you tell us what happened?"

I hardly knew where to begin. Sam must have taken my hesitation for reluctance. "You don't have to talk about it if you don't want to," she told me.

"No, I—it's been quite an eventful week. And I have some questions for you. How did you know where I was, and what was happening at Botkin's?"

Sarah answered. "Botkin's has been under remote surveillance for days, inside and out. We have a videotape of everything they did to you. That's how we were able to stop them before they did too much damage—I hope. Agents were dispatched, and Jones-Harris called us, the minute the tape monitors saw them bring you in. I'm only sorry it took as long as it did for us to get there."

I was amazed.

"How does it happen that you—and Sam—are in on this?"

This time, Sam answered. "Colin Jones-Harris asked you to help him expose a trade conspiracy, right?"

"Yes . . ."

"Well, my government asked me to do the same. And Sarah—well, I'll let Sarah speak for herself."

"I'll tell you all about it later, Alex."

We rode in silence for a moment before I asked the real question.

"Well . . . who was it?"

"You don't *know*?" Sam exclaimed.

"NO, I *don't know*!" I shouted angrily.

"We didn't realise," Sarah said quietly. "Alex, I'm sorry—it was Matt Ireland."

"*Matt Ireland?!* But he's in hospital, he's—"

"He *was*. He obviously recovered quite nicely." She gave me a moment to absorb this. Something in her voice implied her belief that the knock on the head had been deliberately arranged to put him beyond suspicion. "Alex, why would Matt Ireland—an old family friend—do this to you?"

Now that I knew about Matt, many things became painfully clear. Ireland, who'd stormed out of the PA meeting after accusing Trevor of having killed Botkin and others.

Ireland, who had been the one to ring me in such a panic about a conspiracy in the bookselling business, right around the time Wellbrook's acquired Hanford Banner from Megacom.

Ireland, who had rung me to say, "It wasn't the publishers, it was the booksellers"—again, as in Wellbrook's, a firm Trevor was now part of.

Ireland, who I was certain would prove to have hired Nate to ring me to say it was Hanford Banner who'd killed Montague.

Ireland, then, who had hired the Sarah impostor to break me down . . . and told her to walk towards the Stones' house, to turn me against the Stones and suspect them. All to turn me against Trevor Gravesend and Sam Stone to keep me from selling Plumtree Press to them, with its Botkinload of books. I felt certain it had been Ireland who rampaged through Botkin's, furious that he couldn't find the hidden Cotton Collection remnant. And no doubt it had also been Ireland who arranged for Botkin and me to be threatened with eviction from our ancestral leaseholds, to break us down enough to want to sell. Now it occurred to me that perhaps Whitticombe, involved with the sale of Botkin's himself, had come to suspect his old friend Matt. Perhaps that's why he'd been snooping around the shop that night. Perhaps—and sadly, I thought it even likely—Ireland had killed his old friend, Botkin. But Botkin's death had been made to appear a fall . . . and that's exactly what Hammonds's had been made to appear. Had Matt Ireland killed them *both*? But Ireland had nothing to do with the *Beowulf*/Judith issue . . . at least that I knew of. I shivered at the thought.

No; surely all of this chaos, created by one obsessed elderly bibliomaniac publisher, didn't relate to Hammonds's death and the cover-up of the Judith changes. And Ireland almost certainly had nothing to do with the world of high finance and megamergers. That meant that the people trying to kill me weren't done yet . . . because Ireland had merely tried to drive me out of my mind, it seemed.

Well, one out of three conspiracies settled was better than none. At least I knew who'd been trying to drive me round the bend. And I still had my mind, my life, my Press, and Botkin's—which, combined, might allow me to untangle the other two conspiracies involving *Beowulf*/Judith/and the monopoly.

I tried to momentarily shelve all the other things I still didn't know, such as who had arranged for "Father Mike" to appear in the old house in Malconbury . . . and a few other disturbing details.

Sarah, I realised belatedly, was still waiting for an answer to her question: *Why Matt Ireland?*

"Books," I answered. "Matt wanted my books—the ones that used to be Botkin's. But I still don't quite know why . . . if there *is* a reason, beyond his pathological obsession."

Diana! My synapses made a connection from the thought of obsession to thoughts of Cotton Vitellius A.xv . . . which took me back to my last glimpse of Diana Boillot disappearing into the British Library. How could I not have thought of her before this? *Dear God, please let her have fared better than I have tonight.*

"Do you have a phone that I could use?" I asked. I heard the excessive formality in my voice, but I didn't know how formal or informal to be . . . didn't know if Sarah was my fiancée or my ex-fiancée.

"Here," Sarah said. Her voice, soft, rich, lovely, and calm, was the voice of my dreams. I heard a subtle rustle next to my ear as she passed the phone back to Sam.

"What number?" Sam asked.

Of course: I couldn't see to press the buttons.

"Directory enquiries, for Diana Boillot's office number. Please."

Sam passed me the phone when Diana's office number was ringing. Being blind made me feel defensive and ashamed.

A woman's voice answered. "Diana Boillot."

"Diana. Alex here. Are you all right?"

"Yes! But what about *you*? When I couldn't reach you I was afraid—I mean you were so eager to hear—"

"Sorry about that . . . I ran into a bit of trouble outside the library." For just an instant my brain connected Matt Ireland to Vladimir Beattie and Desmond Wilcox and their test. But then I realised that even Beattie and Wilcox didn't know I would be at the library with Diana late at night. Ireland must have been following me; perhaps he'd tracked Diana and me all evening. He and his people must have been watching for me when I left the library.

"Everything's fine now," I assured Diana. "No trouble *in*side the library, then?"

"No! None at all."

A wave of relief swept over me. Perhaps Ireland hadn't known *why* Diana and I had been at the library.

"Alex, I have absolutely stunning news about your codex. I know it's late, but can you pop over to talk for a few minutes?"

"Er, that would be a bit difficult just now—could you tell me over the phone?"

"Of course," Diana answered. "You're not going to believe it. In a nutshell, everything that you told me *might* have been changed in Judith *was*! The name of the city was Schechem, not Bethulia. And it *was* Nebuchadnezzar who was killed instead of the general, Holofernes. Your 'friends' who conducted the earlier test were deliberately obfuscating their findings. There's no way anyone who knows the first thing about ultraviolet testing could have said no changes had been made."

Poor Hammonds. It was all too clear now why he

had died . . . his study of *Beowulf* had come too close to revealing the secrets of Judith's politically convenient changes. "Thank you, Diana. Thank you so much."

"I should be thanking you. It's the most excitement I've had in months—and I'd certainly never have got my hands on that codex otherwise! I'll see you soon."

Someone took the phone from me. "Perhaps you already know about this, too," I told Sam and Sarah, "but there seems to be another little issue . . . related to changes made to the Bible around the time of King James. An ancient codex called Cotton Vitellius A.fifteen seems to have proof of this, and might even have led to the death of one of my authors."

There was silence in response. Did this mean that they *did* know about it, or didn't? I opted for the former . . . which drove me to wonder just how the two had become so hand-in-glove with everything I'd told Jones-Harris.

"Here we are," Sarah announced as she slowed the car and turned off the road.

Sarah was out of the car and opening my door before I'd found the door handle. She stood close, gripping my hand, and gently led me forward. It was extremely disconcerting not to see where I was going; at every step I expected to plunge off a kerb or run into a brick wall. But after a bit I realised Sarah wouldn't allow that to happen.

I heard a swoosh, felt warm air, and sensed light; presumably we'd walked through automatic doors into the hospital. "This is Alex Plumtree," Sarah said with authority. "Someone rang to tell you we were coming."

"Yes, Mr Plumtree. Come straight through." I heard soft-soled shoes squelching on the hard floor as we followed her in to what I imagined was an examining room. "Dr Levine will be right with you." The woman squelched out again as Sarah turned me round and helped me find a seat on the examining table.

I'd no sooner sat down than Dr Levine had come in. She informed me that she would be flushing my eyes with a cleansing solution immediately though she understood Sarah and Sam had already done so. She lost no time in having me lie down on the table. "There isn't time to anaesthetise first, but I will the instant we're done. All right?"

I nodded, and the next thing I knew she was holding open first one eye and then the other as tepid liquid coursed over them . . . again. I clung to the edge of the examining table as if it might diminish the pain, but it had no effect whatsoever. My discomfort must have been apparent to Sarah, because she reached out and placed her hand firmly over mine and clasped it. There was some relief in clinging to her instead of the padded vinyl upholstery.

"There, that's done." She quickly administered the anaesthetic drops and I prayed the stuff would work fast.

"Now then. I need you to tell me exactly what happened." She peppered me with calm but rapid-fire questions, asking what I knew about the liquid in my eyes, how long the drops had been in, and how my eyes felt. I learned that it was most likely the surface of my cornea had been burned with the acidic solution, whatever it was. It wouldn't be clear, the doctor said, for several days how much permanent damage had been done. Until the next examination, in two days, I would have to wear bandages over my eyes to let them heal.

In reception we set a time for the next examination, and Sarah led me out once more into the night air. Sam followed close behind. Now that the ordeal with my eyes had been taken care of, I was eager to pursue the precise nature of Sarah and Sam's link with Jones-Harris. I turned to Sarah as we walked to the car.

"Er—if you don't mind my asking—exactly what is your role in all of this?"

An unnatural length of time passed before I prompted, "Anybody there?"

Sarah finally spoke. "Alex, it's a very long story, and I don't think this is the time to go into it. You've been through a lot, and . . . Can you trust me for a little while longer? I promise to tell you, when you're not so tired."

"*No,*" I said with a great deal more force than I expected. "No, I jolly well *can't* trust you for a little while longer. I have waited far too long as it is for a great many things to be explained. I need to know at least this much now."

"All right," she said. "Let's get into the car first."

As I climbed into Sam's car for the ride back to Chorleywood, I could tell I'd hurt Sarah by how careful her voice was. What's worse, I'd actually *wanted* to. What was happening to me?

Taking a deep breath, she began. "Jones-Harris has been working to stop a number of major English publishers from falling under the control of a bookselling chain—you know most of it, because you're involved, too. As is Sam. But no one ever thought this would happen to you. No one ever would have allowed it to happen."

"I wanted to tell you, Alex," Sam piped up. "That's really why I came as a Godwin Fellow. But now that everything's worked out, I hope I can finish the rest of the year as a *normal* Fellow."

"Sarah. Sam. Why didn't you just *tell* me, for heaven's sake?" I could hear the weariness, the disappointment, in my own voice. "What you're really saying is that I was the bait."

"Jones-Harris has had his eye on you as one of his 'people' for a long time," she continued. "This was his test of your mettle, Alex. I can imagine how you might feel—well, *almost*—but think of it: You're saving the entire British publishing—and quite possibly bookselling—industry."

I sighed. "Sam, who on earth is Francis J. McDonald?"

I suppose I expected her to tell me he was a Stone & Stone corporate informant, the sort who would keep Sam senior up-to-date on the empire's on-line commerce partners, television affiliates, radio stations, film companies, and so forth . . . from Rome to Tokyo. What I didn't expect was for her to cackle as if I'd made a particularly good joke.

"Oh, Frank McDonald. One of my father's favourite people." She chuckled again. "Seriously, Alex, now I'm letting you in on a really big secret. You must not tell a soul. *There is no Francis J. McDonald.* My father always has that name listed on the boards of the corporation's partners so he can slip someone in if he needs to. He's gotten away with it for decades—only his closest associates know. No one else has ever seemed to notice."

I was torn between wondering if Sam had the full picture, and admiring Sam senior's little joke.

I knew my own corner of Hertfordshire so well that when at last we turned on to the Amersham Road, I knew we were not going to the Orchard. "Where are we going?"

"Can't put anything over on *you*," Sam said. "Sarah and Ian have been staying at the Bedford Arms since they got back from Germany. We thought it might be best for you to stay there tonight, too, all things considered."

"Fine," I said, feeling utterly powerless. I couldn't very well argue with them. After all, the elegant little inn in Chenies was exactly where I'd *planned* to take Sarah when we were reunited.

But the wedding I'd dreamed of didn't seem at all likely. Even if Sarah had wanted to marry me, things had changed substantially with regard to my fitness for marriage or anything else. We couldn't rush into a wedding—even if she consented—until I knew whether I'd ever be able to *see* her again.

I allowed myself to be led up the path to the Bedford Arms. Sam had the grace to let Sarah do this part, though by now I was beginning to suspect that Sam was along as a chaperone for a fearful Sarah. Sarah took me up to a room that I knew would be perfectly delightful . . . if only I could see it. More than anything, I wished that I could study Sarah. I felt certain that if I could look into her eyes, I would know what she needed, could soothe and comfort her. As it was, I felt at such a distance that I hadn't a clue.

I could discern the softness of the bed, anyway, and a toothbrush and flannel had been provided.

"If there's anything you need, just knock on the wall at the head of your bed. I'm right next door. Bang on the wall when you wake in the morning . . . sleep as late as you can." Sarah gave me a peck on the cheek, and before I could even return it, she was gone.

The bed next door. We were getting closer.

CHAPTER 20

When I awoke, it was to the utterly wretched and irritating tweet of my mobile. I blundered out of bed, wearing a pair of unfamiliar pyjamas that Sarah had borrowed for me from Ian, eyes aching and chest complaining. I tried to home in on the phone's location but tripped over the leg of a chair and fell flat on my face . . . and all the while the damned thing was ringing. I crawled on hands and knees towards the origin of the sound, and eventually found it on a chair under the clothes I'd thrown off the night before. I pressed the *talk* button and nearly snarled something very unpleasant indeed . . . but instead settled upon an irritable *"Alex Plumtree!"*

"Good morning, Alex," Colin Jones-Harris answered cheerfully, sounding ever so solicitous.

Good morning definitely seemed a stretch. I managed a "Hello" and tried to feel my way back to the high bed without doing myself another injury.

"Alex, those tapes of last night were ghastly. It

looked as though they'd roughed you up quite a bit before they ever got you to Botkin's. I'm so sorry. How are your eyes? How are you feeling?"

Clutching the toe that I'd stubbed, I sighed. "I'd be feeling a lot better if people hadn't kept so much information from me. I'd be feeling a lot better if you, for instance, hadn't signed me up to help and then left me twisting in the wind. I'd be feeling ever so much better if Sarah weren't treating me like we'd never met before, and didn't seem so frightfully familiar with you. And finally, I'd be a new man if I could see through these bandages, and if I knew whether I'd ever be able to see again."

"I see—" I imagined him grimacing at this painful faux pas. "Ah—I mean, I *understand*."

"What's going on, Jones-Harris? With Stone, Gravesend, and Kruse? As far as I can see, I've only dealt with a private adversary—and it cost me nearly everything to do it. These others could be nastier yet."

"Ah. You've thought of that, have you? Well, so have we. I'd very much like to come and have a chat, Plumtree. We've got the antitrust issue settled, I believe. Look in the paper—sorry, Plummers, I mean listen to the news today. Now that the attempt has been publicised, I don't believe they'll try it again."

I agreed to see him at the Orchard at one o'clock. I hoped it would be safe enough from the powerful monopolists now that they were washed up—whoever they'd been, and I couldn't wait to find out.

"One more thing, Jones-Harris: You might not care about the fact that King James tried to change the Bible to suit his royal whims, but I presume as an English subject you do care about falsifying antiquities.

Remember plucky little Judith and dogged Beowulf? You know, one of my authors *died*—"

"Yes, Alex—about that. I'd quite like to discuss it in person this afternoon."

I sighed. "Oh, all *right* then," and disconnected.

I knocked on the wall as Sarah had suggested the night before; moments later, the hotel phone rang. Sarah's lovely voice came down the line.

"Good morning, Alex. Sam and I thought we might all have breakfast in the dining room. I'll pick you up in—well, a little while. Okay?"

She was as good as her word. I'd done as much as I could on my own in the way of grooming when she knocked on my door. I could smell her when she drew close and took my hand; I sank into her presence as if into a down bed. It was comfortable; it was perfect. But so much remained unsaid.

Somehow I sensed that what remained was not for me to say; so I contented myself with her presence and a few words here and there as she led me down the stairs.

In the dining room, after greeting Sam, I quickly mastered the technique of first locating the saucer with the left hand before attempting to replace the cup with the right. Five minutes after we'd sat down, my damned phone rang again. Both Sarah and Sam made noises about taking care of it for me, but this was one thing I could do myself. I found the right button and pressed it. "Alex Plumtree."

"Morning, Alex—Diana here. I thought you might like to see exactly what I found last night, and how to proceed. Are you home? Shall I come out to you?"

"Er, I hope to be home quite soon. Yes, that would be wonderful."

"I'll leave straightaway. Wait till you see what I've got to show you."

I didn't enlighten her about not being able to see it . . . somehow I didn't have the heart. Sam and Sarah were certainly free to see Diana's evidence, anyway.

As Sam drove us from the Bedford Arms to the house, I couldn't help but wonder why she was still hanging about. If things didn't change soon, I'd begin to think of her as the mill-Stone. She obviously had been put in the picture about Sarah's and my imminent wedding at the time of Sarah's disappearance, and must have known that we urgently needed time alone, together. But she was resolutely, relentlessly, with us. Even when Sarah and I might have *almost* had a moment alone the night before, however, Sarah had firmly said good night and almost hurried off to her own room.

"Give her time, Alex," Ian had said. *"Think of what she's been through."*

Yes, okay, I thought. God knew, I'd given enough thought to what she'd been through. But wasn't it time to get on with things?

There was no missing the turn into Old Shire Lane, and several minutes later the drive to the Orchard. I knew exactly where I was in this part of the world. "Ever thought of widening your driveway?" Sam asked.

"Historic hedges," I said tersely. "Mediaeval. Not allowed to remove them, even if I wanted to."

"Ah, I see. Hmm—looks as though they're almost done," Sam said.

"The hedges? Done? What do you mean?"

"No!" Sarah laughed at the rising panic in my voice. "Don't worry, no one's touched your hedges. It's just a little surprise we've planned for you."

I didn't much like the thought of a surprise at this point. In fact, I thought I could use a month or two without a single unexpected occurrence.

"Of course we didn't anticipate the eye problem," Sarah said. "But don't worry. We'll take care of everything until you're back to normal."

That was optimistic, I thought grimly.

Sam brought her car to a stop in the gravel parking area; I could hear the fountain. Sarah led me up the path to the front door, and I heard a couple of male voices greet us. The women answered them. Silence reigned as our odd little procession passed.

"Who was that?" I asked as soon as I politely could.

"Those are some of the workmen installing the most advanced, unbreachable security system available on the planet," Sarah said firmly. I heard something in her voice, and felt thick for not realising sooner: She had been abducted from the Orchard. She must have *horrible* memories of this place—

At last, here, I could walk unaided—not that I minded Sarah's hand on my arm. But she stopped leading me and I walked into the library on my own. "Alex," Ian said, and came to give me a hug. Perhaps Sarah had asked him to oversee the transformation of my home into Fortress Orchard. "I'm so sorry, so very sorry."

I wanted to tell him it was all right, but just couldn't get the words out yet. Instead I went to sit down in my favourite chair, enjoying this small act of independence. I felt like shouting, "I want to talk to Sarah! Alone!" but knew that I couldn't press her. Best, perhaps, to remain quiet.

The first person to arrive at the door was Ed

Maggs, bringing my bag of clothes and precious books, not to mention the hire car. I invited him to stay and hear what had happened with Judith, and he eagerly accepted. Ian made coffee, and we filled the time with speculation until Diana arrived half an hour later.

I heard the others oooh and aaah as she showed them where the old markings were in her photographs. In some of the places she explained that she could clearly see "Schechem" beneath "Bethulia," and in the other places she could see King Nebuchadnezzar's name beneath Holofernes. "You'll be glad to know, Alex, that the photographs are quite clear. I have absolute proof."

It was difficult in the extreme for me to know that Sarah sat not six feet from me, on the sofa—but then I had freed her from having to decide how close to come, by sitting in a one-man chair. I could, however, remember that she'd happily planted herself on my lap in that very chair three months before.

I noticed Sam was very quiet during this discussion. What was she thinking?

I thought they might be interested to learn how I knew Judith had been altered. After explaining about the *Cottonia* collection I'd found (I didn't mention the hidden library at Botkin's, and Ed didn't say a word) with the letter from Botkin's ancestor to my ancestor, I told them about "Petrus" corporate and monastic, and how they were related. Ed brought the Malconbury Chronicles out of my bag, and I told them where to look to see the tiny letters surrounding the initial capitals. There was silence all round when I told them about the still inexplicable Father Mike, and the house that hadn't been occupied in years. I secretly suspected that Ian had gone to great lengths to arrange for a "Father Mike," props and all, so that I could feel I'd discovered the revelations of the Malconbury Chronicles myself. But he certainly had *not* arranged the killer in the backseat of my car. No doubt I would find out who'd been behind that all too soon.

"There's more," I said, believing they should know the full story where the books were concerned. "A group of bookmen met in Botkin's in the early twentieth century—my grandfather, one of the group, chronicled it in a book. The group consisted of Kruse's grandfather, Gerhard Quaritch; Sam's grandfather, the last of the Barkers; and Gravesend's grandfather, printer emeritus at Cantabrigian Press."

Jones-Harris arrived on the stroke of one, carrying, I was told, an awe-inspiring hamper of the products his family was famous for packaging into luxury gifts: teas, pâté, jams, ham, cheese, biscuits, gâteaux, and more.

Then, of course, we talked about the things Jones-Harris knew most about. Sarah, I was informed, had been the one to mastermind the changing of company names in order to flummox whoever was trying to gather all the companies together. The financial and legal heads of the firms had agreed to be listed under different and meaningless names for the purposes of the government operation. They still had no proof, Jones-Harris said, of who had been behind the manoeuvring. "But we'll get them," he added confidently.

It had gone out in the paper that morning, he said, that the government was scrutinising all transactions in the publishing and bookselling world for possible criminal activity. The Chief Prosecutor had put a hold on all transactions for several weeks, in view of the attempt.

Around three o'clock, despite Ian's offers of tea,

Ed and Diana left, saying they had to get back. Jones-Harris, a bit ominously, remained. Ian made himself scarce; I heard him rattling in the kitchen.

"There is just one more thing, Alex," Jones-Harris said, when only Sam, Sarah, and I remained.

To my surprise, it was Sam who spoke next. "Yes. My father—who, by the way, doesn't know about my, um, *other* job with the CIA—has suggested a dinner party for tonight. He wants to see everyone one last time before going back to New York. Once I'd heard about the Bedford Arms, I suggested it to him and he loved the idea. I thought it would be easier for you, too."

"Thoughtful of you." I imagined myself ordering a hamburger at the top-ranked, Chaine des Rotisseurs rosette restaurant, so I could manage the transfer from plate to mouth.

"Alex," Jones-Harris began. "You remember I told you that I wanted to talk to you about setting the record straight with regard to the St James scroll and the genizah in Cairo, and Judith. Naturally, this is a matter of some shame for Britons everywhere. It occurred to me that either Gravesend, who still has control of Cantabrigian, or Stone, who of course still has close control of Ecumenical, might wish we *weren't* putting things right."

"Mm," I said. "And, did you know that Sam Stone's ancestor was the King's Printer? Christopher Barker?"

"Yes, as a matter of fact, I did." Jones-Harris's tone told me that this wasn't incidental knowledge . . . it had significance. I thought I might be on the verge of catching his drift.

"And did you know, Alex, that Trevor Gravesend's

ancestor was the head of Cantabrigian back in the seventeenth century, when the King gave Cambridge University a licence to print the Bible?"

"Yes, I did know that—and I get the idea. Look, Colin. I'm blind and feeling quite dumb, as well. You expect me to walk in to that particular group of men—knowing that, given what you just told me, one of these men might kill to keep certain information from coming to light? Information about their ancestors, and their original family firms? The top two publishers of antiquities in the world, and I'm going to face them with the knowledge that they've perpetuated a great historical myth? A fraud? For nearly four centuries?"

I'd been in those family-name-and-honour situations before, and knew that they were the most deadly of all. People killed for far less.

"We'll have someone there to protect you," he said.

"Good—because I could be attacked by a mosquito right now and be quite defenceless."

"Sam and I will be there," Sarah said. "Only—well, Sam will tell you."

I nearly groaned. The mill-Stone.

"I'm to be Henning's date," Sam said, a smile in her voice.

"Ah—good," I remarked, hoping that she'd be occupied enough with the winning Kruse to leave Sarah and me in peace.

As if they sensed what I was thinking, Jones-Harris stood and said, "We'll leave you now—perhaps you and Sarah would like some time alone."

As I stood to see them out, he said, "No, don't get up, Alex." But I noticed that Sarah rose to secure the house as they left. She was taking no chances.

"Eight o'clock tonight, at the Bedford Arms."

"Right." *I'll just wear the bull's-eye on my chest, then, shall I?*

We said our good-byes; everyone—including Ian and Sam—seemed to be leaving us. I heard Sarah pressing the alarm keypad and thought, *This is it.* Now we'd find out what was left between us, if anything.

She started a fire in the fireplace, then sat down on the sofa again with a sigh. "Alex, there's something I have to tell you . . ."

Ah. I knew what was coming, then. Just as well that she couldn't see my eyes.

"But first, how about a glass of wine?"

"Lovely," I said, not trusting my voice to say more. I heard her grapple for the corkscrew in the kitchen drawer, listened to the cork squeak against the bottle as she twisted it out, heard clinking as she gathered glasses, and braced myself for what I was about to hear.

I just can't, Alex, now or ever . . . I've met someone else . . . The fact is, I just don't love you anymore. . . .

Or was all of this about how her hostage experience had "changed" her, as Ian had mentioned? I saw no outward injuries. . . .

She came back then and took my hand, placed my fingers round the wineglass, and said, "Okay?" But she didn't walk away again; she seemed to hesitate. "Would you mind if we sat on the sofa—both of us? I feel so far away from you over there. We've been too far apart . . . for too long."

I couldn't agree more. But this seemed to be a *positive* sign. I moved to the sofa and she sat encouragingly near. I felt like a teenager on a first date. For courage as much as anything, I brought the glass to my lips and smelled the bouquet of one of her thick, buttery

chardonnays—more food than wine. I took a sip and
waited.

"Alex, there's something I should have told you
long ago. But I didn't want it to cause you any more
problems—" A laugh seemed to take her by surprise.
"You always seemed to have enough with the Press.
And everything."

How true. That alone would be reason enough for
her to reject me.

"I'm not who you think I am."

It was my turn for an incredulous laugh. "*What?*
Sarah, what on earth can you mean?"

"Didn't you ever wonder why I travelled so much,
even as the most junior member of the bank's staff?"

This wasn't at all what I'd expected. I shrugged,
shook my head slightly. "You're brilliant. I knew they
could spot a star employee when they found one."

"No. You're very sweet, but that's not it. Didn't you
ever wonder why I held you at arm's length for so
long?"

"It was obvious." I heard the caution in my own
voice. What was she getting at? "You'd just lost your
husband, and—"

"Yes, but I mean for all the years after that. Alex,
please don't be angry with me for deceiving you. I only
did it to protect you."

"*Protect* me? You—protect *me*?"

"Is that so hard to believe?"

"No. *No* . . . Sarah. Darling. What are you telling
me?"

"Well . . ." She laced her fingers through mine and
held my hand tightly. "You know that Jones-Harris
delicately suggested that you might help him on future
projects? If you want to, I mean."

"Yes, but . . ."

"Well, I work for the US government the way Jones-Harris does for your government. Er, sorry, Her Majesty."

An avalanche of memories came then: missed appointments, sudden appearances where she wasn't expected, Jonathan Metcalf's odd reaction on my latest visit to the Foreign Office, the three—four?—times she'd saved my life.

Okay, I thought, okay. That didn't change anything. I could cope with my wife—my love—being a spook.

"And at the moment, everyone thinks I'm dead because of the news reports. So, you see, I'm a rather valuable person just now. I can't stay, Alex."

Now I understood what had changed. I put down my wine, rather successfully, and reached my arm round her. "You—you can't stay?"

I heard the base of her glass on the table, too, but then I heard it go over and bounce off the table onto the floor. She leant against me and began to shake; the sobs caught in her throat. There was so much we hadn't talked about—everything she'd endured, what it must have been like to escape . . . perhaps this was her way of telling me.

But what did she mean, she couldn't stay??

I just held her and loved her. At least she was *here, now* . . . I'd wanted this more than anything else.

I sat wiping her tears and stroking her hair until the sobs stopped. "You know I'd do anything for you, Sarah. And I think we may as well bring everything out in the open. Not knowing how you feel is killing me. I need you to tell me . . . if you can. Are we still planning to be married, or has everything changed? Do you still love me, or am I just the horrid beast who's forever plunging you into mortal danger?"

"Oh, Alex, *yes,* I love you. I love you so much that I was watching your house from down the road, longing to be with you, when I saw the gunmen and rang the police. *Yes,* I want to marry you. But, I'm doing really important work just now. The people and places I know—the way things work—have taken years to become familiar with. I can't just give them all up like that; it's not fair to anyone. Lots of people risked their lives to get me out of Iraq. I owe it to them to bring our work to completion. I made a commitment and I must keep it."

With gentle fingers she touched my face. "Do you think you could ever marry me, knowing that for the foreseeable future I can't be seen with you? If you *did* still want me, a notice of the wedding couldn't even be published in the papers. It would be a strange life . . . and I'd be flitting in and out until I retire. It would be irresponsible to have children until I retire, too—and then it might be too late."

Had she mentioned a wedding?

I brought her close for the most memorable kiss of our entire courtship. It was more a tender conversation than a kiss.

"Yes, Sarah, I could marry you. I could take care of our children, too—but not if I'm blind. Are you willing to take that risk? In three days we'll know . . ."

"I'm very willing. Alex, if your eyes are permanently damaged, you'll still be you. It's you I love, not just your eyes."

"I know, but Sarah, I wonder if you realise what our life would be like—"

"Everything's going to be all right," she said firmly. I smiled.

We sat on the sofa, each absorbed in the other. I was aware of the whole we made when we were together; a whole that was very different from the sum of its two parts.

"Let's get married before anything else can happen to prevent it, Alex," she whispered. "Let's get married at midnight tonight, after this dinner."

I told her of my enthusiastic approval with a kiss, then asked her to dial Martyn's number at the vicarage. I asked him to arrange the wedding that instant, and told him not to tell a single soul.

"Not even Amanda?" he asked.

"No. Not even Amanda."

"All right . . . all right!" he agreed, stammering with surprise and delight. "You do realize that to make this official, it's going to take a bit of song and dance with the Bishop—or the Registrar—if I can even get hold of them. We haven't published the banns, after all. But assuming I can work that out . . . what do you want for music?"

"Don't need music," I answered. "No music. Besides, this needs to be quiet."

"Any special verses?"

"Anything from the Bible will be perfect."

Sarah laughed, that rich, melodic sound for which my ears had been so starved, and I knew what she was thinking: She and her mother had spent every scrap of spare time for months making plans for our September wedding. And none of it mattered now except for being married.

Martyn had one last question: "Does she want to say 'obey'?"

"*I* don't want her to say 'obey.' Not unless we both say it."

Sarah gave me a squeeze.

"Okay; we'll leave out the 'obey.' You know, sometimes a simple yes or no would do nicely, Plumtree. 'Let your yes be yes, your no be no'—you know."

"Lovely. Until later, then, Martyn."

"Right! And well done, Alex. *Well done.*"

Sarah and I continued to enjoy one another in blissful solitude. She leaned her head on me and after a bit fell asleep; her breathing became deep and even. Perhaps I fell asleep, too, because the next thing I knew, Sarah had started in my arms and twisted round to turn on a lamp.

"Alex! It's seven o'clock! We must get going." She stood and pulled me to my feet. Then she drew me close, facing her, and ran her hands through my hair. "I am so very, very happy," she said, with a depth of peace in her voice I'd never heard before. "Remember, Alex— I can't let these people know I'm around. So you won't see me at the dinner; I'll be in a room upstairs, listening. They set up the equipment earlier today. I'll hear every word. If there's the least problem, I'll be there."

"It's very attractive, you know," I told her.

"What?"

"Your power. Your confidence, and capability."

I imagined she was grinning.

"I do have just one question," I said.

"Mmm?"

"Why didn't you let me know sooner that you were alive?"

"Can you understand that I thought it might be kinder to you if I passed out of your life, so you could go on and have a—well, a traditional life? With companionship, and children, the way you've always wanted?

And when I saw you with Nicola . . . I really hesitated. You two would be good for each other, Alex. And if I ever *don't* come back . . ."

I thought I took her meaning . . . if she permanently, forever, *couldn't* come back. "Just don't ever make that decision for me, Sarah. Don't ever *not* come back because you think I don't want you anymore."

She answered with an emphatic embrace; I revelled in it.

As I bathed, making allowance for the bandages, I tried to anticipate the discussion with Stone and Gravesend. This issue of having manipulated the Bible in the distant past must be of very great importance for them indeed, because they themselves had been involved in negotiating with me.

Where Gravesend was concerned, I thought he'd have done almost anything to protect his potential O.B.E.—including hiring assassins to gun me down at home and attack me in my car on isolated Norfolk roads. Had the man Gravesend hired to kill Hammonds been the same one who had either followed me to Father Mike's or hidden himself in my boot for the ride out?

I also couldn't help but wonder if Gravesend had paid Nate Griffith a substantial sum to evaporate into thin air with all his knowledge, and if Nate's one act of protest had been to leave his notebook for me to find.

When I got myself dressed and back downstairs, Sam was there to give me a ride to the Bedford Arms. Sarah, I was informed, had already gone.

"Oooh, you look *killer* handsome!"

"If you don't mind, I think we might avoid the k-word . . . but thank you, Sam. I was worried that the gauze might be a bit flashy . . ."

Sam laughed and delivered us safely to the comfortably elegant brick hostelry. It was greatly to my advantage that I'd been there for meals throughout my life and knew exactly where I was going.

Dinners at a place like the Bedford Arms began with drinks in the bar while we chatted and considered menus. Diners were taken in to the table only once the first course was served. When I drew even with the lounge bar, Stone's booming voice came to meet me. "Here he is—Alex! My God. What's *happened* to you?"

"I say, Plummers," Gravesend exclaimed in his reserved fashion. "What on earth?"

Their voices were close. Concerned, at least on the surface.

"It's nothing," I lied. "A chemical burn. Just a bit inconvenient."

We sat and the barmaid took our drinks orders. I steered conversation away from the inevitable focus on my bandages and on to the weather, American football, Trevor's children. We placed our dinner orders and after another twenty minutes were shown into the dining room. I knew without my vision that the lighting in the intimate room was nicely subdued and heavily dependent on candles; the decoration tasteful, traditional English, down to the Colefax & Fowler chintz curtains. People felt special, plied with the excellent service, food, and drink.

Kruse joined us just as we went in, apologising for his delay and expressing shock at my injury. Once we got over that conversation-stopper again, we drifted along quite nicely on a conversational raft of mutual acquaintance, shared experience, food and wine. I couldn't forget that Sarah was listening to every word; it was very enjoyable to think of her somewhere nearby, part of our conversation and yet not.

When my sole had nearly disappeared—I'll never pretend that eating it had been easy, but mashed potatoes had saved the day—I broached The Subject with a segue from Stone's comment about what an astonishing week it had been, in terms of the mysterious, anonymous monopoly attempt. He'd read Sabera's Bookworm column in the *Bookseller,* and understood it had shaken up the big booksellers.

"Yes, and did you see the article in the *Times* about the new study of Cotton Vitellius A.fifteen at the British Library?"

"Yes," Henning said. "I did see that. Very interesting. Who do you suppose is behind it?"

"I don't know, but I *can* tell you something as remarkable—and disturbing." Very deliberately, I took a sip of my wine to build suspense. "An author of mine—come to think of it, you probably read about him in the *Times,* too—was researching *Beowulf,* which is bound into the same codex as Judith, when he died. He wanted the book to be pulled and studied under UV light. I think he got a little too close to the truth about someone having changed Judith, and was killed for it. You see, I had an independent expert examine the codex, and it *had* been deliberately altered. The study was a fraud."

Stone's first comment was one of studied calm. "Is that right?" A pause. "But why would anyone care about some changes that might have been made centuries ago?"

"Probably," Henning put in, pausing to swallow a mouthful of his dinner, "because it makes someone look bad."

No, no, no, Henning! I thought. Good Lord, he didn't know . . . though he was the one who'd told me about the plan to consolidate the Society of Near- and Middle-Eastern Studies, Antiquities, Orientalia, and Judeo-Christian Scholarship. Perhaps he knew more than I thought—but would he stumble in headfirst? Sam the Younger should have told him beforehand.

"Why? How does it make someone look bad?" Trevor's voice was so cool that I wondered if he had a pulse.

"Surely you saw the news reports about the scroll found under St James's Palace when Prince Charles was having those renovations done. Two years ago, was it? If you recall, the scholarly world was up in arms because this was the only record corroborating the version of Judith in the King James Version of the Bible. King James had cited this scroll, certainly, but no one had been able to find it. Queen Elizabeth presented the scroll to a repository for such things, genizah in Cairo. But in view of this recent discovery—"

Stone the Elder exclaimed, "Fascinating! I feel as if I've had my head under a rock for years. But Alex here seems to be saying that the corrections to the Cotton Vitellius A.fifteen Judith were somehow illegitimate. Tell me, one of you who knows so much about this, why couldn't the corrections in Judith have been *honest* mistakes made by the scribes? Mistakes that they had to scratch out and write over? Even I have read that this was done quite frequently."

I heard the sound of cutlery being set down with finality on a plate. "That would be believable, Sam," Trevor said. "But I'm afraid our friends have caught us at our little game."

I heard the shocked silence; forced myself to say nothing, do nothing. Sarah would be sitting up and taking notice, wherever she was.

Sam the Elder's voice was ice cold. "Oh? And what game is that?"

"Socialising with these people to become better educated," Trevor explained. "Where would we be if you didn't tell us what was happening in the world of antiquarian books?"

I thought I felt all of us relax a bit, though it seemed to me that Trevor had drawn a line in the sand. He wanted us off the subject, *now*. But I hadn't missed a precious evening with Sarah to back off at his request.

"But surely, Trevor, this calls for an objective investigation of both the scroll in the Cairo genizah and the manuscript in the library. And I'm sorry to say it, but your 'mistake' theory doesn't work, Sam. My expert's secret study of the codex contrary to the study publicised in the *Times*—led by your author, Desmond Wilcox—revealed that there's *no* way anyone could have missed the deliberate changes made to Judith."

I grew impatient with playing games. "To be perfectly honest, I have proof that someone close to King James took the Nowell Codex, between 1600 and 1611, and had a monk make the changes to the ancient manuscript."

Trevor snorted. "That's absurd! Why would King James want to make changes to Judith? It had already been in existence for over seventeen hundred years. Everyone already knew what it said from all the *other* versions of the Bible. Including the Vulgate, the very first authority."

"Ah." I heard Henning's thoughtful voice and envisioned him raising a finger. "But you're forgetting the scroll. Naturally he anticipated the question, *Why make the changes?* He had to prevent people saying, 'King James doesn't want his people to read about the King being murdered by a woman, a powerless widow at that, so he's changing the Bible!' He had the scroll made supposedly buried beneath the sands for thousands of years and miraculously discovered in 1611. Now it has been uncovered again, under St James's Palace."

Sam Stone the younger seemed to sense that it was time for us to move on. Now they knew that we knew, we'd served our purpose. If they wanted to say something later, they would. She changed the subject to something completely different that might still have been considered linked to the previous topic: the refurbishment of royal palaces. People were already talking about which might be the most appropriate for Prince William. We carried on through the sweet on that topic and others; we were the very essence of congeniality. I had a divine deep-dish forest berry pie, with heavy cream poured over it. What's more, I could eat it with a spoon.

Upon retiring to the lounge for coffees and liqueurs, conversation turned to politics but remained innocuous. In fact, the evening ended that way, another hour and a half later. I knew because the bells of Christ Church Chenies chimed, putting me out of my misery as I awaited midnight.

We all thanked Sam the elder for the delightful dinner party, and the five of us parted as—ostensibly—the best of colleagues and even friends. Sam senior, who was returning to New York the very next day, had travelled with Trevor from London. They went out to their car together to disappear into the night.

Henning stayed to chat with us for a minute or two at the front of the Bedford Arms. A fine mist was falling, but it felt good to be outside. Henning clearly didn't know whether he could speak freely with me in front of Sam. When she excused herself for a moment before driving me home, he leaned close and wanted to know what had happened to my eyes. I told him the truth; he sounded truly shocked.

"Nice job, by the way, at the Society conference. I heard all about it, Alex. Poor Beattie, eh? I am amazed, frankly, that Stone and Gravesend let us off so easily tonight. I thought we might be bundled into their cars and never seen again." He laughed. "All's well that ends well."

The church clock chimed forty-five past the hour; Sam rejoined us. I began to worry about being late to my own wedding. Sam and Henning made plans to see each other the next day, and when he'd gone, she agreed to drop me at the Orchard and then return to her room at the Arms.

I grew increasingly nervous on the way home; what if something kept us from getting married this time? What if Martyn hadn't been able to get an exception from the rigid restrictions of the Church of England on such short notice?

Sam drove quickly, God bless her, and we were home in seven minutes. I thanked her profusely for the trouble of driving me and urged her to just drop me off, because I knew Sarah was waiting inside. We didn't want to be late for Martyn. But she insisted on walking me up to the door, making sure I could disarm the alarm, and it was another few minutes before I stood alone inside the house.

Sarah came to me as soon as Sam was gone and gave me a lovely bear hug, as excited as I was. We laughed and indulged in a bit of youthful smooching before she giggled and said, "Let's go!"

I climbed in the hire car with her and she pointed it in the direction of Christ Church Chenies. "This is *wonderful*!" she exclaimed.

I laughed in delight. It seemed impossible that we were going where we were going, together, for the purpose we intended. This was a very pure wedding, untainted by anything less pure than our love for one another.

As she pulled into the church drive, which sloped upwards to the right of the church, just between the churchyard and the church lawn, the clock tower chimed twelve. "Twelve bells," I said with happy inanity.

She left the car in the drive; no one else would be coming at this hour. I got out and began to feel my way towards the church; happily, I knew it well, too. But Sarah came round and took my hand in hers, and put her left hand on my back. Ah, wonderful.

"Hello, hello!" Martyn's voice as he came to meet us was a cross between reverence for the task he was about to perform, and boyish excitement for his friends. Then he caught sight of me. "Alex! What's happened to you?!" I told him it was a long story for another, less eventful night. He gave Sarah a hug and then me, and said afterwards, "Well, I don't suppose you want to delay! It's a miracle, but the diocesan bishop came through. I'm ready for you."

Sarah and I, hand in hand, followed him up the centre aisle. The heady smell of paraffin, wet stone, and musty service books surrounded us. "It's beautiful, Alex. Martyn has all the candelabra lit, the length of the church. Thank you so much," she breathed.

"Nothing could make me happier," he said. "Well, here we are. Ready?"

"Very," Sarah and I answered in unison.

"Right. We'll, er, cut to the chase, then, Sarah—as you might say."

"Good."

"Dearly beloved, we are gathered here in the sight of God—"

Sarah shoved me to the ground roughly and screamed, "Get down!" just as the sickening sound echoed through the church. Gunfire. It was absurdly incongruous with this place, this occasion. I heard Sarah scrabble behind the front pew; heard her dress rustle as she—what? "Get him outside, Martyn. The side door. As far as you can into the churchyard." Then I felt his shaking hands grip my arms, hustle me to my knees, and start for the door. We must have been close to the door when a barrage of shots came from the back of the church. Was it Sarah, trying to distract our attackers?

I heard lead smack into wood again as their bullets followed us. But Martyn was still yanking me along the path I knew so well, and we somehow got round the back of the church and into the churchyard. Neither of us said a thing; we didn't want to die. I wanted to marry Sarah. It was only as Martyn pulled me down, presumably behind an especially large gravestone, that I had time to feel cheated.

Angry and cheated.

Martyn had better sense, but then his wedding hadn't just been put off for the second time, after more than eight years of courtship. "Give me your phone!" I passed it to him and heard the beep of the phone as he rang 999. The sound of gunfire still erupted from the church; in a whisper he told the police what was happening and where we were. I felt sick with worry.

The shots ominously stopped; Martyn gripped my arm. *"What could be happening?"* It was quiet for several seconds, which might as well have been several eternities. When we heard the police pull up for the second debacle at Chenies Parish Church in recent memory, it was with great relief. At least we would know. "They're walking towards the door," Martyn reported. "They've got their weapons drawn. They're going in . . ."

One of the constables must have come right back out; across the quiet graveyard I heard him call, "We need two ambulances." Then the crackle of a radio as the constable outside made the call.

I stood up and started towards the sound; Martyn caught hold of my jacket. "You can't go over there, you don't know—"

"Exactly. I don't know, Martyn."

At that he realised what I meant and put a clammy hand at the back of my neck to help steer me over. The police must have caught sight of Martyn's dog collar and my bandages; what a sight we must have been.

Martyn started to chatter. "Martyn Blakely, hello— I was the one who rang you. This is the friend I was marrying—er, to the woman in there—when the shots started. She saved us. They tried to kill us! I—"

The constable must have seen that Martyn was the type who would rabbit on forever if he wasn't stopped and got under control. "A *woman*, you say?" he asked dubiously. His voice sounded like the same one that had asked for the ambulances. So he had been inside . . .

"Is she all right? Has she been hurt?" I was desperate to know. *Couldn't they see that?*

"Who, exactly, do you mean?"

"My fiancée! The woman in the church!" I nearly screamed.

"There is no woman in the church, sir. And what did you say your name was?"

I scarcely heard; my relief at learning that Sarah hadn't been hurt swept everything else away. Just then the ambulances arrived, and we were asked to hang about to answer a few questions. Martyn said into my ear, "They're bringing out a very tall, big guy . . ."

Stone, I presumed.

"Plumtree," Stone's voice called out weakly as they wheeled him over the rough gravel track. "A deal. She made a deal . . . smart woman."

A deal? What could he possibly mean?

"Here comes the other one," Martyn said softly in my ear. "Good Lord! It's Trevor Gravesend, from the Merchant Taylors board of governors! He's unconscious . . . poor fellow doesn't look very well at all."

And so Sarah was gone again. Martyn and I went over and over events with the police, who were understandably flummoxed by the case of the disappearing markswoman. At one o'clock, they insisted upon accompanying me home to see if they could find her there. Martyn followed us to the Orchard in the hire car, to get it back to the house. The police hurried up the front walk, only to find that they needed me to disarm the security system.

"Does she know how to work this?"

"She designed it."

A pause, as I imagined the policemen looking at one another askance. They came inside with me, and though I hoped Sarah was there somewhere, she was too smart to be found when she didn't want to be.

While the police snooped around, I settled in the library and tried again to work out why Sarah would have run away. Martyn insisted upon staying, and I was grateful. I missed Sarah terribly already. I knew she couldn't be seen, but . . . maybe she was just staying out of the way for the moment, and would be back.

Perhaps she would have Jones-Harris, or her American bosses, make some phone calls and work it all out for her with the Buckinghamshire Constabulary (Chenies was just over the line from Hertfordshire into Bucks). She had been working on an assignment, after all, involving Stone and Gravesend. If they tried to kill her, and us, she had every right to defend herself.

In time, the police left, not having found their mysterious woman. Only then did I ask Martyn to look on the tops of the door frames for folded scraps of paper. "Um . . . yes!" he said, finding one on the top of the door leading out of the library.

"Would you read it to me, please?"

"Of course . . . 'Alex, dearest——had to run for obvious reasons. Made a deal to solve problem with friends. Ask Colin. I shall return as soon as possible for another appointment at the church. Do not keep this note. Much love, nearly your wife, Sarah.' " I didn't know whether to laugh or cry. It was wonderful; it was horrible.

But she would be back.

I remembered that, as I waited for two more days to have the bandages removed.

I remembered it as Jones-Harris rang to tell me that Gravesend and Stone would not be prosecuted for their monopoly execution. (They had, after all, managed to be one step ahead of the governments involved.) The deal, which had been struck at twelve-fifteen A.M. in Chenies Parish Church, Jones-Harris said, demanded two things in exchange for immunity: 1) The boys had to put their toys back, along with all the money they made plus a fine, and 2) Stone and Gravesend had to allow the truth to come out about their ancestors and their publishing houses having misrepresented history.

And I remembered that Sarah would be back as Jones-Harris invited me to take a more active role in his work. I thanked him, but declined.

Someone had to run the house.

CONCLUDING NOTE

The truth about both *Beowulf* and Judith remains a mystery. In researching and writing this book, I have consulted scholarly tomes about *Beowulf,* Old Testament scholars, rare book experts, books on the history of bookselling in London, scholars of eighteenth-century English, and experts in the use of ultraviolet light to examine palimpsests (and many, many more). This dizzying year-plus of research has taught me one thing for certain: There are as many points of view about literature and the dating thereof as there are people. If you happen to be an expert on *Beowulf* or Judith and your views differ from those of Alex Plumtree's experts, please be assured that I have made every effort to consolidate the wide spectrum of views into one that is both representative of the truth and accessible to readers.

Authentic details give life to a story, whereas inaccurate details detract and offend. Therefore every effort has been made to make the details authentic, with one caveat: Part of the fun of writing Alex Plumtree's sort of fiction is using history and literature as a jumping-off point. In this book I have mixed fact and fiction where Judith is concerned, and it is only fair to point out where and why.

Fact: The Book of Judith has always been questioned

as an authentic historical account because of certain obvious and puzzling inaccuracies. For instance, in the real Judith, the geography is blatantly wrong, and Nebuchadnezzar is said to be the king of Assyria when, in fact, he was king of Babylon. Some scholars feel this is a deliberate message to the reader to view the book as a story, rather than as a historical account. In the real Book of Judith, as you or I would read it today, Judith slays Holofernes, not Nebuchadnezzar.

Fiction: For the purposes of *Unsigned*, I wanted to make it appear that perhaps this was not the original story. Aside from the intriguing thought that works we consider authoritative today might have been altered to suit the political whims of past kings, it seemed reasonable to me that King James might have wanted to forestall any more murdering of kings by women for political purposes. I also chose Judith because it is a fascinating and entertaining story, but is not considered an especially significant part of the Bible. As part of the Apocrypha, it is left out of many versions. It allows us to have some fun with the idea of publications being changed for political purposes without beginning to raise questions of the authenticity of the whole Bible.

If you are interested in *Beowulf* and ancient manuscripts, a fascinating book to read is Kevin Kiernan's *Beowulf and the Beowulf Manuscript*. It is also interesting to note that Kiernan's dating of the manuscript varies significantly from that of the experts who have recently written reviews of Seamus Heaney's new *Beowulf* translation. It remains a mystery. . . .

About the Author

JULIE KAEWERT worked for book publishers in Boston and London before starting her writing career with a London magazine. Her series of mysteries for booklovers has topped mystery bestseller lists around the country, and she is at work on her sixth Alex Plumtree adventure, *Uncatalogued*.

If you enjoyed Julie Kaewert's
UNSIGNED, you won't want to
miss any of her *Booklover's
Mysteries*. Look for them at your
favorite bookseller's.

And don't miss the next *Booklover's
Mystery*, **UNCATALOGUED**,
coming in Spring 2002!